SCATTERED LIES 3

"Finally, the Truth..."

WRITTEN BY

MADISON

5 Star Publications
PO BOX 471570
Forestville, MD 20753

ISBN -13: 978-0985438623
ISBN-10: 0985438622
Library of Congress Control Number: 2012938556
First Printing: October 2012

Printed in the United States

www.5starpublications.net
www.tljestore.com
www.iammadisontaylor.com

Follow Madison for the latest updates: on *www.facebook.com /iammadisontaylor* and *twitter.com/madisonme*

Acknowledgements

As always, I would like to thank **GOD** for His blessings. Without Him, there would be no me. To my family and friends, thank you for always being there for me.

To reviewers: **Joey Pinkney, OOAS Book Club (Anna Draper), Literary Wonders, Tom "Slim" Clover of Grind Mode Magazine, Myra Panache of Panachereport.com, Melody Vernor-Bartel Reader's Paradise 5 bookmarks,** and **Cyrus Webb.** Thank you for your reviews.

To book clubs: **Girls Bay Area (GBC), Sister of Unity (SOU), DMV** and **Columbia S.O.C.I.A.L.** Thank you for selecting my book.

To bookstores: **The Literary Joint (Shawn, La Quita), Horizon Bookstore (Quita), Urban Book Knowledge (Karen, Mondell), Sidi (125th Street), Antoine Inch Thomas (Amiaya Entertainment).** Thank you.

I also give thanks to my team: **Publicist Makeda Smith, Editor Carla M. Dean, Candice Coleman, Tonya Patterson, Keisha Green,** and **Kayon Cox.** We did it again!

To my muse, the best is yet to come! Thank you for supporting and believing in me all these years.

Readers,

The final installment of the *Scattered Lies* trilogy is here! As its predecessors, *Scattered Lies: Where Lies Are Really the Truth* and *Scattered Lies: Lessons Can't Be Learned When Lies Prevail*, we continue to explore the ups and downs of Madison and her cohorts as they encounter unexpected experiences.

All of our favorite characters have returned for this final showdown that will be both shocking and illuminating. In the finale, all questions will be answered and all lies will be disclosed. Some will triumph and some will fall. If you're like me, you will not be content until you know it all!

I hope you enjoy reading *Scattered Lies: Finally, the Truth*, where deceptions, intrigues, and consequences are finally revealed.

As Always, Love,

Read On!

SCATTERED LIES 3

"Finally, the Truth..."

INTRO

"**M**rs. Carrington, can you hear me?" the doctor said as they rushed her into the examination room. Right before passing out one last time, Christina cried, "Please save my baby."

Nervous, Tony watched as they wheeled Christina into the other room. *Damn, I hope she'll be okay. She lost a lot of blood.*

Tia and Mookie came running down the hall a short while later.

"Yo, Tee, we just heard what happened. Is Chris alright?" Mookie asked.

"They're still working on her."

"Do you need anything?" Tia asked.

"I'm good," Tony responded in a zombie-like state.

Seconds later, Joyce and Diana, Christina's assistant and publicist, arrived.

"How's she doing?" Diana asked.

"Don't know," Tony said, walking away to be alone.

Joyce, who was too distraught to speak, took a seat in a nearby chair.

"What's wrong with her?" Diana inquired.

Tony sighed. "Christina is pregnant."

"What?" they said in unison.

"Yeah!"

"You and Christina were going to have a baby and not tell nobody?" Mookie asked.

"I didn't know until she blurted it out when they were taking her into the examination room. I guess that's what she wanted to tell me over dinner." His voice cracked as he spoke.

Mookie walked over and placed his hand on Tony's shoulder. "Don't worry. She's gonna be fine."

Tony nodded and then forced a slight grin.

"Well, the media is out there, so let me go handle them. As soon as you hear something, though, you come get me. A'ight?" Diana told him before walking out.

When the doctor finally appeared in the waiting area, the look on his face let Tony know the news wasn't good.

"Hi. Can we go some place and talk?" he whispered to Tony.

Once they were in the privacy of a small conference room, the doctor sighed before asking, "Did you know she was pregnant?"

Tony flatly replied, "Not before this evening."

"Well…she lost the baby."

Damn. Tony lowered his head. "Is she awake?"

"Yes, but she needs to rest."

"Does she know? When can I go see her?"

"No, she doesn't know. Would you like for me to tell her?"

"Please. I don't think I'll be any good at doing it."

"Sure."

Christina's eyes were closed when Tony and the doctor entered the room.

"Chris," Tony softly said.

Sedated, Christina fought to open her eyes. "Tony…is…" she tried to say.

Tony looked at the doctor and then back at Christina.

"Chris, the doctor wants to talk to us."

"Is my baby alright?" she finally found the strength to ask.

The doctor moved closer. "Mrs. Carrington, I'm sorry. We tried, but we couldn't save the baby."

"NO! NO! PLEASE, OH GOD!" she screamed.

FOUR YEARS LATER

Chapter One
Denise

Six years and two kids later, Denise and Derrick were still going strong. After DJ was born, Denise finally agreed to marry Derrick. She had grown tired of everyone calling her a forever fiancée.

While growing up, Denise witnessed the downside of marriage. To her, it seemed like once two people got married, things changed, and it seemed to always change for the worse. Afraid Derrick would change once she married him, she secretly saw a therapist, who suggested that she also attend premarital group sessions. After completing a few sessions with the therapist and the group, Denise decided the only way to find out if things with Derrick would change was to marry him. On August 12, 2004, Denise wed Derrick in Las Vegas with their family and closest friends in attendance.

Derrick wasn't like most men. He was supportive, secure, and always attentive to her needs. Another thing Denise adored about Derrick was that he didn't mind taking the backseat. When she won the Information Technology Manager of the Year Award, her job held a dinner in her honor. At the dinner, Derrick didn't mind falling back and letting his wife shine. He didn't get jealous when she danced and flirted with other guys. He even winked at her from across the room a few times.

Derrick's lovemaking skills were awesome. In her previous relationship, Denise used to fuck, but with Derrick, he showed her the true meaning of making love. In return, she exposed him to "thug lovin'", as she called it. Many nights, they would have sex for hours.

Just when Denise thought life couldn't get any better, along came Lil' Derrick! Because Denise had several abortions when she was younger, she figured she couldn't get pregnant, and being that she and Morris had unprotected sex that didn't result in a child being conceived, she believed she would never be a mother unless it was through adoption. God had bigger plans for her, though. On July 24, 2005, Denise gave birth to Derrick Johnson, followed by Halle two years later.

Once Lil' Derrick came, Denise changed her life and became very dedicated to raising her son. She resigned from the Department of Information Technology and decided to focus solely on real estate. Owning forty buildings throughout the tri-state area, she really didn't need to work for the city anymore. Also, Derrick's consultant firm had signed a six-figure deal with Paramount Pictures.

Most couples who were not financially strapped would have hired a nanny, but Denise was old school. Since she hadn't been raised by a nanny, neither would her children. Besides, this was her firstborn. Everything she didn't have as a child, Denise wanted to make sure Lil' Derrick did. Denise was only four months pregnant when she started looking into daycare centers, but after a few interviews, she decided just to open up her own.

Denise drove Derrick crazy. She smirked at the thought of how he had such a huge impact on her life. She finally understood what Gabrielle meant when she said Greg was her better half. Being the total opposite of Denise, Derrick kept her grounded. Though Denise brought in over three million a year in revenue from Taylor Management, she kept a low profile. Even with all their accolades, they still managed to live a simple life. Denise didn't splurge like she did years ago. Instead, she invested her money in new business ventures, which was something she learned from Derrick and Greg.

Derrick was an excellent businessman. Being around him, Denise learned so much. Together, they were building an empire. Some might say they were in competition with each other, but Denise and Derrick begged to differ. They supported each other's ideas, but kept most of their businesses separate. That was another unique thing

about their relationship; they didn't fight over money. When they finally decided to get married, both sat down with their attorneys and drafted a prenuptial agreement. In the event of a divorce, both would walk away with what they came into the marriage with, and anything they purchased together before and during their marriage would either be sold or put into the children's names.

After they were married, Denise and Derrick purchased a house in Englewood, New Jersey. Denise wanted to be close to the city. However, she still kept her apartment in Manhattan.

As Denise watched her kids play in the yard, she thought about her friends who were no longer there. Looking up at the clear blue sky, she couldn't help but smile.

"Hey, guys, I made it. I made it for us," she mumbled.

Strangely, after Paul died, it seemed like everything started looking up for everyone. Greg owned a franchise of nightclubs and restaurants across the states. Tony branched out into a clothing line, movies, cologne, and real estate. He was named in *Forbes Magazine* as one of the top ten richest people under forty. Even still, when they got together, none of that mattered. They still acted like they were in the projects hustling. Whenever their schedules permitted, they would hook up at one of Greg's restaurants, laughing and snapping on each other like the good ole days. Sometimes they would talk about their friends who were no longer with them, but Greg would quickly change the subject, something he did when he was secretly investigating people.

As for Denise's family, their bond was tighter than ever, especially since Jasmine's diagnosis of breast cancer. It had been a year since the family found out, and Denise still had a hard time accepting it. Just the thought of losing her sister scared the hell out of Denise, who prayed she would give up all her success and accomplishments if God would make Jasmine better.

To make matters worse, Morgan went totally crazy. Instead of going away to college, she surprised everyone when she decided to attend NYU. However, it was when she announced she was pregnant that Denise knew she had completely lost her mind.

"Baby, Jasmine and Gabrielle are here," Derrick announced.

"Tell them I'm out here," she told him, then turned around and yelled, "DJ, Auntie Jasmine and Cousin Gabby are here!"

All of a sudden, Denise heard loud clapping and cheering. She turned around to see it was Jasmine and Gabrielle being funny.

"Mother of the year," Jasmine said, busting out laughing.

"Shut up!" Denise joined in the laughter while walking over to them. "What's up, y'all?" she asked, giving her sister and cousin a hug and kiss. "Damn, Gabby, they are getting so big."

"And grown," Gabrielle added before telling her children, "Go and play with your cousins."

While the kids played in the yard, Denise, Gabrielle, and Jasmine went into the screen house.

"Jasmine, you're looking good," Denise commented.

"Well, sis, I'm trying. Chemo is kicking my ass, but I'm not letting that stop me."

Denise's eyes immediately filled with tears, causing her to lower her head. Gabrielle looked at Denise and then at Jasmine, who had a somber look on her face.

"Denise, are you okay?" Jasmine asked.

Denise sighed. "Yeah, I'm good," she mumbled.

There was a moment of brief silence before they heard Derrick yell, "There's plenty of food! I'm gonna throw some hamburgers on the grill for the kids. Y'all want some?"

At first, no one responded. Then, Denise snidely said, "Derrick is a pain in the ass. Ever since we remodeled the backyard, he's been dying to use the grill."

Her remark caused everyone to laugh.

"Yes, babe," Denise finally yelled back to him.

"Denise, the house is gorgeous. You remodeled it, too?"

"Yeah, you know Derrick is always looking to spend money." She flashed a devilish grin.

"Bullshit! I know it was your ass!" Jasmine yelled, and once again, everyone laughed.

"No, really, we only redid the kitchen and this part. Shit, remodeling is expensive. The next time we're remodeling is when the kids turn ten."

"I love the view," Gabrielle said admiringly.

"Well, I learned from the best." Denise looked over at Jasmine, making her smile.

"Hey, Aunt Dee!" Monique and Michael yelled.

Denise jumped up. "Oh my God! Look at you guys! Monique, you're so big and pretty. You look just like Jasmine."

"Everyone says that," she replied.

"And look at my handsome nephew. I know you're driving the ladies crazy down there."

Before he had a chance to respond, Jasmine blurted out, "He better be driving those books crazy. Denise, don't fill their heads up with nothing."

Denise looked over at Jasmine, who had a serious look on her face but remained quiet.

After they were gone, Denise asked, "Is everything okay?"

"Yeah. I just don't want them to follow..." Jasmine replied, her voice trailing off.

Denise nodded.

Once Morgan got pregnant, Jasmine became strict with her other kids. A part of her believed if Morgan had been living with her instead of Denise, she wouldn't have gotten pregnant.

"How's Morgan?" Gabrielle blurted out.

Jasmine sighed, while Denise noisily exhaled and rolled her eyes.

"Alive," Jasmine replied. "She was supposed to come, but who knows with Morgan nowadays." Disappointed, she shook her head. "I don't know what's gotten into that child."

Just then, Greg, Tony, and Christina arrived.

"Must you always make a grand entrance?" Denise smiled. "I didn't think you guys were gonna make it."

"Of course, we would. There's free food, right?" Tony responded with his hand out.

"Shut up, fool! Hey Chris, how are you doing?" Denise said, kissing her on the cheek.

Christina giggled. "I'm good! Where are the kids?"

"They're running around with their cousins and being a pain in the ass. When are you and Tony gonna pop out some damn kids? They need playmates."

Christina and Tony looked at each other, flashing fake smiles, and then in unison, they replied, "Don't know."

"Mrs. Brightman...Hey, Jasmine," Tony greeted with a smile.

"Tony," Gabrielle snidely replied, and then warmly said, "Hey, Christina," as she kissed her on the cheek.

With the music playing and the kids running around knocking over stuff, Greg and Tony played a game of Cee-lo. They even got Derrick to join in.

Denise shook her head. *You can take a dude out of the ghetto, but you can't take the ghetto out of the dude.* She thought about joining them, but decided to stay with the girls.

A short while later, a couple of guys from Derrick's job arrived with Mookie, while Mike trailed behind.

When Morgan finally popped up, everyone was busy laughing and talking shit.

"Ayyy, Morgan!" they yelled upon noticing her.

"Hello..."

"Wow, Morgan, you're getting so big," Gabrielle stated.

"Yeah, tell me about it. I can't wait to give birth."

Since there were guests around, Denise decided not to say anything. She just looked at Jasmine from the corner of her eye before glaring back at Morgan. Judging by Jasmine's look, she was still upset with Morgan. When Morgan announced she was having a baby, Jasmine flew into a rage, urging her to have an abortion and explaining how having a baby would hold her back.

"Wow, you came. I didn't expect you to show up," Denise snidely stated.

"I told you that I was coming."

"Yes, but you've said that plenty of times. Anyway, it's great to see you."

Morgan shook her head, choosing not to respond to Denise's comment.

"How's school?" Jasmine asked.

"School is wonderful. I have a 4.0 GPA. Mommy, don't worry. I only need twenty credits to finish," Morgan informed her.

"That's wonderful. When did you start college? I just started taking college classes, and it's killing me," Christina blurted out.

"Chris, I didn't know you were in school," Gabrielle said.

"Before Paul died, he encouraged me to go back to school," she replied in a saddened tone.

"Paul was a good dude," Denise mumbled.

"Yep, he was." Christina beamed before walking out of the screen house.

"So, Ms. Morgan, are you ready to become a mother?" Gabrielle asked, switching the subject.

"She better be," Denise snapped.

Morgan cut her eyes and giggled. "Ready as I'll ever be. After the baby is born, I'm going to finish up undergrad before applying to law school."

Denise loudly sucked her teeth while cutting her eyes. "Oh really? So you have it planned out, eh?"

"Morgan, who's gonna watch the baby while you're in school?" Jasmine asked, remaining calm.

"The babysitter. Mommy, I'm going to law school," she responded, getting annoyed.

"I know you are, even if you have to carry that child with you," Jasmine protested.

"And I will. I'm not taking any time off after the baby is born. Mommy, I will finish college and go on to law school. I promise."

"You better," Denise snapped.

"I will, Auntie." Morgan leaned over, kissing both of them.

"Any word from the father?" Denise inquired.

"Nope."

"So he just up and left?" Jasmine said.

Irritated with them grilling her about the child's father, Morgan sighed. "Yes. He said he wasn't ready to be a father."

"What about his family?" Denise asked.

"I don't know anything about his family. They live in Chicago," Morgan replied, growing upset.

"Chicago? You go out and fuck a nigger that's not even from New York? Shit, if that's the case, I know a couple of losers that could've knocked you up," Denise snapped, making Gabrielle and Jasmine giggle.

"Very funny. HA! HA! I don't need any man to help me raise my child," she proclaimed, causing everyone to stare at her.

"So you're gonna raise this child alone?" Jasmine asked.

"Yep."

"You sound like them other silly bitches. Excuse my French, but I'm sick of chicks saying they don't need a man. Then they're the first ones to jump on the welfare line or run for child support. Honey, you may not need a man, but your child is gonna need a father. What are you gonna tell that child when he or she asks about their father?" Denise stated, while everyone nodded their head in agreement.

"The father didn't want to be in my child's life. Either way, my child is going to be fine."

"For a person who's so smart, you're saying some dumb shit right now. You're not making any sense," Denise said.

"That makes two of us who thinks she's not making sense." Jasmine glared at Morgan.

"Really? That's funny coming from you, Aunt Denise. It's because of you..." she blurted out, but then caught herself. "You know what? That's the main reason I don't come around. I feel like I'm being interrogated. It's not like I'm living with anyone. I'm twenty now. I can make my own decisions, and I decided to have a child!" she snapped.

Just as Denise was about to say something, Jasmine threw her hand up, stopping her.

"First of all, who do you think you're talking to? I don't give a damn how old you are, young lady. You better watch your mouth. I'm still your mother, and just because I'm sick, it doesn't mean I won't get up and knock the shit out of you."

"So, because you don't live with anyone, we don't have the right to question you?" Jasmine continued. "It's only because we care about you, Morgan. We want to make sure you know what is about to happen. Having a child doesn't make you a woman, young lady," she said, grabbing Morgan's face. "Instead of being defensive, you need to start listening. Because the reality is, it's not your problem. It's *our* problem."

Jasmine was yelling so loud that Tony came to see what the problem was.

"Y'all alright in here?" When he looked over at Morgan, he noticed the tears running down her face. Immediately, his blood started boiling. As bad as he wanted to say something, he couldn't.

After struggling to get up from the chair, Morgan said, "Excuse me," and left.

"Morgan!" Jasmine yelled.

"Jas, leave her," Gabrielle suggested.

Tony took a deep breath. "What happened?"

"Why?" Denise snapped.

"I just asked. Why y'all going in on her like that?"

"And how's that's your business?!" Denise said, glowering at him.

"Nah, it isn't, but there's a time and place for shit like that."

"Tony, go sit down. This shit has nothing to do with you. This is between Morgan and Jasmine."

"Then why are you so involved?" he shot back, pissing Denise off even more.

By this time, Christina had returned and was trying to figure out what was going on.

"Tee, don't go there!" Denise shouted, jumping in his face.

"Nah, you don't go there. I'm not the same Tony, Dee..."

"You think that matters," Denise whispered in his ear.

Both glowered at each other before Tony walked away, which was probably for the best, because in two seconds, Denise was about to hook off on him. Laughing to herself, she sat back down. She knew Tony was only showing off.

As the sun started to set, everyone retreated inside except for Greg, who remained in the yard chilling alone.

"What are you thinking about?" Denise asked, walking up on him.

With his shades on, he laughed and replied, "Thinking? How did you know?"

"Come on now. How long have we been family?"

Greg smirked. "What was that all about with you and Tony?"

"Nothing. He just tried to flex." She brushed it off. "You know I don't pay him no mind. He was upset that we were yelling at Morgan."

"Why?"

Denise sighed. "Because she got pregnant."

Greg nodded and gave her the side eye. "Dee, you gotta let Morgan figure things out for herself. If she feels like having a baby, then just be there for her."

"Yeah, but…"

"But nothing, sis. Yelling at her isn't going to help. You of all people should know that. Remember Perry used to say that to you a lot."

Denise giggled. "Yeah, he said I'm emotional."

"And that's not good."

Denise lowered her head. Greg always had a way of making things make sense.

Greg took a deep breath. "I think about Perry and Paul every day."

"So do I…especially Perry. I can't believe…"

"Dee, when I came into the game, this old timer told me that at least one person on my team was gonna cross me."

"Fucking Alex! Didn't he come home?"

"He made the board. Too bad he didn't make it home." Greg winked.

Denise laughed and was about to say something, when Greg nudged her, alerting her to Tony, Mike, and Mookie walking towards them.

"So this is where the party's at?" Tony joked. "Yo, sis, I'm sorry for acting out."

Denise smiled. "It's cool. Just don't let it happen again. Tony, don't let this…" she said, pointing to her house, "fool ya. I'll still put that work in, especially when it comes to my family and friends."

Tony lowered his head. He wanted to respond, but didn't want anyone to start questioning him.

There was a moment of silence before Mookie said, "Greg, can I ask you a question?"

Greg nodded. "Shoot."

"Everyone I've talked to that knows you loves you. Not one person has anything negative to say about you. Is it because they fear you?"

Greg smirked. "Nah, my parents just raised me to treat everyone with respect. To know me is to love me."

"Were you always this laidback?"

"Yeah, Mookie. Dudes that wanna be loud and seen are insecure. When I was younger, I hung around a lot of older dudes, and I remember this one dude who was always by himself. The most he hung with were two people. He didn't like a lot of people around him. One day, I asked him why, and he told me having too many people around draws attention. As long as you know you're important, who gives a shit about what others think? There's no need for me to walk around with my chest poked out."

"That's true. You know, I've been around plenty of dudes, and none of them are like you. You're not flashy."

"For what?! Mookie, there are two things people want in life; that's money and power. Some believe power will get them the money. That's why a lot of them are incarcerated. For others, it's money. They think the money will get them power, which isn't always the case either. For me, it's a balance. I knew my strength. That's why I'm still here. I wouldn't allow anyone to do something I

wouldn't do; we ride together. That flashy shit has never been my style. That's when the haters come out."

"Mookie, I think I speak for all of us when I say this is the good life. Money doesn't equal happiness, and we all had to learn that. I know my family is more important to me than money because I had my share of both. Money is a tool we use in life," Denise explained.

"Yep. Only rappers go around stunting. No offense, Tee. You don't see Bill Gates or Mike Bloomberg talking about how much money they have. I know a lot of dudes that are rich but miserable because mo' money mo' problems," Greg stated.

Everyone nodded.

"Mookie, I want you to read one of Warren Buffet's books. It's really good. I read it while in prison," Greg suggested.

"A'ight, I will. Thanks. I remember growing up and watching you. If you wasn't with your crew, you was always by yourself, and I used to ask myself were you scared."

They all laughed.

"Nah, I'm always on point. Dudes knew better. Mookie, it's rare that you find a dude like me. I don't play both sides of the fence. A lot of dudes, jump ship when shit hits the fan. That's not me, and that's another reason why I'm still here."

"Now you see why I love this man. He's the realist nigga on the planet. There's no one like Greg Brightman," Tony blurted out, giving Greg a pound.

Immediately, Tony started reminiscing about the olden days, having everyone in stitches. Denise was laughing so hard that she had to excuse herself to the bathroom.

"Damn, I wish Paul and Perry were here," Mike said.

"Dee and I were just talking about them. Perry still owes me from that dice game." Greg giggled while shaking his head.

"Don't forget about Felicia," Tony added.

"Oh yeah, big Felicia," Mike said, raising his hands. "Damn, do they know who killed any of them?"

"What is the police saying?" Mookie asked, causing everyone to give him a weird look.

"Police? Nigga, we don't do police. They don't give a fuck. To them, it's just another nigga," Tony voiced in a nasty tone.

"True, but they gotta know something," Mookie continued.

Then, out of the blue, Tony asked, "Yo, Greg, did Denise tell you that faggot-ass nigga Moe tried to holla at me?"

"Moe..." Greg said, twisting up his face. "For what?"

"He wanted some cash. Don't worry. It's cool. I had Paul take care of him. Remember, Mike?"

Mike squinted. "Oh yeah, I remember Moe."

"When did this happen?" Greg inquired.

"A couple years ago. I was gonna come up there to tell you—you know, keep you in the loop—but Denise said I needed to handle it myself," Tony explained nervously.

Like always, Greg put on his poker face when he didn't want anyone to know what he was thinking. "That's cool. So is everything good?" he asked.

With his shades covering his eyes, Tony nodded and replied, "Yeah, I haven't heard anything from him."

Mike looked over at Tony, who looked over at Greg and awaited a response.

Greg sighed. "Yo, Mike, the last time you spoke to Paul what did he say?" he inquired, changing the subject.

"He said he had something to take care of. He told Chris that he was meeting an old friend. Why?"

"Nothing. When y'all approached Moe, how did he take it?"

"Well, I stood outside while Paul went and spoke with him, but everything seemed cool from what Paul said."

Greg just nodded. His silence scared them. Tony and Mike knew the wheels were turning. Mookie sat there confused. There was a brief silence until Denise returned.

"Tony, you're a fool, for real," she said, holding her stomach.

Just as Denise was about to continue, Morgan emerged from the house and said, "Derrick asked if anyone wants any more food before he puts it away."

Mookie turned around. "Oh shit, she's pregnant again?" he mumbled loudly.

"Who?" Denise asked.

Mookie looked over in Tony's direction before responding, "Nah, I thought she was someone else," in an attempt to clear it up.

"Put your damn contacts in. That's a little girl you're talking about. All this money he got and his cheap ass won't buy any glasses!" Tony yelled, trying to make a joke.

Everyone laughed but Greg. He was in deep thought.

Feeling a little uncomfortable with Greg's silence, Tony rubbed his stomach and said, "I don't know about y'all, but I'm gonna get me another plate."

"I'm with you on that, playboy," Mookie said, while Mike jumped up to follow them.

Once the three men had gone inside the house, Greg looked up at the sky. "Dee, Tony had a problem with Moe?" he asked her.

"Yes, he did a couple of years ago. Why, he has a problem with him now?"

"Nah, I was just curious as to why I'm just finding this out and why you told him to handle it himself."

Denise looked down at her manicured grass. She knew where this conversation was going. Wanting some privacy, she said, "Greg let's go into the screen house."

Once they were seated inside, she continued. "Yeah, I told Tony not to go up there to the prison with that bullshit to you. He's a grown-ass man. We've been carrying his ass for years. We were already handling that shit for him with Felicia."

"Why didn't you tell me, though? You know I was locked up with Moe's cousin. If I would've known that, I would have sent the word out. A motherfucker can't smile up in my face and try to extort my crew."

"You're right, but you can't handle everything. We've been doing that shit for years for Tony. He had Paul talk to Moe. Why, something happened?"

"No. He just brought it up today to me, but I'm thinking if Paul stepped to Moe..."

Denise cut him off. "You're not thinking Moe killed Paul, are you?"

Greg just looked at Denise.

"Shit!"

"Nah, I'm not saying that...yet. Moe knew Tony was down with me, so even if I was locked up, Moe knew better than to play games with anyone on my team, especially since his cousin was within arm's reach of me." Greg stood up. "This shit is not making sense to me. If Moe felt threatened, he would've killed Paul on the spot or hollered at me about the situation."

"Greg, you were locked up."

"Just because I was locked up doesn't mean a motherfucker won't respect me. You think because I was locked up my reach isn't long?" he said, upset.

"No, but people change. Please, dudes thought you had life. They didn't give a fuck. I'm not saying Moe felt that way, but it's true."

Greg sat back down. "You might be right, because Moe is just like us."

Denise took a deep breath. "So what you wanna do? You want me to talk to Moe?"

Greg removed his shades so he could stare Denise in the face. "Talk?" he simply replied.

Denise laughed. "Yeah, you're right. Fucking with Moe, I might have to kill his ass."

"Or make him kill himself. Dee, we have families now."

"Shit, I know! What, you think I'm gonna kill the nigga in Times Square in broad daylight? Come on, Greg, this is me. Let me talk to him."

Greg pondered her words for a second. "Nah, if he did have something to do with Paul's death, I don't want him to know we know. Feel me?"

"Alright, but you know I'm always here."

"I know, sis, but let me do some investigating first—see if he was in town when Paul was murdered."

"And if he was?"

Greg just looked at Denise. The question didn't require an answer.

After putting the kids to bed, Denise and Derrick went back into the yard for some quality time.

"Now this is what I call fun." Denise smiled and kissed him.

"Yep. Hey, is everything alright? When you and Greg came back in the house, you seemed to have something on your mind."

"Really? We were just talking about our friends that passed away."

"Oh, how did they die?"

"Like every black man—someone killed them, but enough about them," Denise responded, taking off her shirt. "Mrs. Johnson wants you to fuck her."

Derrick, who instantly became rock hard, released a giggle. "Oh yeah? Now that's what I like to hear," he said, then yanked her on top of him.

*****

Over the next couple of weeks, Denise thought about her conversation with Greg. She really hoped Moe didn't have anything to do with Paul's death. After handling Perry, she was done with that killing shit. She had a family now. However, a part of her felt it could've been her lying in that casket. Another thing that popped into her head was why Tony told Greg after all of these years. Was he trying to be funny? She made a mental note to check his ass.

As Denise drove into the Lincoln Tunnel, she looked at her kids in the rearview mirror and sighed. They were her everything, and they deserved to be raised by their mother. Therefore, she might have to sit this one out. Lil' Derrick played with his toy, while Halle looked out the window. Those were the only two people she would come

out of retirement for. After dropping them off at the daycare, Denise headed to the office.

Although she loved running her own corporation, it seemed like she worked harder. Unlike her city job, she had to give a hundred percent all the time. There were days when she wanted to walk out of meetings, but she knew it wouldn't look right. Though she hired an executive committee to handle most of the business, she didn't fully trust anyone. Her motto was no one can count her money better than she could.

Denise was about to make a call, when her assistant told her Mike was there to see her.

Apprehensive, Denise repeated, "Mike?" Once her assistant confirmed the name, Denise took a deep breath and said, "Send him in".

"Mike, what brings you here?" Denise stood to kiss him on the cheek.

"I wanted to talk to you."

"Sure. What about?"

"I wanted to tell you that I didn't tell Greg about Moe. It was Tony."

"I know. Greg told me."

"Oh, I didn't want you to think I said something."

Denise giggled. "No, it's cool. I have nothing to hide."

"That's cool."

"Mike, let me ask you something. How did that meeting go with Moe?"

"What do you mean?"

"What did he say?" she asked him.

"Nothing. I stood outside while Paul went in, but Paul did say Moe told him someone had already hollered at him. Moe is cool, though, Dee. I hang out with him all the time."

"Huh?" Denise was confused.

"Nah, we just hang out from time to time. Moe is looking to get into the business. You know I'm showing him the ropes."

"Alright, but be careful. Moe is still a street nigga. So tell me what went down between Paul and Moe," Denise said, getting back to the subject.

"When we saw Moe, everything was already cool. Apparently, Tony reached out to someone else to talk to him. So, when we saw him, it was all love."

"Did he say who?"

"Only that the dude was from the NYC."

Denise frowned up her face. "So why did Tony say y'all holla?"

"We did, but it wasn't like that."

Denise nodded and asked one more question. "How was Perry at the job?"

"P was cool. You know P; he didn't care about that rapping shit."

"How was his relationship with Tony?"

"Good. They hardly saw each other. When they did, it was all good. Why?"

"I was just thinking."

"I do know Tony set P's wife and kids up with some money," Mike informed her. "He brought them a house and set up a trust fund for the kids."

"Tony did all of that for Perry?" Again, Denise was confused.

"That's what I said."

"That's good!"

"Shit, Tony even helped Felicia."

"What?" Denise nearly shouted.

"Yeah, she came up to the studio a few years ago. Tony gave her a few dollars."

"Wow! They didn't even get along like that."

"That's what I said, too, but Tony gave his number to her and told her to hit him up if she ever needed anything."

"Did she?"

"Nah, she never came back around."

Now Denise's wheels were turning. She could understand Perry and Paul, but Felicia. Tony knew Felicia hated him, so why did he give

18

her money? Was Felicia extorting Tony? Denise was thinking so hard that she didn't hear Mike call her name.

"Hey Dee, are you alright?" He tapped her desk.

"Yeah, I'm good. I'm just surprised."

"Why? Tee was just showing his love like Greg use to do."

"Yeah...yeah. Mike, do you know if Felicia had any brothers?"

"I saw her with this dude one time. She said he was her brother. I haven't seen homeboy in years. He didn't even come to the funeral."

"So, she did?"

"Yeah, he used to come around. Damn, I can't remember dude's name. Felicia's mom doesn't know?"

"Last time I check, she didn't."

"Oh. Well, you know she doesn't live in Melrose anymore. Word is she moved to Manhattan Avenue after she got Felicia's insurance money."

"What money?'

"She got like two hundred thousand from the policy."

"Damn. Do you have her information? I need to talk to her."

"Not on me, but I will make some calls and get back to you," Mike told her. "Oh, you know who would know about Felicia's brother? Bruce and Joe. You know them niggas know everything."

Denise threw her head back. "That's right. They are the neighborhood newsmen." She giggled. "I didn't even think about them. Mike, get me Millie's information."

"For sure," he said, then left.

Damn, I forgot about those dudes, she thought.

Chapter Two
Gabrielle

Gabrielle felt as if her prayers had finally been answered. With a great husband and two beautiful kids, what else could she ask for? Not only were they financially comfortable and successful like Denise and Derrick, they, too, maintained a normal life.

However, Gabrielle had to admit her mother was right when she said that she and Greg had a lot to learn when it came to marriage. Though married for over ten years, they had lived separately for the past nine of those years.

Of course, the first ninety days after Greg's release from prison were wonderful. They went on romantic vacations, took long strolls in the park, and had candlelight dinners followed by hot steamy sex. Then the babies came, and it became all about them. For the first year, Gabrielle and Greg didn't get any sleep, let alone spend any quality time together. Whenever she suggested going out, Greg always wanted to bring the children along. It wasn't until the babies were able to speak that just the two of them went out to dinner.

It also didn't help that both of them had demanding careers. Gabrielle's clientele increased once people knew Greg was home. Tony also referred a lot of his colleagues to her. Greg opened up a couple of clubs, restaurants, and sports bars in addition to owning apartment complexes in Newark, New Jersey. *Brightman Incorporated* was the company's name. Initially, Gabrielle was going to leave her law office to solely handle their business. Then the conversation she had with her mother popped into her head, and she quickly changed her mind.

Although proud of her husband's accomplishments, Gabrielle got upset when she learned it was Tony who gave him the money. When she first questioned Greg, he got annoyed and asked her what was with all the questions. Had it been back in the day, he would've checked her, but since she was his wife, he obliged her interrogations.

Since Gabrielle and Greg both had strong personalities, they often clashed. Gabrielle had become so accustomed to driving that she didn't know how to take the passenger seat. Eventually, Greg had to show a different side of him, which made her chill out. While Greg would never hit a woman, his silence scared her.

One thing they did was devote their lives to their children by taking turns caring for them. Although the club required Greg to be there at night, he never missed a night having dinner with his family. If Gabrielle cooked, Greg tended to the kids, giving them a bath and getting them ready for bed. If Greg cooked, Gabrielle did the same, but it seemed like when it was her turn, the kids gave her a hard time. After Greg read them a story, they were fast asleep. However, Gabrielle had to go back into the room three and four times before they finally settled into a slumber.

Now that the twins were four years old, Gabrielle and Greg would have what they called "date night". Most times, they went to the movies or would catch a Broadway play, followed by freaky sex. There was a time when they were so caught up in their careers that they forgot the romance in their marriage. One time, they didn't have sex for three months, and when they finally did, it was a quickie.

As usual, Gabrielle prepared breakfast while Greg got the kids dressed. She chuckled to herself when she heard him yelling at Greg

Jr. Thank God she had finally convinced him to hire a nanny and a part-time housekeeper.

Paranoid, he didn't want anyone in their house or around their kids. After his birthday party, Greg decided they would purchase a new house because, according to him, too many people knew where they lived, which in his eyes was a safety issue. He even made her sell all the cars. At night, Greg would conduct a walk-thru before putting the alarm on. He was so cautious, and Gabrielle hated that about him. After a while, she gave up and just accepted the fact that her husband was crazy.

Though they had a nanny, Greg or Gabrielle would drop the kids off to preschool every morning. She wanted the kids to attend Denise's daycare, but Greg didn't think it would be a good idea.

Unlike everyone else, Gabrielle and Greg moved to Rye, New York. Although the commute was long, the town was quiet. On her way to work while listening to the radio, Britney popped into Gabrielle's head. The last time she'd heard from Britney, she was engaged to a black computer analyst. Gabrielle smirked. Britney loved her black men. Often, Gabrielle thought about telling Greg about Britney, but she was scared of how he may react.

Instead of heading to her office, Gabrielle headed to the Manhattan Criminal Courthouse. She was appearing on behalf of Abigail, who was still out of the office since her mother had died of an overdose. Gabrielle signed in and went to the holding pen to see her client, Jaquan Donaldson. He was seventeen years old and being charged with murder in the first degree.

Making her way to the holding cell, Gabrielle yelled, "Jaquan Donaldson!" Ignoring the COs checking her out and the inappropriate comments the inmates blurted out, she yelled one more time. That's when she heard a soft voice yell back, "Over here!"

Trying to figure out where the voice was coming from, Gabrielle walked over to a nearby cell, when the CO pointed and yelled, "He's in cell number four."

"Jaquan," she repeated.

A thin, small boy walked toward her. "Yes," he answered, causing Gabrielle's eyes to widen.

Noticing her reaction, the CO commented, "Yeah, they're getting younger and younger," before opening the cell.

"Hey Jaquan. My name is Gabrielle Brightman, and I will be representing you on behalf of Abigail," she said, while leading him to a private room.

"Okay," he whispered.

Gabrielle looked at him before opening the case file and briefly scanning through it. "It says here that you were seen running from a crime scene."

Jaquan looked around before responding. "I was running because shots were being fired. Mrs. Brightman, I didn't kill anyone," he replied, his voice cracking.

Gabrielle stared into his eyes. Something about him seemed different. "Jaquan, tell me what happened."

"A group of my friends was coming from a basketball game. We stopped at Kennedy's Fried Chicken to get something to eat. A couple guys came in and started staring us up and down. A few words were exchanged, so we left. The dudes followed us, but we didn't think nothing of it. When I stopped to tie my sneakers, some dude came out from between two cars and shot at some guy. I dropped my food and ran. Next thing I know, the police are chasing me. They said they had a witness that said I killed him, but I didn't, Mrs. Brightman. I swear," he cried.

Speechless for a few seconds, Gabrielle opened the case file again. "It says here that you were caught running from the scene, but no gun was found. You had the victim's blood on your sneakers and clothes. Two people claim to have seen you have words with the victim, and they say you then went behind a car and shot the victim," she stated.

"I didn't kill anyone."

Gabrielle sighed. "Jaquan, where are your parents?"

"I live with my grandparents. Are they out there?"

"Oh, they come to your court appearances?"

"Yes…"

"Awww shit! Get off me! CO, help!" someone cried out, making Jaquan flinch.

"Mrs. Brightman, can you get me out of here…please?"

"Let's see what we can do."

*****

"Hey, Nancy, pull everything you have on the Jaquan Donaldson's case," Gabrielle instructed once she arrived back at her office. "I want ballistic and police reports and all the witnesses' statements. Call West and have him go back to the crime scene. Then schedule an appointment with Jaquan's grandparents. I want to know more about him. Lastly, make sure the Department of Corrections moved him to a juvenile facility."

It was going on three o'clock, and Gabrielle still had two more clients to see. One of them was Olay, an artist on Tony's label that he had referred to Gabrielle.

Gabrielle walked into the conference room. "Good afternoon, Olay. Sorry to have kept you waiting."

"It's cool." She smiled back. Olay was an attractive girl; she resembled Lauryn Hill.

"I reviewed the contracts and made some minor adjustments—stuff like they have to consult with you first before any changes are done. Also, I made it so you own ninety percent of your publishing and brand. "

"Wow! Thanks."

"All you have to do is sign, and I will forward them back to Tony."

"Great, because he's expecting them. Thank you again."

"You're welcome. If you have any questions, please feel free to call me."

"Well, I did have one question."

"Okay. What is it?"

"I want to hire you as my personal lawyer to handle all my business affairs."

Gabrielle nodded. "Okay, if that's what you want. Nancy will give you all of my contact information and some forms for you to fill out."

Mentally exhausted, Gabrielle checked her appointment book. *Damn!* She forgot she was supposed to meet her mother for dinner that evening. She thought about canceling, but knew her mother would be disappointed.

While waiting for her mother to arrive at her office, Tommy popped into Gabrielle's head. It had been five years since he died in a car accident. She didn't find out until two weeks later, and by then, they had already buried him. It bothered her that she didn't answer the phone that night. Knowing Tommy, he had found some additional information. After Tommy's death, Gabrielle buried all the evidence with him. Once Greg was released, Gabrielle couldn't keep anything pertaining to how he came home. Therefore, she stored it in her office.

Trying to kill time, Gabrielle walked over to her private cabinet and pulled out some of the tapes. As she listened to them, it was the familiar voice again.

"Damn, why don't you say his name…Robin?" she mumbled. She was listening so intensely that she didn't see her mother standing in the doorway.

"Gabrielle."

She jumped upon hearing her mother's voice. "Oh, sorry, Ma. I didn't hear you come in. Is Nancy still here?"

"No. She let me in on her way out. Are you ready?"

Gabrielle nodded. "Yes. Let me turn this off and put it back."

As she was about to turn the tape off, Sadie asked, "Who is that?"

"It's work," Gabrielle responded, shutting it off.

*****

Dinner was great. Gabrielle and her mother had a wonderful time. Since Noel was out of town, Gabrielle drove her mother home.

Out of the blue, Sadie asked, "Who was that person on the tape?"

"What tape?"

"The tape you were listening to."

"Oh that? It's for a client. Why?"

Sadie shook her head. "Nothing."

"So where's Daddy?"

"Your father is out of town at a conference."

"Oh, and you didn't attend with him?" Gabrielle replied in a shocked tone.

"He didn't ask me."

"Now there's a surprise. He didn't take his gorgeous wife," Gabrielle teased.

"Nope. He stopped asking me years ago," she said, fighting back tears.

Gabrielle faced her mother for a brief second. "Ma, is there something wrong?"

Sadie smiled weakly. "No."

"Are you sure?"

"Yes."

Gabrielle offered to walk her mother in, but Sadie declined.

*****

The last couple of weeks had been stressful. Besides working Jaquan's case, Gabrielle was retained for a sexual harassment suit. It had been five years since Greg and Gabrielle went on vacation without the kids, and boy did she need it. Grateful for her blessing, she couldn't wait to hop on a plane to Bora Bora. While finishing up a couple of things in her office, she heard Nancy scream, "Bitch, stop lying!"

"Nancy!" Gabrielle called out.

"Sorry, boss lady, but this chick online is badmouthing Tony."

"Tony who?" Gabrielle asked.

"Tony Flowers."

"Huh?"

Embarrassed, Nancy walked over to Gabrielle's desk. "Don't judge me," she giggled, then continued. "I've joined Tony's fan site, and this chick is always badmouthing him on there."

With her eyebrow raised, Gabrielle slowly replied, "Alright…"

"No, she's saying how Tony is cheating on Christina, that he's a woman beater, and other stupid shit like that."

Gabrielle didn't know if she should burst out laughing or knock some sense into Nancy. All she could do was shake her head before they both busted into laughter.

"Don't judge me," Nancy repeated, then laughed and left.

*****

Fresh from her vacation, Gabrielle was informed by Nancy that her favorite client, Kyle, was waiting for her in the conference room. Gabrielle sighed, "Early in the morning," and then went into her office to put down her things. On her way to the conference room, she bumped into Thomas.

"Welcome back, Gabrielle. I left some contracts on your desk. Please review them when you have a chance."

Gabrielle nodded. "Okay."

Taking a deep breath, she opened up the door. "Kyle!" she cheered.

"Gabrielle!" He smiled and kissed her on the cheek.

"I'm sorry. I didn't know we had an appointment. I'm still in vacation mood." She playfully tapped him.

"It's fine. I actually made the appointment when you were on vacation. So how's the hubby and kids?"

"Everyone is wonderful. Thanks for asking. So what brings you here?"

"Well, I wanted to thank you for everything."

Gabrielle smiled and nodded. "Okay. You could've sent me a card, though," she joked.

"I know, but I wanted to let you know I'm getting married."

"Really?" Gabrielle raised her eyebrow.

"Yes. We met a couple of years ago, and she's the one. I want you to meet her."

"Wow! You found someone to put up with your ass? It would be my pleasure to meet her."

"She's been handling all of my affairs, being that you dumped me."

Gabrielle playfully patted his shoulder. "No...you know I'm always here if you need me."

"I know. I'm just busting your chops. However, she's wonderful."

Gabrielle nodded. "Well, let me know. I can't wait to meet her."

Kyle smiled. "She can't either. When we get back from London, let's go out to dinner."

"Sounds like a plan."

Kyle got up to walk out, but then stopped and turned around. "Will Greg be joining us?"

Gabrielle smirked. "Of course."

Like any other day, Gabrielle reviewed case files and contracts before heading out to pick up her kids. On the way to her car, she laughed. *Kyle finally found someone to tolerate his ass.*

While walking, Gabrielle noticed a black Jaguar parked across the street. Normally, she would not have paid it any attention, but sitting inside was a lady wearing a pair of shades. Gabrielle stood there for a second staring at the car, while the person looked back at her and then drove off.

Ooookay, she thought.

Chapter Three
Morgan

What they say about wine getting better with time must be true because that was surely the case with Morgan. Although, she still had her beautiful baby face, she had gotten prettier over the years. While most women accredited their beauty to great skin products, Morgan had been blessed with great genes.

By the time Morgan turned seventeen, she was in college. She had been offered a full scholarship to almost every Ivy League school in the world. However, when Tony found out about it, he went ballistic.

Afraid, Morgan turned down the colleges and enrolled at NYU instead, taking twenty-four credits per semester. Initially, she was staying on the campus in Soho, but once Tony found out, he made her get an apartment. According to him, college campuses were dangerous, but Morgan knew he was lying. It was just another way of controlling her.

To avoid a fight, she got a little apartment near the west highway. Still, Tony complained about her being away from him. Morgan even had to check in with Tony every hour. If she didn't, he would beat her.

To escape the madness in her life, Morgan threw herself into school. Her family thought she was crazy, but Morgan was determined to maintain a perfect GPA. Of course, Tony wasn't satisfied. He felt like school was taking up too much of Morgan's time. So, one night, he showed her just how frustrated he was by sending Morgan to the emergency room. Sadly, it wouldn't be the last time.

When he wasn't beating Morgan, he was impregnating her. Before finally keeping this baby, Morgan had been pregnant four other times. Three of them she miscarried, and she secretly had an abortion with one. Tony blamed her for the miscarriages, claiming Morgan was purposely losing the babies. So, after Morgan would come home from having a D&C, Tony would have unprotected sex with her. The first time she objected he gave her a black eye.

The day after Morgan turned eighteen, they secretly filed for a marriage license and were wed shortly after. Once married, they moved into a mansion in Alpine, New Jersey, an area so exclusive that you have to go to the post office just to pick up your mail.

Most girls would have given up their firstborn to live there, but, for Morgan, it was a nightmare. Every night it was something different with Tony. If he came home in a bad mood, he took it out on her. If he was unable to reach her, it was a problem. Morgan had practically begged him to allow her to get a job that was only three buildings down from his office.

Tony was happy when he found out they were having a boy, but his excitement only lasted a few months. He was so insecure that he accused Morgan of messing around while pregnant. Flabbergasted, she would just shake her head since there was no point arguing with him.

Another thing Tony did was keep Morgan from her family. If Jasmine hadn't gotten sick, Tony would've never allowed Morgan around them. When he did, it was only for a brief time. With Jasmine living in Atlanta battling cancer and Felix locked up in Italy for drugs and other charges, Tony really acted up. He wouldn't even allow Morgan to accept his calls. There were days she thought about running away, but Tony assured her that he would find her.

"Goodnight, Al," Morgan said as Al pulled up to the house.

"Goodnight, Mrs. Flowers."

Morgan walked in to find Tony standing in the foyer.

"What took you so long?"

"It was traffic," she said, looking at her watch.

"I'm fucking starving."

"I'll heat up your food now."

"Never mind. I wanted to eat dinner with my wife before I go meet up with Christina."

Frightened about how he would react, Morgan just nodded. "I'll be home early tomorrow and will make it up to you."

"I don't know why you're working anyway. It's not like you need the money."

Morgan sighed, then went into the kitchen.

"Ay, yo...you hear me talking to you?"

Morgan swiftly turned around. "I hear you, Tony. You have made it very clear that you don't want me to work, but what am I suppose to do? Stay home with my legs spread open all day?"

Tony giggled, thinking that wasn't a bad idea. "No, but once my son is born, you're quitting."

Morgan glared at him for a second. "Anything else, Sir Tony?"

"No," he replied with seriousness.

Morgan stormed upstairs. "Fucking asshole," she mumbled after slamming the bedroom door.

Morgan studied for an hour and then read to her unborn son. As she was finishing up the story, Tony entered the room.

"I thought you were staying with Christina," she snidely commented.

Walking over to her, he replied, "Nah," while forcing her onto his lap as he took a seat on the bed. "I'm sorry about earlier. I didn't mean to snap at you. Baby, I just want the best for you and my son."

Morgan lowered her head. She had heard it all before.

"It's fine."

Tony took the book away from Morgan, rubbed her stomach as he finished reading to his son, and then followed sex.

The next morning, Tony made breakfast for Morgan, which is something he always did after he acted up. Over the last couple of months, Morgan had gotten really big, but because she was athletic, the doctor said she wouldn't have any problem losing the weight. During her pregnancy, Morgan worked out. She walked at least three miles on the treadmill and did yoga three times a week. Although she had some crazy cravings, Morgan managed to eat healthy. Tony loved it. Unlike most women, she looked even more attractive being pregnant. Her skin glowed, her hair grew down to her ass, and she stayed horny. There were days when she and Tony would have sex literally all day.

"Good morning," her boss said.

"Morning, Mrs. June."

"You look like you're gonna pop any day now."

"Tell me about it," Morgan replied, giggling. "I can't wait."

Morgan worked for a major law firm who handled high profile cases. Last year, they took on Getty's Oil Company and won. Morgan received a huge bonus from that case, which Tony wasn't happy about. At times, she wondered if he was jealous of her.

Morgan went about her daily business which included making calls, scheduling meetings, and typing up memos before heading to school. Just as she was about to get in her awaiting car service, Gabrielle was coming out of a café.

"Oh my god, Morgan!"

Morgan turned around. "Hi, Gabrielle," she said in a state of shock.

Gabrielle walked over and kissed her on the cheek. "How are you?"

Morgan looking around, then smiled. "I'm doing great. What are you doing around here?"

"Meeting with a client, and you?"

"Oh, I work in this building."

32

Morgan's phone rang; it was Tony. "Excuse me," she said before answering it. "Hello."

"Hey, babe, are you on your way to school?" he asked.

"Not yet. I bumped into my cousin Gabrielle coming out of the building."

"What does she want?"

"Nothing."

"Well, you need to get to school."

"I know."

Click!

"Gabrielle, I really have to get going."

Confused as to why Morgan was so quick to leave, Gabrielle replied, "Okay. Well, keep in touch. Maybe one day when I'm down here again we can have lunch."

Morgan leaned forward, kissed her, and replied, "Sure," before hopping in the car.

*****

It was seven o'clock, and Morgan still had one more class. She also needed to catch the library to get information for a paper that was due next week. As she was crossing the campus, one of her classmates ran up to her.

"Hey, Morgan! Thanks for covering for me," he said.

Morgan snickered. "It's no problem, Jasper. Professor Canon can be a jerk at times."

They both laughed.

"Well, I'll catch you around. Hey, when are you due?"

Morgan laughed. "Any day now."

When Morgan got home, Tony hadn't gotten there yet. So, Morgan hurried up and prepared dinner. She then went upstairs to change. That's when she heard the door slam, and a few moments later, Tony stormed in the bedroom.

"Who the fuck was that guy you were talking to?"

"Huh?" she answered.

Tony grabbed her by the arm. "You think I'm playing with you? Who was that?"

Morgan struggled to snatch her arm from his grasp. "You're hurting me."

Tony released her, but waited for an answer.

"He's in my class. He thanked me for answering a question for him."

"Really? Well, you seemed to be smiling all up in his face."

"Tony, it's nothing... Wait. You were watching me?"

"Morgan, you're my wife, and that's my fucking son you're carrying. I'm always watching you. You should know that by now," he said, then asked, "And what did Gabrielle want?"

"Nothing," she replied before walking back to the kitchen.

During dinner, Tony's cell phone rang; it was Christina. After glancing at it, he turned it off. Showing his more loving side, he cleaned up while Morgan went into the other room to type up a term paper. Tony was so afraid of someone finding out about them that he didn't allow anyone in their house, except for a cleaning company that came once every week.

Morgan was typing, when she heard her cell phone. It was almost eleven o'clock. *Who the hell could be calling this time of night?* She thought. It was her little brother, Michael.

"Hello."

"Morgan, they're taking Mommy to the hospital," Michael informed her.

"What? Why?"

"She can't keep anything down."

"Alright, I'm coming out there."

"No...wait! Let's see what the doctor says first. I'll keep you posted."

"Okay."

Click!

Tony stood in the doorway with his arms folded. "What happened?"

"They took my mother to the hospital."

"You're not going…"

Morgan glared at him, cutting him off. "If she needs me, yes, I am."

"Is this the same mother that went off on you at Denise's cookout? Get the fuck outta here! You're not going."

"Yeah, well, can't say I blame her. I mean, look at me," she snidely replied.

"Yeah, look at you! You still have more than them. They wish they had all of this."

"You're so clueless. You think it's all about money…that everyone wants to be rich," she argued.

"Them? Yes."

Morgan smirked. "Newsflash, Tony! Not everyone wants this lifestyle! I sure as hell didn't want it!" she said, then brushed past him.

Tony stood there in shock. Morgan had never yelled at him. He flew up the stairs behind her. "I'm sorry. If you need to fly out, I'll have the private jet on standby."

Pissed off, Morgan went into the bathroom and slammed the door.

With Morgan's words having scared the hell out of Tony, he tiptoed around the house for the next couple of days. He washed clothes, prepared food, and didn't stress Morgan out by calling her a hundred times a day. He didn't want to upset her, especially with their child due any day now.

As promised, Tony had the private jet waiting to take Morgan to Atlanta. When she arrived at the hospital, she was greeted by her brother.

"Dag, sis, are you carrying twins?" Michael joked, kissing her on the cheek.

Morgan giggled. "It feels like it. How's Mommy?"

"She's good now, but you know she's gonna be pissed when she sees you."

"Why?"

"Because you flew all the way out here. Morgan, you're pregnant."

Morgan wobbled to the elevator. "Well, she just has to get over it, because I'm not leaving."

Michael laughed. "Y'all two are just alike...stubborn!"

As they were about to enter the elevator, some girls were coming out.

"Hi, Michael!" the girls said in unison, while smiling broadly.

Morgan glared at Michael, who had a Kool-aid smile on his face.

"Hey, what's up?" he replied coolly.

Shaking her head, Morgan teased, "Aren't we popular?"

Michael laughed. "I can't help it if the girls love Mike Love," he joked, rubbing his chin.

"Yeah, whatever! You just better make sure you treat women right and don't have any babies."

"Huh? Babies? Are you crazy? I'm only fifteen years old."

"Good. Keep thinking like that."

After receiving assurance that Jasmine was okay, Morgan spent some time with her brother and sister. It wasn't often they got to hang out with their big sis.

Morgan was getting undressed when Monique knocked on the door.

"Morgan, are you sleeping?"

"No. Come in."

"Wow! Your stomach is huge." Monique smiled while touching her sister's enlarged stomach.

Morgan smiled, also. "Tell me about it."

"Are you scared?"

"A little."

"Well, I'm here if you need me," she said, attempting to comfort her.

Morgan giggled. "Awww, thank you!"

Knock! Knock!

"What are y'all doing?" Michael asked, jumping onto the bed.

"Talking about the baby," Monique told him.

"I can't wait!" Michael said, clapping his hands with excitement.

"Me either! Where's the father?" her sister inquired.

"I don't know," Morgan replied in a somber tone.

"You mean, he just up and left?" Michael frowned.

Morgan sighed. She didn't like lying to her brother and sister, but she couldn't tell them the truth.

"Yes. He said he didn't wanna be a father."

"Forget that dude. I'll be my nephew's father. We don't need him. I better not run into him," Michael angrily stated, punching his fist into the palm of his hand.

"Yeah, we don't need him," Monique repeated.

Morgan's eyes got watery. "Awww, thanks, guys. You know being an uncle and an aunt is a big responsibility, right?"

"We know, and we can't wait." Michael bopped his head, causing Morgan to laugh.

"I told all of my friends at school that I wanna be just like my sister when I get older," Monique chimed.

Morgan looked away and then back at her siblings. "No, don't be like me. I want you guys to be better than me. I'm having a baby…" Morgan stressed.

"So? I know a lot of young girls who have children, and they're not in school. Morgan, you're in college," Michael pointed out.

"I know," Morgan mumbled, then replied, "Enough about me. Tell me what you guys have been doing."

Excited, Morgan talked with her siblings into the wee hours of the morning.

*****

It was a bright Sunday afternoon, and Tony was out of town. With nothing to do, Morgan decided to visit her favorite aunt. The last time they were together, it wasn't good.

"Wow! Is it my birthday already?" Denise said sarcastically.

Morgan poked out her lip and folded her arms. "No. I just came back from Atlanta and was in the neighborhood, so I figured I'd stop by."

"Well, you know you're always welcome. How's your mother doing?" she asked, while leading her into the living room.

"She's doing well. They released her from the hospital."

"That's good! So how are you doing? Are we ready to drop that load?"

Morgan giggled. "Yes. How are Derrick and the kids doing?"

"They're fine...getting on my damn nerves." Denise winked.

There was a brief silence in the room, both unsure of what to say. Then Denise blurted out, "Are you scared?"

Instantly, Morgan's eyes filled with tears. "Yes!"

"Well, don't be. I'm here if you need me."

"Thanks. Aunt Denise, have you ever regretted some of the choices you've made in life?"

Caught off guard by the question, Denise replied, "All the time, Morgan. I think seventy-five percent of the choices I made in life I regret. Why? Do you regret getting pregnant?"

Morgan exhaled while trying to get more comfortable on the sofa. Taking another long, deep breath, Morgan stared at the floor as her eyes filled with tears again. *If only you knew, Aunt Denise,* she thought. Staring into Denise's eyes, Morgan decided it was time to talk, but where should she start? How does one tell their aunt that they were raped by her best friend? Right when she went to open her mouth, Lil' Derrick came running in.

"Mommy...Mommy, look!"

Immediately, Morgan snapped back to reality and looked down at her stomach. If she said something, her child would be motherless. Tony vowed if she ever uttered a word, he would kill everyone in her family, including her.

"Sorry, Morgan," Denise said once Lil' Derrick ran back out of the room. "What were you gonna say?"

"Oh, I was saying I don't regret getting pregnant. I just wish I would've waited. Aunt Denise, have you ever been pregnant before?"

Now it was Denise's turn to lower her head. Though Morgan was an adult, in Denise's eyes, she was still her little niece. While waiting

for an answer, Morgan stared at Denise, who sat there with her eyes closed.

Taking a deep breath, Denise blurted out, "Yeah, and one day I'll sit down and tell you about your aunt."

"You've gotten pregnant before by Derrick?" Morgan asked, seeking more information.

"No, but I wish. I got pregnant when I was young."

"Why didn't you keep it?"

Denise smirked. "Well, for one, I was young, and the guy that I got pregnant by wasn't father material. Morgan, I was pregnant several times, and it just didn't seem like a good time to have a baby. I wanted more out of life."

Nodding, Morgan replied, "Yeah, I know. I know everyone is upset with me, but I'm going to finish school."

"It's not you finishing school that we're worried about, Morgan; it's you. It seems like you just did a three-sixty. At one point, you were talking about attending Oxford University. I guess it took us by surprise when you decided to attend NYU."

"Aunt Denise, it's so complicated..."

"What is? Morgan, you should know that no matter what you are going through, you can always come to me."

"I know," she responded, getting choked up.

"Morgan, talk to me. Help me understand."

"I can't. Please don't."

"Has someone hurt you?" Denise asked with concern.

"No."

Denise went over and sat next to her, embracing her.

"Listen. No matter what it is, we will get through it. Alright?" Lifting Morgan's face up by her chin, she added, "I promise I will always be there for you."

As Morgan sobbed in her aunt's arms, Denise simply exhaled and left it alone. Whatever Morgan was hiding, she wasn't ready to reveal, but whatever it was, it scared the hell out of Morgan.

Chapter Four
Tony

Singing the "Good Life" by Kanye West while walking into his lavish office, Tony had just that—a good life. He was married to the love of his life and expecting his first child, all while transforming himself from a local rapper into an international mogul. His net worth was over two hundred million, and he was featured on Forbes' list of The Rich and Famous Under Forty. The industry said Tony had the Midas touch because everything he touched turned to gold. Every artist on his record label went platinum. To add to his fortune, his clothing, cologne, and movie production company grossed over fifty million in its first six months.

Even though Tony was sitting on top of the world, the only thing that mattered to him was the time he spent with Morgan. Their relationship started off wrong, but he did everything in his power to make it right. They had a fleet of homes all over the world and even a private island. When it came to Morgan, he didn't spare any expense. If Tony had it his way, he would fly away with her and never return.

The only regret Tony had was marrying Christina. After Christina suffered the miscarriage, Tony decided to make it up to her by proposing. Once his attorney informed him that the United States doesn't recognize marriages performed in the Bahamas, that's where he wed Christina.

Initially, Tony only planned on staying married to Christina for a year. However, it turned into three years too long. He didn't know how much longer he could continue living a double life. Career wise, it was a great move; people couldn't get enough of them when they made appearances together. However, the sight of her made him sick. There were days when Tony wouldn't say a word to her. In his eyes, she wasn't anything but a stinking bitch. That's why every chance he got he treated her like shit. On the night of their wedding, Tony slept in the other room. Tia practically had to force him to take Christina on a honeymoon. If it wasn't for the money Christina brought in, Tony would've dropped her years ago.

Tony figured since Greg was home, things would've gone back to the way they used to be, hoping Greg would become his manager and accompany him everywhere. Oddly, that didn't happen. After Perry and Paul were killed, it seemed like everyone branched out into their own little world. They rarely came out to support Tony, and when they did, they didn't stay long. Greg and Denise were the only two people in the world that Tony looked up to, and even they were too busy to support him. Some days, Tony thought they were jealous of him.

When Tony found out that Mike was going around asking questions about Paul's murder, he quickly promoted him to Wild Child's marketing manager to keep him occupied.

Greg had put the word out asking for any information about Perry and Paul's deaths, but when he didn't get any feedback, he left it alone. *That's strange. It's not like Greg to just drop something. I guess married life has really changed him,* Tony thought.

Once Tony found out he was about to become a father, he cancelled a lot of his projects. Like Greg and Denise, Tony's view on life was different. It wasn't just about making money. Nowadays, being in the house with his wife was what Tony considered a good time. If it wasn't a business appearance or hanging with Greg and Denise, you didn't see him.

Some nights, Tony would come home from a hard day's work to a gourmet dinner, followed by a nice bubble bath and passionate sex. Morgan made Tony's life feel normal. She didn't see him as Tony Flowers.

Since Morgan was in Atlanta, Tony decided to hit up a party for E-Money at Greg's club.

"Tony Flowers!" E-money cheered.

"What's good, playboy?"

"I'm chillin' man. Glad you came through."

"Of course. You know I'm here to support my boy," Tony said.

"How's Christina?"

Tony smiled. "She's wonderful. Greg's here?" he replied, changing the subject.

"Yeah, he's up in his office."

While making his way through the crowd, Tony shook a few hands.

Knock! Knock!

"Come in!" Greg yelled so he could be heard over the loud music blasting in the club.

Tony walked in only to find Mookie in the office. "Greg Brightman," Tony chimed, ignoring Mookie's presence.

"What's up, Tee?" Mookie yelled.

"Oh shit, Mookie! What's good? Greg, I see the club is packed— big moves." Tony laughed.

Greg glanced over at Mookie and then back at Tony. *Still the same old Tony,* he thought, but replied, "You know it. Nothing's changed. What brings you out?" he asked as he guided them out of the office.

"I came out to support E...and of course, you," Tony said, while following closely behind him.

While Greg went to make his rounds, Tony and Mookie headed over to the VIP section. Though Tony had his shades on, Mookie felt his vibes.

"What's up, Mookie?" Tony snidely asked.

"Chillin'," Mookie replied, pissed.

 42

Greg came back sipping on a drink. "What's with the long face?"

Like a child, Tony had his lip poked out. "What do you mean?"

"You're sitting there pouting."

Tony looked over at Mookie and E-Money, who had impish grins on their faces while trying not to laugh. He started to say something slick out his mouth, but then remembered who he was talking to.

"I have a lot on my mind," he simply replied.

Being a father figure, Greg asked, "You wanna go somewhere private and talk about it?"

Tony shook his head. "Nah, I'm cool," he responded, while glaring at Mookie from the corner of his eye.

Greg shrugged his shoulders. "Well, I'm always here. E-Money, are you enjoying yourself?" Greg blurted out, hoping to change the mood.

"Hell yeah! Yo, thanks, man. The club is off the chain. In fact, I'm about to invite some honeys up here now and see if I can fuck something tonight. You wanna join me? The ladies are feeling you."

Greg laughed. "Nah, I'm good," he said, shocking everyone.

"Word? They're fine as hell," E-Money emphasized.

"I'm good. I don't need that headache," Greg protested.

Confused, E-Money stared at him. Most dudes would have been happy to have sex with some bad chicks.

"Greg, are you alright, man?" Mookie joked, touching his back.

"Yeah," Greg said, laughing at their reaction. "Yo, man, I've fucked enough chicks for ten niggas, feel me? That shit ain't about nothing. I have too much to lose, and nowadays, the way these chicks be tryna blow niggas up, I'll have to pull an O.J. on them for real."

"I feel you, but don't you get tired of fucking the same pussy?" E-Money asked.

"No, especially when it's good and all yours. E, anything those chicks are willing to do, my wife will do. You think I wanna be fucking just to be fucking? That shit gets boring after a while. Like I said, I've been there and done that. I'm on a different level."

"So you never thought about slipping on your wife—having something on the side?" E-Money pressed.

Greg screwed up his face. "NO! For what? Wifey and I are good. We have it all. Listen, when you start creeping, you have to keep that shit up. Both homes have to be happy, right? Sooner or later, the jump off is gonna want some kids or start pressuring you to make a choice. I could never do that to my wife. After all we've been through, she deserves more."

"Damn, that's what's up," E-Money stated, agreeing.

"Listen, that *thing* is out there. I didn't fight for my freedom to catch the monster," Greg explained.

"Real talk," Tony voiced. "I see what you're saying, Greg. At some point, you just have to grow up. Fucking a whole bunch of bitches is whack."

Once again, Greg had dropped knowledge on the young men.

"I feel ya, Greg, and when I find that special someone, hopefully I'll feel like that. But, tonight, I'm tryna have two bitches suck my dick," E-Money said, making everyone laugh.

Two seconds later, a group of girls joined them, but Greg wasn't interested. So, he got up and went to the bar, with Tony following him like a little puppy.

"It was getting a little hot over there." Greg laughed.

"I was feeling what you said back there about fucking chicks," Tony said with a chuckle.

"You know me, Tony. I don't front for no one. I'm real all day, every day. That shit isn't about nothing. Half these broads in here are looking for a baller. Speaking of which, when are you and Christina gonna have some babies? Life can't be all about money."

"In due time..." Tony smirked. "In due time."

"You sure you're alright?" Greg asked. "You seemed upset earlier."

"Yeah, man. I'm just surprised to see Mookie all up in your face. You know how I think."

Greg laughed, then patted Tony on his shoulder. "Tee, you haven't' changed a bit. Mookie is cool. You know if I suspect something..." Greg emphasized.

Tony nodded. "I know."

Instead of going back to the private section, Tony and Greg played the bar the rest of the evening. As they sat, everyone kept coming up to shake their hands. Tony was in his glory; it felt like back in the days.

Greg looked at his watch. "Yo, it's getting late, and I have to get up early to take the kids to a birthday party."

Tony laughed. "You're such a family man."

"You will see when you start having kids. This shit means nothing, Tony. This shit," he said, pointing to the scene in the club, "doesn't love you back. You think this shit cares about you? NO! That's why this shit can't be your life."

Nodding, Tony replied, "Yeah, I'm with you."

With that being said, both men headed out. Tony offered Greg a lift, but Greg had driven himself. After giving each other a hug and pound, the two men went their separate ways. On the ride home, Greg's words penetrated Tony's brain. *He's right. It's all about family.* Another thing that crossed his mind was Mookie. *Is he trying to be slick? It's funny how he's always underneath Greg's ass.* Tony made a mental note to start watching him.

Arriving at his immense house, Tony hated sleeping alone, but he hated sleeping with Christina more. It was going on two o'clock in the morning, and he still couldn't sleep. Missing his wife, he decided to call her.

"Hello," she answered in a sleepy voice.

"Hey, baby. How are you?"

"I'm fine. I called you several times."

"Yeah, I know. How's Mom doing?"

"She's fine. Is something wrong?"

"Nah. I just miss you. You know I can't sleep without you."

With nothing to say in response, Morgan remained quiet.

"Go back to sleep. I'll talk to you in the morning."

"Okay."

"Love you!" he said.

"Love you, too," she replied flatly before hanging up.

Hearing Morgan's voice aroused Tony, so he went into his private living room to watch one of his many tapes of them having sex. Once Morgan learned how to fuck, Tony started secretly recording them. Even after having watched the tapes a thousand times, he still got excited. Once he finished pleasuring himself, he went right to sleep where he lay.

*****

Why the hell did I hang out last night? Tony thought. It seemed like he had only closed his eyes for five seconds. Now he was on his way to an interview with *Wake-Up America* and then off to shoot the cover for his next album. However, those things didn't matter. His joy came from the thought of his wife returning home that evening. To show how much he missed her, Tony planned a romantic evening. A candlelight dinner to start, followed by an old black and white movie, Morgan's favorite.

Tony was leaving the photo shoot when Tia called him.

"Tony, are you ready? We're leaving in two hours."

"What are you talking about?" he snapped, confused.

"You and Christina are scheduled to perform in Denver at the governor's party."

"Oh shit! It's tonight?"

"Yeah. Did you forget?"

Tony threw his head back. *Shit, my wife is flying in tomorrow.*

After checking his BlackBerry, he said, "It's tomorrow, Tia."

"I know, Tony, but you have to do a sound check. Plus, you're scheduled to make a couple of appearances," she responded, sounding annoyed.

"A'ight. What time are we leaving?"

"In two hours."

"A'ight. I'll meet you at the airport."

"We're not using the private jet?"

"Nah."

"Gee...thanks for telling me. See you at the airport."

Click!

Morgan was due any day, and Tony didn't like going away. Until after the baby was born, he specifically instructed his team, along with Christina's, not to book anything out of town. His biggest fear was him not being there to see his son enter the world.

Tony called Morgan. "Baby, I have to fly to Denver for a couple of days."

"Okay."

"If you need anything, call Al or hit me up on my cell."

"Alright."

"Love you."

Morgan sighed. "Love you, too."

Tony took a deep breath and then dialed Christina. "Chris, what's up?"

"Hey," she answered dryly.

"You know we're scheduled..."

Before he could finish, Christina interjected. "I know. I'm already down here."

"Really? So when were you going to tell me?"

"Hmm, maybe if I had seen you more often, I would have told you. Anyway, I wanted to spend some time alone."

"I hear that. I'm scheduled to be there in a couple of hours. You wanna grab something to eat?"

"Don't care. Just call me when you're here," Christina replied, then hung up.

Tony chuckled. *Silly bitch.*

Before heading to the airport to meet up with Mookie and Tia, Tony ran a couple errands. Unlike most rappers, Tony didn't travel with a huge entourage. He learned from Greg that doing so drew too much attention.

A couple hours later, they arrived in Denver, Colorado, and Tony immediately pulled out his cell phone to check in with Morgan, but it went to voicemail.

"Hey, I just arrived. I'll call you when I get to the hotel. Love you," he whispered into the phone.

They headed straight to the suite only to find Christina wasn't there. Happy, Tony kicked off his shoes to relax, but Tia came to inform him that the director of the party wanted Tony to do a sound check that night. When he got there, Christina had just finished. They exchanged hugs before she was whisked away by her team. Surprisingly, Christina had become more popular than Tony. She was an American sweetheart.

Like always, Tony breezed through his sound check. When it came to work, he was such a professional, and people enjoyed working with him. He even managed to have everyone laughing as he cracked jokes.

Tony and Christina were scheduled to appear at a children's fundraiser. As usual, Tony got dressed in one room, while Christina got dressed in another. During the car ride over to the venue where the fundraiser was taking place, Tony checked his phone, making sure he didn't miss any calls from Morgan.

Upon their arrival, they posed for pictures before proceeding inside. Among the rich and powerful, Tony and Christina shook hands with the top officials in Denver. Everyone loved them. Smiling for the cameras, they worked the crowd, with Christina dancing with the governor a few times. One patron mumbled, "Tony is one lucky son of a bitch," which caused Tony to smirk.

After having such a wonderful time, Tony and Christina returned to their hotel room, and with them both being a little tipsy, they had sex. Christina's skills had improved, but she was nowhere near being on Morgan's level.

Tony turned over to Christina, who was butt naked, and then got out the bed to check his phone. He had three missed calls from Morgan, so he went into the other room to call her back. Since it was

five o'clock in the morning, he figured Morgan was probably working out.

"Hello," she answered groggily.

"Ma, you still sleep?"

"Yeah, I just fell asleep."

"Why?"

"Because the baby was sleeping on my side."

Tony chuckled. "Sleeping on your side?"

"Yeah, he had his head pressed up against my rib cage."

"Oh. Are you okay now?"

"Yes, but I have to get up in an hour."

"Why? Stay home and get some rest."

"I can't, Tony. I have school tonight. Besides, this is my last week at work."

Tony sighed. "A'ight, but take it easy and call me when you get home."

"Will do."

"Love you!"

This time, Morgan hung up without saying those two words back to him.

Instead of going back to bed, Tony got dressed and headed to the gym. Even though he and Christina had sex, Tony didn't want her getting the wrong idea about them. After the gym, he headed to the studio. Like Christina, Tony preferred to record in different states. Also, he liked working with new producers. As Tony recorded two tracks for his *Finding Flowers* album, he decided it would be his final album followed by a tour, which he planned on announcing in a couple of weeks. The industry didn't matter anymore. Entering a new chapter in his life, Tony realized being a good husband and father was more important. It was time to grow up.

It was also time to have a sit-down with Christina. Tony knew Christina could never love him the way she loved Paul.

They did one more sound check, this time with Christina cheering him on, and afterwards, they had lunch before returning to the hotel to get ready for that evening. Both were exhausted and decided to

take a short nap first. Christina fell asleep in the bedroom, while Tony crashed on the couch. When he woke up, Tony noticed his phone was almost dead. That's when he realized he had forgotten to pack his charger, so he ran up to Mookie's room.

"Yo, Mookie, I need you to charge this."

"A'ight, but I'm charging mine now. I'll put yours on it when mine is finished and then bring it down to you."

"Cool. I only need it to charge for an hour."

"I got you."

It seemed like the time flew by because they were running late. Rushing out to the car, Tony forgot his wedding band and phone. He instructed Tia to go back for them. Five minutes behind schedule, Tony went straight to the stage and performed. Christina immediately followed. Afterwards, they were ushered to an exclusive party to join the governor and his wife. Meanwhile, back at the hotel, Tia searched everywhere for Tony's phone. After a while, she gave up. *Tony must've lost it,* she thought.

*****

The next day, it was going on twelve o'clock noon when Tony finally woke up. As he dragged his tired ass into the bathroom, it hit him that he hadn't spoken to Morgan. He flew out of the bathroom and started searching for his phone.

"Where the fuck is it?" he yelled, getting frustrated.

At that time, Christina, Joyce, Tia, and Mookie walked in.

"Tee, what's up?" Mookie asked, confused.

"Yo, has anyone seen my phone?" he said, tossing everything around.

"Oh shit! It's in my room," Mookie stated.

Tony glared at him. "How did you get my phone?"

"You left it in my room to charge, remember?"

"Oh damn, I forgot." Tony slapped himself upside his forehead.

"What's the big deal about your cell phone anyway?" Christina asked with an attitude.

Disregarding Christina's remark, Tony exhaled. "Mookie, can you get my phone for me?"

Christina and the others just shook their heads and then headed into the other room.

Tony paced back and forth while waiting for Mookie's return.

"Yo, sorry..."

Tony snatched the phone, not caring to hear Mookie's apology. *Shit!* He had fifteen missed calls from Morgan and ten from Al.

His heart started racing as he ran into the other room and closed the door. Scared, he dialed Morgan's cell phone. It went to voicemail.

"FUCK!" he shouted.

Next, he called Al. It rang three times before he answered.

"Al, what happened?"

"She had the baby."

"What! When?!"

"Last night, she called me. But, don't worry. They're fine."

Whew! Tony thought. "Thanks, Al. Can I talk to her?"

"Sure. She has her phone."

Just then, Morgan beeped in on the other line.

"Al, that's her. Let me hit you back," Tony said before clicking over. "Baby, I'm so sorry..." he mumbled.

Morgan giggled. "It's fine. I'd tried calling you all night."

"I know, ma. I left my phone in Mookie's room on his charger."

"Really?"

"Yes! You know I would never leave you and my son," he responded in a defensive tone.

"Let's forget it. Your son, Anthony Omari Flowers, was nine pounds, fourteen ounces, and twenty-three inches long."

"Damn! He's a big-ass boy!"

"Yep! Tore my butt up!"

"Like father like son," he joked.

Somehow, Morgan didn't find that funny. They talked for a few more minutes, and then it was feeding time for the baby. Tony promised to catch the next flight out before hanging up.

Due to bad weather, he was unable to catch a flight until two days later. When he tried to have his private jet pick him up, FCC refused the request. So, he watched television, played video games, and slept to take his mind off of Morgan and his newborn son.

Once they landed, Tony didn't even bother to say goodbye. He jumped into his awaiting car service and headed home.

With sweaty palms and his stomach in knots, Tony was about to see his son for the first time. He looked up at the sky through the window, smiled, and said, "Thank you." The car didn't fully stop before Tony jumped out and ran inside the house. He heard Morgan upstairs and thought about shouting to let her know he was home, but then he thought about the baby.

He walked into the baby's room. It was a sight he had dreamt about for so long. Morgan was in the rocking chair nursing their son. Tony's eyes immediately filled with tears.

Morgan looked up, smiling. "Hey."

Scared, Tony slowly walked over to them. "He's beautiful just like his mother."

Morgan blushed. "He's greedy," she replied, making Tony laugh.

He kneeled down and kissed his son, then his wife. "Thank you," he said, while staring into her eyes.

Confused, Morgan replied, "For what?"

"For making me the happiest man in the world."

That night, Tony held his wife and son in his arms. Life was finally perfect.

Chapter Five
Christina

*K*nock! Knock!

"Christina, ten minutes before you hit the stage," Joyce announced after opening the door.

Staring into space, Christina nodded and then got up to lock the door. Exhaling, she rested her head against it.

"What the hell is wrong with me, baby? Why am I in this dysfunctional marriage? I know you're looking down on me and so disappointed. I don't know! When I lost you and then the baby, Tony was there for me. I guess a part of me felt like I owed it to him to stay. But, baby, that doesn't mean I don't yearn for you. Paul, I think about you every day. I would give it all up just to hold you again," she cried.

Knock! Knock!

"Christina, it's time," Joyce said from the other side of the door.

Wiping away her tears, Christina replied, "Okay. Give me another sec."

She went over to the vanity set and checked in the mirror to make sure her make-up wasn't smeared. Giving herself one final look, she smiled. "Let's do this," she told herself in an attempt to get into a better mood.

*****

Sitting in her luxury hotel, Christina kicked her feet up, hoping to relax. It was the first night of her international world tour, with the first stop being Australia.

On her last tour, she remembered how Paul made sure she did normal things, like sightseeing and eating at different restaurants. In his opinion, that's what kept people grounded. Life can't be all about work. Christina missed him. If he were there with her, they would have been up early visiting historical places. Being that Christina had the night off, she decided to get some homework done. No one in her camp knew she was secretly taking college courses. Knowing their asses, they probably would've leaked it to the media. In this business, Christina didn't trust anyone, especially since a lot of them worked for Tony.

That's why she made it clear to everyone that on her nights off she didn't want to be disturbed. She made sure Joyce booked her a suite that had a kitchen stocked with food, and it had to be located away from her team, who had to call before coming to her room. Many of them thought she was crazy, but it was the only way Christina could focus on school.

Turning on her laptop, Christina chuckled when she thought about her and Tony having sex. *God, I can't believe I thought he was great in bed. No wonder it hurt. The motherfucker doesn't know what he's doing. I can't wait to get off this tour. I'm getting a damn divorce.*

Christina dove into her schoolwork that she was two days behind in. She loved the fact that she was able to interact with *real* people. Some thought she was THE Christina Carrington, but when asked, she would say it was a coincidence.

As she finished up her online class, her cell phone rang.

"Hello."

"Hi. Can I speak to Christina?"

"This is she.

"Chris, it's Rashid. How are you?"

Christina's face lit up. *Oh my god,* she thought, but replied, "I'm great! And you?"

"Chillin'. I ran into your friend, Asia, and she gave me your new number. I hope you don't mind."

Smiling, she responded, "No, it's fine."

"So how's married life?"

"You called to ask me about married life? Why? Are you about to take the plunge?" she snidely replied.

Rashid laughed. "Only with you. You know I was just joking since you cut a brother off...broke my heart."

"I broke your heart? Please! You weren't interested. Besides, married life isn't all that great." There was a moment of silence before she continued. "So tell me what's been going on with you, Mr. Three-Time Champion."

Rashid chuckled. "I'm chillin', taking things easy. I just started taking some classes at John Hopkins University."

Christina beamed. "Really? I'm taking online classes with Ashford University."

"That's great. I've always wanted to attend college, so I figured this is the best time to get my degree so my kids will know there's more to life than playing ball. When did you start?"

"I started two years ago, and I love it, Rashid."

"Yeah, it's cool. Well, Christina, I just called to holla at you. I would offer to take you to dinner, but I know you're married."

Christina immediately interjected. "It's not like that..." she grumbled, then paused for a second and thought about what she was about to say. *Fuck it.* "Rashid, my marriage is more of a business relationship. Tony and I are not like that. We haven't been in years."

"So why did you marry him?" Rashid asked in a confused, yet disappointed voice.

"It felt right. I mean, after I lost the baby..."

"You were pregnant?" he asked, not letting her finish.

Exhaling, Christina responded, "Yes, that's a long story. Anyway, I was depressed and thought Tony was the one who I was supposed to be with."

"And now?"

"I'd rather be depressed," she replied, causing both of them to laugh. "Rashid, I truly regret getting married to him. I mean, it's bad enough we're not together, but we aren't even friends. The only time we see each other is at social functions. Other than that, I don't see him and don't care to. I know it's crazy, but that's how I feel."

"Damn," was all Rashid could say.

Strangely, Christina didn't cry. In fact, she accepted the situation a long time ago. She just needed to say it out loud to believe it.

"So what are you gonna do?"

"Now that's the crazy part. I don't know. What I do know is that it's time for me to move on."

"Well, you seem to be headed in the right direction. Like I said years ago, I respect you, Chris. I know you thought I was just trying to sleep with you, but I wasn't. Everyone in the business knows Tony doesn't deserve you."

"Really?" Christina's eyes widened.

"Yeah! That's why everyone was surprised when you married him."

"They weren't the only ones," Christina joked. "So are you in a relationship?"

"I was kinda seeing this chick, but I'm pulling back."

"Why?"

"Because she's trying to capitalize off of me."

"Oh, one of those..."

"Exactly! But, enough about her. Are you in town?"

"No, I'm in Australia. I just started touring."

"That's what's up. Maybe I'll fly out there and catch a show."

"Maybe you should," she flirted back.

"Is that an invite?"

"You don't need one...never did."

Rashid laughed. "Alright, Mrs. Carrington, let me see what I can do."

"You do that."

"Later, sexy."

"Later." Christina smiled as she hung up. She ran through her room screaming and laughing, then jumped on the bed.

It had been two months since she'd been on tour, and she couldn't wait for it to be over. While the fans were wonderful, they didn't have a clue as to the preparation that went behind the scenes. It seemed like every day there was some drama with the crew. On top of that, her new manager kept her busy. On the night of her shows, Christina was up early in the morning doing interviews and then it was off to rehearsal. Some days, she went hours without eating. Drained, she slept all day on her days off, too tired to even study.

After returning from doing some shopping, Christina walked in her suite only to be greeted by Tony and Mookie.

Frowning, she told Joyce, "Can you put this in the room for me?"

"What's up, Chris?" Mookie asked, planting a kiss on her cheek.

"Hey, Mookie," she replied, but stared at Tony with her shades on.

Mookie looked at Joyce and then both looked over at Tony, who was on his phone with his back turned.

"Oh shit, Chris, I didn't see you."

"You never do," she snapped.

Brushing her comment off, Tony kissed her on the cheek. "It's good to see you, too. You wanna go and get something to eat?"

Plopping down on her couch, Christina removed her shoes and placed her BlackBerry on the table. "No, thanks. I want to relax."

"Okay. That's cool," he said, taking a seat next to her.

Judging by the tension in the room, Mookie and Joyce decided to leave. Being that Christina and Tony didn't spend any time together, they didn't have anything to talk about. When they did talk, it was about work, but even that changed. Christina stopped seeking any advice from Tony years ago.

She went to remove her clothing while Tony watched a movie. When her phone rang, Tony picked it up and took it to Christina.

"Here, Rashid is calling you," he said with a hint of jealousy.

"Thanks. Hey, Rashid," Christina answered, closing the door in Tony's face.

*****

The next couple of days, Tony and Christina spent some quality time together. They went on shopping sprees, attended a few exclusive parties, and chilled out on the beach. The media soaked it up, but little did they know, Tony and Christina barely said two words to each other. Both played into the hands of the media, smiling and waving as the paparazzi snapped pictures of them.

Getting ready to take the stage, Tony came into Christina's dressing room.

"I'ma chill for the show, but after that, I have to fly back," he informed her.

"Why? Is one of your jump offs calling?" Christina replied sarcastically.

Tony glared at her. "Nah. I just don't want to take up the next man's time with you."

Both glared at each other for a few moments before Christina said, "You know what, Tony..." Then she stopped herself. "You're right. I don't want you to take up a *real* man's time."

Tony chuckled. "Yo, you have a lot to learn."

"So do you. Don't bother staying for the show. You can leave right now. I'll see you in a couple of months," she angrily stated. "This marriage is a fucking joke," she grumbled before walking out.

Since Christina had two weeks off before starting her next phase of the tour, she decided to take a vacation. However, this time, Rashid would be joining her. Since Tony had eyes and ears all over, they decided to meet up in Greece. So no one would get suspicious, Christina gave everyone the week off except Joyce, who she brought along with her. She knew Joyce was aware of her conversations with Rashid. In fact, she was happy that Christina was finally cheating on Tony.

 58

Instead of staying at a five-star hotel, Rashid rented a private villa on Vouvalis Island just off the Gulf Coast. Christina was sure no one would recognize them there. He was already there when she arrived.

Nervous, Christina smiled. "Hello," she said, while trying not to stare at his rock-hard abs.

"Mrs. Christina," he replied, kissing her on the lips.

Their eyes met briefly until Joyce cleared her throat to remind them that she was in the room. Both Christina and Rashid laughed.

"Oh, Rashid, this is Joyce."

"Hello," Joyce greeted as she tried not to stare, also.

"Hey, what's up?"

"Well, Christina, I'm gonna get back to the hotel. Call me if you need anything, but judging by him, you're in good hands." Joyce then licked her lips and left.

Rashid blushed, shaking his head.

As he guided her over to the sofa from behind by her waist, Rashid whispered, "I missed you," and planted a wet kiss on the back of her neck.

Christina flinched before turning around to stare into Rashid's eyes. Besides Tony, she hadn't slept with anyone after Paul's death. Unsure if she was ready to take it to the next level, Christina grabbed Rashid's hand.

"Rashid," she mumbled, "I haven't been…"

"Shhh…it's cool. We don't have to have sex." He kissed her on the cheek.

"No, I want to, but it's just…"

Rashid jumped up off the sofa. "Hey, it's getting late. Let's go in the kitchen."

"You're gonna cook?"

"Ya boy got skills."

Christina and Rashid talked over dinner; he had such a sense of humor. Not only was he sexy, but he was funny, reminding her of Paul. Following dinner, they went to the balcony and snuggled into each other's arms. After a few minutes of cuddling, Christina quietly exhaled and stood up, looking down at Rashid who had a puzzled

expression on his face. Without a word, she removed her blouse and kneeled down to kiss him.

"Are you sure?" he asked.

"Yes."

Rashid pulled her into his arms and gently kissed her. While he wasn't Paul in the bedroom, he sure knew his way around her body. The only thing she didn't like about him was he came too fast.

Christina and Rashid spent the next couple of days making love under the sun. Up until then, she didn't think someone could take Paul's place. Like Paul, Rashid was loving, caring, and although young, he was very mature for his age. Christina liked that he didn't try to impress her, and it was his conversation she loved the most. They didn't talk about the industry. Instead, they studied together like college students. It was the first night of her U.S. tour, and Christina was on cloud nine. She had just come back from spending a couple of days with a good man who gave her multiple orgasms. Throughout rehearsal, Christina could not stop smiling.

"So this is what vacation does to a person?" Mookie clapped, surprising her.

"Hey, Mookie. What do you mean?"

"Chris, your ass is glowing."

"Well, a few days off will do that to ya. What brings you here? Oh wait, Tony sent you to spy on me, huh?"

Mookie frowned. "Nah, it's not like that. Actually, he doesn't know I'm here."

"Hey, Mookie," Joyce said, walking over to them.

"What's up, Joyce?"

Mookie and Joyce watched as Christina rehearsed. She'd come a long way, but unlike most artists, she practiced her ass off. They were just finishing up, when Christina's phone alerted her that she had a text message from Rashid. Instantly, her face lit up as she giggled like a schoolgirl.

Tonight's show was very special to Christina because her parents were coming. It was the first time they would see their little girl perform. Surprisingly, her parents were happy and proud of their

daughter, who put on one helluva show. Exhausted, Christina was in her bedroom getting ready for bed, when her mother knocked on the door.

"Christina, are you sleeping?"

"No, Ma. Come in."

"Love me or leave me," her mother sang, causing Christina to blush.

"Mommy," she laughed.

"I love that song." She danced before taking a seat on the bed. "Christina," she said in a serious tone, "what's going on with you and Tony?"

Christina was about to lie, but couldn't. If you can't confide in your mother, then who can you?

"It's that obvious?"

"Yeah," her mother replied.

"Ma, Tony and I aren't together. I mean, people think we are, but we live in two different worlds."

"Do you love him?"

Christina exhaled. "I'm not in love with him. I do care about Tony, though."

"Then why marry him?"

"I don't know. After I lost the baby..."

"Christina, haven't you learned anything from your father and me. We've been married for twenty-nine years. Yes, it's been a struggle, but never once were we unhappy with each other."

"I know, but we were so perfect..."

"To who? The media? Your fans? Those people don't know you. They only know what they see."

Christina remained quiet as tears rolled down her face. Her mother was right; she was only staying with Tony to keep her image.

"Mommy, I have something to tell you," she said, wiping her snot away with her hand. "You know the baby I lost a couple of years ago? It wasn't Tony's. It was my bodyguard Paul's."

Her mother's eyes widened. "Christina!" she blurted out in shock.

"Mommy, I know, but it wasn't like that. Paul and I fell in love. We were engaged, but he was killed."

Christina broke down in tears, and her mother embraced her. "It's okay, baby."

"Mommy, I swear to you, it wasn't like that. I never meant for this to happen. Paul was my everything. He helped me get my GED, and because of him, I'm taking college courses."

"Why didn't you tell us?"

Christina got up and went over to the window. "I don't know. I was ashamed. Mommy, Paul was so different. He didn't see me as Christina Carrington. It was never about money with him. Right after Paul died, I lost the baby. I was devastated, and Tony was there for me."

"And you felt like you owed it to him? You fell in love with Paul for a reason." She walked over to her daughter. "Christina, your father may not be rich, but I love him to death. I wouldn't trade him for all the money in the world. Always remember true love has no price. It's not a fancy car, big house, or diamond ring. Real love is free."

"So what do I do now?"

Her mother softly exhaled. "I can't make that decision for you, but no matter what, your father and I will always be there for you. Now, let's get some rest."

Before exiting the room, Christina's mother stopped and turned around. "Let the choices you make today be the ones you can live with tomorrow."

Christina thought about her mother's words and decided it was time to divorce Tony, even though she knew he would try to ruin her career. *Damn, I'm gonna need a good attorney, but who has the balls to take him on?* She paced back and forth while thinking. *There's only one person I know that's not afraid of Tony, and that's Gabrielle Brightman.* From what Tony had told her, Gabrielle didn't take shit from anyone. Plus, he couldn't stand her, so that was even better.

Before she lost her courage, Christina got up early and headed over to Gabrielle's office. During the car ride there, she thought about Rashid. *Is it too soon for me to get in a relationship?*

While on her way to Gabrielle's office, Tony called her.

"Hey, I'm at the house. Where are you?"

"I had to run some errands. I should be back shortly. Why? What's up?"

"Since I missed your concert last night, I figured I'd take you and your parents out for breakfast."

"Okay. That sounds wonderful. Tell my parents to get dressed, and I'll meet y'all at the restaurant."

"A'ight."

"Christina," Nancy greeted.

"Hi. Is Gabrielle in?"

"Yes, but she's on the phone. I'll let her know you're here."

"Thanks."

A few seconds later, Gabrielle opened the door to her office. "Hello, Chris."

"Hi. Sorry for popping in, but I need to see you."

"Sure. Come on in. So what can I do for you today?" Gabrielle asked, taking a seat.

"I wanna divorce Tony," she blurted out.

Astounded, Gabrielle simply replied, "Okay..."

"I know this is sudden, but Tony and I haven't been happy for a long time. I understand you and him are friends, so..."

Before she could finish, Gabrielle cut her off. "Christina, Tony and my husband are friends. I could care less about his ass," she snapped, cutting her eyes.

"So will you represent me?" Christina asked.

"Of course," Gabrielle replied, then both women laughed.

Chapter Six
Denise

It had been almost a year since Denise and Greg talked about Moe. At times, Denise thought about asking him, but that part of her life was history. She had a family now, and with her temper, it would be easy to fall back into that lifestyle. However, knowing Greg, he was still investigating. Denise remembered how Greg plotted on Grant for two years before they carried out the hit.

"Oh shit," she mumbled as she ran out to meet Greg.

Today, they were going to Delaware to check out a housing complex that, according to Greg, was a goldmine. As always, Greg was on time and waiting in front of her office building.

"What?" Denise laughed while getting in the car.

"You know your ass is never on time," he replied with a chuckle.

"Yeah, yeah," she said, joining him in laughter.

Denise read over the information Greg had given her while he drove.

Looking out the window, she giggled and said, "You know, this highway brings back a lot of memories."

"Tell me about it. Oh, did I tell you that Christina is filing for a divorce?"

"For real? Does Tony know?"

"Not yet. Chris asked Boo to handle it."

"You think that's a good idea? You know Tony is like family."

"And he has to understand that this is business."

"I don't know why she married him in the first place. You know her and Paul were engaged before he got killed."

"Yeah, she told me. I was tight because it's close to home. If Tony found out, it would've been a problem."

Denise laughed. "Yeah, his ego would've been crushed. You know he's sensitive. Paul would've probably had to beat the hell out of him."

Greg nodded. "Most likely. He came to the club acting up because Mookie was in my office. Can you believe that?"

Denise squinted. "Because of Mookie?"

"Yeah...you know Tony always has to be in the limelight. He acts like a little bitch sometimes. I asked him what was wrong. I know he wanted to say something slick, but he knew better."

Shaking her head in disgust, she replied, "That's Tee for ya. You know Mike told me that Tony had someone check Moe before he and Paul hollered at him."

"Huh?"

"That's what I said, but you know Tony. He's scared of his own shadow."

Greg nodded again. "Those are the ones you have to watch."

Once they arrived at their destination, Denise and Greg fell in love with the area. Although it required a lot of work, it would be a great investment. This would also be the first business deal Denise and Greg invested in together.

Just as they did back in the day, they went out to celebrate at Ruth Chris Steakhouse.

While waiting for their food, Denise asked, "Any news on Moe? Was he in the city?" She prayed for some good news.

Greg looked around. "No. Moe was locked up on a parole violation."

Inwardly, Denise smiled. *Yes!* she thought, but replied, "Damn. So we know it wasn't him. Oh, did I tell you that Mike told me Felicia's mother moved out of the neighborhood? She came into some money and bought an apartment on Manhattan Avenue. He also told me that Felicia did have a brother. He couldn't think of his name, but he was sure Bruce and Joe would know," Denise informed Greg, changing the subject.

"Really? Then we need to holla."

"I went out there, but didn't see them."

"Knowing them, they're probably in rehab or something. Keep going around there. You're bound to catch them," he suggested.

*****

Denise pulled up in front of the building and looked down at the piece of paper Mike had given her. *This is the address,* she thought. She wished Mike had the number. Denise didn't want to pop up on Millie like that. *Oh well,* she thought.

Taking a deep breath, Denise knocked on the door, and five seconds later, Millie opened it. *Damn, she looks different* Denise thought.

"Millie?" Denise said with some hesitation in her voice.

Surprised, Millie shouted, "Denise!"

"Yes."

"Come on in!" she said, opening the door wider.

Denise smiled and kissed her as she walked inside. "Mike gave me your address. I didn't know you moved."

Leading her to the living room, Millie took a seat on the sofa. "Yeah, we moved maybe six months after Felicia died. It was too much for the boys."

Denise looked around. "I see. This is a nice apartment."

Millie nodded. "It turns out my daughter had a policy after all."

"Really?" Denise responded, hoping Millie would provide more information.

"Yeah, it was for two hundred thousand. Tony was the one who encouraged me to buy this apartment and put something up for the boys."

"Which Tony?"

"Tony Flowers. After Felicia died, he came to see me and asked if I needed anything. I told him about the money, and he set me up with someone that helped me get this apartment."

"I'm surprised he did that, because he and Felicia didn't get along at all."

"He told me, but that was nice of him."

"Yeah, it was. Did any of Felicia's other siblings come around?" Denise asked.

"No, but she knew them. She had pictures of them hanging around. She also had their address."

Denise's eyes widened. "Millie, do you still have that information?"

"It's probably in here somewhere, but why are you so concerned with Felicia's siblings?"

Damn, Denise thought as she exhaled and looked away. There was no way she could tell Millie the truth.

"Denise, why are you so concerned about Felicia's siblings?" Millie repeated, while staring in Denise's face.

"Nothing."

"Denise…."

"For real, Millie. I just need to talk to them."

"Denise, I know Felicia was meeting you the night she was murdered. It's been six years. Don't you think it's time for you to be honest with me? I deserve it."

"What do you mean be honest?" Denise asked.

"About the night Felicia was killed."

"What about the night she was killed?"

"She went to meet you, right?"

Denise paused, but she had to quickly say something. "Millie…"

"Denise, please, this is me."

Denise nodded, exhaled, and then responded, "Who told you?"

"Mike. He was with Felicia before she told him she had to meet you."

"Yeah, I saw her that night."

"And?"

Aware that Millie was from the streets, Denise knew lying to her would be a waste of time. "There's something I need to tell you."

Millie waited, allowing Denise to continue. "Just before Felicia died, she contacted me, telling me that something we did back in the day had surfaced. The person wanted a lot of money or they would go to the police." Denise stood up and started pacing the floor, contemplating if she should continue.

"And?" Millie blurted out.

"Well, it turned out to be a lie. There was never anyone. It was a set up. Felicia was going to kill me."

Millie gasped and put her hand over her mouth. "Why?" she managed to say.

"Because I....killed her father."

"What? You didn't kill Grant. No, Denise, someone tried to rob him..."

"I did. I staged it so it could look like a robbery, but it was me."

"Why?"

"Millie," Denise said, taking a seat next to her, "Grant was my first boyfriend. He took my virginity. He also pimped me out to men."

Millie's eyes teared up. She knew Denise wasn't lying, because Grant had done the same thing to her.

"I'm sorry," Denise said.

"Don't be. Grant did the same thing to me. That's what he would do—date either naïve women or little girls and then pimp them out. I'm glad the bastard is dead," she said in disgust.

"Millie, I was there the night Felicia was killed. I met her in Central Park. She brought along two guys, and their plan was to kill me. She said it was because I killed her father, and that she and her brother were seeking revenge."

"You killed Felicia?" Millie asked loudly.

"No, someone beat me to it. Someone else was there and killed her. They shot her from a distance."

It was all too much for Millie, who jumped up and went into the kitchen to pour herself a glass of water.

Worried, Denise immediately followed behind her. "Are you okay?"

"I'm fine, but why did you have to wait until I stopped drinking to tell me this shit?" Millie said, attempting to be humorous. "Why didn't you tell me this years ago?"

"I don't know. At that time, I didn't trust anyone."

"You could've trusted me! Denise, I knew you and Felicia were out there doing dirt. Do you think I was stupid? I'm not like the rest of the mothers out here pretending like their daughters are sitting at the right hand of God. I knew Felicia was into a lot of shit. So, it didn't surprise me that someone killed her. But, you knew this. You could've told me. Instead, you had me thinking it was someone else. As much as I saved your ass, you felt you couldn't come to ME?" she emphasized, hitting her chest.

"How would you have reacted, Millie? This isn't some stranger we're talking about; it's your daughter. How could I look you in the face at her funeral and tell you that I was there?"

"Easy. The same way you're doing it now."

Denise sighed. "You're right, so now what?"

"What do you mean?"

"You're from the streets. You know what I'm talking about."

"Nothing. You said you didn't kill her, right?"

"I didn't."

"Well, it's over. But, I better not find out you killed my daughter. I mean it."

"That's the problem, Millie. It's not over. Felicia's brother is still out there waiting."

"What do you want me to do? Grant had thirteen kids. How are you gonna find out which one of them wants to kill you?"

Denise laughed. "By using my killer instincts," she responded, causing Millie to laugh, too.

"I will look through what's left of Felicia's things and let you know if I find something."

"Thank you!"

As Millie was walking Denise to the door, she thought about something. "You know, Denise, the police said Felicia was killed by a rifle."

"A rifle?"

"Yep."

Baffled, Denise didn't say anything more.

"Can I ask you a question?" Millie said, while standing in the doorway.

"Sure."

"If someone didn't beat you to it, would you have killed Felicia?"

Denise thought for a second and honestly replied, "Yes."

Millie nodded. "I figured that," she said, then closed the door.

Shaken, Denise headed over to see Greg. On her way there, she called Derrick and told him that she would be home late. Greg was in his office when she arrived. Denise knocked on the door before entering.

"Hey, are you busy?"

"Dee! What's up?"

Denise took a seat in the chair and tried to calm herself down. She looked at her hands; they were trembling just like they did when she carried out her first killing. Greg noticed it and went over to her.

"What happened?"

"I just need a second," she responded, gathering her thoughts. "Greg..." she muttered.

"What's up?" he said, worried.

"I told Millie about Felicia," she blurted out.

"What did you tell her?"

"I told Millie about Felicia and Grant."

Greg jumped up to lock the door "You did what? Have you lost your fucking mind," he responded, standing over her.

"I just left Millie, and I told her the truth about Grant and Felicia."

"What the fuck! Are you trying to go to prison?" he yelled.

"NO! She knows I didn't kill Felicia, and she doesn't give a fuck about Grant. Besides, I didn't say you were down with it."

"And that's supposed to make me feel better? Why did you feel the need to say anything? What the fuck is your problem? Are you on some Usher *Confessions* shit now?"

"No, but I need to know who Felicia's brother is. Remember, he's still out there waiting…"

Greg exhaled, rubbed his head, and sat back down. "Talk to me."

"Greg, every day I think about Perry. This shit is killing me—that I put my brother in the dirt. I accused him of being Felicia's brother," she said, crying. "Do you know how that feels? P and I had been through so much, and because of me, he's not here."

"Dee, I know, but you can't…" Greg paused to rub her back.

"I can't what, Greg? I can't allow her brother to attack again. I have a family now. The stakes are higher."

Greg closed his eyes and leaned his head back. "Is someone following you? Why are you feeling like this all of a sudden?"

"Remember that time before everything went down with Alex and I had that bad feeling? Well, I'm getting that same feeling."

"I remember, but real talk, Dee. I spent nine years in prison away from my wife. I refuse to let someone take me away from her and my kids again. So, you're right about the stakes being higher."

"I know. You think I don't feel the same way? I have a family now, too. I can't have them pay for something I did. That's why I went to Millie, hoping she knew something, but she didn't."

"So what did she say about Felicia? How did she feel?"

"She was upset, but she knows I didn't kill her daughter. Besides, Felicia was killed with a rifle. I don't think she's gonna say anything."

"Really? That's the same thing Perry, Paul, and a lot of motherfuckers in the ground or who are serving life in prison thought. That's the problem with people. They don't think until it's a thought, and by then, it's too late. But, I'll tell you this. If I even think…" Greg angrily stared at Denise. "Trust me, it will not have a chance to become a thought," he finished, then walked out.

Denise threw her head back on the sofa. *Damn,* she thought.

*****

Denise entered her house in a fog, which Derrick noticed. She didn't even kiss him. She went straight to their lounge area to pour herself a drink. Taking a seat in the chair, Denise exhaled and thought, *Greg is right. What if Millie does go to the police?*

"Are you okay?" Derrick asked, sitting next to her.

"I'm fine. I just had a rough day."

"You wanna talk about it?"

"No," she said, getting up and walking away.

Derrick sighed.

The next couple of days, Denise walked around on pins and needles, snapping at Derrick and even the kids, worried that Millie might go to the authorities. After all, it was her daughter who had been killed. Standing in her doorway, Denise looked down at her family who was sound asleep in her bed. Millie could ruin everything, and Denise wasn't about to let that happen.

Chapter Seven
Gabrielle

*F*igures! Gabrielle knew once Tony sicced his lawyers on Christina, she would change her mind. Even after Gabrielle assured her that she was not afraid of them, Christina wasn't ready to take on the challenge. Gabrielle knew it wasn't about the money, because even if Christina left, she still would be well off. Therefore, it had to be something else. *Tony is such a bastard!*

The one thing that baffled Gabrielle was how he found out so quickly. Hell, the papers hadn't even been prepared. She exhaled and started preparing for court. Taking over the case while Abigail was out, Gabrielle discovered many things about Abigail's work performance. For one, she didn't follow up and she would handle the case based on the defendant's race. If the defendant was an African American or Hispanic with very little money, Abigail would just settle, and most of the time, the defendant got the short end of the stick. The most shocking thing were the accusations two clients made about sleeping with Abigail when they couldn't pay their bill. One client even had her on his camera phone performing oral sex. Of course, both defendants were minorities. *I guess they're not good enough to represent, but good enough to sleep with,* Gabrielle thought, shaking her head.

★ ★ ★ ★

Abigail's behavior created bad feelings in Gabrielle. She knew it was only a matter of time before someone sued her office. This reminded Gabrielle of Jake Lawrence, which wasn't a good thing. That's why Gabrielle fired her and reported her to the Bar Association, especially after Gabrielle took over the Jaquan Donaldson case. Abigail's negligence could've sent that boy upstate for twenty-five years. Once Gabrielle took over, she immediately got all the charges dropped and his record sealed. Now, Jaquan was on his way to college.

Tonight, Gabrielle and Greg were having dinner at her parents' house. Strangely, after Greg's return home from prison, her parents accepted him. Gabrielle figured they would rather have him in their lives than miss out on their grandchildren growing up. Surprisingly, Greg and Noel got along fine. They had a lot of things in common and both loved sports. A few times Noel hung out with Greg at the sports bar.

Gabrielle was walking to her car, when she noticed that same Jaguar parked across the street. This time, she made sure she got the license plate.

Everyone is here, she thought, pulling into her parents' driveway. Gabrielle walked in to find her husband, brother-in-laws and father watching a football game. Greg was so into the game, he didn't even notice his wife.

"Hello!" she yelled, trying to get their attention.

"Hey, Gabby," her brother-in-laws said in unison, but her father and Greg continued to watch the game.

"GREG...DADDY...HELLO!" she loudly repeated.

Greg jumped up. "Oh damn, boo, I didn't even see you," he said, kissing her on the lips.

Gabrielle giggled. "Yeah, I bet you didn't. Where are the kids?"

"Somewhere running around," he replied as he sat back down to continue watching the game.

She threw her hands up and looked at Grace, who laughed.

"Girl, you know it's pointless talking to these men when the game is on," Grace told her.

They both laughed while heading to the kitchen.

After greeting everyone, Gabrielle pitched in to help prepare dinner.

"This reminds me of when we were growing up. Mommy, you would make me peel the potatoes," Giselle grumbled, then giggled.

"That's the only thing you knew how to do," Gloria teased, as everyone laughed.

As usual, over dinner, Noel talked about raising his girls. Finally acknowledging how proud he was of them, it caused Gabrielle and her sisters to look at each other, then give him the side-eye look.

"So, Grace, are you and Wayne planning on staying in the city or re-enlisting for another seven years?" Giselle asked.

"Well, we have thought about it. I don't want to be away from my family when the baby comes."

"Wherever you're located, your mother and I will come to you. Besides, it will feel good to be on the base again." Noel beamed.

"I didn't know you were in the Navy," Greg said.

"Yeah, I enlisted right out of high school," Noel responded. "At that time, it was the only way a black man could attend college. I stayed for about seven years and left. That's when I met my wife. I used to take my girls to the shooting range all the time."

"I hated it," Giselle and Gloria grumbled together.

"Why?" Wayne asked.

"All of that loud popping...no, thanks. Gabrielle was good at it, though. Right, Gab?"

"You shot a gun before?" Greg asked.

"Years ago," she said, brushing him off.

Noel reminisced about the girls' upbringing, but while everyone laughed, Gabrielle was in another world. For the rest of the night, she remained silent.

Driving home, Greg noticed his wife was very quiet. "Boo, are you okay?"

"Yes. Why?"

"You didn't say a word at your parents' house."

"I just have something on my mind. It's work."

Greg looked over at his wife and knew better. "Are you sure that's all it is?"

"I'm sure."

He looked at her from the corner of his eye, but decided to let it go.

Gabrielle put the kids to bed while Greg caught up on some work. As she poured herself something to drink, Greg entered the kitchen and hugged her from behind.

"You think when we get to be that old our children will visit us with their families?"

Gabrielle giggled. "They better."

Guiding her over to sit on his lap at the kitchen table, Greg kissed his wife on the lips. "Well, I must say your parents did a good job raising y'all."

"Why you say that?" she asked, twisting up her face.

"Look at y'all. All of y'all are successful and married with families. It's hard to achieve that nowadays."

"Please! That's because they forced us."

"Your parents were probably strict, but that's because they wanted the best for y'all. Don't forget they grew up when a lot of things didn't exist for black people. They grew up in that Brown vs. Board of Education era."

"Let me find out you know about that."

"Just because I sold drugs doesn't mean I wasn't smart. My mother made sure me and Samantha went to school."

"I guess you're right. You think we're going to last that long?"

"Why not? I'm not going anywhere, and I know you're not. We came too far to stop now. Whatever it is, we can work it out. Besides, we have children now. The only thing that can break us up is trust."

"Trust?"

"Yeah! Boo, we can work on anything from sex to communication, but if there's no trust, then the marriage is over. Always remember I'll keep it real with you no matter what. All I ask is

for you to do the same," Greg explained before kissing her goodnight.

Gabrielle sighed.

*****

Gabrielle walked around for the next couple of weeks pondering on Greg's words. *Why didn't I tell him?* At this point, he couldn't be mad. He was home, right? Conversely, he would still hit the roof. One thing she learned about him is he couldn't stand being lied to.

She was meeting her mother again that evening, and they were going to a kickboxing class. Strangely, they had been hanging out a lot since Noel was always away on business. Reflecting back to her mother's words about Noel not asking her to accompany him whenever he went out of town, Gabrielle wondered if there was someone else. Nah, with her father, it was all about image. Unless he was screwing Queen Elizabeth, there was no one who could hold a candle to Sadie. She didn't look a day over fifty, not to mention she made more money than Noel.

Gabrielle was meeting with a client when Sadie arrived. Kyle had recommended a friend to her, and he begged Gabrielle to meet with him at the last minute. Miguel Roman was just as arrogant as Kyle, believing they were God's gift to women. Gabrielle had to admit Miguel reminded her of Antonio Sabáto Jr. He was sexy as hell.

"So, Mr. Roman, I will be in touch with you," she said, shaking his hand.

"I look forward to hearing from you. Thank you for seeing me last minute, but I have a plane to catch."

Gabrielle flashed her political smile. "It's fine. Give Kyle my best."

"Will do," he replied while walking out.

"Hey, Mother," Gabrielle said, summoning her to come in. "Give me a second to get my things ready. Nancy, can you create a file for Mr. Roman?"

"Sure, boss lady. He's so sexy," Nancy teased, licking her lips.

"Nancy, file please." Gabrielle laughed, raising an eyebrow.

"Oookay," Nancy whined, causing Gabrielle and Sadie to laugh.

*****

Although Gabrielle was sore as hell, she really loved the class.

Exhausted and sitting in the sauna, Sadie blurted out, "I'm leaving your father."

"What?"

"I'm leaving your father," Sadie repeated.

Gabrielle scanned the room, wondering where her mother's words had come from. "Ma..."

Sadie jumped up and locked the door. "Gab, before you say something, let me explain. Your father and I haven't been happy in years."

"I didn't know. You seemed so..."

"We've pretended for so long that it's natural for us."

"What made you come to this decision?" Gabrielle asked, puzzled with her mother's revelation.

"My daughters. Gabrielle, I look at y'all and see love. I finally realized Noel and I never had that. Yes, he loves me dearly, but he's not for me. He doesn't look at me the way Greg looks at you. His face doesn't light up, and it hasn't for years."

"Ma, I'm so sorry," Gabrielle said sympathetically.

Sadie patted her on the hand. "Awww, don't be! We managed to raise some beautiful daughters. I'm just happy you guys didn't follow in my footsteps. Greg is a good man. You're a lucky woman. Don't lose him."

Gabrielle lowered her head and took a deep breath. Since her mother felt comfortable to confide in her, maybe she needed to do the same.

"Ma, I have something to tell you." She sighed again. "I helped Greg come home."

Sadie gave her a puzzled stare as if to say, *Okay. What's the problem?*

"I mean, I forced the ADA and judge to release Greg."

Still with a confused look, Sadie twisted up her lips. "You didn't break him out, did you?"

"No. Remember those tapes I was listening to when you came by the office? Well, that was the ADA discussing Greg's case. I got a hold of the tapes and blackmailed her to release my husband."

"You blackmailed her?"

"Something like that," Gabrielle replied, not going into all the details.

"Well, you did what you had to do for your family."

"Yes, I guess you're right, but Greg doesn't know."

"What do you mean Greg doesn't know?" Sadie said.

"He thinks Jake Lawrence brought him home. He doesn't know I was behind it."

"I'm confused. Why didn't you tell him? I'm pretty sure he would love to know. He would want to know."

"I can't..."

Her mother raised her hand, causing Gabrielle to stop speaking in mid-sentence. "You can't what?"

"Ma, you know how Greg is. If he finds out, he's gonna give me the long lecture."

"At least he will find out from you. Gabrielle, one thing I've learned is if you lie and lie, all you have is a bunch of scattered lies."

Gabrielle lowered her head. As always, her mother was right. "I know. I promise to tell him."

"Don't lose Greg over no bullshit, Gabrielle. Men like him are hard to find."

She thought about what her mother said and decided to tell him the truth. However, every time she got the courage, something came up. Gabrielle knew once she told Greg, he was going to interrogate her ass. *He's gonna wanna know everything from conception to abortion.*

Another thing that bothered her was her mother; she couldn't believe she was leaving her father. Gabrielle knew they had their ups and downs, but divorced? She didn't see that coming. That's why she decided to have lunch with her father to find out what was really going on. They were meeting at Sylvia's, his favorite restaurant. Noel was already there when Gabrielle arrived.

"Hello, Daddy." She greeted him with a kiss.

"Brielle," Noel said, using her childhood nickname.

It was strange. Gabrielle and her father were never close. In fact, this was the first time they spent time together.

She blushed. "You haven't called me that in years."

Noel smiled.

Knowing her father would get defensive, Gabrielle didn't want to get right into it, so she asked, "What's new, Daddy?"

"Nothing. I'm ready for retirement."

"Really!"

"I just put my papers in."

"How long have you been working for Yale?"

"Twenty-five years."

"Wow! So I guess Mommy is gonna retire soon, too?"

"I don't know what your mother is gonna do. I think she has a couple more years."

"So what are you going to do? I know you always wanted to travel. Maybe you and Mommy can do that together."

"Maybe. How's Greg and the kids?" he asked, totally disregarding Gabrielle's suggestion.

"They're great! Greg and Gail are getting big and bad. Greg is wonderful."

"That's great!"

"Dad, are you and Mommy alright?"

Noel was about to respond, when his cell phone rang. He glanced at it before sending the call to voicemail."

"Is everything okay?" Gabrielle asked.

"Yeah," he responded, but his phone rang again. This time, Noel answered. "Hi. I'm having lunch with Gabrielle."

Whoever had called knew Gabrielle. Noel listened to the caller, then responded, "Stainless steel is better, but let me call you back."

"Is everything okay?" Gabrielle asked again, while glaring at him after he ended the call.

80

Noel flashed a smile. "Yeah. That was your mother. She's remodeling again."

"Oh, didn't y'all just remodel?"

"Yep, but you know your mother." He chuckled.

"Yes, I do. So, Daddy, I was thinking about sending you and Mommy on a vacation...my treat."

Noel's eyes lit up. "A vacation?"

"Yep," she chimed, putting her fork down. "It's time that you and your wife start spending some quality time together."

Noel shot Gabrielle a leery look. "What makes you think we don't?"

Gabrielle put her hand up, laughing. "Alright, but I wanna treat you guys to some place nice. Pick any place in the world."

Smiling, Noel stared at his daughter. "Are you serious?"

"Yep!"

"Let me think about it and get back to you."

Gabrielle remained silent. Something was definitely up with her father, and she hoped it wasn't another woman.

Instead of going back to the office, Gabrielle picked up the kids from the daycare center. Gail wasn't feeling good, so Gabrielle headed straight to their pediatrician. Although it was nothing serious, Greg said he would meet her there. As they suspected, both children had ear infections.

Once they arrived home, Gabrielle fed the kids and then tucked them into bed. Greg decided to stay in since the kids weren't feeling good, but Gabrielle thought he was overreacting. With Greg in the living room watching television, she felt it was the perfect time for her to tell him about Britney.

"They finally fell asleep," Gabrielle said, snuggling into his arms.

"Who would send their kids to school sick?" he angrily stated.

"Greg, kids get sick all the time. I don't think their parents did it intentionally."

"How do you know that?"

"Boo..." Gabrielle rose up, laughing.

"For real! You laughing, but I'm dead serious. I better not find out who the parents are."

"What are you gonna do to them?"

"Check their asses. Boo, you don't understand. I don't play with you and my kids. I don't give a fuck what it is."

She laughed, but she knew her husband was speaking the truth.

Gabrielle worked from home the next couple of days. Although she could've called the babysitter, she didn't. She knew all she was going to do was call every five minutes to check on them. The twins were cranky while sick. It was bad enough when one child was sick, but she had two crying, miserable babies on her hands. *Finally,* she thought after putting them down for their noon nap. Gabrielle wondered how people did it back in the day. Having eight and nine children, she would've lost her mind.

While sipping some green tea and staring out of the window, Gabrielle noticed that same black Jaguar sitting outside of her house. She quickly closed the curtain and went to call Greg. She dialed his number, but then hung up. After what he said the other night, Greg would kill someone. When she went back over to the window, the car was gone.

Shaken, Gabrielle started pacing the floor. With her children sleeping upstairs, their safety was her main concern. What if they came back? Just then, she remembered she had their license plate number. So, she ran in the other room to get her briefcase. Gabrielle then called a friend of hers that worked at the DMV. *This person doesn't know they're playing a deadly game.*

It turned out the car was registered to someone in Canada— Margaret Weinstein. Gabrielle didn't know anyone from Canada, let alone a Margaret Weinstein. Maybe the person had the wrong address, but that couldn't be the case since they showed up at her office and home. She decided that if she saw the car one more time, she would tell Greg, which wouldn't be good.

*****

It was three o'clock in the morning when Greg got the call that three of his clubs were robbed at gunpoint. Surprisingly, they would do it on a night that Greg went home early because the kids still weren't feeling well. Also, they were all robbed at the same time, which meant someone was watching the clubs. According to the manager, the robbers made off with a million dollars. Burning inside, Greg remained calm at the scene. Gabrielle wanted to go with him, but he made her stay at home.

For the next couple of weeks, Greg monitored the surveillance tapes, looking for anything out of the ordinary. Prior to the club getting robbed, Mike and Wild Child had an after party there, but that wasn't nothing. Moe and his crew came through a few times, but Moe knew better than to play games. It was killing Greg because the person had to be someone he knew. Given his reputation, people knew not to mess with his establishments. All the real stickup kids were either dead or in prison.

Meanwhile, the police were all over this crime because of Greg's criminal background, and it didn't help matters that he was not cooperating with them. To him, they only made shit worse. Greg had his own special way of handling shit like this. When the word got out about Greg's spots being robbed, people were calling from all over offering their help. Some even offered to put that work in once Greg found out who was behind it, but Greg denied their offers. The last thing he needed was some bullshit hanging over his head. Everyone would pop that tough-guy shit, but when shit hit the fan, all the Diana Ross came out of dudes.

Greg knew Gabrielle was worried about what he was going to do. When he was at the club, she called him a million times. Also, she stayed up late waiting for him to come home. Although he reassured her that everything was good, she was far from stupid. He didn't care about being robbed because money wasn't a problem. He was more upset about some dudes thinking they could do anything to Greg. If they thought they could rob him and get away with it, what would they do next? Greg had run up into many dudes' cribs while their

families were there, but he wasn't about to let that happen to his family.

If they thought Greg was on point back then, he was like the CIA now. He installed more security cameras at his house and business. He even did another background check on all the managers.

Greg was in the back doing inventory, when Gabrielle and the kids surprised him.

"Daddy!" they yelled.

Greg looked up and smiled despite being upset inside.

"Hey," he said, while kneeling down to their level.

"They wanted to see you," Gabrielle explained, noticing Greg's wary expression.

Immediately, he ushered them into his office. He turned on the TV for the kids and then looked over at Gabrielle. "Why did you bring them here?"

"They wanted to see their father. What's the problem?"

"What's the problem? You know we were just robbed."

"Okay! A lot of places get robbed, Greg."

"Well, not mine. Until I find out who's behind this, do not come around here."

"Greg, you're overreacting."

He snatched Gabrielle by the arm. "What the fuck you mean I'm overreacting? We're talking about my family here. Of course, I'm gonna overreact. DO NOT BRING YOUR ASS AROUND HERE!"

Gabrielle stared in Greg's face. She had never seen him so upset, and by the way he had a tight grip on her arm, she knew it was best not to say anything. She took a deep breath and gently pulled her arm away.

"Come on, kids. Daddy is busy."

Greg didn't mean to come at her like that, but he had a lot on his mind. The last thing he needed to worry about was someone harming his family.

When Greg arrived home, Gabrielle and the kids were watching television.

"Daddy!" they cheered.

"What's up?" he said, putting them on his lap. "What's up, boo?"

"Hi," she replied dryly before walking out.

Greg talked with the kids for a while before going into the bedroom with Gabrielle. "Boo, I didn't mean to yell at you like that."

"It's fine."

Greg lovingly grabbed her by the waist. "I'm sorry. Right now, I don't want you and the kids nowhere near the business."

Gabrielle sighed. "I heard you, but..."

"But nothing, boo. I would die if something happened to y'all. I will kill everything that's moving."

Gabrielle chuckled. "Everything?"

"Fo' sure. Until I know who's behind this, I want you to keep a low profile."

She thought about telling him about the car that was parked in front of the house and office, but she didn't want to hear a long lecture from him.

"Fair enough," she said, kissing him as he started fondling her. "Greg, the kids are in the other room."

"So? They're watching TV," he responded, closing the door. "Don't worry, I will cum quick."

He winked, and Gabrielle laughed.

*****

It was the middle of the night, and Greg did another walk-thru of the house. On his way back to the bedroom, he checked on the kids. Sighing, he thought, *Whoever did it knows me, but one thing is for sure. The person is about to get a visit from the Angel of Death.*

Chapter Eight
Morgan

It had been eight months since finding out, and Morgan still couldn't believe she was pregnant again. After Anthony was born, Tony found it hard to abstain from having sex with her, but promised to pull out. However, that didn't work. When Morgan went back for her six-week checkup, she was pregnant. Four weeks to be exact. If she didn't have Lil' Anthony in her arms, she would've passed out. Tony was ecstatic, especially since it was a girl, while Morgan's family thought she had completely lost her mind.

Jasmine suggested Morgan see a psychiatrist, while Denise didn't speak to her. However, things seemed to have calmed down. There was one thing that did surprise Morgan, though—Tony. He was such a good father to Anthony; he was involved in everything from feeding him to changing his diaper. He even read to him at night. After Anthony was born, Tony brought so much stuff—clothing, toys, and even diamond earrings. That's when Morgan had to put her foot down. First, Tony objected, claiming his son should have the best, but after Morgan threatened to throw it away, he stopped.

Morgan had to admit, Anthony was a doll and a happy baby. He actually made her living nightmare bearable. While she didn't love Tony, she wouldn't trade her son for the world. One thing she didn't allow was a world full of chaos. Morgan wanted to raise her children like her mother did, which was full of love and joy. Although he was on tour, Tony managed to see them twice a month and communicated via the webcam.

With Tony gone, Morgan stayed in her apartment on the Westside. Since it was her last semester, it made it much easier for her to get around from school, work, and the babysitter's.

As promised, at eight months pregnant, Morgan graduated from NYU, receiving a Bachelor's degree in Economics and named valedictorian, which she also was in high school. In addition, she was the only student accepted for the Woodrow Wilson School of Public and International Affairs at Princeton University. This program allowed students to obtain a Master's in Public Administration and their Juris Doctorate. While most students had to be a first-year law student to apply, the school was so impressed with Morgan that they waived that requirement for her. Even though Jasmine and Denise were pissed about her pregnancy, they were proud to see her walk across the stage during graduation. Tony was upset that he wasn't there to share in his wife's moment.

To celebrate Morgan getting her degree, they went out to dinner. As the family was laughing and joking, Jasmine handed her cell phone to Morgan. "Here, it's for you."

Surprised, Morgan reached for the phone. "Hello."

"Congratulations!" her father and grandmother shouted in unison.

"Thank you!"

"Princess, I'm so proud of you. I know you took plenty of pictures."

"Yes, I did, and I'm going to send them to you. Did you get the other ones I sent?"

"Yes, my grandson is getting so big. He looks just like his granddaddy."

"He does. Everyone says that." Morgan giggled, getting up so she could have a little more privacy.

"Bella, when are you coming to see us? I wanna see my great grandbaby," her grandmother chimed in.

"I know, but the doctor said I can't travel until I have the baby," she explained, causing them to get quiet.

Like Jasmine, Felix was also upset with Morgan, but what could he do? Besides, a part of him felt like he didn't have the authority to dictate her life, especially when he didn't take his mother's advice and move Morgan with him.

"Well, I can't wait to see my baby. I miss you so much."

"I miss you, too. I can't wait for you to see the kids."

Morgan talked for a couple more minutes before joining her mother and family. After dinner, everyone returned to Denise's apartment, while Jasmine and Morgan took a stroll through Central Park. Jasmine felt it was a good time to have a long, overdue talk with her daughter, hoping to get some of her questions answered.

"Are you okay?" Jasmine asked.

"Yes, I'm fine. How about you?"

"I'm okay." She paused before saying, "Morgan, we need to talk."

Morgan sighed. She knew this was coming. Normally, she would get defensive, but this time, she just listened.

Jasmine took a long, deep breath. "First, I wanna say how proud I am of you. I know for the last couple of months we haven't seen things eye to eye, but a part of me is to blame for that. I feel like it's because of me that you're pregnant."

Morgan stopped walking and stared at her mother with a confused look. "Why do you say that?"

"I don't know. Maybe if I had kept you closer to me, you would have come to me. You were my firstborn, and I should not have allowed Denise to raise you," Jasmine explained, while leading them over to a nearby bench.

"Denise didn't raise me, Mommy. Remember, it was for school."

"I know, but I feel like I should've been there, and I want to say I'm sorry."

Morgan lowered her head, thinking she should tell her the truth about her situation. *Mommy, it's not your fault. I was raped,* she thought.

"Mommy..." Morgan whined.

"No, Morgan. Let me finish. I want you to know that I only wanted the best for you. Everything I do is for my kids. I love y'all so much."

"I know, Mommy."

"If something should happen to me..."

"Mommy, don't talk like that. You're going to be fine."

"But, if something should, please take care of your brother and sister. You understand me."

Morgan nodded. "Yes."

*****

In an attempt to lift her mother's spirits and indirectly make up for not telling her what was going on in her life, Morgan threw Jasmine a birthday party, inviting friends and family only. Of course, Tony made sure he was available to attend. Throughout the party, Tony and Morgan stood on opposite sides of the room, which was hard for Tony. Unlike some pregnant women, Morgan looked stunning. Her hair was pulled up in a tight bun, and her skin was flawless. However, it was her outfit that drove Tony crazy. She had on a black and white maternity dress designed by Diana Von Furstenberg. Thank God Tony had on shades, because he would've been caught staring. Periodically, they danced with each other, but other than that, Tony kept Christina close.

Jasmine was really enjoying herself, but the party came to a halt when Lil' Anthony reached for Tony while crying and yelling "Da Da" as everyone looked on. Morgan almost went into labor.

Michael saved the day when he laughed and said, "He says that to everyone."

As the party came to an end, Tony went into the kitchen with Jasmine.

"Hey, Jasmine, how are you feeling?" he asked, helping her clean up.

"I've had better days."

"Well, you know your kids adore you, even Morgan," he joked.

Jasmine smiled and then sighed. "Tony, I don't know what has gotten into her."

Me, he thought, but didn't dare say it out loud. "What do you mean? She finished college and is about to go to law school."

"I guess you're right, but she's gonna have two babies without a father. You and I both know how hard it is to raise a child alone, and I'm in no position to help her," she said, choking up.

Tony reached out to embrace her. "I know, and if it's alright with you, I wanna help. Whatever she needs me to do, I will."

"That's thoughtful of you, but you have your life..."

Tony interjected. "Jas, stop it. Morgan is family. The kids will have a father."

"An uncle/father," Jasmine replied, laughing.

"Yeah, they're not gonna want for nothing, trust me," he said, hugging her.

"Thanks, Tony."

"Anytime."

Everyone left a short while later, leaving Christina and Tony there. Christina was upstairs helping Morgan with Lil' Anthony.

"Morgan, he's so cute. He looks just like you."

"Thank you. He's bad, though. Right, papi?" She smiled and kissed her son.

"Do you know what you're having this time?"

"Yeah, a girl."

"I wish I didn't lose my baby," Christina mumbled sorrowfully.

"You were pregnant?"

"Yes, a couple of years ago, but I lost the baby."

Morgan stood quietly until Tony walked in.

"What's up, little man?" he said, picking up Lil' Anthony.

Glaring at him from the corner of her eye, Morgan snatched Lil' Anthony away from him. "Give me my son."

Surprised, Tony stared at her. "Is everything okay?" he asked, confused.

"Christina just told me that she was pregnant years ago," she said, still glaring at the wide-eyed Tony.

He stood there just staring at Christina and not saying anything. Silence filled the room, and then Monique busted in.

"Christina, can you come and sign my CD?"

"Sure," she said, following Monique out of the room.

Once alone, Morgan angrily said in a low voice, "She was pregnant by you?"

Tony turned around to make sure no one was behind him. "No," he said, picking up his son.

"You're lying," Once again, she attempted to snatch the baby from him. "Let go of my child."

"No, I'm not. She was pregnant, but not by me. Morgan, you know I wouldn't..."

"You wouldn't what?! You wouldn't go around raping girls and getting them pregnant?"

Tony stood quietly. Morgan had never spoken to him like that before. "Baby..." he moaned, trying to calm her down, "let's not do this here."

Morgan glared at him, then at their son, and sighed. "Do what, Tony? Isn't she your wife? You think I'm stupid."

"No... Can we talk about this later? I swear to you that it's not what you think."

Pissed, Morgan finished undressing their son to give him a bath. Suddenly, she started feeling contractions. Morgan fell on the bed, and staring, Tony reached out for her.

"Are you alright?"

Unable to speak, Morgan smacked his hand away while breathing heavily. A few seconds went by as she thought, *Please don't tell me I'm going into labor.*

"Morgan, what's going on? Talk to me," Tony demanded in a scared tone.

Ignoring him, Morgan got up, but the contractions hit her again. This time, they were severe.

"Oh God!" she gasped. "I think I'm going into labor."

Scared, Tony yelled, "Oh shit! Jasmine!"

Five hours later, London Paris Flowers was born. She was eight pounds, four ounces and measured sixteen inches long. Ironically, Tony was in the delivery room. Jasmine was too sick and Michael was too young, which left Tony. Overwhelmed with emotions, Tony broke down when he held his daughter.

After London was born, Morgan stayed in Atlanta for two months before returning home. While she was grateful for the help from her grandmother and mother, she couldn't wait to get home. Plus, Tony had a couple of days off and wanted to spend time with her and the kids.

Tony was standing in front with a big smile on his face when they pulled up to the house.

"What's up, big man?" He playfully picked up his son. "Daddy missed you." He then leaned over to kiss his wife. "I missed you, too, babe."

Still pissed, Morgan flashed a fake smile and walked into the house with London. Tony put his head down. He knew he had some serious explaining to do.

After putting the kids to bed, Morgan started sorting the babies' clothes, when Tony came in.

"Can we talk?" Since silence meant consensus to him, he continued. "Morgan, Christina wasn't pregnant by me. I know you don't believe me, but it's the truth. Yeah, she was pregnant, but it wasn't mine. When we got together..."

Morgan interrupted. "You mean when you raped me."

Speechless, Tony's eyes widened. He didn't know how to respond. "Morgan..."

"What, Tony? We didn't get together. You raped me; you forced me into this marriage. There's a difference. My life was perfectly fine until you came into it."

"I know. I'm sorry."

"Sorry? I have two kids, Tony. I think sorry is a little too late."

With his hands in his pocket, Tony didn't know how to respond. Morgan was right.

"Why?" she asked, glaring at him with tears rolling down her

 92

face. "Why did you rape me?"

He closed his eyes. "Morgan, I'm sorry for what I've done."

"You said that already. Now tell me why."

"I don't know. I fell in love with you, and I didn't want anyone to have you."

"So you raped me?"

He reached out for her hand. "Baby, it wasn't like that. Morgan, I have never loved anyone like I love you. You're everything I wanted, and I thought by being your first, it would help you see that."

Morgan shook her head. "You thought?" she repeated. "You know, Tony, I look at our kids and worry. Worry that someone like you is going to harm them."

"I will never let that happen."

"You just don't get it. For every Morgan, there's a Tony," she said, then started to walk out the room.

"Morgan," Tony shouted, "what do I have to do? Just tell me."

Their eyes met briefly.

"I don't know. A part of me wants you out of my life forever. But, we have kids together, and no matter how much I despise you, I could never take my children away from their father," she replied, then left.

Hoping to spend some quality time with his wife and kids turned out to be just the opposite. Morgan barely said two words to Tony. When she did, it was only pertaining to the kids.

It got to the point where Morgan didn't acknowledge Tony in the house. In the morning, she worked out before heading to work, leaving Tony with the kids, which he didn't mind. When she returned, she prepared dinner and then it was off to study.

It was the last night before Tony went back on tour, and he was in the room playing with the kids. From afar, she watched him interacting with their children. He was such a good and loving father. He had given her the most precious thing in the world—her children—yet, Morgan viewed him as a monster.

Morgan went downstairs to the living room and glanced at their family portraits. Sighing, she closed her eyes and thought, *How can someone that causes me so much pain create something that brings me so much joy? Is it possible that good comes from evil?*

"Baby girl," Tony said, standing behind her, "I know you don't wanna hear it, but I'm sorry for everything, and I will die trying to make it up to you."

Morgan turned around. "I don't know if you're capable."

"So what are you saying? You want a divorce?"

She took a long, deep breath. A divorce would be her way out of this nightmare. She stared deeply into his eyes. *Is he sincere?*

Tony gradually walked towards his wife. "Ma, I'm sorry," he said, getting choked up. "Please don't leave me. Don't take my kids away from me. I'll do whatever it takes to prove to you that I'm a good person."

Hesitant, Morgan stood there quietly as tears rolled down her face. "Tony..." She lowered her head. "I..."

"Morgan, please...I love my family," he said, embracing her.

"Even if I wanted to, I could never take our kids away from their father. If I do stay, things have to change."

Tony nodded while smiling inside. "Okay. Whatever you say."

"For one, we need to tell my parents. We can't continue living like this."

"I know, but let me get some things together first. Your mother is not in the best of health, so I think we should wait. Morgan, I know we started off wrong, so I want us to start over again. Let's be friends."

Morgan nodded. "It's going to take me some time, but I'm willing to try for our children's sake. If it doesn't work out, though, I want a divorce."

"Okay."

"And I want to do normal things. I want my own car so the kids and I can travel on the weekends."

"Travel where?"

"Anywhere. I wanna take them to the zoo and other places."

Tony sighed. He didn't want anyone around his family, but right now, he didn't have a choice but to agree with her demands. "Alright, but I want someone to travel with you."

Morgan screwed up her face. "For what? Tony, no one knows about us. They don't know those are your kids. If you assign bodyguards, people will start asking questions . No, the kids and I are fine."

"I guess I don't have a choice."

"No, you don't."

That night, Tony and Morgan worked on becoming friends, and she sent him back on his tour with a smile on his face.

As promised, Tony really changed. Although he still called a lot, he didn't question Morgan about her whereabouts, allowing her to drive herself and the kids to the park and other places. She also was allowed to hang out with the few friends she had, and some nights Denise watched the kids. Finally, Morgan had a life.

Being that Tony turned over a new leaf, Morgan took another job at a prestigious law firm called Wachtell, Lipton, Rosen, and Katz. At first, Tony objected, claiming it was going to take too much of her time away from the kids. However, Morgan had to remind him about their conversation. She didn't know it, but it wasn't the job Tony was scared about; it was the men. While Tony probably had more money than any of them, he knew it wasn't about money. For Morgan, it was about personality and respect—something Tony didn't allow her to see.

Morgan had to admit working a full-time job and raising two kids was a lot of work. Some days, she didn't know where she got the strength. Lil' Anthony was walking into everything, while London put everything in her mouth. It was during times like this that she missed Tony.

One night, Morgan was preparing dinner, when her cell phone rang. She brushed it off, thinking it was Tony. When it rang again, once more she ignored it. She had just gotten in with the kids and was running behind schedule. She wanted to feed them and then put them to bed so she could get some studying done.

However, it rang again, and she sighed. "You know your father is a pain in the butt."

She giggled, kissed London, and then searched for her phone. It was Monique, but before Morgan could call her back, Monique called again.

"Hello," Morgan answered.

"MORGAN! Mommy is not moving! The paramedics are here working on her!"

"What?! Calm down! What are you talking about?"

Monique took a deep breath. "Mommy...she's not moving."

"What are they saying? Let me talk to someone."

Monique handed her grandmother the phone. "It's not good. I think you better come now."

When she arrived at the hospital, Morgan was greeted by her grandmother. "How is she doing?"

With tears in her eyes, she responded, "Not so good. She's asking for you."

Morgan handed the kids over to her grandmother and then went to see her mother, who was on a respirator.

"Ma," Morgan said.

Jasmine opened her eyes. "Morgan..." She struggled to speak. "You made it."

With tears pouring down her face, Morgan grabbed her mother's hand. "Yes. Ma, I love you so much and I'm sorry."

"I love you, too."

Morgan smiled. "Ma, I have something to tell you." She took a deep breath. "I was raped when I was fourteen."

Jasmine cried, "Oh God..."

"I wanted to tell you, Ma."

In pain, Jasmine wept. "I'm sorry I didn't know."

"No one knew. Ma, the person that raped me was...Tony. Those are his kids, and he's my husband."

The machine started to go off as Jasmine gasped for air. By that time, Denise had arrived.

"Jasmine!" she cried.

Morgan ran out the room to get the nurse, while Jasmine looked at Denise and said, "He hurt my baby. He hurt my baby," then took her last breath.

"Who hurt your baby? Jas...Jas! Please no," Denise cried, holding Jasmine's head.

Morgan returned to the room with the doctors, but it was too late.

"She's gone," Denise wept into Morgan's arms.

Chapter Nine
Tony

It had been ten months since Jasmine's death, and Tony was worried about Morgan. Since her mother's death, she'd become withdrawn from the world. At Anthony's birthday party, she barely spoke to anyone. It also didn't help that Tony was on tour when all of this took place. Every night, he called home to check on her. Some days she seemed great, while others she was frustrated.

Tonight was his finale show in Madison Square Garden, and everyone came out to support. However, Tony couldn't wait for it to be over so he could get back home to his wife. At the end of his show, he gave a secret shout out to Morgan. Initially, he was supposed to be on a romantic vacation with his wife, but at the last minute, Tia informed him that Christina was throwing him a birthday party. Livid, Tony decided he would not attend. While the thought was nice, he had other plans. Nonetheless, Tia convinced him to grace the party with his presence. Tony agreed, but he made sure Morgan was invited.

It was a star-studded event; Christina spared no expenses. The party was in Singapore's luxurious new Marina Bay Sands Hotel. Wolfgang Puck prepared a French cuisine for the partygoers. She also hired Aerial dancers.

The party was a blast. Everyone from sports players to moguls attended. Tony was having a good time until Morgan showed up in a one-strap, sea blue Versace dress. He paused mid-sentence when he saw her come in, and he wasn't the only one. When one of the CEOs from another company inquired about Morgan, Tony quickly informed him that she was taken.

Throughout the night, Tony watched Morgan like a hawk. Mookie was sweating her, unable to control himself. As Tony joined Morgan on the dance floor, it took every ounce of him not to grab and kiss her. Forgetting how well Morgan could dance, Tony was in a zone. They danced for about five songs before Tia interrupted them.

Meanwhile, Denise, Derrick, Gabrielle, and Greg were having a ball on the upper level. When Christina wasn't greeting people, she was on her BlackBerry. Tony figured she was talking to Rashid, who was across the room. Morgan was standing on the balcony when Tony found her.

"Are you having a good time?"

"Yes. The party is nice. Christina did a good job."

"Yeah, I guess," he said, staring at her. "You look sexy as hell. I can't take my eyes off of you."

Morgan blushed and was about to say something, when Denise walked up to them.

"Hey, niece, I saw you out there dancing."

"Yeah, I was doing a little something. You and Derrick were getting down, too," Morgan replied with a smile.

Denise laughed. "Girl, please! Back in the day, your mother and I used to party our asses off."

Morgan lowered her head. "Mommy…I guess that's where I get my dancing from," she said, then started to walk away.

"Morgan…" Denise reached out to touch her arm. "Sweetie, you have to stop blaming yourself."

"I can't, Aunt Dee."

"I know, sweetie. I do, too," Denise mumbled, hugging her niece tightly.

"Excuse me," Morgan said, leaving them.

Standing there like a lump on a log, Tony lowered his head. It killed him to see Morgan hurting. It hurt him even more that he could not console her.

"I'm worried about her," Denise said.

"She'll be alright. She just needs a little more time."

Concerned about Morgan, Tony planned a nice vacation to their private island in the French Polynesia with the kids. *Maybe being away will make her feel better,* he thought.

Morgan arrived with the kids a day prior to Tony. Before the questions started from his camp, Tony hopped on a plane, leaving his staff puzzled, as usual. The sun was setting when Tony arrived. He walked in and found Morgan with the kids standing at the table with a cake.

"Happy birthday!" they yelled.

Smiling, Tony was in awe.

"Happy birthday, Daddy," Lil' Anthony said.

"Thanks, man!"

After kissing his kids, Tony gazed into his wife's eyes. "Thank you."

"You're welcome. I know it's not what…"

Quickly, Tony cut her off. "Hush. This is the best party I've ever had," he said, planting a kiss on her lips.

"Come on, Daddy," Lil' Anthony said, grabbing his father's hand, as Morgan and Tony looked at each other and laughed.

Tony played with the kids while Morgan prepared dinner. Whereas Christina had spent thousands of dollars on her party for Tony, this was worth more to him. Spending time with his wife and kids was priceless.

After the kids were asleep, Morgan and Tony had a romantic dinner on the deck. At first, it was silence, with Morgan in a daze and Tony afraid to talk.

"Were you surprised?" she asked, breaking the silence.

"Yeah, I was."

"Well, I'm happy."

"How are you doing? I'm worried about you."

"I'm great."

"Are you sure? The last time…"

"No, I'm good. I had a long talk with my grandma, and I have to stop blaming myself."

"That's true. Your mother would be proud of you."

Nodding, Morgan flashed a slight grin. 'So how was your tour?"

"It was good, but I'm glad it's over."

"Why?"

"I'm tired of being away from you and the kids."

"Tony…"

"For real, Morgan! I missed the birth of my son and almost missed my daughter's birth, too. I missed your graduation…and Jasmine…" he mumbled, getting choked up. "You don't know how I felt."

Morgan reached for his hand. "You can't blame yourself."

"I do, ma," he said, rubbing her hand. "When I started out in the business, I wanted to make so much money, thinking I would be happy, but you've changed all of that."

"Me?"

"Yes, you! Morgan, before I met you, I was out there sleeping with a lot of chicks, thinking that was the good life, killing myself. Now I see that's not the good life. Coming home to my wife and kids is the good life. Reading to my son at night, that's the good life."

"I didn't know that."

"Well, now you know! All that matters to me are you and the kids."

Morgan lowered her head. Since the death of Jasmine, she never talked about it. Maybe it was a good time now. She had to admit that Tony's words seemed genuine. Morgan looked up to find him staring at her. Taking a deep breath, Morgan let down her guard and confided in her husband.

Over dinner, they talked about everything. At times, they laughed and then cried. For Tony, it was a sign that they were heading in the right direction. After dinner, they took a long stroll on the beach. With the beautiful evening sky and the gentle breeze blowing, Tony wrapped his arms around his wife while carrying her sandals in his other hand.

At first, there was a brief silence while both enjoyed the scenery, but then Morgan blurted out, "Oh, *Time Magazine* wants to interview me."

Tony stopped walking. "For real? That's what I'm talking about," he chimed, picking up Morgan as she giggled.

After putting her down, he stared at her. It was the first time he felt loved. Happy, Tony twirled his wife up in the air again and then ran into the ocean.

"Tony!" Morgan laughed.

Tony looked into his wife's eyes. "I love you," he moaned. "I love you with all my heart."

"I love you, too," she replied and kissed him.

There they were standing in the middle of the ocean kissing and fondling each other. It had been months since they had sex, and both were extremely horny. Morgan shoved her hands down Tony's pants.

"What does daddy want for his birthday?" she moaned, turning Tony on.

He grabbed her by her face, staring deeply into her eyes. "I want you forever. Morgan, I don't care if I lose everything. As long as I have you, I'm fine. You have to believe me when I say you own me, ma. You have my heart and soul. I live for you," he said with a single tear rolling down his face.

Morgan leaned forward, kissed his tear, and then passionately kissed him on the lips. She unbuckled his pants and pulled out his penis. As they gazed into each other's eyes, Morgan slid down and started performing oral sex on her husband. Weak, Tony damn near dropped to his knees. He lifted his wife up, kissed her, and then picked her up, wrapping her legs around him.

"I'm not wearing any panties." She laughed in the heat of passion.

"Just like I like it," he said, inserting himself inside her. "Damn, I missed you," he loudly moaned.

"I missed you, too," she gasped, riding him.

From the beach to the house, Morgan and Tony made love into the wee hours of the morning. The way the two were talking and yelling out, they would've wakened everybody up had anyone been on the island with them.

The next day, Morgan slept while Tony took the kids out to the beach. As he laughed and played with his kids, Tony thought about Morgan's words. *Will karma come back to my kids?* He looked over at London, who looked just like Morgan. Tony would die if someone raped his little girl.

"Look, Daddy!" Lil' Anthony yelled.

Tony laughed and then joined him.

When they returned, Morgan was in the room looking at some photos of her mother.

"Mommy!" Lil' Anthony yelled, pulling on her.

"Yes, baby. Did you have fun with Daddy at the beach?"

"Yes."

"Tell Mommy what you did."

"We made Spiderman," he replied, laughing.

Morgan clapped her hands. "Yay! Look at you, though. You're filthy. Let's get you cleaned up."

Lil' Anthony was smart and talked very well for his age. Just like her mother did when she was that age, Morgan read to him and enrolled Lil' Anthony in school when he was just an infant. Morgan put the pictures on the bed so she could take London out of Tony's hands. Meanwhile, Lil' Anthony ran over and picked them up.

"Mommy," he said, while pointing at one photo.

Both Tony and Morgan turned around.

"No, that's your grandma," Tony informed him.

"Grandma?" he repeated back.

"Yes, baby, your grandma. She's in heaven," Morgan said, pointing up in the air.

"Why?" he asked.

Morgan sighed and looked over at Tony. "She was sick," she replied, hoping he didn't ask any more questions.

There was a brief silence, until London started fidgeting for Morgan to put her down. This caused everyone to laugh.

*****

The next couple of days, Tony had a joyful time with his family. When it was time to leave, he didn't want to; he couldn't take living his life in secrecy. Being with her made him realize it was time to tell the truth.

Tony went back to work—semi retired as he called it. Tia had a schedule and a slew of interviews for him. Since he announced his retirement from the game, everyone wanted to know what was next for him. Being that Tony had his hand in everything, some reported he was branching out into movies.

Calculating every step he made, Tony made sure he informed Denise and Greg of his conversation with Jasmine. Before publicly helping Morgan with the kids, he also informed Christina of his so-called good deeds. He didn't need her to start speculating. Her naïve ass thought it was nice of him. Tony knew Christina didn't give a rat's ass; she was too busy fucking Rashid.

With a new job and starting law school, Morgan got home late a lot, leaving Tony to play Mr. Mom. Although the kids were in school for most of the day, Tony looked forward to picking them up and taking them home.

Since Morgan was out of town helping with Monique's birthday party, Tony stayed in the city with the kids. Surprisingly, Christina was home when they arrived.

"Oh my God! Is that London and Anthony?" she asked, coming down the stairs.

"Yep. Morgan went away, so I told her they could stay with us for the weekend. You're cool with that, right?"

"Sure," she said, kissing them on the cheek.

With London in his arms and Lil' Anthony holding on tight to his leg, Tony went into the other room. He laughed and told his son, "She's not gonna bite you."

"I want Mommy," he whined.

"She's in Atlanta with Aunt Monique."

"Awww!" Christina smiled. "You want some ice cream?"

Lil' Anthony nodded.

"Go with Chris and get some ice cream."

For the rest of the evening, Tony and Christina acted like proud parents. He had to admit she was great with kids. She bathed London and read to Anthony before he went to sleep.

The media had a field day when they saw Tony and Christina in the park with the kids. Some even speculated that she was pregnant. On the other hand, Morgan didn't like the idea of her children being exploited, and she made sure Tony knew this.

Tony took the kids over to see Denise, who had just returned from the grocery store when Tony pulled up with the kids.

"Tony," Denise greeted, smiling as she put away the groceries.

"Sis," he said, kissing her on the cheek. "With all the money you're making, why don't you hire someone to do that shit for you?" he jokingly suggested.

"Oh hush! I love taking the kids food shopping. It reminds me of when I was a little girl. And for your information, just because I have a couple of dollars doesn't mean I can't do shit for myself."

Tony put his hand up. "A couple of dollars? Okay, Donald Trump. But, I feel you about living a simple life. I was just joking. Where's Big Derrick?"

"You just missed him. He went to pick up his car from the dealer. I see you're really enjoying my niece and nephew."

"You know, Dee. Anything I can do to help."

"That's all you better be doing."

"What is that suppose to mean?"

"You know what I mean," she said, glaring at him.

"Morgan is an adult..."

"Tony!" Denise yelled. "I'm serious. I don't mind you helping out my niece with the kids, but that's all your ass better be doing."

"Damn, Dee, why are you coming at me like that?"

Sarcastically twisting her face, she replied, "Because I know you like pretty girls."

"And?"

"And, motherfucker, Morgan is my niece."

"Yeah, I know! You think I'm not good enough for her?"

With a solemn stare, Denise replied, "No, I don't! I love you and all, Tee, but you are something else. You're married to Christina and cheating on her."

"That's Christina. She's a piece of shit," he said, waving his hand and making Denise giggle.

"Tony, you heard what I said," she warned.

"Dee, I'm not into your niece like that. Besides, she has a man."

Denise eyes widened. "She does?"

"Yes!" Tony snapped, lying.

"You've seen him?"

"Nah, but I know."

Denise could tell she hurt his feeling "Tony, don't take it like that. That's my niece we're talking about."

"I know. It's cool. It's just fucked up that you would think of me like that."

"Nigga, please! Who are you kidding? Your ass is a dog."

"People change, Dee," he stated.

The nerve of that bitch. People change. Shit, her ass changed, he thought on his way home.

Denise's words weighed heavily on his mind. After all he had accomplished, he couldn't believe she felt like that about him. Even if he hadn't raped Morgan, Denise still wouldn't have approved of their relationship. *Oh well, she better get used to it, because there is no way I'm giving up my family.*

Since the daycare was closed that day, Tony brought the kids to his office. Because he didn't talk about his personal life, no one dared ask him about the kids. Even though he had huge pictures of them all around his office, they pretended not to see them.

Tony was in his office with his kids, when Mookie knocked on the door.

"Come in," Tony said.

Lil' Anthony and London were watching *Barney*.

"Oh, you're still watching the kids for Morgan?"

"Yeah, she'll be back tonight. What's up?"

"Nothing. I wanted to go over contracts."

While going over the contracts, Lil' Anthony blurted out, "Daddy, I'm hungry."

Forgetting Mookie was there, Tony responded, "Okay. Daddy is going to heat up your food now, okay?"

"K."

Confused, Mookie asked, "He calls you daddy?"

Tony's eyes widened. He had to think quickly. "Yeah. His real father isn't around."

Mookie nodded and went back to reading.

"Mookie, watch them for me," he said, exiting to heat up the children's food.

Looking around, Mookie noticed the many pictures of the kids.

Tony returned shortly. "Lil' Man, are you ready to eat?"

"Yes, Daddy."

Watching, Mookie sighed and shook his head. *Who the fuck is he kidding? These are Tony's kids,* he thought. "Tee, can I ask you something? And be real with me, man."

"Shoot."

"Are these your kids?"

Tony paused, swallowed hard, and then glanced over at Mookie. "Nah...I told you."

"Tee..." Mookie said, raising his voice, "come on. Look at all these pictures of them. Tell me the truth."

Tony took a deep breath and closed his eyes. The game was over. Unable to verbally respond, Tony nodded.

Stunned, Mookie voiced, "These *are* your kids. What the fuck?"

"Yeah, man!"

"Yo, this shit is crazy. So all this time you was fucking with shorty?"

"It's not what you think, Mookie," Tony said, getting up to lock the door.

"How long?"

"How long what?"

"How long have you been messing with her?"

Tony remained quiet.

"It was you who got her pregnant years ago? How long, Tee?" he shouted.

"Since she was fourteen," he mumbled, looking away.

"Fourteen?! What the fuck is wrong with you? She was a kid. Are you crazy? Yo, what about Chris? Does she know?" Mookie asked.

"It's not what you think. It just happened."

"Just happened?! You just happened to have two kids by Denise's niece. Does she even know?" Mookie stood up with his hand open. "What about Chris? You're married to her."

Tony exhaled loudly. "Let me explain."

Mookie shook his head in complete repugnance. "Explain what? Tee, you have two kids by this little girl. How long do you think you're gonna keep living like this? It's only a matter of time before everyone finds out."

Tony leaned his head back. Mookie was right. How long could he keep up the charade?

"Mook, I know you don't understand, but I love her. She's the one I wanna be with. I don't give a fuck about anything else. Those two people right there," he said, pointing to his kids, "and Morgan is all that matters. She wasn't just some shorty I was fucking. I've been with her for eight years, and we've been married four years. Yeah, I fucked up because shorty was young and my best friend's niece, but I couldn't help it. Once I laid eyes on her, I knew she was the one."

"What about Chris? You're fucking married to her."

"Nah, I'm not! Chris and I never signed any legal papers. We got married, but it's not legal. I'm legally married to Morgan. She's my wife."

Mookie rubbed his head. He didn't know whether to congratulate Tony or get him a straightjacket. One thing for sure, he never heard Tony talk about anyone like he was talking about Morgan. So, she had to be someone special.

"Tee, man, listen. I hear what you're saying, but you're going about this all wrong. What do you think is gonna happen when everyone finds out how old she was when you started fucking her?"

"Don't know." Tony rubbed his head. "I do know I'm not leaving my wife and family."

Mookie giggled. "Yo, you're one crazy-ass nigga. So all these years, she's been the one who had your ass acting crazy?"

Tony laughed. "Yo, Mookie, she got a nigga open. I can't breathe without her. And now she has given me two beautiful kids," he said, looking over at them.

Mookie nodded. "I can't front. Morgan *is* bad. She's on Michele Obama's level—elegant and sophisticated. You do have some beautiful-ass kids, too."

Tony beamed. "Mookie, she's different. Do you know this chick has me locked down? She got a nigga reading, cooking, and cleaning. I'm even thinking about taking some college courses." He laughed. "I know it's fucked up about me and Chris, but Chris is just eye candy. Once that shit fades, it's over. I want someone with substance, and Morgan has it all. Real talk, she keeps me focused on normal shit. Why you think my ass don't go nowhere anymore? It's because of them."

Mookie smiled and nodded. "A'ight, man, I got your back, but I'm telling you, you need to holla at Denise and Greg. Don't let them find out on their own."

Tony nodded.

"What about Chris?" Mookie asked.

"What about her? Please! She and I haven't been together for years. She wants out of this relationship just as much as I do. She's too busy fucking with Rashid."

Mookie's eyes widened. "Nah, Chris?"

Tony smirked. "Yeah, Chris. You know that baby she lost a couple of years ago? That wasn't my kid. She was pregnant by Paul. Can you believe that shit? They were engaged, so I seriously doubt she'll be heartbroken."

Mookie shook his head. "Y'all are crazy."

Both men laughed.

Afraid Mookie would open his mouth, Tony hung out with him more. While they had been partners for years, a lot of people overlooked Mookie. Other CEOs really didn't conduct business with him unless Tony was around. However, that all changed. Tony personally made sure everyone knew Mookie was the man.

Another thing Tony did was start taking his kids around his side of the family. One day, he left them with his mother, and when he came back to pick them up, his mother asked if they were his kids. He was about to lie, but knew his mother already knew the truth. First, she was upset because they weren't by his wife. His father, on the other hand, advised him to get a paternity test. Tony hated lying to his mother, but he knew she would've been upset if she knew the truth about their mother. There were days when Tony wished he could turn back the hands of time. Maybe if he would've waited, things would've been different. Now he was forced to live his life in concealment.

Christina was out of town allegedly on business, which meant she was with Rashid. So, Tony went home to the smell of some good Italian food.

"Mmmm," he said, walking into the kitchen and giving his wife a kiss. "What's this?"

Giggling, Morgan replied, "Shrimp linguini with lobster sauce." She kissed him back. "I know I've been working late and neglecting my family."

Tony grabbed his wife. "It's cool, ma. I know this is important to you. The kids and I are fine, but I have some good news."

"What?"

"I'm taking online business college classes."

Morgan's eyes opened wide. "Really? That's great! But, what made you?"

"I've always wanted to go to college. Before I started hanging out, I wanted to be a Business Administrator."

"Well, it's never too late. I'm proud of you." She kissed him again, and he smiled.

As usual, Tony cleaned up while Morgan got the kids ready for bed. For Tony, taking care of their kids was the closest thing to normalcy. By the time Morgan came into the bedroom, Tony was laying on the bed watching TV.

"I want you to meet my mother," he blurted out.

"You think she will like me?" she asked, snuggling under his arms.

Tony kissed her on the forehead. "No, she will love you."

* * * * *

Once Tony told Mookie the truth, it seemed like Mookie was always avoiding him. One time, he even used the excuse that he had a meeting. Of course, Tony didn't believe him. Therefore, he had him followed, which turned out to be nothing. Paranoid, Tony wasn't satisfied. *What if Mookie tries to blackmail me? What if he slips up and tells Greg?*

Instead of going home, Tony headed over to visit Greg at the club since he hadn't seen his man in a while. Upon his arrival, Tony was greeted by some adoring fans. He smiled and waved, then headed straight to Greg's office.

Greg was on the phone when Tony walked in. Motioning him to come in, Tony took a seat on the couch.

"What's up, Tee?" Greg said, giving him a pound.

"You, playboy. I figured I'd stop by and say what's up to my boy. I heard what happened."

"Oh yeah, it's cool."

"You know you have my assistance."

"Of course, but I have the situation under control."

"Alright, but I'm here."

"That's what's up. It's always a pleasure. You want a drink?" Greg asked.

Tony nodded, and Greg poured them both a glass of Hennessy.

"So how's retirement life treating you?"

Tony chuckled. "It's going well. You know I've been helping Morgan out with the kids."

Greg nodded "Yeah, I heard. Mookie and Denise told me. That's good. You know shorty is stuck with those two babies."

Mookie, Tony thought, but replied, "I promised her mother before she left this earth that I would step in and help out."

"That's good. You used to mess with Jasmine, right?"

"Yeah, and before you go there..."

"Nah, I'm just saying," Greg said, giving him the eye.

Both men laughed.

"Yo, I've been meaning to ask you how old Gab was when y'all started messing around."

"Oh damn! Umm, I think she was around sixteen or seventeen years old. She was in high school."

"She wasn't eighteen?"

"Nah, she was young."

"How did you know she was the one? I mean, Gab was a youngster."

"Yeah, she was jailbait. To tell you the truth, I just did. She was different," Greg replied. "Although Boo was young, she was mature and not fast like the other girls in the hood. She brought out the best in me. Why?"

"I was just thinking about how y'all got together. I can't believe someone locked you down." Tony laughed.

"Yep, for life. Tee, man, like I said at E-Money's party, I'm a grown-ass man. I'm not afraid to let the world know my feelings for my wife. I would be stupid not to. You know how some dudes wanna be married and a player? That shit is for the birds. It's all about me and my wife. She has my last name for a reason. Your wife is supposed to be your equal. She's not supposed to walk in front of you or behind you, but right beside you. If not, then she's not your equal. Do you have that with Chris?"

Tony shook his head. "Actually, Greg, I don't know what's going on with Chris and me. We haven't been together for years, and real

112

talk, a nigga is getting tired of her. She's good eye candy and all, but I'm ready to have a normal life. I want some kids, feel me? We're like two ships passing in the night. Plus, she's fucking around with Rashid," he grumbled.

"Are you giving her a reason to fuck around?" Greg asked, causing Tony to look at him. "Come on, Tee. If we're gonna talk, let's keep it real," he said, while pouring them another drink. "Are you faithful?"

"I'm not gonna front. I'm not, but..."

"But nothing. That's why she's out there loose like that. Home is always supposed to be taken care of. I don't give a shit who you're fucking," Greg stated, staring into Tony's face.

"Home isn't fucked up. Home isn't with Christina either. Yo, remember mad chicks were after you back in the day?" Tony said, changing the subject.

Greg grinned and nodded. "Those chicks were after the lifestyle. They didn't give a shit about me. None of them hollered at me when I went to prison. Boo was the only one who stayed with me, and she had a lot to lose."

"True. What about Britney? She didn't help?"

"Britney? I haven't heard from her in years."

"Word? I thought she helped you with the case."

"Nah, I came home on a 440 motion-*Newly Discovered Evidence*. You know Jake doesn't play."

"Oh, so Britney didn't help after all."

Confused, Greg looked at Tony. "Britney? What made you think that?"

"Because Dee told me years ago that Gab found out about her."

"What? I didn't know."

"Yeah, Gab found a letter and asked Dee. I figured she had helped. I'm sorry. I thought you knew."

Unable to hide his emotions, Greg frowned. "I didn't, but she wasn't the reason I came home."

Inside, Tony smirked. *Yeah, Gabrielle, take that bitch,* he thought.

Chapter Ten
Christina

Christina had been seeing Rashid for a little over two years, and things were getting serious. Rashid, who was in love, demanded that Christina get a divorce from Tony. At first, she agreed, but then she quickly changed her mind. While she wasn't in love with Tony anymore, a part of her cared about him, especially after she lost the baby. Every time Rashid brought up the subject, she brushed him off. Despite Rashid slowly winning her heart, Christina refused to be forced into a decision. He was aware of her situation beforehand. Besides, she wasn't sure if he was faithful while he was on the road.

On the set of her second movie, Christina thought about Paul, and on days like this, she missed him. Although grateful for Rashid, she preferred a guy who wasn't in the industry. She and Rashid made an effort to see each other, but their busy schedules sometimes made it impossible. It also didn't help that they had to sneak around.

Sitting in her trailer, Christina picked up a magazine and started scanning it, when she came across a picture of her and Tony in the park with Morgan's kids.

She chuckled. "Hmm, I guess pictures are worth a thousand words."

She had to admit she and Tony looked great together. Too bad it wasn't real. There were times Christina thought about trying to make it work, but so much had been said and done. They were so different. Tony barely stayed at home, and when he did, he slept in the other room. He didn't even come out to support her anymore.

Knock! Knock!

It was Rashid.

"Hey, baby," he said, greeting her with a kiss.

Smiling and surprised, Christina peaked outside of her trailer to make sure no one was looking. This made Rashid upset.

"Why are you looking around? It's not like everyone doesn't know."

Christina folded her arms and pouted. "You know it's not like that, Rashid, but I'm still married."

"Yeah, I know! When are you going to divorce him? I've been waiting for over a year now."

Christina threw her head back. She didn't feel like hearing that. "I know, but it's not that easy."

"Yes, it is. Either you're gonna divorce him or..."

Christina silenced him with a kiss. "Baby, I am," she said, kissing him again.

Rashid chuckled. "You think you're slick. Your kisses are not gonna work," he told her, while kissing her back.

"Well, I have something else that will," she moaned, removing her robe.

Usually, Christina would be cautious with Rashid, but this time, she didn't care. Following sex, they decided to go to the exclusive Ivy Restaurant for dinner. Knowing the spot was a magnet for paparazzi, Christina went anyway. Her mother was right; it was time she stopped living a lie. She also gave Joyce and her bodyguard the night off; she didn't need them meddling in her business.

As always, Christina looked fierce, wearing white wide-leg pants, a matching tank top, a pair of Giuseppe Zanotti sandals, and carrying a Prada clutch. Her hair was pulled back with a band, and her face without make-up. Like Paul, Rashid preferred Christina make-up free.

Laughing and talking while cruising in Rashid's silver Bentley coupe, Christina was on cloud nine.

Upon their arrival, just like she expected, the paparazzi was there. "Christina!" they yelled, trying to get her attention. Christina just waved and smiled as Rashid opened the door for her.

"Is it true that you and Rashid are an item now?" one of the reporters blurted out.

Christina was about to respond, when Rashid jumped in.

"Nah, Christina is my cousin," he lied.

"Yeah, more like kissing cousins," the reporter retorted, making everyone laugh.

Being that they were in public, Christina and Rashid refrained from being affectionate. Mostly, they just laughed and snapped on people. The night was still young, so they decided to hit up a few clubs. In the back of Christina's mind, she knew it didn't look right for them to be together, but it felt so good. Rashid was such a fun person; he made her feel young and normal—something Paul did when they were together. Christina had to admit she was falling in love with Rashid, and for the first time, she felt it was okay to love again.

Since they didn't have any bodyguards, the bouncer of the club ushered them over to the VIP section, where they chilled for a little before heading to the dance floor. Before you knew it, Christina and Rashid were in their own little zone. This time, there wasn't anyone to stop them. At one point, she even kissed him.

While looking lustfully into his eyes, Christina whispered, "Let's get out of here."

Rashid grabbed her by the hand and exited the club. On their way to his condo, Rashid played Maxwell's "Fortunate". The next morning, Christina woke up beaming. Rashid had already left for practice.

That day, Christina was completely free; she didn't have any meetings planned. Therefore, she decided to lounge around. She thought about going back to her hotel, but she didn't feel like being bothered. After fixing herself something to eat, her cell phone rang. Her first thought was to let it go to voicemail, but she didn't want anyone to worry.

"Yeah, Joyce," she answered dryly.

"Turn on the TV."

"For?" Christina asked.

"It's all over the news."

"What?" Christina grew annoyed with the hidden clues.

"You and Rashid."

Christina turned on the TV, and sure enough, plastered on the screen was a video of her and Rashid leaving dinner and entering the club.

"Chris, they're calling you guys an item."

"And?" Christina snapped.

Joyce sighed. She wasn't in the mood for Christina's bullshit. "Fine. I was just letting you know," she snapped back.

"I don't mean it like that. I'm just saying…"

"And I was just calling you before anyone else."

Beep! It was Christina's publicist on the other line.

"Joyce, let me call you back. It's Diana."

"Okay. Wait! Are you…"

Christina released a chuckle. "At Rashid's place? Yes, and I need you to bring me some clothes, and don't tell anyone where I am."

Click!

"Yes, Diana," Christina answered snobbishly.

"Chris, have you lost your mind? If you're gonna go out with someone, don't you think you should tell me so I'm prepared for stuff like this?"

"Like what?" Christina retorted.

Diana sighed. "Doing stunts like this can ruin your career."

"Hmm, this isn't a stunt. Last time I checked I hired you to handle my *career*. This doesn't sound like it has to do with my career."

"If you keep doing things like this, you won't have one."

"Is that a threat, Diana? Because…"

"No, I'm just warning you. Chris, you're married to Tony Flowers. Doesn't that mean something to you?"

"No, but obviously it means a lot to you. I tell you what; call me back when you start working for me."

Click!

"Fucking bitch! You're married to Tony Flowers," Christina mocked. "Big fucking deal. You would think he was the fucking president for crying out loud," she angrily mumbled.

Exhausted from hanging out, Christina decided she wasn't going to let any of them ruin her day. She notified her parents of the situation and then turned off her phone so she could go back to bed. *It's funny, Tony can run around playing daddy, and no one asks him shit. I have one little dinner date, and I'm making the evening news,* she thought.

The sun had just set, when she was awakened with a kiss by Rashid.

"You slept all day?" he asked, then kissed her again.

"Yeah, well, you wore me out last night." She smiled.

As Rashid walked to the bathroom to take a shower, Christina said, "You know we're all over the news, right?"

Taking off his clothes, Rashid replied, "Are you surprised?"

"No, but all over the world?"

Naked, he walked over to her. "It doesn't bother me. What about you?"

"It's fine. I'm just saying."

"You're saying what? Oh wait. You're married?"

"Well, yeah..."

"Were you married last night when you were fucking my brains out? Did you think about your husband then?"

Christina jumped up. "That's not fair, Rashid. You know..."

"I know what, Chris? I know I'm in love with someone else's wife. That's what I know. It's been over a year now, and you're still stringing me along," he protested.

"You know how I feel about you. I'm not stringing you along."

"Then why haven't you left?" he asked, getting in her face, causing Christina to look away. "Yeah, I thought so."

Rashid was right. Her marriage to Tony had been over years ago.

"Rashid," she whined, touching his chest, "I love you, too."

"So what's the problem?" He pushed her away. "It's either me or Tony," he stated, walking into the bathroom.

★ ★ ★ ★ 118

Christina fell on the bed crying. She loved Rashid, but was scared of leaving Tony. In a strange way, Tony was like her safety net. However, she wasn't happy with him. She couldn't even remember the last time they had fun together. Sitting there in deep thought with tears rolling down her cheeks, Christina decided it was time to leave Tony. She didn't want to lose out on another good man.

With a towel wrapped around his waist and dripping wet, Rashid asked, "Are you hungry?"

"No," she mumbled. "Rashid..." she stood up to face him. "I've decided to leave him. You're right. I can't keep asking you to wait. I did that before and lost someone special."

Rashid stormed over to her, stared into her eyes, and without uttering a word, he ripped off her t-shirt. Unsure of what was going on, Christina just stood there in heat. He picked her up and carried her outside to the balcony.

"This is what I think of your marriage to Tony Flowers" he moaned in an angry voice, then shoved himself inside of her.

Christina loudly groaned, choking on her saliva. Instead of being gentle, he pounded her. He was filled with many emotions and needed to release them. For Christina, it reminded her of when she and Paul used to have sex. She loved the assertiveness.

Rashid pulled out and then kissed her hard. "Suck my dick," he ordered. Any other time, his demand would've been a killjoy for Christina, but something about the tone of his voice turned her on. He gently grabbed her head, guiding her down on her knees. Obliging, she gave him head, but right in the middle of the act, he said, "Chill. I want you to put your hands down and open your mouth."

Doing as she was told, Christina opened her mouth wide. Rashid palmed the back of her head, then shoved his penis down her throat, making her regurgitate. She tried to say something, but was unable. Horny, Rashid did it again.

"Open wide, baby. Take all of this in your mouth," he said, then pushed it down her throat once more. This time, Christina gagged and spit out a blob of saliva. "Yes, spit it on this dick," Rashid ordered. "That's what I want. You want me to stop?"

With tears coming out of her eyes, Christina shook her head no while licking the spit off his cock.

"That's what daddy likes. Fuck Tony Flowers!" he said, thrusting in and out of her mouth.

Christina gave him head until he released in her mouth. Other than Paul, this was the second time she enjoyed giving oral sex. Rashid collapsed into the chair trying to catch his breath and pulling Christina on him. They stared into each other's eyes for a few moments before Rashid kissed her.

"How did it taste?" he asked.

"Good," she replied, wanting more. "Now it's my turn." She smiled and climbed on top of him, putting her pussy in his face.

Rashid released a sexy chuckle before returning the favor.

*****

In Hollywood, this too shall pass, Christina thought.

Back on the set of her movie, paparazzi were lurking outside of her trailer, which pissed off the director. Meanwhile, Christina didn't pay them any attention. She also instructed her team to focus on her career and stop worrying about her personal life. Joyce, on the other hand, was different; she was more like Christina's friend. She shared relationships with her. Amazingly, Joyce was happy that Christina was finally stepping out on Tony. Most of the people in the industry were joyful when the rumors started about Christina and Rashid. Everyone knew Christina was too good for Tony.

Avoiding the media, Christina stayed in her trailer when she wasn't shooting a scene. As she prepared for the filming of the next scene, her cell phone rang. It was Tony.

"Hello," she answered.

"What's up, Chris? How's the movie coming along?"

"Great."

"I know. You're all over the news," he said with a chuckle, letting her know he knew.

Oh, two can play that game, she thought. "Yeah, Rashid is wonderful. He's the perfect leading man," she snidely replied.

Tony laughed. "Yeah, so I've heard. See ya when you get back."

Click!

"Asshole," she mumbled.

"That was Tony?" Joyce asked.

"Yeah. He knows, but do you think that bastard cares? He's too busy playing daddy."

"Who are those kids he's taking care of?"

"Denise's niece. You know he worships the ground Denise walks on."

"How does her niece look?" Joyce asked, knowing Tony's history.

"Oh, Morgan? She's gorgeous."

Joyce gave Christina the side eye.

"Oh wait. He's not seeing Morgan. She's not on his level. Besides, she's just a child in Tony's eyes."

*****

As usual, Tony wasn't home when Christina arrived. This made her happy. She was meeting with her accountant and needed to discuss some business. Christina was in the dining room when the doorbell rang. Assuming it was her accountant, she ran to get it, but it was Greg and Denise.

"Hi," Christina greeted in a surprised tone.

"Hey Christina," Denise said, kissing her on the cheek. Greg kissed her, as well.

"We were looking for Tee. Is he here?"

"No."

"Are you sure? He wanted us to meet him here," Denise asked, looking at Greg.

"I've been here a while. Come on in. Maybe he's on his way. You know Tony."

Greg and Denise looked at each other before following behind her. In the living room, Christina offered them something to drink. Greg declined. Denise, on the other hand, wanted some water.

"So what brings you here? Is Tony in trouble?" she jokingly asked.

"No, he actually wanted us to come and see him," Denise informed her, then laughed as she noticed the pictures of Morgan's kids. "Damn, do you think he has enough pictures of my niece and nephew?"

Greg looked around. "For real. I didn't even notice that."

"Oh yeah, he loves those kids," Christina snidely remarked, making Denise give her the side eye. "I didn't mean it like that, Denise. I meant Tony would do anything for you."

Denise frowned. "Do anything for me? He's not doing this for me," she stated.

"He's not?"

"No. Tony used to mess with my sister years ago. Before she died, he promised her that he would help my niece with the kids. What made you say that?"

Greg stared at Christina. Remaining silent, he knew there was more to the story, but she wasn't saying.

"He messed with your sister? I didn't know that. Then again, there are a lot of things I don't know about my husband."

"You would if you weren't out there running around," Greg blurted out, making Denise and Christina look at him.

"Greg..." Denise tried to say, but he gave her the 'shut up' look.

"Chris, I know you haven't been happy with Tony," Greg said. "That's the same shit we heard when you were messing with Paul. Is that the justification you use when you wanna creep?"

Denise looked at Christina, nodding in agreement with Greg.

"Tony may be a lot of things, but he's not disrespecting you like that. You're all in the papers with another dude."

"So...just because he's not making the papers doesn't mean he's not cheating," she tried to explain, but Greg threw his hand up.

"No, that's not what I'm saying. Unlike you, ma, he's not out there like that. It's not what you do, but how you do it. You keep saying you're unhappy, but you're still with him. Maybe the problem isn't with Tony. Maybe it's you."

Speechless, Christina glared at Greg. Until now, she had never heard him really talk. "Tony must pay you well," she remarked snidely, not knowing who she was talking to.

Greg was about to say something, but Denise jumped in to defuse the situation. "Pay us? What you think, we don't have a mind of our own? Tony doesn't control shit. Greg is right. If you're unhappy, then you need to leave Tony alone. I told you that years ago when we talked in the store. I love Tony to death, but if he's treating you like shit, leave! Because if you think messing with other guys is hurting him, you're wrong. What you're looking like is a whore. No offense. "

Christina sighed. They were right. Even though she wasn't happy, there was a way to go about doing things.

"Tony is a motherfucker. He's not going to let me go that easily…"

"How would you know?" Denise asked.

"Mrs. Carrington, your accountant is here," the maid announced.

"Where's Carmen?" Denise inquired.

"She quit," Christina informed her. "Excuse me."

After she exited, Greg and Denise looked at each and thought the same thing. *Tony sure knows how to pick 'em.*

Chapter Eleven
Denise

*W*hat the hell is the problem now? Greg had called her early in morning. Supposedly, Mohammad needed to see them. *This better not be any bullshit.*

The Millie situation had Denise on her toes. Even though Millie assured her that she would keep her mouth shut, Denise was still worried. Greg was right. Telling Millie was a fucked- up move. For the first time, Denise felt like she was slipping.   Also, something was definitely up with Greg. Ever since that night, he had been quiet, which meant he was thinking, and when Greg started thinking, it meant someone was going to die. While their bond was tight, after Alex, Greg wasn't allowing anyone to cross him again. Right now, she was looking like the weakest link in Greg's eyes.

Denise knew the day was going to come where she had to answer for her actions, but one thing was for sure—she would not be the only one answering.

The babysitter was watching the kids, while Derrick worked late again. So, Denise agreed to meet Greg, who was waiting for her outside of her office building, which was strange.

"Am I late?" Denise asked, walking over to the car.

"Nah!" he said with a serious look on his face while staring straight ahead.

Denise sighed and said a silent prayer before hopping in the car. When they pulled up to Mohammad's store, there was a group of people outside chilling. So, Greg called Mohammad and told him to meet them around the corner. Giving their notoriety, Greg didn't feel like talking to anyone. Besides, if something was about to jump off, he didn't want anyone to see him and Denise around there.

However, Denise sat there silently watching Greg's every move. *Damn, I'm not even strapped,* she thought. She was slipping for real. Staring out the rearview mirror, Denise watched as Mohammad walked to the car.

"Here he comes," she said.

"Greg and Denise!" he said in his strong Arab accent after getting in the backseat.

"What's up?" Greg asked in a serious tone, while Denise smiled.

Mohammad pulled out a DVD player. "I wanted you guys to see this."

"You're selling movies now?" Denise asked.

"No! I wish. But, check this out."

It was Millie, Joe, and Bruce in the back of Mohammad's store plotting to extort Denise and Greg. Millie told them that Denise and Greg had killed Felicia and Grant.

"Turn it off!" Denise snapped.

"But there's more," Mohammad told her.

"Turn it off! I've seen enough!" Denise yelled.

Greg, on the other hand, didn't utter a word. He simply glanced at Denise from the corner of his eye.

"When is this supposed to take place?" she asked.

"Someone is going to contact you this week. You can have the DVD. I don't need it."

"How did you get this?" Greg asked, not trusting anyone.

"You know I have slot machines in the back of the store. People were getting robbed back there, so I had cameras installed."

"Has anyone else seen this tape?"

"No! Are you crazy? Hey, guys, this is me! You know I would never do anything like that. That's why I called you, Greg. I don't give a shit about Bruce and Joe. Hell, they owe me money. That's the only copy."

Greg looked at Denise and then at Mohammad through the rearview mirror. "Alright, good looking. Someone will be in touch with you."

"No, this one is on me, Greg. It's because of you that my kids are in college. No one touched my store when you and Denise were around, so this is my way of saying thank you."

Greg smirked. "That's real. Well, you know I'm always here if you need me."

"Yeah, Mohammad, just call us for anything."

"Alright! Thanks, guys," Mohammad said, then hopped out of the backseat.

"I fucked up, huh?" Denise said, looking at Greg.

Greg giggled. "Yeah, Dee, you fucked up, but what are you gonna do about it?"

"What else is there to do?"

With that, Denise knew it was on.

*****

Like Mohammad said, Millie called Denise asking to meet her in Hunts Point in a warehouse. So Millie would not suspect anything, Denise hesitated, claiming she had something to do, but Millie insisted. Finally, Denise gave in, but she told Millie it had to be after nine o'clock because she had a meeting she couldn't miss.

Immediately, Denise called Greg to give him the location of the meeting. As they thought, Bruce and Joe would be attending the meeting. Their plan was to threaten Denise and make her go tell Greg, thinking that because Greg had just come home from doing time in the state penitentiary that he had a lot to lose. They couldn't be more wrong. Because Denise and Greg had families, it made them more dangerous.

The meeting would take place in an abandoned meat warehouse. Denise, who was dressed in an all-black tailored business suit, wanted Millie to think she had just come from her meeting. It was still cold outside, so Denise hid the shotgun under her wool coat.

Greg had arrived two hours earlier and was hiding in the cut with his shotgun. One thing for sure, they were serious about their business. Normally, they would use guns, but for snakes like them, it was shotgun style.

"Millie!" Denise yelled, walking into the place.

"Denise…" Millie said, emerging from behind the door. "Sorry we had to meet here, but I didn't want anyone to hear."

"Hear what? Millie, what's going on?"

"Denise, you took something that was very special away from me, and now you have to pay."

"What?"

"I want three million dollars or I'm going to the police."

Still fronting, Denise pretended to be scared. "Millie…I can't believe…"

"Believe what? That you're out here living the good life while my daughter is in the ground."

Quickly scanning the room, Denise had to stall. According to Greg, Bruce and Joe were there probably recording everything.

"Millie, I don't know what you're talking about. Have you started back drinking?"

"Don't play fuckin' dumb with me. You told me that you killed my daughter and her father."

"I don't know what you're talking about."

"Well, let's see if the police believe me," she threatened.

"I don't think you wanna do that."

Boom!

Millie jumped and looked around quickly to see what the noise was, but by that time, Denise had pulled out her shotgun.

"I told you."

Millie's eyes widened as if she had seen a ghost. "Denise…"

Greg had found Bruce and Joe, who were in the other room videotaping Denise. The shot they heard was Greg shooting the equipment.

They ordered them to kneel down with their hands behind their backs. Scared to death, they did as they were told. Bruce was so

scared that he defecated on himself. Just like a bunch of cowards, they all started pointing their finger at each other. Denise stared at Millie. She couldn't believe she tried to extort her. *This bitch must have a lot of balls.* Denise was so angry that she busted out laughing.

"You gotta love it, Greg."

Greg joined her in laughter. "All the time."

Terrified, Bruce, Millie, and Joe looked at each other. Back in the day, they heard the rumors when people used to say the reason why Greg's team never got caught is because they practiced black magic. Now they were about to witness it firsthand.

"I told you this was a bad idea," Joe said. "Hey, Greg, it wasn't me," he pleaded.

"Denise," Millie cried, "please."

With an empty soul, Denise raised her shotgun and blew Millie's head off. Brain matter splattered on Bruce and Joe. When the two men saw that, they wept.

"Dee…" Bruce whined, "Greg, we didn't mean no harm."

"We know you didn't," Greg responded.

"Greg, for real! Listen, I know who robbed your clubs."

Greg paused. "Who?"

"Mike and Moe. The word is they're the ones behind it. Word is Moe is going to come after y'all."

Greg looked at Denise.

"This nigga is lying," Denise said. "Why would Moe come after Greg?" she asked Bruce.

"Something about his cousin getting cut in prison. You haven't heard? Mike and Moe have been hanging tight. Wild Child just hired Moe for security."

Greg stared at Bruce; he couldn't have been lying. Moe's cousin had been stabbed in prison. Greg was on his family visit when it happened.

"You said Moe and Mike are hanging out?" he reiterated.

"Yes, we saw them a couple of weeks ago chillin'."

Denise didn't believe them, though. She figured they were willing to say anything to save their lives.

Joe blurted out, "He's not lying. I was there."

"Yo, who is Felicia's brother?" Greg asked.

"Huh?" Bruce said.

"Who is Felicia's brother? I heard he use to come around," Denise said

"Moe…"

"Moe?" Greg and Denise responded together.

"Yes, Moe," Joe stated.

"Moe?" Denise asked again just to be sure.

"That's right. His name is Moe."

Greg and Denise looked at each other. The only Moe they knew was their Moe.

But it makes sense. Moe is the only one who had the power and courage to pull this shit off, Denise thought.

Without warning, Greg opened up Bruce's chest cavity and then his face.

"Please! It was Millie and Bruce's idea," Joe screamed.

Boom!

Denise let off a single round, causing Joe's skull to open up.

"Can you believe these motherfuckers?" Greg said, pouring gasoline over them.

"Do you believe that bullshit about Mike and Moe?"

Greg looked at Denise. "Let's talk about that later," he said, lighting a match.

While speeding down the highway, Greg asked her, "What do you think about Moe being Felicia's brother?"

"It doesn't make sense, but he's looking good for it."

Greg nodded but didn't respond. Instead, he focused on the route to Denise's house.

*****

Troubled over what had just happened, Denise informed Derrick that she would be staying at her apartment. Sitting on the couch

staring out of her panoramic windows as the light from the other apartments shined on her, Denise leaned her head back.

"This can't be happening," she muttered to herself.

Taking a deep breath, she glanced over at the family picture on the end table. *What the fuck am I thinking? If this shit gets out, I will lose everything.* Shaking her head, Denise wanted to kick herself in the ass. Greg was right. She played herself when she told Millie about Felicia. Real killers take their crimes to the grave. That's the first thing she learned from Greg. Silence is golden. Another thing that worried her was Greg. While things may have seemed cool on the outside, Denise knew he was tight on the inside.

Ring!

Disheartened, Denise ignored the ringing doorbell, hoping the person would go away. However, they rang it again.

"Hey," she said, surprised to see Greg.

"What's up? I came to check up on you."

Denise stood there for a second before speaking. "So you just came here to check on me? Greg, stop with the bullshit. Yeah, I made a mistake, but I'm cool. You don't have to worry about me," she stressed in an annoyed tone.

Greg laughed; that was the Denise Taylor he raised. "You know, I gotta make sure."

They both laughed.

"True! I fucked up, but you see I handled my business," she said, taking a deep breath.

"I knew you would. I just wanna make sure this shit doesn't happen again. Like you said, we have much more to lose now. You know I was tight with you, ready to kill your ass. But, I needed to give you one last chance before I made my decision."

"I figured that, and real talk, I would have no choice but to respect it. All I would ask is for you to take care of my family."

"Of course! So what are we going to do about Moe and Mike? You know, now that I think about it, Mike and Moe were at the spots a few days before the robberies happened."

"Really?"

"Yeah. I thought it was strange that Moe was there, figuring that's not his style, but Mike…"

"Like you said, it's always the ones we love and trust," Denise reminded him. "You know he gave me Millie's information."

He sighed. "Yeah."

"I don't know, Greg. I mean, a part of me…" she started before pausing.

"You know you were never good at hiding your feelings from me, so talk," he joked.

"I just have this weird feeling that something big is about to happen."

"What do you mean?"

"That's the thing. I don't know. You know before Jas died she kept repeating to me that someone had hurt her baby. That shit has been fucking with me ever since."

"Dee, your mind is just playing…"

"No, let me finish. Greg, I didn't make it out of the game to end up dead or in prison. I have a fucking family now."

"And I don't? Do you realize if we would've paid them, it wouldn't have stopped? People like Bruce and them are like sharks that smell blood in the water. You think if we still lived in the projects they would've tried that bullshit? Denise, a nigga can't rob me and think he can get away with it. If he believed that, he would never stop. I knew it was someone close, because a stranger would kill themselves before playing with me. Sis, you can't be as scared as I am. I spent years in prison."

Denise nodded. Greg did have a point. "I'm not saying that, Greg. It's just…"

"It's just what?! Dee, it is what it is. Like you said, we have families now, so I won't think twice about putting someone in the dirt for my family. So what are you saying? We should've paid them off?"

"No, but we should have paid someone to handle it. It's not like we don't have the money. We're not in the fucking hood, Greg. We're millionaires. It's nothing to give a nigga a hundred thousand to

wipe motherfuckers off the planet. What's the sense of having money and not using it?" she protested.

"Pay someone?! Pay who?! Who do you know keeps it official? No one! The ones we did know are dead. You and I both know dudes aren't built like that. The first sign of police coming at them, and they're folding like chairs. Why do you think niggas are in prison? Because people talk! One thing I know for sure is that we're not going to tell on each other. Now that I do know!"

Greg made a lot of sense. Whether Denise wanted to hear it or not, he was right. Nowadays, you can't trust anyone. Felicia showed her that.

Denise got up to pour them a drink. After handing him the glass, she asked him, "So how do you wanna handle Moe and Mike?"

"Like we do everything else—follow their asses. Their lives become ours, and then we come up with a plan. Nothing changed, sis, but the players."

"I can't believe Mike."

"I can! When was the last time you seen Mike? Mike is my man and all, but dudes change."

"Yeah, but he has a great job. Isn't he Wild Child's manager or something?"

"Yes, but sometimes that's not enough."

"True! But, I don't think Moe is Felicia's brother. I mean, we've known Moe for years. Why come at us now?"

"Why do people do the things they do? Like you said, we made it, and now dudes feel like just because we made it, we're weak. Always remember there's somebody out there that wants to make a name for themselves. Moe is actually the only one that's crazy enough to come at us like that."

"True. So what you wanna do?" Denise sighed, sitting across from Greg. "You know Moe; he's like us. He's gonna be hard to get to."

"Don't believe that. It's gonna be like stealing candy from a baby."

Denise giggled at Greg and his analogies. "More like a fucking kid. He has a crazy team, Greg."

"Naw, Moe is the strongest one on his team. Kill his ass and everyone will die along with him. I can handle this."

"Nah, we'll ride this together," Denise said, while staring into Greg's face. Then she asked, "Do you believe in God?"

"Of course, but I also believe in the Angel of Death."

Shaking her head, she joked, "And let's not forget the Devil."

"Dee, let me ask you something. You told Boo about Britney?"

Here we go again with this bullshit, she thought. "I had no choice. She found some love letters from Britney, and you know Gabby she doesn't let up. Why?"

"Nothing," Greg surprisingly answered.

"Damn, who told you?"

"Tony."

"I see Tony is telling a lot of things."

"You know Tee."

"Maybe I don't."

After that night, Denise went back to her daily routine of being a wife and mother by spending a lot of time with her family, who were the most important people in her life.

*****

For a couple of months, Denise and Greg watched Moe and Mike. Bruce and Joe were right. Something was up with them.

To avoid any questions from Gabrielle and Derrick, Greg and Denise took turns following Moe. Sadly, Moe wasn't as on point as they thought. Although he traveled with a team, he always had the same routine and left the spot at the same time. When they finally settled on a plan, Greg and Denise went over it a dozen times exploring everything that could go wrong— something they did back in the day.

That evening was family night. So, Denise and Derrick took the kids to Chuck E. Cheese's. While watching Lil' Derrick and Halle play, Denise thought about if something would ever happen to them how she would kill water, and she got teary-eyed.

"What's going on with you?" Derrick asked, noticing her getting emotional.

"What do you mean?" she responded in a snappish tone.

"You've been acting funny lately."

"I have a lot on my mind, but it's nothing for you to worry about," she replied and tried to walk away, but Derrick reached out and grabbed her arm.

"Denise, be honest with me. Is there someone else?"

Puzzled by the question, Denise looked around before answering. "Where did that come from?"

"You tell me."

She couldn't believe they were having this conversation. "Derrick, I'm not having an affair," she responded, frowning.

"Then what is going on with you?"

Denise was about to respond, but Lil' Derrick screamed for them. Snatching away her arm, she went over to join the kids, leaving Derrick fuming.

Days went by, and there was still tension in the Johnson's household. Denise focused on the kids, and Derrick worked late. It was like they were playing the roles in the movie *Mr. & Mrs. Smith*; they were both cordial towards each other, but that was it. Once this was over, Denise decided it would be time to come clean with Derrick. All of the lying was starting to take a toll on her. He was such a good man, and she didn't want to lose him.

*****

It was the end of the day, and Denise was reviewing the monthly board finance report when Jasmine popped into her head. It seemed like only yesterday they were playing in the park together. Right now, Denise could use her sister's advice. Other than Greg, Jasmine was the only person she could confide in. Also, Denise was still puzzled by what Jasmine meant by *he hurt my baby*. She glanced at her watch; it was going on five o'clock. So, she packed up and ran out, heading to the cemetery.

Upon her arrival, Denise's body got warm, and she experienced a jittery feeling. It had been months since she had been there. Strangely, she felt Jasmine's presence; she felt her conviction. She kneeled down at the gravesite and had a long overdue conversation with Jasmine. She went from crying to laughing and then back to crying.

Once she returned home, she and Derrick had a nice talk. Although she lied about what was on her mind, they managed to patch things up.

*****

The time has come. Enough with this procrastination bullshit, Denise thought while sitting in her office. Since Derrick had accused her of having an affair, she didn't want to put off the business with Moe and Mike for much longer. In an attempt to ease Derrick's suspicions, she lied and told him that she was hanging out with her sister, De'shell.

Everything was supposed to have taken place on Friday. However, Greg called and changed the plans at the last minute because someone told him Moe was leaving Thursday night to go out of town for a month.

Moe was at one of his bars on 137th Street in Harlem. According to Greg, he exited around eleven o'clock every night, which meant in twenty minutes one of his men would come out and scope the area. Parked directly across from the bar in a black Honda with tinted windows sat Greg. He had been patiently waiting since nine o'clock. Denise glanced at her watch, knowing that soon Moe would be exiting.

Oh shit, Greg thought when he saw Moe get into the passenger side of the front seat. "What the fuck," he muttered.

Greg needed to tell Denise, but it was too late. Denise sped around the corner on her motorcycle, firing several shots before speeding off.

One of Moe's friends chased the bike, firing shots at it, but Denise was gone.

"Fuck!" they yelled.

"Yo, I'm hit!" Moe screamed.

His man jumped in the car, and they drove off. Running a red light, Greg followed. Moe limped out the car and went into Harlem Hospital's emergency room.

"Shit," he mumbled. "Now what am I going to do?"

There was only one thing to do—finish the job. Greg pulled up to the ambulance entrance, scoping out the area. It was only a matter of time before the police arrived. He pulled his hat down low to cover his face and ran through the area designated for patients who arrived by ambulance. Familiar with the hospital set up, Greg knew hospital security would not be covering the area at that time. With his head down, Greg walked into the packed emergency room. The hospital emergency staff was so busy tending to patients that they didn't even ask him any questions. Pretending to be searching for a relative, Greg peeked into each examination room. Then he heard Moe's voice.

"Hurry the fuck up!" he screamed in pain while waiting to be seen by the doctor.

Glancing at his watch, he saw that time wasn't on his side. He knew he only had a few seconds before the police and Moe's team arrived. Like a cat creeping up 'on a mouse, Greg moved slowly towards the room, while putting the silencer on the 9mm.

Greg busted into the room.

"Greg…" Moe said, shocked.

"Nah, nigga, it's the Angel of Death." Greg winked and then fired five shots into Moe's chest cavity, sending him flying into the wall. Tucking the gun back into his waistband, he calmly walked out.

As he was exiting the hospital, he heard loud screams echoing, "Oh my God! Someone call the police!" Greg jumped in his car, busted a u-turn, and smiled as he passed the police.

Parked off of Long Island City, Denise sat on a bench.

"What took you so long, Greg?"

"You didn't see what happened? Moe got in the front seat. His man got hit in the backseat. Moe was only hit in the shoulder."

Denise closed her eyes. "What?!"

"Don't worry. I finished it. I caught him at the hospital."

"Greg…"

"Don't worry. We're good. Let's focus on Mike's ass."

"How do you wanna handle it?" she asked.

"Well, right now, it's about to get hot. So, let's fall back for a while. Let Mike think shit is sweet. For him, it has to be special since he was like family."

"That's gonna make it even sweeter."

"Bitter sweet, sis…bitter motherfuckin' sweet," Greg emphasized.

They burned their clothes and guns before going their separate ways. Denise went to her Manhattan apartment to freshen up before going home. When she arrived, Derrick was in the living room watching television.

"Hey, are the kids sleeping?" she asked.

"Yes. Where were you?"

"I told you that I was going to my sister's."

"Oh, that's right," Derrick replied in a sarcastic tone. "Did you have fun with your sister?" he asked, not taking his eyes off the television.

Denise smirked. She knew Derrick was trying to be funny, but she was too tired for his bullshit. She headed upstairs, stopped in her kids' room to give each of them a goodnight kiss, and then headed to bed.

A week had passed, and it was still all over the news. *Kingpin Killed at Harlem Hospital* read the headline of the newspaper, and the police had no leads. Denise laughed. *Kingpin?* She shook her head. *He was a fucking homo*, she thought.

Hopefully, she could close that chapter of her life now.

Chapter Twelve
Gabrielle

Greg was still upset about what Tony revealed to him. Why hadn't Gabrielle told him about Britney? *Something isn't right,* Greg thought. However, he was more concerned about Denise and what was going on with her. Every time Greg turned around, something popped up and her name was always involved. Shaking his head, he knew shit was about to hit the fan.

Greg pulled up to Mr. Rubin's office. The receptionist announced his arrival and told him to go in.

"Greg Brightman," Mr. Rubin cheered, walking over to hug him.

"Mr. Rubin..." Greg smiled.

"How are you?"

"I'm great! You know, staying out of trouble."

"Yeah, you better! You have a beautiful wife and kids now. Twins, right?

Greg beamed. "Yep."

"You heard about Moe. It's sad because I had just spoken with him a few weeks ago. I warned him."

"Sometimes that's all you can do," Greg replied.

"So what can I do for you?"

Greg sighed. "You know I came home on a 440 motion."

"Yeah, I heard. I couldn't believe it. Judge Barron ruled in your favor. That son of a bitch never did that."

"Really?"

"Yes. He's a conservative judge. For him to rule in your favor, you must've had some strong evidence. You know how many people went in front of him with hardcore evidence and the prick still refused their release? He's probably the only judge in the Bronx with the most overturned cases in the federal court system."

Greg's puzzled expression made Mr. Rubin explain further.

"You went back in front of a judge who never rules in the favor of the defendant. Not only did he rule in your favor, Greg, but he released you. Boy, he must have been real sick," he said, releasing a chuckle.

"He's sick?"

"Well, that's the joke. Your case is what must've made him sick, because he died maybe two months later," Mr. Rubin joked.

"Mr. Rubin, I didn't have time to talk to Judge Barron before he died. How can I get copies of the brief from my case?"

"Oh, I can get that for you. Why? You think they made a mistake?" He laughed.

"Nah, I just need to know something."

"I'll have my secretary get it for you and send it over."

"Thanks."

"Greg, why didn't you just ask your wife?" he inquired, raising an eyebrow.

When Greg smirked, Mr. Rubin simply laughed.

*****

Greg had been coming home late every night for the past two weeks. Gabrielle sensed something was up. Therefore, she decided to pop up on him at the club. Even though he told her he didn't want her around for safety reasons, Gabrielle wanted to make sure someone wasn't occupying his time. Once Mark, the bouncer, recognized Gabrielle, he immediately escorted her into the club and upstairs. As usual, Greg was in his office reviewing paperwork. Instead of knocking, Gabrielle barged in, hoping to catch him doing something. Sadly, she didn't.

"Boo, what's up? I thought I told you..." he started in a laidback tone.

"Yeah, I heard what you said," she said, cutting him off while looking around.

Greg laughed. "You gonna have me kill your ass." He grabbed her by the waist and kissed her. "You know that?" he said, rubbing her butt.

"Good, because if ..."

He silenced her with another kiss. "If what?" he said with a short giggle.

Knowing what his wife needed, Greg kissed her again. Between killing people and working at the club, he hadn't dicked her down in a couple of weeks. Gabrielle always acted up when they didn't make love at least once a week. Although she hated saying it, Gabrielle was whipped—open like the front door, as Greg would say. While he hated jealous females, it was kind of a turn-on to watch his wife act out.

Gabrielle pulled away from him to lock the door and then unbuttoned her trench coat while smiling. "You like?"

Greg's eyes almost popped out of his head. "You're naked," he said, walking over to her.

"Yep. I figured since you're working so hard, you may need some R&R." She touched herself.

"You know what, Mrs. Brightman? You're such a freak." He joined in with touching her.

"I'm your freak," she moaned before kissing him.

Gabrielle let her coat fall to the floor and took Greg to heaven. Freaky, Gabrielle dropped to her knees, giving him pleasure, and then pushed him over to the sofa.

"Okay, you're trying to turn daddy out," he moaned.

"I did that ten years ago," she commented, inserting him inside of her. "Why you think you married me?" She leaned forward and started sucking his bottom lip.

Greg smirked. She was right; he was just as open as she was. He had never seen his wife like this. She was talking dirty to him and even doing a little dance. Aroused, he lifted his wife up and threw her on the desk.

"Now it's daddy's turn. Let's see if you can handle this cock."

Thank God the music was loud, or else everyone would have heard Greg screaming her name.

Baskin in their love, Gabrielle looked into her husband's eyes and asked, "Boo, what's going on with you?"

"What do you mean?"

"You're reserved."

Greg looked at his wife with distrustful eyes. "I'm good. I just have something on my mind."

"You wanna talk about it?"

"When I'm ready, you'll be the first to know," he replied, kissing her on the forehead and taking her back to dreamland.

*****

Greg received the information from Mr. Rubin and was furious. Just as he suspected, Britney's name was all through the brief. Gabrielle was in the kitchen when Greg walked in.

"You're home early," she said.

Greg put his keys and the large envelope on the counter. "Let me ask you something," he said in a calm voice, while Gabrielle stared at him in silence. "How did I come home?"

Oh shit, she thought. With a panic-stricken look, she asked, "What do you mean how did you come home?"

"You heard me? How did I come home?" he repeated.

"You won your case."

He lowered his head, taking a deep breath. "Boo..."

"Greg, what are you..?"

"Don't fucking lie to me!" he angrily shouted.

"I don't know what you're talking about!" she yelled back in a frightened tone.

Greg smirked. "You're still lying, eh?" He picked up the envelope and tossed it at her. "Maybe Britney can help you out."

Picking up the envelope, Gabrielle swallowed hard. She was caught. Her worst nightmare had just come true. Greg glowered at her while she read over the papers.

"Are you still gonna lie to me?"

"I don't know what..."

Greg charged her. "You don't know what? What is it that you don't know?"

Baffled and at a loss for words, Gabrielle tried to explain, but this only made him angrier.

"Did you reach out to her?" he screamed at the top of his lungs.

"Yes, I did!" she shouted, then said in a lower voice, "So what I contacted her. Why didn't you tell me about her?"

Pissed, he tightened his lips and responded, "Why didn't I tell you about her? There was nothing to tell."

"How about telling me that she was the reason your ass was in prison. Let's start with that!" she shouted, tossing the dishcloth at him.

Angry, Greg paced back and forth. "You go and contact her without telling me? I'm your husband. You were supposed to tell me. What the fuck else are you hiding from me, huh?"

"Hiding? Motherfucker, do not come in here with that when your ass was messing around with her. I did what no one else wanted to do. So, instead of yelling at me, you need to be thanking me."

"Thanking you?! Get the hell out of here! You were supposed to confide in me. I trusted you. What if something would've gone wrong? Then what?"

Now she interjected. "Trust? Give me a damn break! Did you trust me enough to tell me about her? Unlike you, I went to school for my craft. You think I'm some amateur? Of course, I had everything covered. That's one of the reasons I didn't tell you, because if your hands were involved, then you probably would've still been in prison," she retorted.

"Is that what this is about? You proving your loyalty to me? You think I care about that?"

"No! It's your way or the highway, Greg. Let's face it. You think you know every fucking thing, and you don't."

"You think I would be here if I didn't?"

"You don't get it. Even the president seeks advice from others. You can't do it alone."

"Neither can you."

She shook her head. Greg was totally missing the point. "Oh, you would still be here, just not standing in our kitchen."

"So you're making decisions for *us* now?"

"Yes, the same way you did ten years ago."

Both glared at each other before Greg stormed out.

*****

Greg hadn't been home in two weeks, and Gabrielle was losing her mind. He had been staying at their Riverdale apartment. She tried calling him, but he wouldn't speak to her. When he did call, it was to speak to the kids.

Sulking in her office, Gabrielle couldn't believe Greg found out about Britney. Wallowing in her sorrow, she poured herself another drink. *How the hell did this happen?* The only people that knew were Tommy, who was dead, and Denise.

"That fucking bitch," she grumbled.

A tipsy Gabrielle put on her coat and then hopped into her car. While speeding down the street, she grumbled, "I can't believe she opened her mouth."

Fuming, she banged on Denise's door. "Denise!" she shouted.

Stunned, Denise opened the door. "Gabri..." Before she could get her name out, Gabrielle had slapped the shit out of her.

"You stinkin' bitch! You told Greg about Britney!" she shouted, wildly swinging at Denise.

While blocking and trying to make sense of Gabrielle's words, Denise replied, "What are you talking about?"

"Don't play dumb with me!" Gabrielle shouted, then swung and caught Denise in her face.

Gabrielle threw another punch, but this time, Denise blocked it and knocked the shit out of Gabrielle.

"Bitch!" Gabrielle said, out of breath and disorientated.

"What the hell is wrong with you? What are you talking about? And lower your goddamn voice. Derrick and the kids are upstairs sleeping."

Gabrielle tried to catch her breath. "You told Greg about Britney."

"What?!"

"Don't fucking lie to me. You told him because no one else knew but you."

Confused, Denise yelled, "No, I didn't! It was Tony!"

Incoherent, Gabrielle continued yelling. "Yes, you did! After all I have done for you...after all we've been through, you go and do this?"

Denise grew more upset. "Gabrielle, I didn't say..."

"Stop fucking lying! You did! You tell him every fucking thing, just like you told him about Felicia."

Denise narrowed her eyes.

"Oh yeah! You think I didn't know that. Have you ever asked yourself what if the person taking that shot missed?" Gabrielle said in a composed tone, while staring intensely at Denise.

"You were there?" Denise asked, stunned.

"Of course, I was. Why you think you're still standing here?"

"It was you?" Denise probed.

"It's amazing what you learn growing up. My father used to take us to the gun range on his naval base. Since he didn't have any sons, he forced us to take up gun lessons, which is the best thing he ever did."

"You shot a gun before?"

"You seem surprised." Gabrielle laughed. "There are a lot of things you don't know about me."

Gabrielle pranced around as if she was performing on a Broadway stage. "Felicia came to me first. The little bitch had the nerve to tell me that she wanted a million dollars in cash or she was

gonna tell the police about some other murders that Greg did. Can you believe the bitch had the audacity to say this to me?" She pounded her chest.

Stunned, Denise just stared at Gabrielle.

"I'm Gabrielle Brightman. I don't get extorted." Gabrielle smirked. "So, I waited. Felicia contacted me with a time, and I was supposed to meet her in Central Park."

Denise thought back to that night. She hadn't noticed it then, but Gabrielle had on all black, too.

"Once I saw you at Justin's, I figured you were meeting her there, too. So, I followed you. I watched how Felicia made you kneel down like a d-o-g," she said, getting in Denise's face.

Intoxicated, Gabrielle slowly paced back and forth as if she was in a courtroom. "So, I pulled out my .50 caliber sniper rifle." She giggled deviously. "By the time she realized what happened, it was too late!" she yelled, reenacting that night. "I watched as that bitch dropped to the ground."

"Gabrielle..." Denise mumbled.

"But Jake...he was different. With him, it was personal," she said, pointing her finger.

"You killed Jake?" Denise's eyes widened.

Gabrielle turned around, glaring at Denise. "No, I watched Jake kill himself. That motherfucker deserved to die. He didn't give a damn about his clients. He allowed my husband to sit in prison for nine years. So, he had to pay...with his life. I doubt if the police will ever find Larry and Miguel." She flashed a devilish grin. "That's the difference between you and me. You perceive to be something you're not, because if you were what you perceive to be, Felicia would've never set you up. Oh yeah, I heard about your rep back in the day. Funny, you don't live up to it, though."

"Gab..." Denise struggled to search for the right words. "What have..."

"What have I done? I saved your life. I was protecting my family. Isn't that what you do, Dee?" she said, while walking like a thug. "Gabrielle, why do you want to be down so much?" she mimicked.

Swiftly, Gabrielle turned around and in a whining voice said, "What's the problem, Dee? You think I can't walk in your shoes?" She giggled. "Shit, you can't walk in mine either. Unlike y'all motherfucker, I have the law on my side—best of both worlds, chica!"

This was something straight out of the movies. Denise was aware that Gabrielle was drunk, but enough was enough. She was starting to piss her off.

"You're drunk, Gabrielle."

"You stay the fuck away from me and my family, or..." Gabrielle threatened.

Denise laughed. "Watch what you say. I don't..."

"Don't what?"

Putting her hand up and backing away, Denise stared at her and started clapping. "Nice performance. You deserve an Oscar, but this is not the movies, Gabrielle. So, don't..."

"If you come near my family..."

"What are you gonna do, huh? I warned you. Cane killed Abel."

Both stood staring into each other's faces. Denise could smell the liquor on Gabrielle's breath.

"Like I said, stay away from me and my family, or..."

"Or what?!" Denise glared at her, causing Gabrielle to snap back to reality. "I didn't think so. Now, you better leave before we both do something we'll regret."

After gathering her things and straightening her clothes, Gabrielle walked over to Denise. "Everyone has a defining moment. Remember that," she said and then walked out, leaving Denise speechless.

*****

It was Saturday morning, and Gabrielle woke up with such a hangover that she couldn't remember how she got home. When she finally opened her eyes, she saw her mother standing over her.

"Where the hell have you been? I've been calling all over town for you."

"Ma, where's the kids?" Gabrielle asked, ignoring the question.

"With Greg. He came by last night and picked them up. What's going on with you and Greg?"

Gabrielle sucked her teeth, cut her eyes, and tossed the covers off of her. Scratching her head, she tried to recollect the previous night while staggering into the bathroom.

"Gabrielle, what's going on with you and Greg?" Sadie repeated.

"Married stuff!" she yelled, slamming the bathroom door.

Since Greg took the kids for the weekend, Gabrielle stayed in bed the entire time recovering from her hangover. Also, she tried to remember what had happened. She called the kids a few times, praying that Greg would at least talk to her, but he didn't. His ass was so stubborn.

Can't cry over spilled milk, she thought. While she knew she was wrong, she felt Greg was wrong, too. Maybe if he would've told her about Britney, none of this would've happened.

Monday morning, Gabrielle walked into her office and greeted her receptionist. "Good morning, Nancy."

"Morning, boss."

As Gabrielle read over some documents, Nancy spoke through the intercom. "Mrs. Brightman, there's a lady here to see you."

Confused, Gabrielle asked, "Who?"

"I don't know. She's related to Tommy."

Gabrielle paused for a second. "Tommy?" she asked. "Sure, send her in."

"Hi, my name is Margaret. Tommy was my brother."

Gabrielle nodded. "I've seen you outside of my office. You drive a black Jaguar, right?"

Margaret blushed. "Yeah, that's me. I wanted to make sure…"

Gabrielle laughed and then interjected. "I know. I didn't know Tommy had a sister," she said, shaking her hand.

"Yeah, my brother likes to keep his work separate from his family," Margaret joked.

"Well, have a seat. It's a pleasure meeting you."

Gabrielle led Margaret over to the conference table so they could get better acquainted. After chatting about Tommy, Margaret handed her a small box.

"I found this with your name on it. I figured my brother wanted to give it to you before he died."

Gabrielle's eyes filled with tears. "I'm so sorry about Tommy. He called me the night he was killed. If I knew..."

Immediately, Margaret interrupted her. "Gabrielle, it's not your fault. My brother was killed by a drunk driver. There's no way you could have known."

"Yeah, but I just wish I would've answered the phone."

Margaret had a few more stops to make before flying back to Colorado, so she had to cut her visit short. "Well, I have to get going. It was a pleasure to finally meet you. My brother talked about you so much. Hopefully, when I come back into town, we can have lunch."

Gabrielle smiled. "I would like that."

After Margaret left, Gabrielle looked at the small box. "I'll look at that later," she mumbled. "Right now, I have to get some work done."

On her way to the pantry to heat up her food, she noticed Nancy's face screwed up.

"Are you okay?" she asked.

Nancy, who was reading an email, blurted out, "Oh my! Tony Flowers is an asshole!"

Shocked by her comment, Gabrielle asked, "Huh? What made you say that?"

Not realizing what she had said, Nancy replied, "It's nothing."

He must've slept with her, too, Gabrielle thought, shaking her head and laughing as she continued to the pantry. On her way back to the office, Nancy stopped her.

"Boss lady, you're good friends with Tony, right?"

Gabrielle chuckled. "I wouldn't say good friends. Why? Is that same girl badmouthing him again?'

"No! But, I befriended the girl. We talk over the net, and he's a monster."

"What?"

"Remember I told you how she badmouths him on his fan page. Well, I emailed her about it, and she told me that she's been messing with him for years and that he's a woman beater."

With a somber look, Gabrielle replied, "She told you all of that?"

"Yes. We've been talking for over a year now, and I believe her."

"Okay, so what has she been saying?" Gabrielle asked, pretending to care.

"She started telling me how Tony is abusive."

Nancy handed Gabrielle some of the emails she printed out from the girl, and Gabrielle read over them.

"Wow! This is some disturbing stuff."

"I know. Do you think it's true?"

"I don't know. I mean, why hasn't she gone to the police, or has she sold her story to the tabloids? Tony is very famous. If he was doing these things, someone would've known by now. How does she look?"

"I don't know, but I believe her," Nancy stated.

Unsure of how to respond, Gabrielle just shook her head. *Please tell me that person isn't Stevie,* she thought while walking back into her office. Before going inside, she stopped, turned around, and said, "Nancy, tell her to send you a picture."

Once inside her office, Gabrielle shook her head and then picked up the phone to call Stevie. It rang two times before she answered.

"Hey, sis!"

"Hey, Stevie. Listen, you're not on any of Tony's fan sites, are you?"

"What?" Stevie giggled.

"Nancy just told me that she met some girl on Tony's site, and the girl told her that Tony is abusing her."

"Are you serious?"

"Yep!"

"And you thought it was me? Gab, give me some credit. The last thing I need is to be on some website bashing his ass."

"I don't know what to think."

"The abusing part I believe. That does sound like him. It's probably someone playing a joke. You never know with people."

"And especially with people on the internet," Gabrielle agreed. "Listen, I gotta go. I'll talk to you later," she said, ending the call.

★ ★ ★ ★ 150

Chapter Thirteen
Morgan

It was almost six o'clock, and Morgan and her co-worker Rodney were still preparing their brief. Glancing at her watch, she thought, *It's gonna be another long night. Better call home.* Morgan called to inform Tony that she was going to be late. Abiding to his promise, Tony was okay with it.

"Hey, Morgan, I was gonna order something to eat. You want something?" Rodney asked, looking over a menu.

"Uh, sure. I'll have a Greek salad and bottled water."

Throughout the evening, Rodney kept staring at Morgan, wondering if she had a man. *Someone that beautiful probably does,* he thought.

For the past couple of months, they had been working on a case together and gotten extremely close. However, Morgan only saw Rodney as her fun co-worker, where as Rodney had a huge crush on her. In fact, most of the men at the company did. Rodney Robinson was twenty-seven, half Black and Latino, and after graduating from Harvard Law School, he was hired as a junior attorney for the firm.

There were plenty of days Morgan walked in her office and found a bouquet of roses; she had a feeling they were from him. Nonetheless, she didn't dare take them home. The last thing she needed was Tony acting up. It had been months, and Tony had done a complete three-sixty; he was kind, loving, and the best father in world. At times, she still found it hard to believe that something good could come from evil.

"Morgan, can I ask you a question?"

With her head buried in some papers, Morgan nodded.

"You have kids, right?"

"Yes, I have two beautiful babies." She looked up and smiled.

"Are you married to the father?"

"Why?" she asked.

"I was just asking. I know someone as beautiful as you isn't single."

Morgan blushed. "I'm with someone. What about you?"

"I'm with someone, also."

"Is she special?"

"Yeah, she is," he replied. "I wanna get her something. What do you think I should get her?"

"As a gift?"

"Yeah. Do you think I should get her a pair of diamond earrings?"

Morgan frowned.

"That's not good?"

"Yes, but why don't you take her to a nice Broadway show, a romantic dinner, and then ride through Central Park?"

Rodney thought about it for a second. "Damn, that sounds good. I didn't even think of that."

"It's not always about an expensive gift," Morgan explained.

"True."

Morgan heard her cell phone ringing; it was Tony. "Hey," she answered, excusing herself.

"Babe, Al is downstairs waiting for you when you're ready."

"Okay. It's not gonna be too much longer."

"Morgan, are you gonna finish your drink?" Rodney yelled to her.

"No, you can throw it away."

"Who's that?" Tony asked, hearing a man's voice in the background.

"That's my co-worker, Rodney. He's here working with me."

"Just you and him?"

"No, there are other people in the office."

Fuming, Tony replied, "Alright. Well, Al is downstairs."

Morgan finished up and then headed home. When she arrived, Tony was in the bed.

"Hi." She leaned over and kissed him.

"What's up?" he answered dryly.

After placing her cell phone on the nightstand, Morgan went into the bathroom to wash her hands and then checked on the kids.

"How's London?" she asked when she returned to the bedroom. "Is she still cranky?"

Flicking through the channels, Tony screwed up his face. "She's good."

Noticing his body language, Morgan shook her head and went to take a shower. While in the shower, her cell phone chimed with a text message from Rodney, who was thanking her for her help.

Tony read it and then barged into the bathroom. "Yo, who's Rodney?" he asked.

Morgan, who was drying herself off, jumped. "Tony, he's my co-worker," she stressed, brushing past him.

Tony snatched her by the arm. "Why is he sending you text messages thanking you? What the fuck are you doing?"

"You read my text message?"

Tony yanked her toward him, glaring at her. "Of course. Is there a problem?"

Yanking her arm away from his grasp, Morgan snapped, "He was thanking me for helping him plan something for his girlfriend, if you must know."

"So you're the expert now?" Tony said, following her.

"No, Tony, I'm not, considering I've never been anywhere," she spitefully replied.

"What do you mean? You have access to anything."

"Is that all you think about is money? You think I give a shit about your money?"

"It's not mine. It's ours."

Disgusted, Morgan shook her head. "It's not mine, Tony. It's yours. I don't want anything from you."

"I'm not saying that. You're missing the point. You have everything of mine, Morgan. You're my wife," he pointed out.

"Wife? I'm your secret. A wife goes to the movies and out to dinner, Tony. That's what married couples do. When's the last time you took me anyplace?" she shouted.

"I'm working on that."

"Oh yeah? When? You just don't get it. You think just because you put me up in this big house and buy me expensive things that I'm supposed to be happy...that I'm supposed to think you're a wonderful husband. Newsflash, Tony! It takes more than that," she said, jumping into bed.

Stumped, Tony stood there for a moment before taking a seat on the edge of the bed. "Morgan..." he mumbled.

"What?" she snapped.

"You're right. It takes more than that. I know we need to start doing things together, but..."

"But what?" Morgan sat up. "Tony, what's done is done. At some point, you have to tell the truth. We can't keep living like this. We don't do anything publicly together with our kids. You want me to forgive and learn to love you, but how can I when we don't do anything together? I'm tired of living this lie."

Nodding, Tony replied, "Me, too. We're gonna start doing stuff."

"We better or else Rodney is gonna bring me home one night," Morgan jokingly stated.

He laughed. "Yeah, and you'll both get killed," he said while tickling her, which led to them making love all night.

Tony had really changed, allowing Morgan to express her feelings without getting angry. Years ago, he would've closed both of her eyes. However, her warning caused him to step his game up. He even personally picked Morgan up from work. Even though the windows were tinted, it was nice to see him outside. There was so much he wanted to do, but his celebrity status prevented him. The last thing he needed was his picture all over the tabloids.

Tony had the evening all planned out, though. He was taking Morgan to a play and out for a romantic dinner. Unfortunately,

Christina and Mookie were tagging along. It was the only way Tony could pull it off. Initially, Mookie said no, feeling it was too risky, but like always, Tony convinced him.

It was awkward for Tony and Morgan throughout the night as they avoided each other. But, it was extremely difficult for Tony because, like always, Morgan looked stunning and the scent of her perfume turned him on.

On the other hand, Mookie had a blast. He finally had a chance to talk with Morgan, and astonishingly, he understood why Tony was so enamored with her. Morgan demonstrated that old Hollywood class and was extremely intelligent. If he had to choose between Christina and Morgan, he would pick Morgan, too.

The play was fantastic; Denzel Washington was excellent. After shaking hands backstage with the cast, they headed to the restaurant. Morgan rode with Mookie.

"I can see why Tony is so in love with you," Mookie mumbled.

"Excuse me," Morgan said.

"I said I can see why Tony is so in love with you," he repeated.

Morgan glanced up at him. "He told you that?"

"Yeah."

"Hmm," she said, nodding.

"I didn't mean anything," he exclaimed.

Morgan laughed. "No…I'm just surprised he told you."

"Well, it's hard not to see the way he treats his kids."

Morgan blushed, wondering how much Mookie knew. "Yeah, he loves his kids."

"Yep, and you, too." Mookie smiled.

Instead of going to a five-star restaurant, Tony chose a small, intimate place. Once seated, Tony broke the silence.

"So, Morgan, how's law school?"

Caught off guard, she stared at him before responding, "School is going great."

"I don't know how you do it. Going to school, raising two kids, and working full time is a lot," Christina stated, then took a bite of her roll.

"Yes, it is, but Tony has been a big help," she responded, playing along.

"Yeah, Tony loves your kids," Mookie joined in. "They are some beautiful kids."

"Yes, London looks just like you," Christina said.

"Blame that on my Italian side." Morgan laughed.

"You're Italian?" Mookie and Christina asked in unison.

"Yes. My mother is Greek and African American, and my father is Italian."

"I didn't know that," Christina said.

Tony was quiet, beaming inside.

"How's school with you, Christina? Did you finish?" Morgan asked.

Mookie and Tony looked at each other, then at Christina.

"You're in school?" Tony asked.

"Actually, I'm in college. I'm just about finished. I have one more semester," Christina stated, brushing off their stares.

"I didn't know that," Tony said.

"Yeah, well, there are a lot of things you don't know," she snidely replied.

"You think I don't, but truth is, I just don't give a damn," Tony shot back.

"And neither do I."

Morgan glanced over at Christina and then back at Tony. *Is this all an act?* She thought.

Dinner was nice, but Christina and Tony didn't speak for the rest of the evening. However, Mookie and Christina were amazed at how intellectual and humble Morgan was. As the night came to an end, Morgan and Christina exchanged kisses on the cheek before Christina hopped into her awaiting car service. Everyone knew she was still upset with Tony. Mookie had another engagement, so he left by himself. Being a gentleman, Tony offered Morgan a ride home.

"I had a nice time, Mr. Flowers," Morgan said, kissing him in the car.

"So did I, Mrs. Flowers. I'm sorry you had to witness that bullshit with Christina."

"Were y'all serious?"

"Yes, Morgan! Christina and I are together in the public eye only, and that's it. We don't talk or have sex. That's what I've been trying to explain to you. I don't give a shit about her. She's not even my wife."

"Y'all are not married?"

"Hell naw! We had a wedding, but we didn't get our marriage license, and I only did that to please everyone else," he explained, frustrated.

"Mookie knows about us?"

"Yeah, I told him. He knows how much I love you."

"He told me," she stated.

Tony faced her. "Ma, I know I sound like a broken record, but it's real. All my life I just wanted someone who I could share the rest of my life with—someone who loved Anthony Omar Flowers—and you're that person."

"Tony, I can't make you happy. Happiness comes from within."

"I know, but you're a big part of it," he replied, kissing her on the cheek.

Morgan playfully pushed his face away, causing Tony to laugh. "What am I going to do with you?"

"Love me," he replied while staring deeply into her eyes.

*****

Morgan was in the office when she was informed she and Rodney had to fly out to their west coast office to work on a case. Morgan sighed. *Tony already suspects that something is going on. I know he's gonna hit the roof with this news.*

Knock! Knock!

"Morgan, you wanna grab something to eat?" Emily asked.

"Where are you going?"

"A few of us are gonna go out for lunch."

"Sure, give me a second."

While they were eating and laughing, someone noticed Christina and her entourage exiting.

"Morgan!" Christina smiled and kissed her on the cheek.

"Hey, Chris! How are you?"

"Wonderful! How's the babies?"

"They're great. Oh, these are my co-workers Rodney, Emily, and Donna," she said.

"Nice to meet you," Christina said before being ushered to her car.

"So you know the infamous Christina Carrington, eh?" Rodney teased.

Morgan busted out laughing. "Something like that."

*****

With Tony having to work late, Morgan picked up the kids and then headed home. She had just put the kids in the bed when Tony came in.

"Hey," she said.

At first, he didn't say anything. So, Morgan repeated it again, but this time louder.

"Hi."

Tony glared at her. "Yo, you like it when I put my hands on you, huh?" he said calmly.

"What? What are you talking about?"

He flung some pictures at her. "This is what I'm talking about. I want you to quit."

Morgan picked up the photos. The pictures were of her and Rodney from earlier that day.

"Tony..." she mumbled.

In a rage, he grabbed Morgan and tossed her on the bed. He was about to hit her when Lil' Anthony walked in.

"Daddy..."

Tony paused, realizing what he was doing. Morgan pushed him off of her and ran to hug her son.

Rushing over to them, Tony took Lil' Anthony from Morgan and mumbled, "I'm sorry."

That was it! It was one thing to abuse her, but Morgan was not about to have her children witness it. Tony had gone too far. Morgan stormed into her closet to get some clothes. Once he realized what she was doing, he tried to stop her.

"What are you doing?" he asked.

"I'm leaving! I've had enough!" she screamed, while crying.

Petrified, Tony reached out for her hand, but Morgan pushed him away.

"Get off of me! I'm taking my fucking kids and getting out of here! I don't care what you do to me! You will never see them again!"

Tony eyes widened as he gently pushed his body up against her. "Baby, I'm sorry," he whispered, trying to kiss her.

"Get off of me," she cried, pushing him away again.

Devastated, Tony went and sat on the bed as Morgan and the kids left.

For the next couple of weeks, Morgan stayed in her Manhattan apartment. It was small, but at least she was safe from him. She went about her daily routine, dropping the kids off to school and then heading to work. The nights when she had to work late, she called the part-time nanny to pick the kids up and take them home. Begging-ass Tony sent flowers, candy, and even diamonds, but Morgan had heard it all before.

When she wasn't working, she was hanging out with her co-workers. It felt good to get out and live life. She also went back to working out and taking up Bikran Yoga to relieve stress. She was finally getting to know herself. When it wasn't about her, Morgan took the kids out to many different places. Even though they were small and probably didn't understand a lot of what they were seeing, it felt good to just be out with them without having to look over her shoulder.

Chapter Fourteen
Tony

Tony had become miserable. Two months had passed, and Morgan still hadn't come back home. She was staying in her apartment in the city. Stressing, Tony drove by there every night hoping to get a glimpse of them. One night, he got lucky because Morgan and the kids were coming out of the building. He had called her several times, but she sent him to voicemail. Morgan also stopped using Al to chauffeur her and the kids around, which Tony felt was unnecessary.

Today, he was attending an important meeting with the CEO of Society Records, who he sold half of his company to. Sterling had called a last-minute meeting to announce Mookie as the appointed CEO of their west coast office. Distraught over his split with his wife, Tony didn't even notice the law firm that Morgan worked at was in attendance. Reading over some documents, Tony didn't bother looking up as Sterling announced their entrance and everyone got acquainted.

"Hello, everyone. I would like to get this meeting started," Sterling stated.

Tony sighed and almost fainted when he looked up. Across from him was his wife. Mookie, who was aware of Tony and Morgan's separation, smiled as he looked over at Tony. Their eyes met briefly before Morgan diverted her attention to Sterling. Throughout the meeting, Tony couldn't take his eyes off her. He didn't even care who caught him staring. This was the perfect opportunity for Tony to approach Morgan to tell her how sorry he was.

"Hi, Morgan," he said, holding his breath.

"Hello, Mr. Flowers. How are you?" she replied, sounding professional.

"Good. How are the kids doing?"

"They're fine."

"Hey, Morgan, Sterling and them are ordering lunch. Carol said we have to stick around, but I have to go. You know today is Linda's day," Rodney informed her.

Morgan giggled. "Alright. Tell her I said hello."

Tony and Morgan stared at each other, with Tony feeling like a complete idiot. Morgan was about to walk away, when Tony reached for her arm.

"Can we go somewhere and talk?"

"No, Tony," she whispered.

Tony looked around to make sure no one was watching them. "Please," he mumbled with sorrowful eyes.

"Hey, ma." Mookie walked up, kissing her on the cheek.

Morgan flinched and then smiled. "Hi, Mookie. Congrats on your new position."

"Thanks. You're doing the damn thing at that firm. I see ya," Mookie jokingly responded.

"Thank you."

Tony stood there like a sick puppy, just listening.

"How are the kids doing?"

"Wonderful. Missing their father," she replied, looking at Tony for a reaction.

Mookie glanced over at Tony and then back at Morgan. "Talk," he requested before walking away.

After a few moments of standing there quietly, Morgan followed Tony into his office to hear what he had to say. As usual, he apologized for his behavior and promised not to do it again. However, Morgan didn't believe him. While the kids missed him so much, Morgan worried about her safety. Tony was a very jealous person; anything would set him off, and she was sick of it.

"Talk," she ordered, taking a seat in the chair.

"I miss you. I miss my kids. I want y'all back," he pleaded.

Morgan glanced around the office at all the pictures of their kids. "You have a lot of pictures," she commented, ignoring Tony's begging.

When she got up to get a closer look at them, Tony came up behind her and wrapped his arms around her waist. "I miss you, baby girl. Please don't do this to me," he begged, smelling her hair and then kissing her on the top of her head.

Tia walked in. "Excuse me," she said, closing the door back.

"Wait, Tia…" Tony said. "Come in and close the door. I have something to tell you."

Leery, Tia looked at Morgan, then back at Tony. "Okay," she mumbled.

Tony exhaled. "Morgan is my wife and those are my kids," he blurted out.

"What?" Tia said with her hands out.

"She's my wife."

Tia took a seat on the chair. "What do you mean she's your wife and those are your kids? When did all of this happen? Why didn't you tell me?"

"We've been married for a couple of years now. I didn't tell anyone. "

Shocked by his admission, Morgan stood there in a daze. "Tony, this is not good. I mean…"

"I don't care, Tia. She's my wife."

"Hey, I have to go. I'll bring the kids by tonight," Morgan said, walking out.

Tia locked the door after Morgan exited. "Tony, are you fucking crazy? If this gets out…"

Sitting at his desk, Tony rubbed his head while thinking about Morgan. "I don't give a shit about if it gets out," he proclaimed angrily.

Mookie knocked on the door. "Yo, Tony…"

Tia opened the door.

Sensing the tension, Mookie asked, "What's going on in here?"

"I told Tia about Morgan," Tony stated.

Mookie's eyes widened. "Oh…"

"You knew?" Tia asked.

"Yeah, he told me awhile ago."

"And you didn't tell me, Tony?" Tia looked over in Tony's direction and then back at Mookie.

"What's there to tell, Tia?"

"How about telling me that you have a family and are married to two women, or did you forget about Christina?"

Mookie glanced over at Tony with a look that said 'you better tell her the truth'. So, Tony sat Tia down and told her everything, leaving out the rape and abuse. Not only was she upset about Tony keeping this secret from her, but Morgan was a child when he started messing with her, which was something she disapproved of. In her opinion, he was a child molester.

"Does Denise know about this?" Tia asked.

"No, she doesn't know. Promise me that you won't say anything."

"Oh, I'm not going to say nothing. Trust me. The less I know about it, the better," Tia exclaimed, walking out.

Mookie glanced over at Tony who had a damned look on his face. "She'll come around," Mookie said, hitting Tony on his leg.

After leaving the office, Tony went directly home to await Morgan's arrival. As promised, Morgan pulled up to the house with the kids, who he hadn't seen in a while. Tony was coming downstairs as they were entering.

"Daddy!" they both yelled, bringing tears to Morgan's eyes.

"Hey!" He laughed, grabbing his two children into his arms.

Tony played with the kids while Morgan gathered some more things. It was getting late; London had fallen asleep and Lil' Anthony was almost there.

"Anthony, get your sneakers. It's time to go," Morgan said.

"I wanna stay with Daddy," he whined in a sleepy voice.

Tony looked over at Morgan. "Can they stay? I will have Al drop them off to school."

"Fine."

"You can stay, too," he added.

"No! Just make sure the kids are dropped off."

Morgan was about to walk out, when Tony yanked her to him, kissing her.

"You're not leaving."

Morgan wanted to push him away, but she missed him, too.

"I've been so miserable without you," he moaned. "I'm sorry, baby. I'll never raise my hand at you again."

"You said that before, Tony," she responded, attempting to push him away as she came to her senses. "You haven't changed."

"I have, Morgan." He held her tightly. "I was upset. I thought you were cheating on me. I lost it."

"And that's an excuse for you to hit me?"

"No, but..."

"But nothing, Tony. I haven't given you any reason to believe that I'm cheating. Regardless of how I feel, I love my family. So, I would never jeopardize them. Can't you see that?" She walked away. "I'll be home around seven, so you can drop them off by then."

Tony sighed. He thought about running after her, but he knew she needed time to think.

*****

The holidays were just around the corner, and Morgan still wasn't home. Even though the kids spent two nights a week at Tony's house, it still wasn't the same. He was extremely lonely. Christina had become more involved with Rashid, and they were secretly living together. When she wasn't spending time with Rashid, Christina was closing huge deals.

Tony figured if he gave Morgan her space, she would've come back home by now, but that didn't happen. In fact, she appeared to be happy without him and barely said two words to him when she picked up the kids. It was killing Tony inside.

Thanksgiving was two days away, and Tony decided to have dinner alone. While he was invited to everyone's house, if he couldn't be with his family, he would rather be by himself. He was in the living room watching television, when he heard a car pulling up. He glanced at his watch.

"Who the hell is that?" he muttered. Then he heard Lil' Anthony's voice. He ran out to the front. It was Morgan and the kids getting out of the car.

"Hello," she said.

Happy, Tony grabbed the bags from the backseat. Then he looked up toward the heavens and whispered, "Yes."

"Did we interrupt you?" Morgan asked, as Tony placed the bags in the living room.

Screwing up his face, Tony replied, "No, you could never do that. This is your home."

Morgan nodded. "Well, the kids wanted to see you, and I thought maybe we could spend Thanksgiving together. But, if you made…"

"Morgan, stop."

She strolled over to him and gently touched his cheek. Tony closed his eyes, kissing her hand.

"I'm so happy you're here. I missed you so much."

"We missed you, too." She kissed him.

Blissful, Tony and Morgan spent the next couple of days making up. Morgan prepared such a feast that Tony thought she was cooking for an army. After dinner, Morgan and Tony moved to the living room to watch a movie. That night, he prayed to God, thanking him for his family.

*****

Tony was meeting Christina for dinner. He felt like canceling, but didn't feel like hearing her mouth. They met at Mr. Chow's, with Tony arriving first.

Once Christina got there, Tony ordered, not wanting to waste any time. He was dying to get back home to his family.

"So what do you wanna talk about?" he asked.

"Us."

"What about us?" he said in an uncaring tone.

"Don't you think it's time for us to move on from each other?"

"If that's what you want."

"Tony, cut the shit. We haven't been happy for years."

"And that's my fault?" Tony snidely replied.

Tony is such an asshole, she thought. "No, I guess everything is my fault. Anyway, how do you wanna do this?"

Glaring at her, he put some noodles in his mouth. "It doesn't matter to me. You tell me. How does Rashid feel about this?" Tony chewed, giving her a side-eye look.

"What does Rashid have to do with this?"

"Still lying, huh?"

"Lying about what? Yes, I'm with him. You and I both know that."

Tony glanced at his watch. It was getting late. "I tell you what. I'll have my attorney contact Gabrielle and work something out." He smirked.

"Cool. I don't want this to get out of hand and be all over the front pages of newspapers."

"Neither do I." Tony laughed.

It was official. Christina and Tony was no longer an item, which was a good thing for Tony. He was glad she initiated the break-up. That way, when he announced his marriage to Morgan, he wouldn't look like a bad guy. Being that they hadn't gone public yet, Tony accompanied Christina to the Golden Globes. She was up for supporting actress. While Tony would rather be at home, he didn't need the speculation. It was amazing the façade they put on. Everyone truly believed they were the perfect couple. After the awards ceremony, Christina stayed in Los Angeles while Tony hopped on a plane back to New York.

Ever since Tony told Tia about Morgan, she'd been acting differently towards him. Every morning, they would have a thirty-minute conference call to go over his daily agenda. Now, she emailed it to him or left it on his desk before he arrived at the office. Tony thought about talking to her, but changed his mind. *She'll get over it, and if she doesn't, who cares,* he thought.

Natalie, his receptionist, knocked on the door. "Morning, Tony," she said, licking her lips.

Natalie was Tony's quick fix years ago, but he stopped sleeping with her once Morgan came into his life. In fact, Tony left all the girls in his office alone.

"What's up, Nat?"

"I was just wondering if we can have lunch together."

Tony grinned. "Thanks, but I'm good. I'm not gonna be in the office all day."

Disappointed, she flashed a weak smile. "Okay...well, maybe some other time."

Playing with his BlackBerry, Tony didn't bother to acknowledge her response. Just then, Tony's private line rang; it was Mike.

"Yo, you heard what happened, right?"

"Nah."

"Moe was murdered."

"What?!"

"Yeah. From what I'm hearing, they shot up his car. He was hit in the shoulder, and they chased him to the hospital and finished him off."

"Get the fuck outta here. Do they know who did it?"

"No, but they said it was a girl. From what I'm hearing, it's some chick from out of town. Supposedly, Moe was messing with shorty and broke it off. That's not the crazy shit, though. Check this out, Tee. They found Millie, Bruce, and Joe's bodies in an abandoned building."

"What Millie?"

"Millie from around the way. Yo, I heard they blew her shit off. They needed dental records to identify her."

"Damn! For what?"

"I don't know, but shit is hot right now."

"Do Greg and Dee know about this?" Tony asked.

"I haven't spoken to them in a while. You know I've been on tour with Wild Child. But, they probably know, or at least Greg does."

"Well, good lookin'. I'll reach out to them. How's everything with you? How's the tour going?"

"You know me, fam…chillin' and tryna get this paper. Oh, the tour is crazy," Mike replied.

"A'ight, that's what's up. Yo, when you get back, let's hook up."

"Fo' sho, fam. One."

"One."

After hanging up, Tony still wondered if Greg and Denise knew. If they didn't, he needed to tell them. He placed a call to both but was unsuccessful in reaching them, getting their voicemail. So, he left a message.

Finally, Tony was able to hook up with them; they were having dinner at his penthouse in Tribeca Place. Anxious, Tony waited in his office until Denise and Greg arrived.

"Hey, guys." Denise smiled and kissed them on the cheek. Then she informed them that she would have to be out of there in an hour.

Tony and Greg nodded.

"Yo, did you hear about Moe?" Tony whispered.

"Yeah, we heard," Greg replied.

"What about Millie and them?"

"We know about that, too," Denise said, sipping her water.

"Damn! Why didn't you tell me?"

In a subdued way, Greg looked over in Denise's direction. "I didn't think we had to."

Checking himself, Tony responded, "I didn't mean that…"

"Why are you so concerned?" Denise asked apprehensively.

"I was just surprised," Tony answered. "Do y'all know who did it?"

Annoyed, Denise looked around. "What's with all of the questions? You called us out here to ask us this shit?"

Greg looked at Tony with a 'she's right' stare.

"No, it's not like that, Dee. Damn, I was just asking."

"For what? So you can run your mouth?" she snapped.

Tony looked at Greg and then at her. She was still the same Denise—always humiliating him in front of people. It was time to show her things had changed.

"Yo, watch your fucking mouth," he retorted. "I'm just asking you a fucking question."

Greg saw Denise's face and immediately interrupted, because in five seconds, Tony would've been dead. Tony wasn't aware of the shit going on behind the scenes. It was tension, and his slick comments could cause him to get himself hurt.

"Tee, I agree that it seems like you called us to ask a bunch of questions. You know we don't get down like that."

Fuming, Denise glowered at him but didn't utter a word.

"Nah, Greg, it isn't like that. This is Tony, and sometimes I feel like just because I'm a rapper y'all treat me different."

"What the fuck are you talking about treating you different?" Denise blurted out.

Greg held up his hand for her to allow Tony to finish. "Speak your mind, Tee. You know how we do. The floor is yours."

Tony looked over at Denise, collecting his thought. One thing Greg always did was allow them to say what was on their heart. That way, everything would be out in the open. Tony just wondered how he could put it without sounding like a suspect.

"I was just saying...you know, I feel like y'all exclude me from stuff. Just because I'm a rapper doesn't mean I'm not the same person."

"Exclude you from what?" Denise asked.

"Everything, Dee. When y'all hang out, y'all don't call me. If there are some investments, I'm never involved."

"Are you fucking kidding me? This is so high school. It's true. We never included you in anything. Would you like to know why, Tee? Because everyone knows your ass isn't built like that. You were never built for the street."

"You're right, but I have enough money. I own the muthafuckin' streets."

Denise laughed at his comment, while Greg glared at him. "Is that what you think? Just because you have money you think you own the streets?" she asked, as she stood up from her seat, approached him, and bent over, getting in his face.

"Of course," Tony replied, trying to display courage.

Denise looked over in Greg's direction and then turned back toward Tony. "I know niggas like you—straight pussy. They think just because they have a few dollars that they're powerful." Both stared into each other's eyes. "You know how I know this, Tony? Because I put a lot of them niggas in the dirt. On their deathbeds, they begged me for their lives. Sometimes, Tee, not even money can save you. So, like I said before, you may be rich, but your heart..." she tapped his chest, "your heart beats Kool-Aid."

Scared, Tony laughed. "You keep on believing that, Denise. You know, the greatest trick the devil did was make people believe he didn't exist."

"Now you're speaking my language. I am the devil. You of all people should know that. I'm still breathing, and it's not by default. So, Tee, I suggest you watch your fucking mouth before I forget you're my friend," she said before walking away.

Tony was about to respond, but something about Denise's words terrified him.

He looked over at Greg, who replied, "Tony, it's not like that. You know Denise and I have a different relationship that was established from the jump. No offense, but there's some things you're not gonna know, and it's for your own protection. It's nothing personal."

"Oh, I'm not saying that, but, Dee, I wanted to know..."

"Wanted to know what? When did we start answering to you? Tee, this isn't the rap world. This isn't a diss record. You think if we know something we're obligated to tell you?"

"No, I don't, but you're coming out your face for no reason, and I didn't do shit to you. I'm not the same Tony."

"And you say that to say what?" Denise said, getting up again. "I'm not the same Denise. Tony, don't let that gangsta rapping shit go to your head. You better watch your mouth."

"And if I don't?"

Greg jumped up, getting in between them. "Denise, chill. Tony, what's up with you?"

"She's coming at me like that. I didn't do anything."

"Fuck you! I'm outta of here."

"Dee!" Greg yelled, forcing her to chill and talk. He knew if Denise left there upset, Tony was as good as gone.

Greg took over the conversation and forced them to make up. Tony apologized for his behavior. On another note, Greg had to threaten Denise to let it go. After things calmed down, they had dinner as planned before leaving. Tony knew he had fucked up, so as Greg and Denise prepared to leave, he reached out and hugged her.

"Stop acting like that. You know I was just kidding, sis."

"Every joke has some truth in it," she warned, giving him a serious look.

Tony nodded.

While Tony put on a front as if nothing was bothering him, he was burning up inside. Not only did Denise embarrass him again, but Greg didn't do anything about it, which only meant they were hiding something. Either they had something to do with the killings or they knew the person that did. It was time to dismantle this friendship.

Chapter Fifteen
Christina

It wasn't any surprise that Tony didn't put up a fight when Christina asked for a divorce. He wanted out of their sham of a marriage just as much as she did. One thing that was going to be a problem for sure was getting him to give back all of her publishing rights. Being foolish, Christina had signed over seventy-five percent of her royalties to him.

Working on her third album, Christina flew out to Arizona to record some songs. Then it was off to China to promote her new clothing line. After China, she would be back on the set of her movie.

It was coming to the end of the day, and Christina was exhausted. She'd been working nonstop, getting three to five hours of sleep a night. All she wanted to do was order some food and cuddle up into Rashid's arm. Unfortunately, the cuddling with Rashid would have to wait because he was playing in Texas, and with school finals around the corner, she decided to order room service and get down to studying.

Knock! Knock!

"Señora, where shall I put your food?" the room service employee asked after Christina opened the door.

"Oh, put it on the table. Can you have someone bring me some more fresh towels, please?"

"Sure. I'll send the maid right up."

"Thanks."

Christina went back to studying, but a couple minutes later, there was another knock at the door. As she went to answer it, she thought, *This better not be Joyce.* It wasn't. It was Carmen, the housekeeper that worked for Tony.

Surprised, Christina said, "Carmen?"

"Señora Christina," Carmen replied in an unsure tone.

"Yes," Christina said, leading her inside the room. "Wow! It's so good to see you."

Carmen flashed an apprehensive smile and then ran into the bathroom to put the towels away. Baffled, Christina shrugged her shoulders and went back to studying.

When Carmen emerged from the bathroom, she asked, "Is there anything else you need, Señora Christina?"

Christina was about to respond, but noticed Carmen was shaking. "Are you okay?"

"I'm so sorry, Señora Christina. I tried…"

"Sorry about what?" Christina asked, staring at her.

"I…" Carmen said, then ran out of the room.

"Wait!" Christina yelled, but it was too late. Carmen had run out of there leaving Christina puzzled.

Shrugging it off, Christina went back to studying only to be interrupted by Rashid.

"Hey, daddy," she giggled.

"What's up?"

"Nothing. Just studying for my finals."

"Yeah, that makes two of us. Listen, the game is over, so since I have a day off, I was thinking…"

"Of course! I miss you," she whined.

He chuckled. "Alright, I'll be there tonight. It's probably gonna be late."

"So, come."

"I'm sure you're gonna make me."

They both laughed before hanging up.

Christina woke up in Rashid's arms. Since she didn't have to be on the set until that evening, they went on a shopping spree. As always, the fans and paparazzi didn't leave them alone, screaming and snapping pictures of them as they went in and out of stores. At one point, Rashid pleaded for them to stop. Christina, on the other hand, ignored them. As they left a boutique, Christina and Rashid held hands.

"So does this mean you're not with Tony?" a photographer asked.

Shooting a devilish smile, Christina responded, "Why don't you go and ask him?" Then she jumped into Rashid's car.

It wasn't ten minutes later when her publicist called her.

"Have you lost your mind?"

"Excuse me."

"Why are you parading around with Rashid?"

"Diana, if you must know, Tony and I are no longer together. We discussed it and decided to move on. I'm meeting with my lawyer when I get back to New York. Now you can prepare to release a formal statement."

Click!

"What's wrong?" Rashid asked.

"People...I can't wait for this divorce to be over."

To avoid any more unwanted attention, Rashid and Christina stayed at his place until it was time for her to go to the movie set. However, Rashid stayed behind to rest.

Being a perfectionist, Christina nailed her scenes the first time. It was going on three o'clock in the morning when the director called it a wrap.

Worn out, Christina headed back to her hotel, and while on her way up to her room, she saw Carmen. Their eyes met briefly before Carmen ran away again. Something was definitely up, but Christina was too tired to find out.

Winding down, Christina laid in bed flicking through the channel, when she came across *Panache Entertainment Report*.

"After seven years together, Christina and Tony Flowers have decided to call it quits. Stay tuned for more details about their break-up and how they are gonna split their huge fortune," the reporter said.

Christina jumped up. *Oh shit,* she thought. She didn't know Diana would put it out there so fast. She phoned her immediately.

"Hello," Diana answered.

"Why did you put that out there without consulting me first?" Christina barked.

"What? Aren't you the one who told me to release a statement? I only did what you told me to do. What's the problem now?" Diana asked.

"Tony! He didn't want anyone to know yet. I told you to *prepare* a statement, not actually release it."

"Well, it's too late now. I doubt he saw it anyway."

"Diana, be for real. Of course he's seen it, and if he didn't, someone in his camp did. I have to call him."

Click!

Christina dialed Tony, but it went straight to voicemail. "Call me. It's important. Diana released a statement about our split."

She then phoned Joyce, who was sleeping. "Joyce, it's out there. Diana released a statement about Tony and I."

Half asleep, Joyce responded, "Isn't that what you wanted?"

"Why does everyone keep saying that? I wanted to tell Tony first."

"Well, have you spoken to him?"

"No, and I don't want him to find out like this."

"Chris, please, everyone knows about you and Rashid, even Tony. He doesn't care. He probably has someone else, too. It's best that you strike first rather than him."

Christina thought about Joyce's statement. *Maybe she's right.* It was better that Christina put out a formal statement because it showed she had some class.

For the next few days, Christina and Tony were the talk of the town. Her fans were devastated. The golden couple was calling it quits. Many of the fans took sides, blasting each other, and even blog sites joined in.

On another note, Rashid loved it. He was considered *The Man* amongst his peers. People couldn't believe he had stolen Christina away from Tony Flowers. Sure, her record label management company was very displeased with her, but Christina didn't care. Right now, she was hot like fire. No one in the game could touch her, and the record company knew this. Therefore, they bit their tongues and went along with the program for the time being.

It was time to fly back to New York and deal with Tony. Surely, he had heard the news by now. You would've thought he would have picked up the phone and called Christina, but she knew it was all a part of Tony's game. He wanted to come out looking like the victim.

Christina couldn't even make it out of the airport before being greeted by a mob of reports. "Is that you?" a reporter yelled. Unaware of what the reporter was asking about, Christina and her team looked at each other and then jumped in their SUV's to drive off quickly. Simultaneously, everyone's BlackBerry smartphones started going off.

"Oh my God!" Christina yelled, while looking at pictures displayed on her BlackBerry. There were pictures of Paul and Christina having sex and pictures of Christina giving Rashid head. Embarrassed, Christina rushed into her apartment.

"Get Diana on the phone!" she ordered.

"It's all over the blog sites," Joyce said, scanning through her phone.

"Who would do this? How did they get those pictures? I have to call Rashid."

But, it was too late. Someone had already sent them to him.

"Hey," she cried.

"Hi. I've seen it. Is that your bodyguard?"

"Rashid, it's a long story. You have to let me explain," She replied as she continued crying.

"Calm down. When I get back, let's talk. Alright?"

"Yes. Thank you!"

"Hey, I love you. We'll get through this."

Christina nodded. "Okay," she said, then hung up. "Joyce, get me Panache. I wanna know who's behind this."

Panache was one of the hottest entertainment reporters. If Panache didn't know who you were, you weren't anyone. Panache and Christina had a good relationship, and she had been Christina's biggest support.

"Hi. It's Chris. Who's leaking all of this information? What the fuck is going on?"

Panache released a giggle. "I was about to ask you the same thing. First, I get a phone call from Diana giving me the exclusive, and then a couple hours later, I get some pictures of you."

"Who sent you the pictures?"

"That's the thing, Christina. I don't know. Are they real?"

Christina disregarded the question. "Panache, find out who sent you the pictures, please."

"I take it they are. Well, I'll put my team on it, but I want an exclusive with you."

"You got it!"

Christina couldn't believe this was happening. While trying to calm down, she put her thinking cap on, wondering who could've leaked those photos. Paul had been dead for years, and they were so careful when they were together.

"Your fans are saying the pictures are fake. They don't believe them," Joyce informed her.

"They are too delusional," Christina mumbled.

"So these pictures are real? You and Paul were together?" Joyce asked.

"Yes, we were engaged, and that was his baby I lost."

Joyce sat there with her mouth open. "You messed with Paul?"

"No, I was his fiancée. There's a difference," Christina sobbed, correcting her.

Joyce was about to respond, when Tia came in the room.

"Hey, have you seen Tony?"

"No," Joyce answered.

"Figures," Tia sarcastically grumbled, then noticed that Christina was clearly upset. "Did something happen?"

"Oh, you haven't heard about or seen the pictures?"

"What pictures?"

Joyce showed her.

"Oh my God! Is that...you and Paul?" Tia asked.

"Yes," Christina cried.

Tia shook her head. "Are these real?"

"Yes, I was seeing Paul."

"Wow! No wonder..." Tia started to say, putting two and two together.

"No wonder what?" Christina asked.

Catching her comment, Tia replied, "Nothing. Listen, tell Tony that I need to talk to him."

"Is everything okay?"

Tia stared at Christina. She knew Tony had leaked those photos.

"Well, I might as well tell you. I found a job in Miami."

"What!? Why?" Christina inquired.

Tia sighed. There was so much she wanted to tell Christina, but she couldn't betray Tony. Although she thought he was the scum of the earth, he believed in her when no one else did. However, she respected Christina. Even though Christina had cheated on Tony, Tia couldn't blame her. Tony had been dogging her out ever since they got together. He even went and married someone behind her back.

Tia took a seat next to Christina. "Chris, you know I've always loved and respected you, right?"

"Yes."

"I love Tony, too. He's been nothing but good to me. But, Chris...Tony...he's..." she said, catching herself again.

"He's an asshole," Christina said, finishing Tia's sentence.

"Asshole is an understatement. Let's just say I don't know him anymore. Chris, my advice to you is to leave Tony alone," she warned, looking at Christina and then at Joyce. Tia grabbed her bag and was about to leave, but stopped and turned around before exiting. "Those pictures were leaked by someone close to you. Once

you think about who would benefit from doing it, you'll have your answer. It wouldn't surprise me if Tony had his hand in it," Tia said, then left.

Joyce looked over at Christina with a puzzled expression. "You think Tony..."

"With him, anything is possible," Christina said, "but I doubt he knew about Paul and me."

"Well, something isn't right. He's been too quiet about y'all's break-up."

"I know he's up to something," Christina stated.

At the advice from her team, she stayed in the house until things cooled off. Although she had plans to attend Rashid's game in Philly, Diana told her that she needed to keep a low profile and finish up her album. For the first time, Christina agreed. Therefore, she lounged around the house and studied for her final exams.

This gave Diana time to release a power statement and threaten legal action. However, it was Tony who surprised everyone by not coming to Christina's defense. In fact, he, too, released a statement stating he doesn't comment on Christina's personal life. Christina chuckled when she read that. *The motherfucker doesn't even have the decency to support me.*

Since Christina had diehard fans, everything blew over quickly and became yesterday's news. Even though she announced her break-up with Tony, most of them believed she loved him more than he loved her. Either way, Christina had support from everyone. *Like everything else in Hollywood, this too shall pass.*

With Rashid having two days off, Christina decided to make him a nice home-cooked meal. While preparing a southern feast, Carmen and Tia popped into Christina's head. *Why did Carmen say she was sorry?* Thinking back, Christina found it strange that when she came back home from the hospital, Carmen was gone. *And Tia? What happened between her and Tony? Does she know something? Is Tony trying to sabotage my career?*

Chapter Sixteen
Denise

After that last incident, Denise started attending church. Once again, God had brought her through tough times, and she wanted to spiritually get closer to him. She had received so many blessings. Very few made it out of the ghetto, and most people that lived her lifestyle were either dead or in prison. That's why Denise knew it could only be the man above protecting her.

She also wanted to introduce her children to church. Growing up, her parents never read the Bible. Sadly, Denise didn't start reading the Bible until she was an adult. She always felt if she would've been involved in the church when she was younger, maybe things would've been different.

Derrick, on the other hand, was happy. He'd been begging Denise for years to attend. However, she would always brush him off, calling the people in church hypocrites.

Afterwards, Denise and Derrick took the kids to a café lounge in New Jersey to have brunch.

"You were feeling it in church, huh?" Derrick teased.

Denise giggled. "Yes, Sam was preaching today. I felt he was speaking directly to me."

"A lot of people did."

"I guess."

★ ★ ★ ★ 180

"Denise, are you okay?"

"What do you mean?"

"Some nights I hear you crying and pacing the floor," he told her.

"I'm thinking about my sister," she lied.

Truthfully, a whole lot of shit was running through Denise's mind. With that stuff concerning Moe and Millie, Denise was slowly slipping back into that lifestyle. On top of that, Denise couldn't believe Gabrielle was the one who killed Felicia. *I guess you never really know someone.*

Following brunch, Denise and Derrick took the kids to the movies and then to FOA Schwarz Toy Store since Lil' Derrick had been begging to go there for quite some time.

As they pulled up to their house, Denise noticed an unmarked car with New York plates parked out front. At first, she thought it was a hit, but when two people jumped out of the car, Denise knew it wasn't. In fact, she knew who they were. They were detectives from the 40th precinct.

"Denise Taylor," Detective Clyde greeted.

"Detective," Denise snidely answered.

Derrick looked over at Denise and then back at the detectives. "Is there a problem, officer?" he asked.

Glaring at the detectives, Denise said, "Derrick, take the kids into the house."

"Is there..."

"Derrick, just take them, please," Denise stated in a nice, yet stern voice.

Derrick looked at everyone. "Come on, guys. Denise, call me if you need me."

Denise nodded, flashing a forced grin. "So what can I do for you?" she asked, directing her question at Detective Clyde after her family had gone inside.

"Nice house. It's amazing what drug money can buy for a person," Detective Sharon stated sarcastically.

Denise smirked. Sharon had it in for Denise ever since she was a beat cop walking the streets. Years ago, Denise found out that

Sharon was messing with one of her workers, Dino. Sharon was open, so Denise used her to run a few packages across town and then ordered Dino to drop her. She was devastated and threatened to lock Denise and Dino up, but she changed her mind when Denise showed her pictures of her committing crimes.

"Detective Sharon, are we still playing in the hood?" Denise asked.

"That depends. Are you still killing people?"

Denise laughed. She knew Sharon was trying to get under her skin. "Anyway, what can I do for New York's finest?"

"You heard about Moe?" Detective Clyde asked, trying to defuse the tension between the two women.

"Yeah, I heard."

"And what about Bruce, Joe, and Millie?"

"No! What happened to them?" Denise asked.

"They were killed."

"Sorry to hear that. And you came to tell me this why?"

"Well, we know you and Millie were cool, but we have questions about Moe."

"What about him?"

"How was your relationship?" Detective Clyde inquired.

"Last time I checked, we were cool. I haven't seen Moe in a while. I'm not in that lifestyle no more."

"Bullshit, bitch!" Sharon blurted out in anger.

"What's wrong, Sharon? Are you still upset about Dino dumping you?"

"Fuck you and fuck him!"

"You did that to him, among other things."

"And what about you, Denise? You think just because you live up here in the suburb that makes you a model citizen? I wonder if your husband knows who he's married to. No matter where you go, you're still a fucking criminal."

"Is that so? Ummm, and what are you, Sharon? You know that's a two-way street, honey. Even on my worst day, I'm still better than you on your best. Always have been and always will be."

Fuming, Sharon jumped in Denise's face, with her hand resting on her gun and praying for Denise to give her a reason to use it. "You think you're funny, don't you? Let's see how funny you are when I put my gun down your throat, bitch."

"Clyde, you better get her. She's out of her jurisdiction, and I mean literally."

"My badge gives me the jurisdiction."

"Since you know me so well, Sharon, you should know I don't give a fuck about that badge. Clyde, get this bitch out of my face before I come out of retirement," Denise grumbled fiercely, while staring at Sharon.

Detective Clyde grabbed Sharon by the arm, pulling her away. "Sharon…"

Sharon took a deep breath and then backed up, pissed.

He diverted his attention back to Denise. "So, as I was saying, you and Moe were cool?"

Glaring at Sharon, Denise replied, "Yes, we alright. Why?"

"Because a witness said they saw a girl in the room just before Moe was shot, and I know these young cats are not going up against Moe. Since there are only a few girls I know who are capable…"

"You are coming to me…" Denise said, cutting him off.

"Yes. Denise, come on. You act like you haven't been down this road before. Sometimes old habits die hard."

"Well, I'm not in that life anymore. In case you haven't noticed, I'm married with kids. I've been out of the game over ten years now. You of all people should know that."

"Bullshit! Bitches like you never leave the game. It's in your blood," Sharon stated.

Denise glanced over in her direction. "How much are you making now? What, fifty thousand with overtime? Struggling to pay your bills? It's funny how life turns out for some of us. Here I am living the American Dream, with a husband and kids, while you, Sharon, are still fucking around with losers. So who's the bitch here?"

"Denise, do you know anyone that wanted to hurt Moe?" Detective Clyde asked, continuing with his questioning.

Pulling her eyes from Sharon, she looked over at Clyde. "No. Listen, I'm done answering your questions. If you don't have a warrant, get the fuck off my property," she said, walking away.

"Denise, trust me. We will find out," Clyde called out.

"So do that," she replied, not bothering to look back.

"Your day will come," Sharon said.

"It hasn't yet, but I bet you one thing. Yours will come first," Denise yelled back, then slammed the door.

She went straight to the bar to pour herself a drink, only to be confronted by Derrick.

"What was all that about?" Derrick asked with his arms folded.

"It's nothing. A friend of mine was killed a couple of months ago."

"And?"

"And nothing. They wanted to know if I knew anything about it."

"Well, did you know anything about it? Why would they think that?"

Denise screwed up her face. *Is he serious?* "Derrick..." she said, getting pissed off.

"Derrick my ass! For the past couple of months, you've been hiding something. Now the police are showing up at our door. I want some answers dammit!"

"You want some answers? Then go upstairs and ask your children, because the last time I checked I'm not one of them," Denise shot back, sipping on her drink.

"My children?" he repeated. "Fine," he said, storming away.

Denise sighed and sat on the couch. Just when things were starting to get better, Derrick gave Denise the silent treatment. She brushed that off, though. She was happy he wasn't speaking to her. This way, she didn't have to answer his questions.

*****

Sitting in her office the next day, Denise laughed at Detective Sharon. *The nerve of that hoe.* While shaking her head, she giggled and said, "God, I'm trying."

Denise informed Greg, but they had already spoken to him. *Cocksuckers. Same ole Clyde; he's always fishing for shit.* Unfortunately, he was up against a veteran. One thing for sure, Denise didn't fold under pressure. After a couple of meetings, she called it a day, but instead of going straight home, she decided to drive through her old neighborhood. Something told Denise that the rumors were coming from there. Not wanting to attract a lot of attention to herself, she drove to 125th Street, parked, and then hopped on the train.

Damn, things had changed so much since Denise and her crew ran the streets. As she walked, all she could do was shake her head in disgust. *This generation is sad.* Dudes were walking around with a body full of tattoos and skinny jeans hanging off their asses, fronting and thinking they were Lil' Wayne or 50 Cent. The girls were the worst. *Doesn't anybody work out any more?* Some of them looked like they had about ten kids, and many of them probably did. It was dead winter, and everyone seemed to be wearing "two sizes too small" jackets with jeans to match. Every other word out of their mouths was either yo, bitch, son, and Denise's favorite, my nigga. *If these kids knew how stupid they sound, or the history behind it, they would stop talking like that.* The females were harder than the dudes, and what was going on with everyone wanting to be gay? Only if these teenagers knew that being gay is a lifestyle not a fade. Most of them did things just to fit in or be different. While it was like that when Denise was going up, she remembered them being a little more discreet. For Denise, it wasn't what you do, but how you do it.

Walking past a few buildings she owned, she shook her head. It was a mess. There was garbage in front, and someone had broken the glass to the front door. Denise pulled out her BlackBerry and sent the property manager a nasty email. She decided she needed to visit her properties more often. Finally, she was in front of the infamous Melrose Projects. Smiling, she reflected on the past. This was the place Denise once called home.

Going into her favorite bodega, Denise asked the clerk, "Is Mohammed here?"

"Yes. He's in the back."

"Denise Taylor?" an older lady blurted out.

Denise turned around to see Mrs. Davis, her junior high school teacher, standing there.

"Mrs. Davis." Denise smiled and gave her a kiss on the cheek.

"My God, I had a dream about you the other day."

"Really?! I can't believe you remember me."

"Now why wouldn't I? You gave me so much hell." Mrs. Davis laughed.

Denise blushed. "I didn't mean to. You know, I was a kid."

"It's fine! How are you doing? You look good."

"I'm great. I got married and have two beautiful children."

"I always knew you would be okay. That's why I fought with those cops for them to un-cuff you. Remember?"

One night, the police ran up on Denise and found some drugs. They had her in handcuffs and were ready to put her in the squad car, when Mrs. Davis came out of the school and begged them to release Denise. Since the officers knew Mrs. Davis, they complied. Once they were gone, Mrs. Davis made Denise promise to get her life together. It took a couple of years, but Denise kept her promise.

"Yeah, I remember."

"What happened to your friends, Denise? I know about Tony, but what happened to the rest of them?"

"The ones that are still alive are doing well. Greg's married, has kids, and owns a few restaurants and clubs. Perry and Paul died years ago, but Mike is good. And as you already said, you know about Tony."

"Yeah, I know about Tony. You know, I never liked him. He always seemed to be sneaky."

"Tony?"

"Yes. You better watch out for him. He's no good. I get bad vibes when I'm around him."

Denise nodded. "Okay, I will."

"Denise!" Mohammed yelled, emerging from the back.

"Hey Mohammed!" Smiling, Denise hugged him.

"Listen, Denise, you take care of yourself, and don't be no stranger. You hear me?" Mrs. Davis said.

"I promise." Denise kissed her on the cheek again.

"And I wanna see those babies next time," Mrs. Davis added before leaving the store.

"So you heard about Bruce, Joe, and Millie?" Mohammed said.

Denise laughed. "Yeah, I heard about them."

"Oh and Moe, too," he said. "And to think I just saw him."

"You did?"

"Yes. He was here with Mike maybe a day or two before he died. They came in to get a sandwich. They were asking if I heard anything about Greg's clubs being robbed. I told them no."

Before Mohammed started asking a thousand questions, Denise started back home.

*****

Tony gave Tia a farewell party, inviting Denise and Greg. Although she didn't feeling up to it, Denise went anyway. Since they weren't fans of being in the limelight, Greg and Denise chilled upstairs in a private section, smirking at everyone. Unlike everyone else, Denise and Greg didn't wear any bling expect for their wedding bands. One thing she learned years ago was that being flashy attracted a lot of attention.

"How are you doing, sis?" Greg asked.

"Meaning?"

"With everything. Last time we saw each other, shit was hot."

"Come on, Greg. You know I'm fine."

Denise wanted to share what Gabrielle had told her, but that wasn't her style. If Greg found out it was Gabrielle, he would hit the roof and probably kill her ass for being stupid and especially for not telling him.

"Are you? You can tell me."

"Who you think really killed Felicia?"

"I don't know. Why?" he asked.

"Just a question."

"Denise, questions like that already have answers. Do you know something I don't know?"

Unable to lie, Denise turned away. "I got an eerie feeling about that night."

"Talk to me."

Greg was sharp as the Board of Health. Therefore, she needed to choose her words carefully.

"I don't think Moe was her brother."

"Yeah, I was thinking that after one of his mans told me that he grew up with him."

"Damn, so Felicia's brother is still out there? I'm telling you, Greg, shit is close to home."

Both looked at each other before Greg replied, "It's only a few of us left."

"What's good?" Mookie yelled, while approaching them. "This is Olay."

They both nodded.

"Hey, what's up?" Greg replied, greeting the young lady.

"Damn, I'm surprised to see y'all here," Mookie commented.

"Sometimes we come out to support," Greg said with a chuckle.

"Yeah, and to watch these fronting ass people," Denise snidely added.

"Fronting?" Olay repeated in a nasty tone.

"Yes, fronting," Denise snapped, staring at her.

"Do you know who we are?"

Denise looked her up and down. *Is she serious? She better check her history and read about the real gangster,* she thought to herself before saying, "Mookie, get this bird out of here before I..."

Olay stepped forward and was about to wild out, but Mookie stopped her. She didn't have a clue, and judging by Denise's looks, she would soon find out.

"Anyway...Mookie, I'm going to the other side with the rich and famous people. Too many broke-ass haters over here."

Denise laughed. "Haters? Honey, stick to rapping and sucking dick."

"Excuse me! Bitch, do you know who I am? I'll pay someone to pop your top off."

"Send them," Denise replied in a laidback tone, then took a sip of her drink.

"I will knock…"

Mookie covered Olay's mouth before she could finish her sentence and escorted her out.

"Mookie, get your artist, because this isn't a gangster video shoot," Denise told him.

Greg sighed. "It's always something," he said, laughing.

"Fuck her! Let's be real, though. These people in here are fake."

"Yeah, but that's the world. You know how that shit goes."

"I guess, but fuck her. She's lucky Mookie grabbed her ass."

They both laughed.

"What's going on?" Tony asked, walking up on them. "Thanks for coming out. You don't know how much this means to me, for real."

Greg smiled. "Anytime."

Denise, on the other hand, flashed a fake smile. Ever since Tony showed his ass at his house, she hadn't been feeling him, which Tony sensed.

"What's up, Dee?"

"I'm good." Denise glared at him, then smiled.

"You're not still mad at a nigga, are you?"

"Dogs get mad," Denise shot back. "We're good."

Greg looked at Denise. Normally, he would've checked her, but he was getting bad vibes from Tony, too. Maybe Denise was on to something when she commented on whether Tony was the same person. People like Tony believed money brought them power, and Greg knew he always envied Denise on the low.

Greg was about to say something, when Detectives Clyde and Sharon walked up on them.

"What's up? Can we go some place and talk?" Detective Clyde asked.

"Is there a fucking problem?" Tony angrily blurted out.

Detective Clyde replied, "Listen, either you can go with us willingly or by force. You choose one."

Denise and Greg looked at each other and smirked. Both thought, *Fucking police.*

To humiliate Denise, Sharon handcuffed her. "I told you this badge gave me the fucking jurisdiction, bitch," she mumbled, tightening the cuffs.

Denise shook her head. She didn't bother putting up a fight, because the day would come when she would see Sharon again.

Furious, Tony left the party to follow them. At the police station, the detectives grilled them about the murders. Ironically, they didn't think Greg and Denise did it. However, they knew Greg and his crew knew who killed them.

As always, Denise and Greg gave them nothing. Actually, they found it hilarious. Once the detectives realized they weren't going to talk, they released them with a formal warning.

Outside of the station house, Greg snapped. "Where the fuck is this heat coming from?"

Shaking her head, Denise replied, "I don't know."

"Well, we need to find out. Someone is playing a fucking deadly game."

Denise sighed. She knew by the tone of Greg's voice that it was only going to get worse.

Chapter Seventeen
Gabrielle

Still not on speaking terms with Greg, Gabrielle threw herself into work and her kids. It was the only way she could keep her mind off of him. A part of her wanted to call him and say she was sorry, but her pride wouldn't let her. In her eyes, she didn't think she had done anything wrong. In fact, she was upset Greg hadn't thanked her yet.

Meanwhile, this didn't affect their relationship with the kids. That evening, they were taking the kids to see the lighting of the tree at Rockefeller Center. It would have been nice if Denise and her kids came along, but since that night Gabrielle cursed her out, they hadn't spoken. That was another thing Gabrielle was scared about. What if Denise said something to Greg?

Surprisingly, Tony and Morgan were joining them. While everyone thought it was sweet, Gabrielle didn't like the idea of Tony spending so much time with Morgan and her kids. It just didn't feel right in Gabrielle's opinion.

Greg was already downstairs in the car with the kids, so Gabrielle shut off her computer and headed out.

"Hi, Gail and Greg," Gabrielle said, smiling as she got in the car.

"Hi, Mommy!" they yelled.

"Hi, Boo," she said, looking at Greg.

"What's up?" he responded, staring at his wife.

On the ride downtown, Greg and Gabrielle barely said two words to each other. She talked to the kids while Greg focused on traffic. Since it was freezing outside, Greg dropped Gabrielle and the kids off while he went to park.

"Gabrielle!" Morgan shouted, coming down the block with the kids.

"Hi!" They kissed. "Oh my God, Morgan, London is so pretty. She looks just like you."

Morgan smiled. "I know. Tell me about it. She is so bad, Gabrielle. She touches everything."

They both laughed.

"Tell me about it. Gail thinks she's my mother. Say hello to Morgan."

"Hi," the two children said in unison.

"Hello," Morgan said back to them.

"Where's Lil' Anthony?"

"He's with Tony."

Gabrielle frowned. "Hmm," she responded, causing Morgan to laugh. "So how is the infamous Tony doing? I heard he's been really helping you out."

"Yeah, he's been a big help."

"I bet. Well, be careful with him, Morgan."

Gabrielle was about to say something else, but Tony and Greg joined them.

"Hey, Gabrielle," Tony said.

"Hi," she grumbled in response to his greeting, causing Morgan to look at him strangely.

*****

After their outing, Greg dropped Gabrielle and the kids off. He was about to drive off, but Lil' Greg didn't want him to leave. So, while Greg got them ready for bed, Gabrielle went into her office to finish up some work.

As Greg was heading out, he yelled from the foyer, "I'm leaving."

"What?" she said, coming out of her office.

"I'm leaving," he repeated.

Unsure of what to say, Gabrielle asked, "Are the kids sleeping?"

Greg nodded. "Yeah."

As he was turning the knob on the door, Gabrielle reached for his arm. "Boo," she mumbled.

He turned toward her and asked, "What's up?"

"I'm sorry," she said, then leaned forward to kiss him.

Horny, Greg grabbed his wife by her waist. "So am I," he moaned, while kissing her back.

Right there in the foyer, Greg and Gabrielle had the best make-up sex ever. Finally, things were back to normal. Greg was home, and the kids were healthy. What more could Gabrielle ask for?

*****

On her way out of the courthouse, Denise popped into Gabrielle's head. It had been weeks since they had spoken. That was her favorite cousin; it's because of Denise that Gabrielle met the love of her life. Gabrielle sighed. It was time to make amends. She thought about calling, but knowing Denise, she would hang up or not answer. Therefore, she headed over to her office. Denise's assistant announced Gabrielle's arrival.

"Hey!" Gabrielle smiled.

Still pissed off, Denise responded, "You have a lot of fucking nerve coming to my office. What can I do for you?"

Gabrielle looked around, then down at the floor. She knew Denise wasn't going to be that forgiving. "Dee, I'm sorry…"

Denise cut her off. "Sorry about what? That you killed someone or that you threatened me?"

Taking a seat, Gabrielle stated in a defensive tone, "I was drunk and upset."

"You accused me of telling Greg something I didn't. Tony told Greg!" Denise said loudly.

"Tony knows? I didn't know that," Gabrielle mumbled, staring at the floor.

Denise sighed while glaring at Gabrielle. "Yeah, I told him years ago. I didn't know he was gonna tell Greg, though."

"He was upset that I reached out to her and lied," Gabrielle confessed.

With her hands folded and lips poked out, she responded, "You lied about a lot of shit."

"Like?"

"Like killing people. Gab, do you know what you did? By your ass lying, it caused other people to get hurt. This is not a game here. This is life! I take this shit seriously."

"And I don't? Why you think I wanted to kill her ass? Because she was playing with my husband's life."

"Yeah, but why didn't you tell me? I could've went to prison for this shit. You don't go and kill on someone else's playground unless you tell them. Shit like that could get you killed."

Gabrielle lowered her head. Denise was right. What if something had gone wrong?

"Denise..." Gabrielle whined. "I know I was wrong, and I'm sorry."

Denise took a deep breath. "You don't get it. Sorry is too late. You don't even understand what you have done."

"I do. She's gone, so what's the big deal? No one knows."

"The big problem, Gabrielle, is Perry. Because of you, Perry is dead. I killed Perry thinking he was Felicia's brother. That's the problem. I killed my brother."

"What? Oh, Dee! I..."

"What?" Denise's eyes began tearing up. "I killed my brother. How can I forgive you?" she said, and then left her office.

Gabrielle dropped her head. "Damn..."

After leaving Denise, Gabrielle felt like shit. She wanted to go home, but had to finish up some last-minute paperwork.

"Good afternoon, Nancy. Any messages?"

"A few. Kyle canceled dinner. He was called away on business."

"Thank God," Gabrielle said, walking into her office.

She looked at her watch. *Shit! It's almost three o'clock, and I still have a lot of work to do.* She called an emergency meeting with her staff. Following the meeting, Gabrielle got down to business. She only had a couple more days to prepare for court, and she was way behind schedule.

By the time she looked at the time on her computer, it was going on seven o'clock. As she was gathering her things, Nancy spoke to her through the intercom.

"Boss lady?"

"Yes, Nancy."

"Christina is here to see you."

Gabrielle sighed. "Send her in."

"Hi."

"Hello."

"Did Tony's lawyer call you?"

"No," Gabrielle said.

Confused, Christina said, "So no one called you on his behalf?"

"No. Why?"

"Because we talked a couple of weeks ago and decided to get a divorce. Didn't you hear about it? It was all over the news."

Surprised, Gabrielle replied, "Sorry I don't have time to watch the news. So Tony is aware of this?"

Christina giggled. "Yes, we're on the same page. I just wanna make sure I get what's mine. I wanna move on with my life."

Frowning, Gabrielle responded, "You sure you discussed this with Tony?"

"There's nothing to discuss. In fact, I never should've married him, but that's another story. I'm ready to move on."

"Alright, because the last time my office worked their asses off for you..."

"I know. I've been thinking about it for years now, ever since we came back from the Bahamas."

Gabrielle froze. "Wait! You were married in the Bahamas, right?"

"Yeah," she said in an unsure voice.

Gabrielle ran over to her file cabinet to search for Christina's file. *Got it,* she thought. Gabrielle scanned through it.

"Chris, did you and Tony ever apply for a marriage license in the United States?"

"No, we never got around to it. Why?"

"Christina, this means you and Tony are not legally married."

Christina's eyes widened. "I don't understand."

"Although you had a ceremony in the Bahamas, you're still not legally married in the U.S. The United States doesn't recognize your marriage to Tony."

"So now what?"

"Nothing. You don't need to apply for a divorce."

"But we have so much together in our name."

"That's nothing."

"So all of this time I wasn't legally married to Tony?"

"Nope!"

"That's great. So now I just have to remove him from my career."

"What do you mean?"

"Tony owns most of my publishing," Christina told her.

Gabrielle went back to her file cabinet. "Christina, do you remember signing a three-sixty deal?"

Christina shrugged her shoulders. "I signed so many papers. Why?"

"Here." She handed Christina a copy. "Tony gave this to me a couple of years ago. It's a three-sixty deal. It's a deal that states no matter what Tony will always profit from you."

"Not my modeling career, right?" she asked.

"Yes, everything."

Fuming, Christina asked Gabrielle to help her get out of the deal. Gabrielle agreed to help, but she knew it wasn't going to be easy. She gave Christina a copy before walking her out.

Tony will have a hard time explaining this one, Gabrielle thought and laughed.

* * * * *

It was that time again. Gabrielle called Nancy into her office so they could plan the twins' birthday party.

"Okay, Nancy, here's the list of everyone. Please send an email blast to them with the date."

Nancy reviewed the listing and then replied, "Alright. Is there anything special I should add?"

"Nah, it's a kid's party."

Nancy nodded and left.

Just as Gabrielle was about to make a phone call, Nancy busted back in the office. "Oh my God, you know her?!" she shouted.

Startled, Gabrielle jumped up from her seat. "Know who?"

"The girl that's dating Tony. Here's her email."

Gabrielle looked. "It has to be a mistake."

"No. Here are the emails she sent me. I haven't heard from her in a while, but look. It's the same one."

"Do you know her?" Nancy asked.

"No, I don't," Gabrielle lied.

"I got this mailing list from the kids' school, so it could be a mistake. You know how email addresses can look very similar. In fact, scratch that email off the list."

Oh my God, it can't be, she thought.

Chapter Eighteen
Morgan

Morgan was moving fast up the ladder in her firm. Being that she was a quick learner, her boss promoted her to Senior Legal Assistant, and with that new position was a huge pay increase. All the assistants on Morgan's floor now reported to her. A lot of the women in the office were already jealous of her, but once they found out she was making over seventy thousand dollars, the rumors started. Morgan just laughed them off; they were so high school.

Things got better at home. Tony realized Morgan wasn't going to leave him, even after all the bullshit he had done. So happy that she came back home, Tony allowed her to take the kids to Italy. It was either let her take them or lose them again, and that was something he didn't want to go through. He wasn't too happy about his kids visiting their grandfather in prison, but Morgan didn't pay him any attention. *He'll get over it,* she thought.

The kids were growing up so fast. London was a year old going on twenty-one, and Lil' Anthony was nineteen months and bad as hell. She felt it was the perfect time for them to get to know her side of the family and understand where they got their looks from, which was something her mother kept from her. There were days Morgan wished she was close with her cousins on her father's side. Maybe she would've confided in them.

They weren't off the plane yet before Tony started calling to the point where Morgan turned off her cell phone. Morgan and the kids had a blast. Her family embraced the kids and spoiled them to death. Strangely, Morgan always felt at home around them, whereas her visit with her father was a different story.

Felix apologized for his situation and not being there for her during her time of need. However, he expressed his disappointment with her about having kids out of wedlock. Again, this was the perfect opportunity for Morgan to tell the truth. While Felix probably would've been upset, at least he would know the truth. But, Tony told her to wait.

Her grandmother knew Morgan was lying, though, because when Morgan tried to tell her the same thing, she abruptly cut her off and indirectly called her a liar. Once Morgan sensed her grandmother's vibes, she left the subject alone.

Arriving back in the states, Tony personally picked them up at a private airport in New Jersey. Exhausted from their trip, the kids went straight to sleep when they got home. Tony was thirsty to make love. Morgan was tired, but she knew if she didn't, all hell would break loose.

She'd been gone from her job for only a week, but the work was piled up. After placing a few calls and scheduling some meetings, Morgan checked her private email account. She had an email from Gabrielle about the twins' party. Morgan replied, letting her know she and the kids would be attending. She was just about to log off when Gabrielle responded, asking to meet her for dinner that evening. Morgan sighed. It was short notice, and she was still worn out from her trip to Italy. Also, Tony was leaving in the morning to Africa to finish up some rescheduled dates from his tour. Morgan declined and told her Friday would be a better day. Gabrielle agreed to meet her on Friday.

Friday rolled around, and Morgan prepared herself to meet with Gabrielle for dinner. She found it strange that Gabrielle wanted to have dinner with her since they were never close, but she went anyway. It was nice to get out the house. She knew Tony would ask the same thing if she would've told him about their date, so she lied, telling him that she was working late.

They met at some restaurant in the city with Morgan arriving first. Moments later, Gabrielle and another young lady walked in.

"Sorry, Morgan," Gabrielle said, kissing her on the cheek.

Morgan smiled. "It's okay. I just got here myself."

"This is my girlfriend, Stevie."

"Hello," Stevie said with a smile.

"Hi."

"So where are the kids?" Gabrielle asked.

"They are with the babysitter. I'm picking them up afterwards."

"Oh, you mean Tony isn't watching them?"

Morgan laughed. "Not tonight."

The ladies laughed and talked throughout dinner. Morgan didn't know Gabrielle was so funny chatting about everything from Barack Obama to *American Idol*.

As the night was coming to an end, Gabrielle said, "Morgan, I have something I wanna ask you."

"Sure."

She reached in her bag, pulling out a piece of paper. "Is this your email address?"

Morgan looked at it. "Yes."

"How long have you had this email address?"

"I don't know...for years, I guess. Why?"

Gabrielle looked over at Stevie, and both nodded. Gabrielle went in her bag again. "Someone using your email address sent these emails to a friend of mine."

Morgan read them and almost died. *Oh my God,* she thought. "That's not..."

"Morgan," Gabrielle whispered in a serious tone.

"They are not mine. You called me here for that?" she snapped in a scared tone.

"No..."

"Morgan, I dated Tony," Stevie chimed in, getting Morgan's full attention. "We met when he was in the drug game. He used to come out to Atlanta to hustle. One thing led to another, and before I knew it, I was living in New York. It was wonderful in the beginning. Tony was every woman's dream, but like every dream, there's a nightmare lurking. At first, he isolated me from my friends and family, complaining that I spent too much time with them."

Morgan was silent as tears rolled down her face.

Stevie continued. "Then the cheating started. Every night, a different girl called my phone saying she had just finished fucking my man. When I confronted him, he denied it. I threatened to leave him, and from there on it got worse."

Closing her eyes, Morgan couldn't believe what she was hearing. Although she didn't say anything, her tears confirmed that Tony was doing the same thing to her.

"Morgan, you have to tell your aunt," Gabrielle suggested.

"No...I can't."

"You have to. How long do you think you can keep this lie up?" Gabrielle asked.

"Morgan, we will go with you," Stevie offered, reaching out to touch her hand.

Afraid that Morgan would change her mind, Gabrielle located Denise, who was at her apartment. Trembling, Morgan started having second thoughts the closer they got to the door, and she became nausea.

"I have to get the kids," she said, trying to turn away.

"Morgan...you have to tell her," Gabrielle told her, knocking on the door.

Denise opened the door wearing her coat. "Yes," she answered, but when she saw Gabrielle standing there, she added, "I'm on my way out."

Gabrielle forced her back inside. "No, you're not. We have something to tell you."

"I don't have time for you tonight," she said, not realizing Morgan and Stevie were with Gabrielle.

"Denise…" Stevie said, getting Denise's attention, "we need to talk."

She was about to say something when she saw Morgan.

"Morgan…" she said in a concerned tone.

Morgan, whose face was flustered from crying, flashed a weak smile. "Hi, Auntie."

Denise glanced at all of them and knew something was wrong. So, she led them into the living room.

"Alright, what's up?" she said, removing her coat.

Gabrielle and Stevie looked over at Morgan for her to say something. Frightened, Morgan had her head down. Denise looked over at them and then back at Morgan.

"Morgan, what's up?" she asked.

Trembling, Morgan shook her head. "Aunt Denise…" she said, then paused for a few moments. "Remember that night when I came home from school telling you that I was accepted into the Harvard Law School Summer Program?"

Vaguely remembering, Denise closed her eyes and thought back to that night. "Somewhat."

"You were here drinking with Tony."

"Oh yeah, I remember. That's the night I got locked up."

Morgan's eyes widened. "You were locked up?" she said, hoping to change the subject.

"Yes. Why?" Denise asked, wanting to know where Morgan was going with her statement.

"Well, that night, Tony…he…he…," she hesitated.

"Tony what?" Denise asked, scared.

"He raped me!" Morgan cried.

The room froze with Morgan's words. Gabrielle and Stevie held their breath. Denise, on the other hand, wasn't sure if she had heard Morgan correctly. Therefore, she repeated it.

"You said he raped you?"

"Yes, he came into my room and raped me."

Denise closed her eyes tightly to avoid the tears from dropping. She felt like someone had just shot her in the back and paralyzed

 202

her. She was able to hear and speak, but couldn't move. Gabrielle and Stevie put their hands over their mouths in disbelief.

"He raped me, and he said if I ever told anyone, he would kill my family."

"So that's why you had kids by the first guy you met?" Gabrielle said with a hint of sarcasm.

"No...Tony is the father of my kids. He didn't stop. Every day, he would pick me up, take me to this house, and have sex with me. I tried to stop him, but he would beat me."

Still stunned, Denise mumbled, "That's why you had all those bruises?"

"Yes. When I turned sixteen, we got engaged. He came to my sixteenth birthday party. Remember, I told you that I was gonna spend the night with Chloe, but it was him."

"Oh my God, Morgan, why didn't you say something?" Gabrielle said.

"I wanted to. You don't know how many nights I wanted to run in there and tell you, Aunt Denise, but I was scared—scared that Tony would kill you. He promised me that as long as I did what he said, everything would be okay. That's why I married him and had his children."

"You're married to Tony?" Denise asked calmly.

"Yes." She looked away in shame. "He won't let me go. He said I'm his forever."

This was so surreal. Denise needed a moment to collect her thoughts, so she got up and went to the window while everyone watched in silence. Leaning her head on the window, she thought about Jasmine's last words. *He hurt my baby.*

"Jas knew," Denise muttered in a soft voice.

"What?" Gabrielle said.

Denise turned around. "Jas, she knew. On her deathbed, the last words she uttered were 'he hurt my baby'. For months, I didn't know what she was talking about."

"I told her just before you came in the room, because she kept blaming herself for my mistakes."

Denise hit her head against the window, trying to conceal her pain. "I had no idea," she voiced, getting choked up.

"I'm sorry, Auntie, but I was so afraid that he would kill you," Morgan explained while walking over to Denise.

Staring into her niece's eyes, she grabbed her tightly and cried, "I'm so sorry. Oh my God, I'm sorry."

Clearly, Denise remembered that night. It was the night she had an argument with Morris and ran out of there, leaving Tony in the apartment.

"I found it strange that he was still there when I got back, but I just figured he was watching you," she cried, squeezing Morgan. "DAMN! It's okay. He won't hurt you again. I promise."

Gabrielle and Stevie looked at each other and shook their heads.

Morgan pulled back from Denise. "Auntie, he's my children's father," she explained.

Denise was about to respond, but caught herself. She remembered those white girls in her building seeing Tony's driver a couple of years ago. It was all starting to make sense now. He was taking care of his own kids.

Mutherfucker, Denise thought. "Morgan, did anyone know about this besides you?"

"Al, Mookie, and Tia."

"All of them knew about you and Tony?" Gabrielle asked, shocked.

"Yes. Al would pick me up and take me to Tony."

"So Al drove you to the house?" Denise nodded.

"Yes, and Mookie took me to have an abortion."

"You had an abortion?" Denise asked.

"Yes, when I was fifteen years old."

"Morgan, how old was you when he raped you?" Stevie asked.

"I was fourteen."

"He's been doing this since you were fourteen? He's a sick bastard," Gabrielle said.

"How in the fuck did he manage to pull this off? So Anthony and London are his kids? And you're married to him?" Denise said, thinking out loud.

"Oh shit! Anthony is Tony's real name," Stevie informed them. "His name is Anthony Omar Flowers."

"Yep, and we were married a day after my eighteenth birthday."

"How? Isn't he married to Christina?" Denise asked, still stunned.

"So that's why he didn't marry her," Gabrielle mumbled.

"What?" Denise said.

"Christina came to my office. She wanted to file for a divorce, but it turns out that she and Tony were never married."

"That's impossible, Gab. I went to their wedding," Denise protested.

"You're right. You did go to a wedding, but they never applied for their marriage certificate. Boy, Tony is one slick son of a bitch, I tell ya."

Denise glowered at them. "He's slick alright."

Desperately trying not to show her emotions, Denise apologized to Morgan repeatedly, letting her know she was safe now. Having gone through so much in her life, Denise would've never expected this. As they continued to talk, Denise kept fighting back tears while Morgan shared the gruesome details. There were times when she would close her eyes, thinking about how much pain Morgan had gone through. But, most of all, how much pain Tony was about to endure.

Staring at Morgan, she thought about how Jasmine was probably looking down on her and hurting. Jasmine had trusted Denise, and look what happened. Denise thought about her little girl and someone raping her. All of a sudden, Denise got hot and her body started to quiver. Praying in her mind that this was all a dream, she closed her eyes and went back over to the window. *Please, God, wake me up from this dream.* Sadly, it wasn't. Tony Flowers had betrayed her.

"We need to go to the police," Stevie stated.

"No," Morgan said, causing everyone to look at her. "I mean, I don't want him to go to jail."

"Morgan, what he did to you was wrong." Gabrielle got up and grabbed her. "He needs..."

"Morgan is right. No police," Denise said. "What's done is done. Is he hitting you now?"

Besides, Denise was about to deliver more justice to Tony than any law enforcement could do.

"No, he's actually nice. I know it's crazy, but we're a family. He's my children's father. I can't turn him in," she said before going to the bathroom.

"She's just as sick as him," Stevie grumbled.

"No, she's suffering from Stockholm Syndrome and probably Battered Women Syndrome among other things," Gabrielle explained.

A thousand things were running through Denise's mind. Looking over at Gabrielle, she stated, "We're not going to the police. I can't believe Tony. This is not like him."

Gabrielle looked over in Stevie's direction, signaling her to tell Denise why she left Tony.

"Denise," Stevie said, standing up, "do you know why I left Tony? It wasn't because he was cheating. Tony abused me. He blackened my eyes, busted my lips, and even raped me at times."

Dumbfounded, Denise rubbed her forehead. "What? He did that to you? Why didn't you say anything?"

"I was ashamed and thought no one would believe me, just like Morgan."

"I knew y'all fought, but I didn't know he was doing all of that."

"No one knew. Gabrielle found out because she popped up on me and saw my face."

Denise looked over at Gabrielle, who confirmed it with a nod.

"So that's why you never liked him, Gab? This is crazy. First Felicia and now Tony," Denise said.

"Felicia? What does Felicia have to do with this?" Stevie asked.

"You know Felicia?" Gabrielle asked.

"Yeah, she's Tony's sister."

"What!?" Denise said.

"She's Tony's sister," Stevie repeated.

"That's impossible. I know Tony's father."

"No, Denise, that's Tony's stepfather."

Denise damn near passed out. "Now it's all starting to make sense."

"You didn't know Felicia was his sister? I went to their father's funeral," Stevie told her.

"Are you sure we're talking about the same person?" Denise said.

"Grant Tiger was his name. He was stabbed to death in his Bronx apartment."

"Yeah, that's him. Stinkin' motherfucker. So it was him that Felicia was talking about when she said her and her brother wanted revenge for their father's death. Fuck! I would've never thought in a million years," Denise said, thinking hard. "You know, I was thinking he did this to Morgan because Jasmine dumped him."

"Tony dated my mother?" Morgan asked, entering the room.

"Yes. They messed around years ago, nothing sexually. He was hurt when Jas dumped him for Theodore," Denise explained, not even realizing what she was saying.

Once again, silence filled the room, and then Denise's cell phone rang. It was Derrick. She answered and told him that she was on her way. After Denise hung up, Morgan informed them that she and Tony had plans on letting everyone know about them; however, they were just waiting for the right time.

Now composed, Denise instructed Morgan to go back home, but for her not to say a word about what took place. She knew if she went hysterical, it would scare Morgan. She also made Morgan write down the place where she had the abortion and the names of everyone who was involved.

Gabrielle and Stevie were astonished by Denise's reaction, but stayed quiet.

Before departing, Denise hugged her niece one more time and assured her things would work out.

"Aunt Dee, what are you going to do?"

Emotionless, Denise did one of Greg's numbers by calmly replying, "Nothing. I'm going to wait for you guys to tell me," she said, but thought, *I'm going to kill everyone that was involved. Anyone that knew about it, I'm going to kill.* Morgan wasn't aware that the devil was there!

*****

The next couple of days were hard for Morgan. She could not believe Tony dated her mother in the past. To get her mind off of everything, she took the kids to the park. While sitting there watching them, Morgan wondered why Denise asked her to write down everyone's name.

After a while, it began to get dark, and Lil' Anthony was starting to get cold. When they arrived back home, Tony was there.

"What's up, babe?" he said, kissing her.

Unable to hold it in, Morgan turned her face. "Why didn't you tell me about you and my mother?"

Stumped, Tony replied, "What are you talking about?" while removing his son's boots.

"You and my mother—y'all used to date," she replied in a firm tone.

"I didn't think I had to," he said in an unsure tone.

"You didn't think you had to? Really!" Morgan snapped. "What else are you hiding?" she said, then grabbed the kids and went upstairs.

Just as she was told, Morgan didn't say a word about the things she found out. In fact, it tickled her pink that Tony's ass walked around on pins and needles. Prior to all of this, Morgan and Tony had planned to spend Christmas at one of their many houses in Aspen, Colorado. He hoped the holiday season would cheer Morgan up. As always, Morgan arrived there first with the kids. The place was decorated like something out of a magazine. Tony had gone all out. The kids went crazy, running and touching everything, making

Morgan smile. Since it was their first real Christmas together, Morgan put her feelings aside and got into the spirit.

A couple of hours later, Tony arrived with more stuff for the kids. However, they were exhausted from playing with their toys.

"Damn, I got here too late," he said.

"Yeah, they went crazy. London almost knocked over the tree," Morgan told him, making Tony laugh. "Are you hungry?" she asked.

"A little, but I wanted us to talk. I know I have a lot of explaining to do."

"Tony..." she grumbled.

Tony grabbed her by the waist. "Baby girl, please, let's just talk."

Morgan sighed.

Sitting by the fireplace, Tony began to explain. "Your mother and I messed around way before you were born. Actually, she was my first older girlfriend."

"My mother? Why?"

"Your mother was different than all the women in the projects. Yeah, she was pretty, but she had a lot of class. She didn't act like she came from the hood."

"So what happened?"

"She found someone else. Your mother wasn't into guys in the neighborhood," Tony stated, causing Morgan to give him a puzzled look. "I mean, in the hood, everyone either sold drugs or played ball. Your mother wanted more than that. We went out a few times, but we never had sex. One night, I found out she was seeing someone else. When I asked her, she said she didn't see a future with me. Because of her, I stepped up my game," he lied.

"And you didn't think to tell me this?"

Tony exhaled. "I wanted to."

"So that's why you're with me, because of my mother?"

"No, I'm with you because I love you. Morgan, the first time I laid eyes on you I knew you were the one."

"And what about your other girl Stevie?"

Tony's eyes widened. "Stevie?! How do you know about her? Who's been telling you stuff?" he asked.

"No one. I just heard about her. Why did y'all break up?"

What the fuck is going on? Who's been telling her shit? He thought, but replied, "She was my girl back in the day. We were together for years."

"And what happened?"

"I was young and stupid. Cheating and hitting her...she left."

Tony's admission made Morgan believe he had changed and was remorseful. She was quiet for a second. So much had been said and done in their relationship. *Is it worth being in this marriage for the kids' sake? What else is going to surface,* she wondered.

Chapter Nineteen
Tony

*I*t's been one helluva year. Hopefully, this year will be better, Tony thought. Even with Tia leaving the company and questions about his marriage to Christina, Tony still managed to bring the New Year in right. After spending a few days in Aspen, he flew his family to St. Tropez for a couple days where they stayed on their yacht. At this point, Tony didn't give a shit who saw them. It was time to start living the good life, and being with his family was just that.

Tia was going to work for some fashion designer, and Tony figured it was for more money. So, he counter offered her with some additional perks, but she rejected it, claiming it was time to move on. Who was she kidding? Tony believed Tia left because he told her about Morgan. He always felt that Tia had a secret crush on him. She probably thought she had a shot when he and Christina broke up. However, once she saw how serious Tony was about Morgan, she knew she didn't have a chance. Strangely, her leaving couldn't have come at a better time since Tony had been thinking about hiring a whole new team.

Meanwhile, Tony was still upset about what Morgan told him. Who the hell was trying to ruin his marriage? There were only a few people that knew about his marriage—Tia and Mookie. Tia wasn't the type to talk. Besides, she only met Morgan once, which left Mookie's sneaky ass. Tony saw the way he gazed at Morgan.

Also, something was definitely up with Greg and Denise, with the police dragging them down to the precinct. All that talk about they didn't know what happened was bullshit. *So now, they're keeping secrets from me after all these years?* If he wanted to, Tony could've put their asses away years ago. Even when he found out Paul, Perry, and Mike had killed his cousin, he still remained loyal to them. And he didn't give a shit what anyone said; Greg ordered that hit on his cousin. There was no way in the world Perry and the others would've done that without Greg's permission. As for Denise, she was something else. After all the shit she'd done in her life, she had the audacity to tell him that he wasn't good enough for Morgan. He couldn't believe that bitch. She out of all people should know if anyone changed, it was him. Shit, she did.

It was cool because Tony didn't need them. He built his empire on his own. Now he was happy they didn't join his company. Right now, all Tony needed in his life was his family. The rest of them could go to hell. Besides, they just found out Morgan was pregnant with twins. So, the motherfucker that was trying to break up his happy home had better come stronger.

After Morgan graduated from law school, they had plans to relocate. Tony wanted to get far away from the grimey-ass people that he once called friends. But, not before he taught Christina a lesson. She was definitely feeling herself, flaunting around with Rashid and releasing statements about their split without Tony's consent. He was hoping those little pictures would've calmed her down, but it just made her worse. Yeah, he was married and did a lot of sheisty stuff to her, but he did it in private. Even when he was fucking with that actress, he kept it on the low. It was because of him that Christina had transcended in the industry. He connected her with the right people, and this is how she repaid him? She fucked with his man, got pregnant by him, and had Tony believe the baby was his. Yes, it was payback time.

Since Tia left, Tony felt like he lost his right hand because his new assistant was clueless. *She was so damn afraid of making mistakes, yet she made plenty.* Today, Tony was scheduled to appear at his old high school, and then it was off to a radio station to support Olay, his new artist. Olay was sexy as hell and everyone thought Tony was fucking her, but he wasn't. In fact, Mookie was the one hitting that. The thought had crossed Tony's mind, but he had too much to lose. Besides, messing with your artist was a no-no in the entertainment industry, especially a female rapper.

Returning the favor from the time when Mookie went out with him, Christina, and Morgan, Tony agreed to tagalong with Mookie as he took Olay on a date later that evening. They were all attending a basketball game at Madison Square Garden. As promised months ago, Tony and Morgan started doing normal things, and tonight, she would be accompanying him to the game.

By the time Tony finished his appearance at his old high school and the interview for the radio station, which included him talking about his personal life and his breakup with Christina, it was too late to go back to the office. So, Tony ran over to his barber to get a line up. When he got to the Garden, Mookie, Olay, and Morgan were already seated. After all these years, Tony's heart still smiled every time he saw Morgan. *It must be love.*

Following the game, they went and grabbed a bite to eat.

When the ladies went to the bathroom to freshen up, Tony asked, "You and Olay are serious, huh?"

"It seems like that. Yo, I'm feeling her."

Tony nodded. "Okay...okay! Well, be careful. You know she's in the same business as you."

"Yeah, but I think she's different."

Tony chuckled. "Yo, take your time. You know pussy is the demise of all men. That shit has brought down emperors, kings, and presidents. Shit, look at me."

They both busted out laughing.

"Yeah, tell me about it. You and Morgan are going strong, son. And y'all have another baby on the way."

"Two babies," Tony corrected. "I told you I'm good. I'm not running around like that no more. Wifey got me on lock, and I don't even mind."

"That's what's up. So when are you gonna tell Denise and them?"

Tony frowned. "I don't know. I tried, but you know Denise isn't trying to hear it. She thinks a nigga hasn't changed, nah mean? She acts like she's the only person in the world that can change. Besides, she and I are not feeling each other right now."

"Word? Why, because of the shit that happened at the party?"

"Nah, that was some bullshit. Denise thinks I'm still the same Tony. She feels like she can talk to me any kinda way, and I had to check that ass."

"Damn, she's like that."

"Yeah, she thinks she's the only one that can bust her gun."

Mookie was about to say something, but Morgan and Olay returned to the table.

*****

Tony was in Dubai when he got the news of his sisters along with their kids found shot to death in their West Nyack house. The police believe they knew their killer because there were no signs of a break in.

Tony caught the next flight out. His parents were devastated, and his mother had to be sedated.

At his mother's request Tony had a private funeral, inviting friends and family only. Not only was it hard for Tony to be strong, but he wondered who would do this. In fact, it made him wonder if it had anything to do with him. The last thing he needed was someone trying to kill him. Morgan offered to come, but Tony told her no. If someone was after him, he didn't want them to see his family.

After the funeral service, Denise and Greg extended their condolences. Even Christina showed up wearing a huge engagement ring.

"Yo, Tee, you have my deepest sympathy, man." Greg hugged him.

Denise, with her shades on, remained quiet.

"Thanks, guys," Tony said. "You okay, Dee?" he asked, noticing her distant attitude.

"I'm good, Tony. Just have a lot on my mind. How are you holding up?"

"Good. You know, being strong for Moms."

"Of course. Do the police have any leads yet?" Greg asked.

"Nah, but I'm going to hire someone to investigate."

Meanwhile, Tony hired additional security for his mother and family. Until they found out who murdered his family members, Tony wasn't taking any chances. He also started looking for a house out of state; he and Morgan had already discussed moving.

It had been a minute since Tony had been out, and while he would have rather stayed at home, he attended a friend's party, figuring he would stop by for a couple of minutes and then bounce. As always, the party was packed, and everyone in attendance gave him their condolences. He chilled in the VIP section until Mookie and Olay joined him.

"What's up, Tee? I'm surprised to see you here. How are you holding up? How's the family?"

"Everyone is good; you know, doing the best they can."

"Alright. Well, I'm here, fam."

"Thanks."

"On a lighter note, Olay and I are engaged."

"Word!" Tony flashed a surprised look. "That's what's up," he said, lifting his glass in a toasting gesture to them.

"Thanks, Tony," Olay said, giving him a kiss on the cheek.

The next morning, while making some breakfast for his kids, Tony's cell phone rang, and it was Natalie.

"Tony, Mookie and Olay were murdered last night! Turn on the TV."

"WHAT!" Tony yelled in disbelief, while hanging up and turning on the television in the kitchen.

By then, Morgan and London walked in.

"What happened?" Morgan asked.

"Mookie and Olay were killed last night."

"What?!" she said, turning toward the TV.

"Tremayne Harris, better known as Mookie, and Sabrina Anderson, also know as rapper Olay, was found shot in their home. As you can see, the police are searching the area for any leads. Before being appointed to CEO of Society Records, Mookie helped launch the careers of Tony Flowers and Christina Carrington. This is the second time someone close to Tony Flowers has been killed," the reporter stated.

"Oh my God," Morgan mumbled.

Shocked, Tony stood there with his mouth open. "I was just with him," he said. Then he grabbed his cell phone and ran into the other room to call Greg. "Yo, Greg, you heard?"

"Heard what?"

"They murdered Mookie," he said, clearing the lump out of his throat.

"Get the fuck outta of here! When?"

"Last night. I was just with him. Yo, this shit is crazy. First my sisters and now Mookie."

"Damn! You know what happened?" Greg asked.

"Nah. We were chilling. He just got engaged. This shit is crazy, man."

By the sound of Tony's voice, Greg knew he was scared. While Tony may have been rich, he was not built like that, and dudes knew it. Tony needed his team back; they needed to be his muscles.

"Let me put my ear to the street and see if I can find out something. Are you going into the office today?"

"Yeah."

"A'ight. I'll meet you there in a couple of hours. Yo, keep your head up. We'll get to the bottom of this."

"A'ight. Thanks, man!" Tony said with a sigh of relief.

*****

Scared to death, Tony dropped Morgan and the kids off, then headed to his office. Everyone was filled with grief. Unlike Tony, Mookie was loved by all the staff. Tony walked into his office and found Detectives Clyde and Sharon waiting.

"Tony, we are sorry for you loss," Detective Clyde said.

"Thanks," he grumbled, while wondering why they were there. "What's up?"

"We just wanted to ask you a few questions about your friends."

Tony paused for a second, wondering if he should contact his attorney before talking to the cocksuckers. "What is there to tell?"

"Do you think Greg and Denise had something to do with Moe's murder?" Sharon asked.

"No. They aren't into that lifestyle anymore. Besides, Moe was cool with them. He was never a threat to them," Tony stated.

"Word on the street is Moe had something to do with Greg's place getting robbed. Now, you and I both know nobody robs Greg and lives to talk about it. Would you tell us if you knew?" Clyde asked.

Tony screwed up his face. "I don't know where y'all are getting your information from, but Moe didn't have shit to do with Greg's spot getting robbed. He and Greg weren't friends, but they weren't enemies either. People are trying to start shit."

Clyde smirked. "Are you sure about that? It's not like they would confide in you for anything."

Tony returned the smirk and replied, "Listen, man, don't come in my fucking office fishing for shit."

"Oh, we're not fishing for nothing. It's just strange that your family and now your best friend were killed within weeks of each other."

Tony glared at both detectives. He knew they were trying to be sarcastic. "Yes, it is, and that's why the NYPD ain't shit, cocksuckers."

Clyde laughed. Who was Tony kidding? Had he forgotten they knew him from back in the day? Just because he had a few dollars didn't mean he had the heart to go with it.

Knock! Knock!

"Tee," Greg said, entering.

"Figures," Clyde stated. "It's the one and only Greg Brightman."

"Clyde...Sharon," Greg replied in a nonchalant tone.

"Fuck them, Greg. They were just leaving. You wanna talk to me? Come back with a warrant, cocksuckers, or my lawyer is gonna have your badges. "

"Or a body bag," Sharon said as she and her partner exited.

"Yo, what was that all about?" Greg asked.

"Nothing! You know Clyde and Sharon are always fucking with someone."

"Enough about the lames. What's up?"

"Stress, man. I don't know what the fuck to do."

Greg gave him a brotherly hug. "It's cool. Don't worry. We're gonna find out. Have you been receiving any death threats? Anyone tryna extort you?"

"Nah."

"What about Mookie?"

"No, Greg. You know Mookie didn't get down like that. That's why this shit is killing me."

Tony's private line rang; it was Morgan. "Yeah, Morgan?"

"Don't forget I'm leaving early for my prenatal appointment."

"Oh, what time is the appointment? Are they gonna do the sonogram?"

"Yes."

"Alright. Talk to you later."

"Morgan's pregnant again?" Greg asked.

"Yeah, with twins," Tony replied without thinking.

"Hmmm, interesting," Greg mumbled.

After Greg left, Tony sat in his office, rubbing his head and thinking, *Why is this happening?* He instructed his staff not to bother him. Again, Tony's private line rang. This time, it was Tia.

"Hey, Tia."

"Is it true?" she wept.

"Yeah, it's true."

"Oh my God! Who would do such a thing, Tony?"

"I don't know."

"Well, I'm catching the next flight out."

"Alright. Be safe and call me when you get here," he said before they hung up.

Tony took the next couple of days off. Between the media speculations and police questioning him, he was on the verge of losing his mind. Every day the police were harassing his lawyer for a sit down. The fans were turning on him. If it wasn't for his family, Tony would've been killed himself.

After tucking his kids in bed, Tony made a decision for them to leave immediately. The idea of losing them scared the hell out of him. Yeah, talking shit on a track was one thing, but people were actually dying, and it was too much for him. He guessed that's why Greg and Denise never asked him to kill anyone, because they knew he couldn't carry it out.

"Hey, are the kids sleeping?" Morgan asked, while putting the dishes away. "Yeah. Hey, baby, I was thinking about us leaving New York NOW!"

"Now? Tony, I'm in school. I thought we were going to wait until I'm done." Morgan tossed the dishtowel on the table.

"I know, but, baby, let's just go...get up and leave. I saw some mansion in the middle of nowhere."

"Tony..." she said.

"Baby, please let's just go," he said, embracing her. "If something should happen..."

"Don't think like that," Morgan said, sensing the fear in Tony's voice.

He led Morgan over to the chair so she could sit on his lap. "Ma, I'm scared. I can't lose you or my kids. I would die," he voiced as he cried, hugging her tightly.

Morgan sighed. It was the first time she felt sorry for Tony. *Even monsters get scared*. She lifted his face up, wiped away his tears, and nodded.

"Okay, let's move," she told him, then placed a kiss on his lips. "Let's go, baby."

They say crying cleanses the soul, and that night, Tony cried in his wife's arms.

*****

Mookie's funeral was star-studded, and everyone came out to say goodbye. The service was held at the infamous Frank E. Campbell Funeral Home. One would've thought it was an awards show. Christina arrived with Rashid; Greg and Denise brought their mates. However, Tony and Tia came solo. There was no way he was bringing his family.

As Tony sat through the service, he realized this shit wasn't worth it at all. He couldn't wait to get the hell out of there. He and Morgan had found a beautiful mansion in Lake Minnetonka; the house was in the middle of nowhere. Taking extra precaution for his family's safety, Tony planned to install a high-tech security system. Also, he brought all the extra land around it and had it gated off.

Right now, Tony wanted to be as far away as possible from this business. He realized it was the lifestyle that will kill you. All those people were crying and fronting like they loved Mookie, when it was probably one of them who had killed his ass. Well, Tony wasn't going to give them a chance to do that to him. Once he was gone, they would never see his ass again, and that included Denise and Greg. Yeah, those were his people, but deep down inside, Tony didn't trust them anymore.

Once the service was over, Tony kissed Mookie's family and rushed out the door with his bodyguards. He didn't feel like being hounded by the media or the fake-ass industry people. However, he did give Tia a ride to her hotel.

"Hey, how are you holding up?" Tia asked, noticing the stress on Tony's face.

"It's hard, you know. My sisters and now Mookie…"

"Do the police have any leads?"

"No." Tony twisted his face in disgust.

"How are Morgan and the kids holding up?"

"They're good. You know they are keeping me together," Tony said. He thought about sharing his plans with Tia, but right now, he didn't trust anyone. "When does your flight leave?"

"In a few days. I have some running around to do, make a few stops."

"Well, be careful," he told her as they pulled up to the hotel.

"I will. Tony, take care of yourself." She smiled and got out the car.

"Tia!" Tony yelled.

"Yeah?"

"Thank you for everything. I love you."

Tia giggled. This situation was really bringing out the best in Tony. "You're welcome, and I love you, too!"

*****

At his lawyer's advice, Tony finally agreed to talk to the police. They were meeting him at his midtown office. Although he told them he didn't know nothing, his lawyer said he should talk to them anyway. Tony was getting ready for his interview, when his cell phone rang. It was Donald, Tia's new boss.

"Hey, Tony."

"Oh, what's up, Donald?"

"Have you heard from Tia? She was supposed to be back at work two days ago, and I still haven't heard from her. I called her cell phone, but it's going straight to voicemail. I called her family, and they haven't heard from her. The hotel said she checked out a couple of days ago."

This shit can't be happening. Tony swallowed hard. "Nah, Donald. Are you sure?" he asked, shaking.

"Yes."

Just then, there was a knock on Tony's door. It was Natalie with a package for him. Since he was on the phone, she left it on his desk and exited.

"I'll make some calls and get back to you," Tony said.

"Thanks, man. By the way, how are you holding up?"

"You know me. I'm being strong. Anyway, let me make these calls. I'll talk with you soon."

Click!

Tony looked at the box. He was going to open it later, but something wasn't right. He looked at the address; it had Tia's old address on it. Tony ripped open the box and damn near passed out. It was a severed tongue with a note that read: *The devil is here!*

Tony dropped the box and ran out the office yelling, "Natalie!"

Chapter Twenty
Christina

Christina was happy. She left Tony just in time. He was public enemy number one; the police were implying that he was a suspect. According to who you listened to, Tony had Tia and Mookie killed, or Tony had owed some drug kingpin some money and that's why they killed his family and friends. Every day someone was speculating about it. They tried to associate Christina with that mess, but her attorney quickly handled it. In fact, Christina banned all questions about Tony when interviewing.

Shit, Christina was still dealing with her own drama. After someone leaked pictures of her and Paul having sex, and the ones of her giving Rashid head on the balcony, Christina almost died. It damn near ruined her relationship with Rashid, because she thought he had leaked the pictures. What baffled her most were the pictures of her and Paul. Christina was sure they were careful. If someone had the pictures back then, why were they just now leaking them? Why not leak them back when Paul was alive? It didn't make sense.

Even though they weren't on speaking terms, Christina felt bad for Tony. He looked so stressed at the funeral. He had lost so much weight, and even behind his big Louis Vuitton shades, you could tell he hadn't slept in days. Several times, Christina tried to reach out to him, but he would send her call to voicemail. When he did pick up, he would say that he'd call her back. After a while, Christina just stopped calling. She knew he was still bitter about their breakup. Christina knew he loved her; he just had a fucked up way of showing it.

Since it was bad timing, Christina held off on serving him the papers about her publishing rights. Christina was stunned when she found out Tia had been killed. The papers said her tongue was cut out of her mouth. *Who would do such a gruesome thing,* she thought. On a brighter note, Christina's life was almost perfect, career wise and personal.

Today, Christina was going with Joyce house hunting. After looking, they had lunch at Il Sole Restaurant.

While scanning the menu, Joyce asked, "How's Tony doing?"

"I don't know. Every time I call him, he acts like he doesn't wanna talk to me."

"Well, I can't blame him."

Raising her eyebrow, Christina responded, "What is that suppose to mean? Don't blame me. I tried."

"I'm not saying that, but you can't act like you're a saint in this. Chris, you messed around with one of his best friends."

"And he fucked Asia, or you didn't know that?" Christina retorted, causing Joyce to look surprised. "Exactly! I wasn't just fucking Paul to get back at Tony. We were in love, and if he hadn't died, we would be together. Besides, weren't you the one who said I should fuck around? Now that Tony is going through something I'm the bad guy, huh?"

Frowning, Joyce answered, "I'm not saying that, Chris. I'm just saying are you sure Rashid is the one."

"Yes! Joyce, when Paul died, a part of me felt like I lost my soul. Paul was the first man I ever truly loved, and it feels like that with Rashid. What's the sense of having money if you don't have anyone to share it with? Tony and I were great together business wise, but that's it. That's not good enough for me."

Joyce nodded. "I hear ya. I just want you to be happy."

"I am. That's why I had to leave Tony. I got tired of hiding my feelings with Rashid."

"Sorry, but I can't help but to feel bad for Tony."

"Neither can I," Christina said.

"I just hope they find out who killed those people."

"So do I, but Paul has been gone for a couple of years now, and the police still don't know who did it. I think they just stopped looking."

"Do you miss him?" Joyce asked with a slight grin.

"Every day." Christina smiled. "Paul was so different. He was like Greg. He just had a way with people."

"Oh yeah, Greg is sexy as hell. His wife is lucky," Joyce commented with a laugh.

"Yep, Gabrielle Brightman is one lucky woman. You know she can't stand Tony."

"Really? I thought they were one big happy family."

"No."

Joyce looked up. "Speak of the devil. Look at Greg over there," she said, pointing to the bar.

Christina turned around and waved, getting Greg's attention.

"We were just talking about you," Christina said, while Joyce gazed at him.

"Word? I hope it was all good," he replied, kissing both of them on the cheek.

"Of course," Joyce blurted out with a huge smile on her face.

"Actually, we were just talking about my engagement to Rashid."

"So when is the big day?"

"We're not doing that. It's going to be small."

Greg nodded and smiled.

"So what brings you out here?" Joyce said, changing the subject.

"Work. I'm checking on a few things."

"You're thinking about opening up a club out here?" Christina asked.

Greg flashed his trademark smile. "Something like that. Have you called Tony to see how he's doing?"

"Yeah, but I haven't been able to reach him. You know he's bitter about our breakup."

Greg sighed. He didn't feel like going down that road again. "Well, keep trying to reach him. Right now, he needs all the support he can get."

"I will," Christina promised.

Greg's party arrived at the restaurant, so he excused himself. Once he was gone, Joyce took a deep breath.

"God that man is sexy."

"And very married," Christina reminded her.

*****

Christina took Greg's advice and reached out to Tony again. This time, she was successful. In fact, Tony wanted to meet with her. He was scheduled to fly out there to Los Angeles for a business meeting. Therefore, he and Christina agreed to have dinner.

Instead of going to a five-star restaurant, Tony wanted Christina to meet him at a rented house outside of Hollywood. On her way there, she wondered if Tony was up to something. When she pulled up to the house, she was greeted by a team of bodyguards who patted her down and confiscated her cell phone.

She and Tony greeted each other with a fake kiss on the cheek.

"Thanks for meeting me," Christina said.

"It's cool. I figured we could wrap everything up since I'm in LA."

"Yeah, I was hoping for the same thing."

There was an awkward moment of silent as both wondered where they had gone wrong.

Then Christina blurted out, "Oh, I had lunch with Greg a couple of days ago. Does he age?"

Smirking, Tony replied, "I guess not, but don't worry. He doesn't like sloppy seconds."

Christina shot him an evil look and then laughed. *Same ole Tony, and you wonder why you're going through bullshit.*

Brushing the comment off, Christina said, "Shall we get down to business? I have somewhere I need to be."

"Fo' sho! So talk to me," Tony said, as he proceeded to eat his food that had been prepared before her arrival.

Caught off guard, Christina responded, "Okay...well, since we're not legally married, I want you to sell back my publishing rights to me."

"Of course, for a fee."

Christina sucked her teeth. "How much?"

"Hundred million."

"A hundred million?! Are you out of your fucking mind?"

"No, that's how much it's worth. You're hot, babe," he spitefully replied. "Between you and your fiancé, I'm sure you both can come up with it."

Christina rolled her eyes and slammed her hand on the table. "You are such a faggot, you know that. You didn't want me, so what's the problem?"

Laid back, Tony replied, "You're right. I didn't want you, but there are certain things you don't do."

"Oh yeah? Like what?"

Tony laughed. "You figure it out," he responded, putting another forkful of food in his mouth.

Okay, this isn't working, Christina thought. Tony was trying to get under her skin. Taking a deep breath, she gently touched his hand.

"I know you just lost a lot of people, and I'm sorry for you. Hasn't that shown you anything? Life is too short for you to be cruel."

Tony put down his fork. "It has, Christina. It showed me that bitches ain't shit," he said, glaring at her hand that rested on his.

"Well, I guess I have my answer," she said while pulling her hand back.

"I guess so," Tony shot back.

"You will never be happy."

"That's where you're wrong. I am happy."

"Oh, I forgot. Your bank statement tells you that."

"Wrong again. It's not about money," he retorted.

"If not, then why won't you sell my publishing rights back?"

"Because I built you. I'm the one who made you HAWT!"

"And you made a lot of money off of me, so we're even. Tony, either you give me the rights to my publishing company or..."

"Or what?" Tony said, flexing. "What the fuck are you gonna do? I have a fucking team of lawyers waiting to handle bitches like you. Unless you have the money to buy it back, it's not up for discussion." He took a sip of his drink. "Now, is there anything else you wanna talk about? If not, get the fuck out of my face. You're dismissed!"

Christina tossed the napkin, stood up, and charged him. "You will give back my publishing company. I bet my life on it."

"That's a bet I'm willing to take. Tell Rashid he better be careful, because you like fucking with the hired help." He laughed before walking out.

Burning up inside, Christina stormed out. "FUCK YOU, TONY! Your day will come, you bastard!"

Why did I even bother? Instead of going to Rashid's condo, she went back to her hotel. When she arrived, Joyce and Christina's stylist were sorting out her clothes. Pissed off, she didn't even acknowledge their presence.

"Hey, Chris! How did it go?" Joyce asked.

She shot Joyce a displeased look and grumbled, "He's such a bitch," before walking into the bathroom.

Before Joyce inquired as to what happened, she asked the stylist to leave. The last thing she needed was someone leaking information about Christina and Tony.

Once alone, Joyce went into the bathroom. "What happened now?"

While removing her makeup, Christina said, "He's a bitch. Would you believe he said I have to pay a hundred million dollars to get my publishing rights back?"

"WOW! Why?"

"Because he's Tony, the Cunt, that's why. It's not like he needs the money. He's upset that I left his ass and moved on. I can't believe I was in love with him. Someone should've slapped the shit out of me. Gabrielle was right. Tony is a motherfucker. No wonder why Tia quit on his ass."

"Damn! Why is he being like that? A hundred million?" Joyce was pissed off, as well.

"Exactly! Then the motherfucker had the nerve to say I fucked with hired help."

"What made him say that?"

"I don't know."

"Do you think he knew about Paul?"

"At this point, I don't even give a damn."

Finally, the Truth

Chapter Twenty-One
Denise

Denise was like an artist who paints, and Tony was her final masterpiece. For those who didn't know, Denise was highly skilled in the killing department. That's why she was never implicated in murders. Like Greg, Denise carefully planned everything out down to the time a red light changed on the street. No rock was unturned. She ran a multi-million dollar real estate company in the day and was a hit man at night. She was about to bring the world down on Tony's head, and it was going to be biblical.

Denise chuckled to herself when she saw the fear in Tony's eyes at the funeral service. *Just like a bitch, he hired more bodyguards.* He was going to need more than that to stop Denise from getting to his ass, though. What killed her most was how conniving he was, smiling in Denise's face while pretending not to know who Felicia's brother was. Some days, Denise felt like walking up to him and blowing his head off with a shotgun, but that would've been too easy.

Denise had just arrived in her office, when her assistant announced Morgan was there to see her. They hadn't spoken since the night Morgan revealed she was raped. Denise had been avoiding her because she couldn't find the right words to say. Plus, she didn't want Morgan to see how upset she was.

"Send her in," Denise said. "Hey, niece." Denise flashed a fake smile, then kissed her on the cheek.

"Hello," Morgan replied.

"So what brings you here?" Denise asked, acting like there wasn't anything wrong.

"Nothing. I figured since you're not returning my calls, I would pop up on you."

Denise stopped and stared at Morgan. No matter how hard she tried not to talk about it, the fact remained that Tony raped Morgan. Denise exhaled.

"Morgan, I just..." She took a seat across from her. "I keep thinking if I don't talk about it, then it didn't happen, you know?"

Apprehensive, Morgan nodded her head and mumbled, "I know...I know."

"Every day, I keep waiting for you to call me up and say April Fools," Denise said, getting choked up.

Morgan lowered her head as a single tear dropped from her eye. "I felt the same way, too. For years, I kept telling myself it was a dream—that it wasn't happening."

"How did you deal with it? I can't even imagine the amount of pain you went through."

"I don't know, Auntie. I just felt the need to protect my family," Morgan replied, getting up and pacing.

"From who?" Denise snapped.

"From Tony! Aunt Denise, do you know who Tony Flowers is? He's rich and powerful. He has the power to do anything to people."

Denise grinded her teeth while glaring at the floor. "That's what you think. He's powerful? Tony may be rich, but powerful is something he's not. Morgan, let me tell you about..." Denise caught herself. "Yeah, niece, he's powerful alright," she said, changing her expression and the tone of her voice. "I just get upset when I think about how painful it was for you."

"Yeah, it was painful. I mean, we would have sex for hours."

"Hours?"

"Yes, and if I didn't, he would hit me. He told me that I was his forever, and it looks like he was right. We're married with two kids now. I guess God doesn't make mistakes."

"What do you mean?"

"On my sixteenth birthday, you and Mommy said God doesn't make mistakes. So, maybe it was meant for me to get raped."

Denise was silent for a second and then tightly hugged her niece. "In this case, I don't know, Morgan. Did you tell Tony about what you told me?"

"I told him that I knew about my mother and that girl, but I didn't tell him about what I told you. Why?"

"Because I'm not ready to confront him with that yet. Tony was one of my best friends, and what he did was unacceptable. I just need a little more time to digest this. It's not every day you find out your best friend raped your niece."

"I know, Auntie. It's hard for me to accept it, too. I mean, he *is* the father of my kids."

"And?"

"And I don't want anything to happen to him."

Denise paused. *Is this girl fucking crazy? She doesn't want anything to happen to her rapist?*

"Morgan, have you ever thought about seeking professional help?"

"In the beginning..."

"You really should. It sounds like you have Stockholm syndrome. Do you hear yourself? Tony is a rapist. He raped you," Denise highlighted. "He deserves to be in prison, even under it."

"He does, but what about my kids?"

"What about them? They won't be the only children raised by one fucking parent. Today, it's the American way."

"You're right, but can't people change? You were the one who told me good can come from evil."

"Yes, but in this case, fuck that saying. Tony is evil," Denise humored.

Morgan released a little giggle. "Aunt Denise..."

Denise stared at her niece, wanting to knock some damn sense into her ass. *Has she lost her fucking mind? So what she has kids by this nigger? That doesn't change the fact that he raped her.* While Morgan had lost her mind, Denise was focused. Even if Morgan didn't want him to pay, she for damn sure was going to make him.

Once Morgan left, Denise played their conversation over in her mind. *Either Morgan is in serious denial, or she is just as sick as Tony,* Denise thought. The one thing Morgan did mention was Felix. She and Tony planned to tell him about their marriage. Although Denise promised she wasn't going to say anything, there was no way she was going to let Morgan lie to her father by making it seem like they had just fallen in love, when in fact, Tony had raped her.

Since Denise had been on her warpath, she avoided a lot of people, especially Greg. If he found out she was behind this shit, she didn't know how he would react. He would probably arrange a meeting with Tony.

As usual, Denise went about her daily routine while carrying out her next attack. Sadly, some people got caught up in the mix. However, they had Tony to thank for that since he fired first.

Standing in her house outside of New York, Denise thought she would never be there. She had purchased the house years ago, and used it as her lay low spot after committing murders. She went there to plan out her attacks. She also kept all her weapons there. Denise really believed she'd never visit that house again. At one time, she considered getting rid of it, but something told her to keep it, and it's a good thing she did.

She sat back and reflected on the murders of Tony's sisters, Mookie, and Tia. Denise never liked Tony's sisters, with their slutty asses. You would think with all the money Tony had, he would get his sisters facelifts. Denise swore it was them who used to call the police on her when they were younger. So, killing them was a pleasure, but as for the kids, they were in the wrong place at the wrong time.

Mookie and Tia, on the other hand, were directly involved, even though both denied knowing about the rape. Most people deny shit when they are staring down the barrel of a gun. Denise had watched

Mookie for weeks. He and Olay had a love nest up in Dutchess County. With all the money Mookie had, one would think he would've invested in an upscale alarm system. They had just arrived home from the party, and Denise waited. Since it would be their last night alive, she allowed them time to get a nut off. Mookie damn near shitted on himself when he saw Denise standing in the doorway dressed in all black.

"Oh shit! Dee, you scared the hell out of me," he said in a frightened voice.

"Yeah, I have that affect on people," she replied.

Unsure and scared, Mookie asked, "What's up?" While standing there looking at Denise, he hoped Olay didn't see her. But, it was too late.

"Mookie, who's that?" she asked, walking over to join him.

By then, Denise had pulled out her .44 Magnum Desert Eagle.

"Sit the fuck down," she ordered.

Still confused, Mookie stood there staring at her. "Dee?"

"Sit the fuck down!" she yelled, causing Olay to jump.

"What do you want?" Mookie asked, trying to protect his fiancée.

"I'm gonna ask you a question, and depending on how you answer, you might live."

Scared to death, Mookie remained silent.

"Did you take my niece to have an abortion?"

"Yeah, but I didn't know she was your niece at the time. That's my word."

"And now?"

Olay jumped from behind Mookie. "You gotta be kidding me! This is about someone fucking your niece?"

Without blinking, Denise put a bullet between Olay's eyes, causing brain fragments to splatter on Mookie.

"OH SHIT! WHAT THE FUCK!" he cried.

"She talked too fucking much. Besides, her album is whack. Now, did you know?"

Crying like a baby, Mookie yelled, "Yes, I knew, but I just found out! Dee, that's my word. I told Tony to tell you."

In a zombie-like state, Denise nodded her head. "You know, we all need friends like you. I'll let Tony know."

She smiled, then put four shots into his body.

"At least they got their nut off," she said and laughed.

Maybe *Fergie* was right, "Big Girls Don't Cry", because Tia had more heart than a lot of dudes that Denise had put in the dirt. Denise caught her on her way to the airport. Careless, just like the rest of them, Tia was so busy yapping on her cell phone that she didn't notice she was in the wrong car. They were outside of Islip Airport before Tia realized what was going on, and that's only because her phone died.

"Excuse me," Tia said.

"Yes."

"Are we lost?"

"Something like that," Denise replied, pulling over.

Tia still didn't have a clue until Denise opened the door with her gun drawn.

"Get the fuck out."

Tia tried to grab for the gun, but Denise was too quick, busting her in the head with the gun's handle.

"Get the fuck up!"

In a daze, Tia stumbled to get up.

"Oh my God, Denise...what's going on?"

"Oh, you don't know? Well, ask your employer."

"I don't understand."

"You knew about Tony and my niece, and you never said anything."

"Your niece? Denise, I just found out, and when I did, I quit. Why do you think I'm not working with him?"

Denise paused. *Is she telling the truth?*

"That's why you left?"

"Yes, I quit when I found out. He has been messing with her for years. He's no better than R. Kelly."

Denise sighed. There was no way Tia would be walking away alive.

"Damn, Tia, I didn't know. Do me a favor. Curse Tony out when you see him," Denise said before putting a hole in Tia's head and then cutting her tongue out.

Fucking Tony! He doesn't understand the true meaning of loyalty. His staff gave their lives for him. Well, he'll be there soon to thank them.

Since the police labeled Tony as the prime suspect, Denise took a break to regroup and come up with a different plan since Al was going to be special. He reminded her of Grant carrying girls to do tricks.

Denise took a deep breath and called it a day. Morgan had ruined her day, but it was about to get worse. Upon arriving home, Denise was greeted by Detectives Clyde and Sharon sitting in her living room.

"Hey, honey, what's going on?" she asked Derrick.

Smiling, Sharon said, "Thanks, Derrick, for your time."

Annoyed, Denise loudly said, "Derrick," but he ignored her and walked the detectives to the door.

On her way out, Sharon leaned toward Denise and whispered, "I guess your day came before mine."

Denise stared at Sharon, cutting her eyes but remaining silent.

"Are you gonna tell me why they were here?" Denise asked with her arms folded.

"I was about to ask you the same thing, Denise Taylor. Or is that your real name?"

Already pissed off about Morgan, Denise asked, "What are you talking about?"

Derrick tossed her a folder. "You tell me. I didn't know my wife was a gangbanger," he snidely stated.

If looks could kill, Derrick would've been dead, because the look Denise gave him was that of a killer. She figured Sharon had given Derrick a copy of her rap sheet. Therefore, there was no need to front about it.

"Okay, so I've been arrested. What's your point? Most people have been."

"Well, most people don't lie about it. I thought you said you went to college. Or was that a lie, too?"

Remaining calm, she stated, "I did go to school. Just because I got arrested..."

"Is that what you call it? You were arrested over a dozen times. You're a convict," he said, cutting her off. "All that bullshit about you having a hard life, and your lying ass was out there selling drugs to your own people. Oh, and don't give me that white man shit. You knew what you were doing," he ranting, storming back and forth across the floor.

Derrick was upset, so Denise just listened. No matter what she said he wasn't trying to hear it.

"I asked was there anything you needed to tell me, and what did you say? NO! Even that day in the park, I asked. You could've told me then. All that bullshit about you and Greg being like brother and sister was a lie. So what you still work for him. You're still his hit man."

"Derrick..."

"Derrick my fucking ass! I knew something was up when the police came to the house. How could I have been so stupid...so blind? Now I know what people say: you can take a person out the ghetto, but you can't take the ghetto out of a person. This empire you built was built on drug money."

"So what! Does that make you better than me? Don't you dare judge me, motherfucker! I never blamed anyone for the shit I've done. So what I sold drugs, and yes, to my own people. A lot of people did. What's your point?" she shouted, getting in his face.

"My point is you're a lowlife...the scum of the earth!" he angrily yelled.

"Derrick, you're upset."

"Are you gonna do something to me? Are you gonna call your gang team? I know one thing. If anything should happen to my kids because of the stupid shit you did, your ass will regret it."

"That's what you think? Do you really think I would jeopardize my family's safety?"

"I don't know what you would do, but know this: you've been put on notice."

Denise was about to respond, but Halle entered the room. Denise glared at Derrick for a second, then turned her attention to Halle.

"Hi, baby! Mommy missed you," she said while smiling. Then she picked up Halle and exited the room.

Calling himself being upset with Denise, Derrick slept in the guestroom, which didn't bother her since he had started to piss her off. One person who had just been added to her shit list was Sharon. Denise should've killed her years ago.

*****

It took some time, but Denise and Derrick were at least on speaking terms. While he didn't care about her past, he was upset that Sharon's grimey ass told him. On several occasions, Derrick had asked Denise about her involvement with Greg, and each time she lied.

There were plenty of times Denise wanted to confide in her husband. She wanted their marriage to be truthful. However, Denise was a pessimistic person; always seeing the glass half empty instead of half full. She figured if Derrick knew the truth, there was no way he would stay with her. Now, Denise couldn't dare tell him what she had done because his ass might turn her in.

Trying to make things work, Denise and Derrick took the kids to Italy for a vacation, hoping to rebuild their marriage. Derrick figured if he got her out of the country, she would feel comfortable about talking to him. Nonetheless, Denise had different intentions. She needed to talk to Felix. Maybe he could talk some sense into his daughter. When Felix saw Denise, he immediately knew something was wrong.

"What's the matter?" he asked, picking up the phone.

"I need to talk to you."

"Is Morgan alright?"

"If that's what you wanna call it, yes."

"I'm listening."

"I just found out that Morgan…" Denise paused.

"Morgan what?"

"She's married to Tony Flowers, and he's the father of her children."

"*The* Tony Flowers? So what, he's not doing right by her and the kids?"

"No, he's doing fine, Felix. He's giving her the world and is a great father to his kids. But, there's something else." Denise paused again.

"What?" he asked, staring at her with a serious look.

"He raped her when she was fourteen."

Like Denise, Felix didn't comprehend what she said. "What did you say?"

"He repeatedly raped her since she was fourteen. When she turned eighteen, he forced her into marriage and made her have his children."

Felix closed his eyes and swallowed hard. Thank God there was plexiglass between them, or else Felix would've caught a body.

"She's my daughter, Denise. She's the best part of me. She and my grandkids keep me alive in this fucking place. Now you're telling me that someone I know violated my daughter?" he said in his Italian accent while grinding his teeth together.

"Yeah, Felix. I didn't know this shit was going on until a couple of weeks ago. Now she doesn't wanna leave him because they have kids together."

"She doesn't wanna leave him?"

"No. She told me that he's a good husband and father now."

Again, Felix closed his eyes. This was the last thing he needed to hear. It was bad enough he was deported when she was a child. As a father, he was supposed to protect his daughter, and he couldn't. Also, he was in prison now, which didn't help.

"Denise, does Tony know who Morgan's father is?"

"He knows, Felix."

"So you are here to tell me what?"

"I want you to talk to Morgan. Get her to leave him so I can do what I need to do."

"No, I don't want her to know that I know. Leave her with him. Just take care of him," he ordered.

"Felix…"

"You heard me. I want the motherfucker dead and his family, too. I don't care what you have to do. Understand me? No one rapes my daughter and lives! NO ONE!" he yelled, causing everyone nearby to stare.

"I'm working on that."

"You do that! The next time you come here, you better have some good news." He got up and started to walk away.

As the guard led him away, Felix yelled, "Denise, keep your promise, because I'm gonna keep mine." Then he left her sitting there puzzled.

After arriving back home, Denise went to see Tony. She wanted to see the fear in his eyes, expose him for the faggot he really was. Like she predicted, Tony was locked away in his office, with security right outside of his office. Laughing to herself, Denise thought, *It's only a matter of time.*

"Tony, what's up?"

"Denise," he said, surprised to see her.

"I figured I'd come here and check on you. This has to be hard on ya."

"Yeah," he responded, rubbing his head, "but I'm hanging in there. What's good with you?" he asked, trying to be strong

"I'm good. Derrick and the kids are fine, so I'm blessed, you know?"

He nodded. "Yeah, I know. Just trying to focus on work and other things. That's what Mookie and Tia would've wanted me to do."

"True! They were loyal to you, I tell you that. You won't find that kind of support nowhere."

"Word! I love them. How's business with you? Your ass is buying up everything. We gonna have to name a block after you…Taylor Avenue," he said, joking.

Denise flashed a weak smile. "Nah, one after you."

Scanning the room, Denise noticed the pictures of his kids.

"Damn, my niece and nephew are so adorable. How can someone turn their back on those two faces?"

Tony looked around. "Beats me. That's why I do what I can for them. On the strength of your sister, I promised her."

"And I know she's looking down thanking you."

"Yeah, well, it's the least I could do."

"So is it true you and Chris are officially over?"

"Yeah, thank God! Bitch was a real headache. Now she wants her publishing rights back."

"So give it back to her. It's not like she hasn't made you rich. Be the bigger person, unless you're upset about something else."

Tony glared at Denise. *Is she trying to be funny?* "Nah, I'm good. I don't fuck with sloppy seconds. That's something I learned back in the day."

Denise laughed. "Hopefully, that's not the only thing you've learned from back in the day."

The direction of their conversation was starting to change. So, before Denise smashed Tony's head against the wall, she asked, "How's your mother and father holding up?"

"Moms is good. Pops is still in the hospital. He's not doing too well. My brother is down here with them."

"Your brother?" Denise asked.

"Yeah, Marvin."

Wow! She hadn't heard that name in years.

"Damn, Tee, I forgot about him. How's he doing? Does he still live upstate?"

"Yeah. Where else is that nigga gonna live? You know he's blaming me for everything. If you ask me, that nigga could've stayed his ass home."

She nodded in agreement. Marvin was Tony's older brother. Before Tony joined the crew, Marvin moved away. When Denise asked Tony about him, he said he just didn't fuck with him.

Denise pretended to care about Tony for another hour before

heading home. Aware that Derrick was clocking her, she didn't want him to start interrogating her. As usual, Denise prepared dinner while tending to the kids. As she played with her children, Denise's eyes got teary. It's amazing how she could be a cold-blooded killer and a loving mother all at the same time. She truly wanted to put that life behind her, but when Morgan told her what Tony had done, it was like a light switch went off. The demons took over her body, and every Sunday while sitting in church, Denise would pray for forgiveness while planning her next attack. *What people say is true: the devil can quote scriptures, too.*

Maybe after all this was over, Denise could go back to having a normal life. However, deep down inside, she didn't want to. For Denise, this was the only way to survive in this world. It was people like Tony who forced her to be a monster.

Derrick was working late, and the kids were spending the night over Gabrielle's house. Instead of going home, Denise went to her "lay low" spot to prepare for Al's ass. Given the community Al lived in, Denise figured the back door to his house would be open. *Does anyone care about security? These people are making it so easy.* When she unlatched the safety lock on her gun, the granddaughter looked up.

"Oh my God!" she yelled, bumping into Denise.

"Don't fucking move!" she ordered, pointing her gun and pushing the girl back into the living room.

"What do you want?" the older lady asked.

Denise fired a shot into the TV, scaring the shit out of everyone. "I want everyone to kneel on the floor with their hands behind their head."

Someone who tried to be a hero lunged at Denise, but she put a bullet in his leg.

"Are there anymore heroes in the house?"

Screams and crying filled the room.

"What do you want?" Al asked.

"Is there anyone else in the house?" Denise questioned.

"No, I swear."

Denise stood with her back against the wall so she could face the other rooms in the event that someone else jumped out. Al lived in a wooded area, so it was pitch black outside.

"Please, the money is in the safe," Al told her.

Denise laughed. "Is that what you think this is about?"

"If it's not, then what do you want?" Al asked.

Denise looked at him. "Tell them, Al. Tell your wife what you did."

Confused and scared, Al looked at Denise. "I don't know what you're talking about."

"I figured that. For years, you took my niece to be raped by Tony."

"Raped?!" Al yelled.

"Yes, raped!" Denise snapped, hitting him with the gun.

"I didn't know!"

"Really? What did you think he was doing to her, Al? You served her to him every day!" Denise screamed, hitting him again. "Did it ever occur to you that she was underage?"

"No, I swear. I was only doing what I was told."

She glanced at the others. "Play with me if you want, and I'll put a bullet in his fucking head."

Cries continued to echo within the room.

"It's funny how everyone keeps saying they didn't know. Do you know my niece's pain bought you this fucking house? Her pain put your fucking kids through college."

"Please stop!" Al's wife cried when Denise hit him for the third time.

Denise looked over at Al's granddaughter. "How old are you?"

"Fifteen," she answered through her tears, frightened.

"You're about the same age my niece was when her soul died."

"I guess," she cried.

"Tell your grandfather you love him. Tell him that you forgive him. Ask him why? Why did he do this to my niece? Because of his stupidity, my niece had to marry her rapist and have his kids. Tell him you forgive him!" Denise ordered.

The girl continued crying. "Please no," she begged.

"TELL HIM!" Denise yelled, making her jump.

"I love you, grandpa, and I forgive you!"

"You see that, Al? She forgives you."

Denise looked at Al and then at the girl. Then she fired a single shot into the granddaughter's head. Her body dropped to the floor with a thud.

"OH GOD!" they cried.

"You see what you did?!" Denise snapped.

Hysterical, everyone cried while begging for their lives.

"Please…I didn't know!"

"Neither did she."

"Please let my family go. You can kill me," Al pleaded.

Denise looked at the rest of them with fear in their eyes.

"Fuck this." She fired a single shot into each one of their heads, including Al's. "This deal is non-negotiable."

This time, Denise changed up. Instead of leaving the bodies as they were, she started a fire. She knew once Tony got the news, he was surely going to kill himself, which might not be a bad idea considering what Denise had planned for him.

Denise reviewed her hit list. Everyone was gone from the doctors to the driver. There were only two people left—Tony's mother and brother. Word was Marvin and his mother went back to Marvin's house after he and Tony had a huge fight. If Denise's memory served her correctly, Marvin lived in a house off of the thru-way. Either Denise had completely lost her mind, or she just didn't give a fuck.

It was broad daylight when she pulled up to Marvin's place. Not knowing what to expect, Denise tucked the gun into her waistline. She was definitely playing herself. This was not properly planned out, and that's how motherfuckers often got caught.

Denise looked around. There was only one car in the driveway. She rang the bell, and Marvin opened the door.

"Denise Taylor," he said. "What a surprise. Come on in."

"Yes, it's been a long time," she responded while looking around.

"My mother is upstairs resting. She hasn't been the same since the funeral."

"I understand. Is she the only person here with you?"

"Yeah. My father is still in the hospital. They don't think he's gonna make it. Why? Did Tony send you to check up on us?" he asked, raising an eyebrow.

"Something like that, but we need to talk."

"I told Tony that we don't need any bodyguards. It's probably because of him that we're going through this. Anyway, what's on your mind?" Marvin asked, taking a seat on the couch.

"Remember my sister Jasmine? She was a couple years older than me."

Thinking, Marvin yelled, "Yeah, she was light skinned."

"Well, she passed away from cancer. She had some kids. You probably don't remember them, though, because you were gone by then."

"No, I don't remember. I'm so sorry to hear that. I didn't know."

Denise glanced at him and figured he was totally clueless as to what was about to happen.

"Yeah, the oldest is an adult now, but when she was fourteen years old, Tony raped her. You know those kids are his that he's taking care of."

Marvin gasped. "Oh damn! I knew this was bound to happen."

"What was bound to happen?" Denise asked in an angry tone.

Marvin lowered his head. He had never told anyone why he and Tony stopped speaking. For years, he buried their secret. Nonetheless, right now, it was time to reveal it. He got up and started walking back and forth while taking deep breaths.

"I knew he would never be the same after that night."

Now Denise was scared. "What are you talking about?"

"If you wonder why Tony and I are not talking, it's because he's a fucking rapist. When we were teenagers, our father brought home some women. He said he wanted to show us how women were supposed to be treated. At first, the women were into it, but out of the blue, they changed their mind. My father went berserk. He locked the door and told them that they weren't leaving until they had sex with us. Once I saw them crying, I didn't want any trouble, so I said forget it. But, my father said, 'No! You take that bitch in the room and make her your whore.' I was scared out of my mind, but Tony was so excited. He slapped one of them across her face and ordered her to perform oral sex on him. They were in the other room, and all I heard was her screaming and begging him to stop. When she came out of the room, she had a busted lip and her clothes were torn. My father threatened to kill the two women if they ever said anything."

"So that's why he raped my niece, and that's why the two of you don't speak anymore?"

"Well, that's part of it. Another night, we went to my father's place. He was in there yelling at his two workers. They were young and had messed up his money. He pistol whipped them, causing them to bleed from their mouths. They were crying, so my father decided to teach them a lesson. He said since they were crying like bitches, he was going to treat them like whores. Then he told us to pull down our pants and ordered them to suck us off."

"Your father gets a kick out of making women suck him off?" Denise blurted out in anger.

"NOOOO! That's the problem. This time, it wasn't women. They were guys. He said he wanted to take their manhood. Denise, I immediately said no! No man was sucking me off, but Tony dropped his pants smiling. Denise, he was rock hard. The boys were crying and begging my father not to make them do it, but he threatened to shoot them in the head. When I repeatedly told my father it wasn't right, he called me a fucking loser and said I wasn't his son. Tony, on the other hand, enjoyed it. He made both of them suck him off. When they got tired of doing that, Tony sodomized them."

"These two guys...do you remember how they looked or what age they were?"

"One of them had a scar on the right side of his face that my father caused."

That son of a bitch, Denise thought, then laughed to herself. It

was the only way to stay calm. Tony had played them all. The job that Denise and Felicia had taken care of for Tony was a lie. Years ago, Tony told Denise and Greg that two guys had kidnapped him at gunpoint and raped him. However, that was a lie. Tony was afraid that the guys would remember him and spread the word about his homosexuality. So, Tony killed those guys to keep his secret.

Expressionless, Denise lowered her head. Tony had been planning this for years.

"Marvin, you knew Felicia?"

"Yeah, she's one of our sisters."

"So Grant was your father?"

"If that's what you wanna call him. I don't even acknowledge him. He was a piece of shit. I don't know how my mother got mixed up with someone like that."

"I don't know either." It was Mrs. Flowers.

"Ma," Marvin said.

"I heard everything. I can't believe what Tony did. I knew something was wrong when he brought the kids to me. He's just like his father...always gotta have the best."

"Ma, it's not your fault," Marvin said, trying to comfort her.

"Yes, it is. There's more to the story. A few years back, I used to work for the Marcianos, cooking and cleaning their houses for them. One day, some of their jewelry went missing, and they blamed me. Mr. Marciano was going to kill me. They had me in the back alley ready to blow my head off. Grant used to run numbers for them, and he just so happened to be there. He offered to pay for the jewelry, and in return, I would become his possession. That's how I got mixed up with him."

"So this was Tony's way of getting back at them, by raping Morgan?" Denise asked sarcastically.

"Tony found out how I got mixed up with Grant through Felicia. She showed up one day at the door claiming she was his sister. By that time, I was married and had moved on with my life. She claimed her mother told her that story. For years, I denied it, but Tony knew it was true. I'm so sorry," she cried.

Speechless, Denise's eyes started to tear up. Now what the hell was she going to do? It wasn't their fault. Nevertheless, it was their actions that caused Tony's reactions. She had to think quickly. Looking around, Denise noticed a picture on the wall.

"Marvin, where did you get that picture from?" she asked.

"That's my father when he was in the Army years ago. Why?"

"I've seen that picture someplace before," Denise said.

"You probably did! Grant gave that to all the women who had kids by him. He called it his special way of letting his kids know he wasn't a piece of shit," Mrs. Flowers explained.

The last fucking piece to the puzzle! Morris, her ex-boyfriend, was Tony's brother.

Denise started to walk toward the door. "You know, I'm sorry, too. Now it all makes sense. But, I wish I've would known all of this weeks ago," she said before riddling their bodies with bullets. *Fucking Tony!*

*****

A couple days had gone by, and Denise was still hot. Out of all the people in the world, she would've never expected this. Shit like this made her reflect back to a saying she had heard in a movie. *The best thing the devil does is make people believe that he doesn't exist.* Funny thing is that was Tony's favorite part of the movie. After killing Tony's mother, Denise knew things were about to get hot. Therefore, she sent her kids down to Atlanta to stay with her parents. When Derrick questioned it, she lied about her mother missing them.

Derrick, on the other hand, was a different story. Denise wasn't sure if she could trust him. The last time they had an argument, he said some slick words out of his mouth. She prayed he wouldn't be a part of the list.

Meanwhile, Denise scoped out the so-called brownstone that Morris used to live in, and just as she suspected, he still lived there. This must've been Tony's reward to Morris for keeping tabs on Denise.

Oh, I can't wait to put this nigga's head to bed.

It took a couple of days, but Morris finally showed up. He looked like he had just come back from out of town. *Damn, he looks good,* Denise thought. For the next few days, she followed Morris around, learning his routine. She wanted to make sure there was no surprise being that Morris was the silent partner.

First, Denise needed to take care of Detective Sharon, though. *So she thinks that badge gives her jurisdiction.* Either Denise was crazy as hell or a certified genius. On a busy Friday night, Denise walked into the 40th precinct dressed in a police uniform. There was so much going on that Denise knew no one was paying attention, especially not her fellow officers. Detective Sharon was on her way to the ladies' room when Denise spotted her.

Someone had to be on Denise's side because the bathroom was empty. After putting on her black gloves, Denise pulled out her gun with the silencer and waited for Sharon to come out of the stall. When she emerged, she was so shocked she couldn't speak. "De..." was all she could say before Denise opened up Sharon's chest cavity, forcing her body to fly back into the stall.

"I told you I don't give a fuck about that badge. Your day has arrived."

With her mouth and eyes wide open, Sharon took her last breath.

"I told you, you were out of your jurisdiction." Denise smirked, finishing her off with a shot in the head. She then propped Sharon's body up and pulled down her pants, making it look like she was using the bathroom. Denise tucked her gun back into her waist, opened the door on her way out, and then removed the gloves. Giggling to herself, she thought, *Fucking NYPD. Such a joke.*

As usual, Denise went back to her lay low house to get rid of the evidence, only to find Derrick parked outside. He'd been following her.

"Nice uniform. I didn't know it was Halloween."

Denise looked around to make sure there was no police. Once she realized they were alone, Denise played it cool by ignoring Derrick's comment and proceeded inside.

"So you're just gonna ignore me?" Derrick yelled.

"No, actually, I was hoping you would come in so we can talk about it," Denise turned around and said.

"So this is where you've been?" he said, looking around her place.

Denise sighed. She wasn't in the mood for his bullshit. "What is that supposed to mean?"

"I don't know, Mrs. Jackson! Kill anyone lately? I can't believe it. I knew you were up to something," Derrick said, throwing his hands up. "You're the one who's going around killing everyone."

"Derrick...Tony raped my niece!" Denise yelled.

"What?"

"She's married to him. Those are his kids he's taking care of," she grumbled, shaking her head.

Derrick put his hand on the counter as if he was feeling lightheaded. "Whoa," he mumbled, not knowing what else to say. "So that's why you're running around killing his friends and family."

"No, only the people who know. It started when she was fourteen, and it never stopped," Denise responded in an angry voice.

"Killing people is not going to change what he did to her?" Derrick pointed out.

"My sister died blaming herself for Morgan's behavior. She thought it was something she did."

Derrick went to comfort her, but Denise backed away.

"What I want is for you to take the kids out of the country until this is over."

"Denise, go to the police!"

"Derrick, you just don't get it! Where I come from we are the police. I decide who lives and dies. I got more justice in a couple of months than the fucking police have gotten in years."

"Sharon was right. You will never change."

"Sharon?! So now you believe Sharon over me? Is that what you're telling me?"

"Those are your words not mine."

Denise smiled. "You know what? She is right. Some things will never change," she said, shooting Derrick in the chest but not killing him.

"You are..." He struggled to talk, gasping for air.

"Tell me something I don't know. Better yet, tell Sharon she was right." She smiled and put two more bullets in him. "Hopefully in your next lifetime you will learn to stop fucking snooping. WHOA! This is so much better than a divorce," she said, laughing.

Denise then carried Derrick's body into the other room.

Now it was on to Morris. Being that Denise had watched him for weeks, she had his daily routine down pat. Like the others, Morris was careless and carefree. Moreover, he was smarter than the previous victims. If she popped up now, he would start asking questions. That's why Denise pretended to bump into him on the street late one night.

"Denise?" Morris said.

"Oh shit! Hi, Morris! How are you doing?"

"Great now that I've seen you."

Denise laughed. *Same ole Morris, thinking he's God's gift to women.* "Well, it was great seeing you."

"Wait." Morris gently grabbed her hand. "Fate brought us together, so why don't we go and get something to drink?"

"Sure! I know just the place," she said.

"A'ight, you lead the way."

Denise looked around, making sure no one was watching. "Let's use my car."

During the ride, she leaned over and said, "You know, I miss you so much, Morris."

"Yeah, but you went and got married on a nigga. I know that nigga ain't hitting that pussy right." Eccentrically, Morris's words turned Denise on. He did have a point. He sure knew how to fuck her.

"I tell you what. I have a little house not too far from here. Hubby is out of town with the kids. Let's make up for lost time."

"Shit, you got my dick hard already."

"Hmmm! I can't wait to suck it." Denise winked and then licked her lips.

A few drinks and laughs later, Morris and Denise were fucking. She had to admit he didn't lose his touch. He had her screaming his name. Too bad it would be the last time.

After a good nut and a dose of Propofol that she stole from the abortion clinic, he was sleeping like a baby. Denise dragged his heavy, naked body to the other room, where she tied him to a chair. Then she sat across from him patiently until he woke up. She wanted her face to be the first thing he saw.

Semi-conscious, Morris opened his eyes. "What the fuck?" he mumbled.

Bam! Denise hit him with the gun.

"Are you awake?"

"What the fuck?" he screamed out in pain. "What's going on, Denise?"

"You guys almost got away with it."

Bleeding from his head and mouth, Morris looked over in the corner and saw Derrick's body.

Denise chuckled. "Oh, that's my husband. Til death do us part," she said, then winked at him.

"You're crazy. You know that?"

Denise smiled. "Then you should've known better."

"What are you talking about?"

"You're still playing the dumb role. Let's see if this will help you remember." She took out a Japanese sword and chopped off his toes.

"Ahhhh, shit!" he cried out at the top of his lungs.

"Now, are you going to tell me the truth?"

"I don't know what you're talking about," he wept. "That's my word!"

Denise took a deep breath before chopping off the foot.

"AHHH! Oh shit!"

"Do you remember now, motherfucker?"

Morris was losing a lot of blood, and Denise noticed it. "Oh no, bitch," she said, giving him a small dose of Demerol and then stuck his foot in a bucket of ice. "Now are you gonna talk, or do I have to cut off your dick?"

"Denise, I swear!"

"TONY!" she yelled.

"What about him?"

"He's your brother, so start talking."

With blood running down his face, Morris stared at Denise. "What do you want to know?"

"Everything."

Body feeling numb, Morris took a deep breath and started talking. "I swear, it wasn't supposed to go down like that."

"Like what?"

"It was Felicia's idea; she came up with the plan."

"Talk," Denise said, getting frustrated.

"Felicia found me and told me that we had the same father. She came to see me upstate. We talked and promised to keep in touch. When I got out, she introduced me to my other siblings. That's how I met Tony."

"AND?!"

"Yo, out of the blue, she said we needed to get payback for our father. She knew you killed him because you told her."

"How does Tony fit into this?"

"She told Tony the same thing. He was tight and agreed to kill you. It was supposed to look like a drug deal gone bad, but you killed Felicia."

"No, I didn't...but finish."

He gasped. "That's what we thought. Please, Dee, my body is shaking, and I can't feel anything."

Psychotically, Denise kneeled down and started giving Morris head. "You like that, huh? Don't I suck a mean dick? Guess what? I learned it from your father. He made me suck a lot of dick when I was young."

Once she realized Morris was fully erect, she picked up the blade from the floor and swiftly sliced it off. "Now you can't feel your dick either. FINISH!" she yelled, hitting him in the head and tossing his penis on the floor.

Morris screamed like a bitch. Blood was everywhere. "OH GOD, MY DICK!"

"Finish!" Denise said, while pouring acid on it.

"Alright! After we found out Felicia was dead, we decided to set you up for her murder."

"It was you who switched my gun?"

"Yeah. You left the safe open. I tried, but you came in, so I tossed your gun in one of your shoeboxes."

"That's why the gun didn't match, and that night, I got locked up."

"Nah, that was Tony. He saw you grab your gun, and he called the police."

"You did..."

"No! Tony called me at the last minute and said he changed the plans. That was the last time we talked about it until he had me follow you."

Confused, she asked, "Follow me?"

"Yeah. We had a chick in the court system who told us when you were up to see the judge. I made your friend Perry drop me off there so he could bump into you. Then I followed you to some restaurant."

"It was you who left me the note? It wasn't Perry?"

"Yes," he replied in pain, "but it wasn't my idea. Tony found out Perry killed his cousin Marion, and he wanted payback. He knew you would've thought Perry was Felicia's brother and would kill him."

"So, it was you and Tony I saw at Felicia's gravesite?"

"Yeah."

"Your plan worked; I killed my brother. What else?"

"After I killed that other dude for Tony, he paid me off and told me to fall back."

"What other dude?"

"The dude that was fucking his girl at the time."

"You killed Paul?"

"Yeah. Please can I have some more Demerol? Please!" he said, crying and begging.

"NO! Finish!"

"Tony said he had something to do with his cousin and was fucking his girl. So, he told me to kill him."

"Tony knew Perry and them had killed Marion." Denise smirked. "Fucking faggot. So where did Morgan come in?"

"Who?"

"Morgan..."

"She wasn't part of the plan. Tony said he fell in love with her."

"You mean he raped her."

Morris shot Denise a surprised expression. "Raped?! I don't know anything about any rape."

"Yes. Don't play stupid."

"Nah, I don't know nothing about that. It was straight about you, yo! It was get back for killing his cousin and our father."

Denise looked at Morris. *Is he telling the truth?* In a strange way, she believed him. Morgan was a last-minute decision.

Denise kneeled down behind him. "You know what, Morris? I believe you," she whispered in his ear before strangling him to death.

To clear her head, Denise went back to where it all started, and that was Melrose Projects. Sitting on the bench with her hands folded underneath her chin, she was deep in thought and didn't notice Greg walking up to her.

"You wanna talk?"

"How did you know I would be here?"

"When I'm going through something, I come here to clear my head, too."

Denise stayed quiet.

"You alright?"

"Friends...how many of us have them?"

"What do you mean?" he asked.

"I mean, it's always the ones we love and trust. Perry trusted me, and look at him."

"You did what you had to do."

"It doesn't feel like that."

"We lost a lot of people on the team."

"Fuck the team! A lot of niggas are dead or in jail because of their team. Don't tell me about the team, Greg!"

Greg nodded. "Alright..."

"I was always a soldier in your wars! I played my position. Even when I didn't agree with you, I still stood side by side with you. Unlike niggas today, I don't play both sides of the fence. I'm not phony," she proclaimed.

"You're not."

As the tears rolled down her face, Denise stared into space. "How did you feel when Alex crossed you? Did you ever expect it to be him?"

Taking a long, deep breath, Greg replied, "No."

"How did you feel?"

"Tight! I wanted to kill everything."

"Why?"

"Because I would've never expected him, you know?"

"Just like how I felt about Tony. I never expected him to cross me."

"What Tony did was messed up, but Morgan is an adult. If they're together, it's not your business. It was bound to happen. Look at how much time he's been spending with her and the kids."

Denise paused. What the fuck was Greg talking about?

"Greg, Tony raped Morgan when she was fourteen years old. Those kids are his; she's married to him!" she proclaimed.

"WHAT?! GET THE FUCK OUTTA HERE! RAPE?"

"Yeah, what did you think I was talking about?"

Greg threw his head back on the bench. "Are you serious?"

"Yes! I just found out. This nigga...after all I've done for him. I raised him. He also had Paul killed, and you know that nigga Morris I was fucking with years ago, it turns out he is Felicia and Tony's brother. Remember I told you that I thought Perry was following me?

Well, it was Morris. Tony told him to do that, knowing I would think it was Perry and kill him. Boy, I tell you that nigga has patience."

"So Tony was behind this," Greg said, rubbing his chin.

"Yep! Remember those two kids we killed for that nigga? The ones Tony said raped him?"

"Yeah?"

"That was a lie. He raped them when they were younger. The nigga is a homo, Greg!"

Greg released a devilish chuckle, something he did when he was pissed off. "Tony….good ole Tony."

"You knew?"

"I had my suspicions after Moe's man showed me some flicks of this tranny Tina that Tony messed with. He also said Moe and Tony fucked around back in the days. That's why Moe came at him, because he sucked Tony off a few times."

"WHAT?!"

Greg nodded. "That's what I said. So, Tony thinks he's the sharpest tool in the shed, huh?"

"Stay out of it, Greg. This has nothing to do with you. It's between me and Tony."

"He smiled in my face. It's because of me that he is who he is today. He can't do shit to us and think he's gonna get away with it. Are you fucking crazy? I will ruin that nigga. He fucked up the team. Niggas aren't here because of him."

Denise stood up. "You think I give a fuck about the team, huh? If any one of them was here right now, I would put a bullet in their fucking head. So, don't tell me about the fucking team. It's the team that crossed me. A fucking stranger would think twice before crossing me, but my friends? They'll do that shit all day. I had more heart than any of them. None of them could do what I've done. NONE OF THEM! Anytime they needed me, I held them down, even when the shit didn't have anything to do with me. It's because of me that they made it past the age of twenty-five. I would respect them more if they had come up to me and said, 'Fuck you,' before putting a bullet in my head. Keep it in the street; that's the rule."

"You're right! You've always been down for whatever, and that's even more reason you need me now. Always remember, sis, I'm here for a reason. I told you before many tried, but many died. This is payback for his father?"

"I don't know. There's a lot of shit. All I know is Tony should've come after me. I'm the one who murdered his father, not Morgan. Come and get me! I'm here! He had plenty of opportunities to kill me. He didn't have to do it himself. Pay someone. Morgan didn't have shit to do with this, Greg! He took her innocence. My sister died because of this shit; she blamed herself. On her deathbed, she said, 'He hurt my baby.' For months, I wondered what she meant. Jas knew! You know how fucked up I feel? That was her firstborn. She trusted me with Morgan's life. After all the shit she did for me, I let this shit happen. No matter what, Morgan is fucked up forever. She will never be right. She used to say it was because of me that she was pregnant. This nigga raped her in my apartment. He smiled in my face and violated my niece for years. How could I not see that? I knew something was wrong. I was supposed to be on point." She sobbed in anger.

"Dee…"

Shaking her head, she continued. "If I can't trust my friends, who can I trust? He raped her, Greg. Someone I called family raped her."

"Then let's handle this shit together like we did his father. Remember that night, Dee?"

She took a deep breath. "I can't, Greg!"

"Dee, do you know why I'm still here and not in prison or dead like most niggas? It's because I realized no one can do it alone. Why do you think I made sure y'all were good when I got locked up? Because it was y'all who helped me build my empire. You think you built that shit on your own? Everyone needs someone. My wife made me realize that shit."

"It's too late. So much shit has been done already. The only person left is him."

"Then let's give him an encore performance so we can go home to our families."

"What family? I only have the kids now."

"What about Derrick? Y'all broke up?"

Denise gave him a leery look. "Something like that. He was asking too many questions."

Greg's eyes opened wide like quarters. "You didn't..."

Denise released a devilish chuckle. "Till death do us part, right? Besides, he believed Sharon's ass over mine. So, fuck 'em both."

Greg shook his head. "You pushed Sharon's shit back, too? Get the fuck outta here. She was killed in the bathroom at the precinct."

"To protect and serve." Denise laughed.

"What the fuck am I going to do with you?"

"Ride," she said.

"Fo' sho! So who killed Felicia?"

"You don't wanna know," she replied while laughing and hugging him.

Chapter Twenty-Two
Gabrielle

L ike Denise, Greg felt played. Tony was the last person he would've expected to cross him. Steaming, Greg closed his eyes. After all he had done for Tony this was how he repaid him. Greg released a devilish chuckle. *Boy, I tell ya. Niggas only respect one thing, and that's violence.*

As Denise stated, they would've respected him if he had come after them. Keep it in the street, and let the best man/woman win. That's the rules of engagement, but dudes always say that until shit gets hot. Then they're either running to the police or doing some other shit like Tony.

Sadly, Greg respected Tony for pushing Perry and Paul's shit back once he found out they had murdered his cousin. Though he didn't like the way he handled it, at least it was payback for his cousin. However, to rape Morgan and force her to marry him was something Greg frowned upon. While he knew there was more to the story, either way, Tony was going to pay, and it was going to be with his life. Denise was a protégé of Greg. He taught her everything she knew. So, he knew she was going to bring the heat.

As for Gabrielle, she didn't feel sorry for Tony's ass. After what he did to Morgan, he should be horsewhipped and then hung from a pole outside. She was worried about Morgan, though. Gabrielle felt

Morgan needed to seek professional help for not wanting anything to happen to Tony.

Another person who surprised her was Denise, who was calm. Gabrielle thought she would've gone ballistic and killed Tony's ass by now. *Damn, she has really changed.*

With all the allegations concerning Tony, Gabrielle was happy that Greg's name wasn't mentioned. It was bad enough the police dragged his ass in for questioning. She already warned Greg that the second he fucked up, she and the kids were gone. There's no way in hell she was doing another state bid by his side. *He better call Britney,* she thought.

Since her parents announced their separation, the kids had been going over there every weekend. This weekend, Sadie and Noel were taking the kids to the museum. Therefore, Gabrielle and Greg planned a romantic dinner at home. With all the drama that was going on, Greg just wanted to spend a nice, quiet night with his wife.

Arriving home to the smell of southern food, Gabrielle dropped her bag and ran into the kitchen.

"Mmmm!" she moaned, kissing her husband. "You're home early."

"Yeah, I wanted us to get started early so I can get in that ass all night," he teased, winking at her.

"I bet. You know, this reminds me of the first time we made love. Remember?"

"You mean the night you raped me?" Greg jokily stated.

Playfully punching him in his side, she replied, "The night I raped you? Oh please! You were the one all over me."

"Get the hell outta here! You begged me to take you upstairs to give you the love muscle."

They both laughed.

"Oh well, your ass never left," she said, walking to the sink to wash her hands.

"That's right! You had me open." He kissed her.

Over dinner, they discussed everything from work to the kids' activities. They were having a great time, until Greg received a call from Tony. Usually when Greg was at home, he didn't answer his phone, but since Tony was going through so much, he answered this time.

"Tony, what's up?"

"Chilling. I wanted to know have you found out anything."

"Nah, no one knows where it's coming from, but don't worry. You know I'm on it. Keep your head up."

Click!

"How's Tony doing?" Gabrielle asked, pretending to care.

"Scared to death."

"Well, he should be," she grumbled.

"Boo, come on. He just loss a lot of people," he said, pretending to sound concerned.

"And, Greg? After what he did to Morgan, and not to mention Denise..." she started but stopped herself.

"I know."

Gabrielle stared at Greg. "So you know?"

"Yeah, Denise told me. That's fucked up."

"It is, but what is Denise gonna do? She can't let him get away with it."

"Morgan doesn't want anything to happen to him."

"So!" Gabrielle slammed her hand down. "Morgan needs help, if you ask me. Denise needs to get her far away from Tony. He has brainwashed her."

"True, but Boo, Denise has a family now. She has to respect Morgan's decision," he explained, lying.

"I guess. I know if it was my child..."

Greg glared at her. "It wouldn't happen. I will kill a nigga, for real."

After dinner, they moved into the family room to watch a movie and then spent the rest of the evening making passionate love. Greg had a lot of frustration built up, and he took it all out on Gabrielle.

*****

It was a Saturday, and no one would be in the office. Gabrielle went there to catch up on some paperwork. She glanced at her watch. Seeing that it was going on four o'clock, she started to clean off her desk. While filing clients' folders, Gabrielle came across the box Margaret, Tommy's sister, had left her. Immediately, her eyes filled with tears as she grabbed the box and sat down.

Gabrielle sighed and then opened it. Inside, there were letters and tapes of the stuff they had presented in Greg's case. With tears rolling down her face, Gabrielle smiled.

"Tommy," she muttered.

She was about to seal the box up, when she noticed a large envelope. *This doesn't look familiar,* she thought. She opened it to find pictures and some documents. Closely examining the pictures, Gabrielle almost fainted.

"This can't be true." She continued reading, and then she ran over to the cabinet, grabbed one of the tapes, and played it.

"Oh my God!" she screamed, covering her mouth.

She grabbed everything and sprinted out of there. Driving like a mad woman, Gabrielle pulled up to the house, jumped out, and banged on the door.

"Where is he?" she asked, searching through the house once she was inside. "Where is he?" she said louder, while advancing toward the family room and flinging the door open. "You bastard!"

"What?" he said in shock.

Given Gabrielle's behavior, Sadie asked the housekeeper to take the kids into the other room.

"Gabrielle, have you lost your mind?"

"Ma, I want you to listen to this." Gabrielle pressed play on the handheld digital recorder she had brought with her. She looked fiercely at her father as the tape played. "Doesn't that voice sound familiar, Ma?"

Still, Noel pretended to be clueless, while looking at her and then Sadie. "I don't know what you're talking about," he said.

"Don't insult my intelligence!" she exclaimed.

"What are you talking about?" Sadie said.

 264

"Maybe this will help refresh it!" she snapped, throwing the pictures and other documents.

Sadie knew the voice sounded familiar. "Is that you on the tape, Noel?"

"Tell her, Daddy. Tell her the real reason Greg was sent to prison!" she cried. "TELL HER GOTDAMNIT!"

Shaken, Sadie asked, "Noel, what is she talking about?"

"Ma, you know what you're hearing. It's my father discussing my husband's case with the assistant district attorney."

Wearing a grave look, Noel remained silent.

"What?! Noel!" Sadie shouted in an angry tone. "Is that true? Noel, how could you?"

"No, there's more. Tell her why you were discussing my husband's case, Daddy," Gabrielle angrily grumbled.

"You did this all to keep him from your daughter?" Sadie asked in a baffled voice.

Gabrielle released a phony laugh. "HA!" she blurted out. "That's what I thought. Daddy, tell Mommy the real reason why you were discussing my husband's case." She glowered at her father.

Noel looked like a deer caught in headlights. He tried to say something, but couldn't find the right words. It was as if someone had removed his tongue. Thus, Gabrielle helped him out, while her mother stood there bewildered.

"It's because Greg was dating my sister. Isn't that right, Daddy?" she cried.

Still, none of it was making sense to Sadie. "You mean Gracie, Gloria, or Giselle?"

"No, Ma, his other daughter. Papa was a rolling stone. He was having an affair with the assistant district attorney."

Feeling weak, Sadie leaned on the chair. "What? Noel, what is she talking about?" she gasped, getting upset.

"Sadie, you have to understand..." he replied as if he was struggling to breath.

"Understand what? Noel, what did you do? Answer me gotdamnit!" she demanded.

Frightened, Noel looked over at Gabrielle and then back at Sadie. He was caught.

"Tell us, Daddy! Help us understand."

"Gabrielle, I never meant to hurt you. If anyone found out, I would've lost everything."

"Now it's all starting to make sense. When Daddy found out that Greg was seeing me and Britney, he knew it was only a matter of time before he got caught. That's when you decided to set up Greg. Tommy warned me this wasn't about a murder or drugs; it was about the money. Isn't that right, Daddy!" she said, handing her mother a copy of Britney's birth certificate.

"Is this true?! You fathered another child?" Sadie shouted.

"Sadie..."

"Motherfucker, answer me! Did you?" she shouted, getting in his face.

"Yes," Noel exhaled.

Silence filled the room as Sadie sighed and then read the name on the birth certificate. Starting to feel lightheaded, she grabbed onto a chair. "You never stopped seeing her."

Now Gabrielle was confused. She looked over at her mother and then her father. "You knew?" Gabrielle asked.

Sadie started to explain while crying. "Two years into our marriage, I found out your father was having an affair with his ex-girlfriend. She was white, just like your father liked them. I'd always wondered why your father chose me. I guess I was the closest thing to being white. Isn't that right, Noel?" She chuckled. "All these years, you were still seeing her. Boy, was I naïve."

"Sadie..."

"My gut kept telling me that you weren't the man for me. I gave up my life for you, and this is the thanks I get. You ruined your daughter's life. What do you have to say, Noel?"

"You're still seeing her?" Gabrielle asked.

"Yes, she needs me. After all you did to her, Gabrielle..." Noel stated.

Sadie ran over and slapped him across the face. "You bastard! Don't you fucking dare say this is Gabrielle's fault! Don't you fucking blame this on my child! If anyone should be the blame, it's your cheating ass!" she screamed. "I gave up my life for you. All these years…" she paced the floor. "Thirty-nine years I gave you, and this is how you thank me. How could you? How could you do this to your own daughter?"

"I did this for both of my daughters. This wasn't supposed to happen."

"So y'all are together?" Gabrielle asked.

"Yes. I never left her. I'm sorry, but I love her. She's the one I want to be with. Sadie, I never meant to hurt you or my family."

Gabrielle felt like she was in the twilight zone. This couldn't be happening.

"You did this for yourself, Noel! This was never about your daughters," she yelled, slapping him again. "I want you out of my house. Get the fuck out!"

"Sadie…"

"GET OUT! I want you out!"

Noel lowered his head and nodded. "I did what was best for my family," he tried to explain.

"You're a disgrace to this family. I'm ashamed to call you my father, but I swear on my children that I'm gonna make sure you pay!" Gabrielle shouted.

"Sadie…" he tried to say.

"Sadie my ass! I want you out of this house!"

Gabrielle stormed over to him. "I will never forgive you for this!"

Sadie fell into her daughter's arms and wept.

"I'm so sorry," Gabrielle cried.

"Don't be. I should've left his ass a long time ago."

Gabrielle and Sadie talked for a couple of hours before she left. She was going to take the kids home, but her mother begged her to let them stay. She needed something to take her mind off of what had just taken place.

*****

It was three o'clock in the morning when Greg came home from the club. "Boo, you're still up?"

Gabrielle looked up at him with her puffy eyes. "Yes."

"What happened? Are the kids alright?"

"Yeah, they're fine. Greg, we need to talk."

"What's wrong? Did anything happen to the kids?"

"No. It's about your case and other things," she replied while leading him into the other room.

Taking a seat in the living room, Greg was scared but not showing it. So many things were running through his mind.

"After I found that letter from Britney, I reached out to a private investigator named Tommy Tulip," she told him.

"The guy who was killed in the car accident?"

"Yes. He was the one who helped me with the case."

"Okay."

"During our research, we came across a lot of information. Boo, I know Britney was supposed to testify on your behalf. That's what you were counting on. She would've, but Jake informed her mother, and they kidnapped her until the trial was over."

"Jake?"

"Yes! Boo, everyone knew you didn't kill Charlie. It was never about Charlie."

"What do you mean?"

Gabrielle sighed. "The judge, detectives, Jake, and Robin all plotted to send you away. For the judge and detectives, you knew too much. You were supplying them with drugs and hookers, so they couldn't risk you talking. As for Jake, he got trapped off. He wasn't a part of it at first, but they backed him into a corner and made him join."

"What about Robin?"

"Now she's a different story. At first, I thought it was because you were messing with her daughter. But, tonight, I found out that was only part of it."

"What do you mean?"

"Apparently, Robin was secretly recording her conversations with everyone. I figured she did that in case shit hit the fan, because she identified all of them by their names on the tape except for one person. She never revealed his name, so we figured that was the mastermind behind everything, the one she was protecting. Before Tommy died, he found out who the mysterious voice on the tape belonged to," Gabrielle said, getting up to play it.

Greg listened, but didn't recognize the voice.

"You know who that is?"

"Nah, I don't."

"It's my father. Greg, Britney is my sister."

"What?"

"My father was having an affair with Robin. When he found out you were seeing me and Britney, he thought he would get caught. That's why they set you up."

Greg stood, placed his hand on the wall, and shook his head. "You gotta be fucking kidding me. How did you find out all of this?"

"I came across her birth certificate," she cried.

Angry, Greg asked, "Where's your father now?"

"With Robin. Tonight, my mother found out that he never stopped seeing Robin."

"Your father took my freedom away, huh?"

"Yes. I'm sorry."

"It's cool," he said, hugging his wife. "So Britney is your sister?"

"Yes, but there's more to the story." Gabrielle pulled away from him.

His eyes widened, and he took a step back. "There's more?"

Gabrielle took a deep breath and paused.

"You wanna tell me what?"

"When I found out what they did, I kinda reacted."

"You reacted?"

"Yes! Just before you came home, I paid all of them a visit, starting with Jake who was supposed to protect you. This motherfucker lied to me in my face and took my money. I don't take well to people doing that bullshit. He thought if he gave my money back to me everything would be fine, but it wasn't. That's the same thing with Judge Barron and those fucking corrupt detectives. They took your life, your freedom. They all owed us, and the settlement was their life."

"Boo, you..."

"Yes! I had to! No one fucks with us. When you went to prison, a part of me went with you. I prayed every night for you to come home. I cried myself to sleep. They weren't going to get away with that. Let the choices we make today be the ones we can live with tomorrow. That's what my mother use to say."

Greg was quiet. He couldn't believe what he just heard. His bourgeois-ass wife was a stone-cold killer. Greg scanned the room thinking it was a joke and that he was on *Candid Camera*, but it wasn't. Gabrielle was dead serious.

"Damn, Boo! I didn't know that."

Gabrielle nodded. "I wanted to tell you, but didn't want you to be upset with me. I didn't want you to think it was about loyalty or me wanting to be down."

Still stunned, he responded, "Nah, I would never think like that. You did what you had to do. And it's a good thing you did it, because if I would've found out..." he started.

They both laughed.

Gabrielle sighed. It felt good telling the truth; her heart felt free.

Greg stood up and grabbed his wife. "You know I love you, right? I love you with all of my heart and soul. I don't want you to ever feel like you can't come to me. Boo, it's us against the world."

She smiled. "I know, and I love you more. You're my everything, Boo."

"You, too."

They kissed.

"So you never stopped going to the gun range, huh?" Greg said.

"Nope! That's the one thing I did like doing with my father. Funny it paid off. Oh, there's one more thing, Boo. I'm the one who killed Felicia."

"What?! Get the fuck outta of here! You?"

"Yes. She came to me demanding a million dollars or she was going to go to the police."

Greg just busted out laughing. *This shit is so surreal. Tony's a homo, raping little girls. Denise is killing everything that's moving, and my wife is a sniper. Boy, I tell ya. What else is going to surface?*

"Is there anything else you wanna tell me?" he asked.

Gabrielle pondered for a second. "Nah, I've confessed all of my sins."

They both laughed.

Although Greg was upset with Gabrielle, a part of him was turned on. She was truly his ride-or-die chick. Never in a million years would he have suspected his wife to put in work like that. *Damn, I guess the world is full of scattered lies.*

However, Noel and Robin were about to get a visit from the Angel of Death. Noel had smiled in Greg's face knowing he was the one who put him in prison. Greg didn't care about him being his father-in-law. He wasn't going to let that slide.

*****

It was as if they never had the conversation. Gabrielle and Greg were even closer. In fact, Greg convinced Gabrielle to forgive her father, which was a part of his plan. They went over to Noel and Robin's house to settle things. Greg wanted to know why they did that, and after a long talk, Greg shook Noel's hand. Sadie, on the other hand, wasn't that forgiving. She burned what was left of Noel's belongings and took all of his money out of the bank. She reported him to the IRS and changed the locks on all of their property. She was so upset that she moved to Florida with Gracie. Gabrielle's sisters felt the same way. They disowned their father and wondered why Gabrielle hadn't either.

Greg told Denise what happened, and together they planned revenge. Denise couldn't believe Noel's shiesty ass. Shit like that pissed her off. She was already on a warpath. Being that Morgan was pregnant again, Greg convinced Denise to fall back from Tony. He wanted Tony to think he was safe again and then catch him with his pants down. While they were doing that, they carefully plotted on Noel. Gabrielle was out of town visiting her mother. He also heard Britney was visiting Robin. So, it would be the perfect weekend to execute things.

One thing Greg learned in prison was to think smarter. It's not what you do, but how you do it. If half of the dudes thought about what they did before they did it, a lot of them wouldn't be in prison. Murder was the easiest case to beat, especially if you didn't have a body.

Noel and Robin had purchased a home in Buffalo, New York, and they had just finished eating dinner, when Greg and Denise surprised them.

Knock! Knock!

"What's up, Dad?" Greg said, barging in. "Since Denise and I were in the neighborhood, we figured we'd stop by."

Stumped, Noel let them inside. "Sure, come in."

"Noel, who is it?" Robin asked, while coming down the hall.

"Robin Cox." Denise winked.

"What's going on here?" Noel asked.

"Where's your daughter Britney?" Greg inquired.

Noel looked at Greg and then Denise. Something about their demeanor wasn't good. He looked them up and down. Both were dressed in black and had on black gloves, too. Something was up.

"The food is getting cold," Britney announced, joining them in the foyer. "Greg!" she said in a startled voice.

"What's good, ma? Now that we have everyone, I think we need to have a sit-down. Don't ya think?" Greg said, signaling Denise to pull out the shotgun.

"Greg..." Noel said, holding his breath while standing in front of Robin and Britney to protect them.

When Greg noticed that, he was fuming. "Look at the motherfucker protecting his white family."

"Greg, we've been through this. I thought we smoothed everything out," Noel said.

"*You* thought we did. Motherfucker, you took my freedom. You think I'm gonna let you get away with that."

"What is he talking about?" Britney asked.

"Why don't you tell her?" Greg suggested. "Tell her, Noel. No, why don't you tell her, Robin?"

"Tell me what?" Britney asked, staring at them.

"Britney, Noel is…" Robin started.

"Is what?"

"He is…" Robin hesitated.

Frustrated, Denise fired a shot in the air, causing everyone to jump. "Tell her the whole truth, you lying bitch."

Robin looked at Greg and then Denise. "He's Gabrielle's father."

"What?" Britney backed away from them. "Greg's wife Gabrielle?" she asked in disbelief.

Noel looked at Britney. "That's why you're here. So we can tell you."

"Britney…" Robin reached out for her hand.

Britney backed away some more. "I can't believe you lied to me. How could you?"

"We did this to protect you."

Britney looked at Greg, then Denise, and then back over to her mother. "Kill this lying bitch," she ordered, catching Denise and Greg off guard.

"Britney!" Robin screamed in shock.

Bom! Bom!

An aggravated Denise fired two shots, hitting Robin in the stomach and chest. Greg ran over to Noel and knocked the shit out of him. He then grabbed Noel by his shirt and beat him to death. Blood was everywhere.

"Greg, chill! He's dead," Denise said, grabbing his arm.

"Fuck that nigga," he said, kicking him before walking into the other room to clean up.

"Greg, what you wanna do with your sister–in-law?" Denise joked.

"What did you say?" he asked, returning to the foyer.

"What do you wanna do with this broad?"

Greg stared at Britney, pulled out his gun, fired two shots into her, and then went to finish cleaning up.

Denise smiled. "I don't ever wanna be on your bad side."

Before leaving, they poured acid on the bodies and cut the gasoline pipe.

Still fuming, Denise drove back to the city. "Are you okay?" she asked Greg.

Taking a long, deep breath, he responded, "Now I am."

Chapter Twenty-Three
Morgan

Things were finally settling down, and the police no longer had Tony as a suspect. Now, if only Morgan could get rid of the morning sickness she was still experiencing at eight months. That evening, they were attending a charity event where Tony would be receiving an award for his outstanding work.

It was the first time the public had seen Tony since the death of his family and friends. He and Morgan walked the red carpet.

"Tony! Tony! How are you holding up?" a reporter asked.

Tony smiled. "I'm good. Between my wife and kids, they are keeping me sane," he replied, then laughed.

"Your wife?" the reporter questioned.

"Yes. This is my beautiful wife, Morgan Flowers."

Morgan smiled. "Hello."

"Hi, Mrs. Flowers."

Instead of answering a bunch of questions, Tony and Morgan posed for pictures before going inside. Joining Denise and Greg, Tony smiled and greeted them.

"What's up, Tee?" Greg laughed. "You and the things you do..." he said while shaking his hand.

"Morgan..." Denise said, pretending to be surprised.

"Hi, Auntie." Morgan smiled but the worried look was still evident on her face.

Tony cleared his throat. "Dee, can we go someplace and talk?"

Noticing Morgan's protruding stomach, Denise smiled and replied, "Sure."

Shaking hands as he walked through the crowd, Tony led Morgan, Denise, and Greg to a private room.

"Dee, I need to tell you something. Morgan and I are together; we are married."

Morgan's eyes widened. She was shaking and thought for sure she would go into labor.

Denise looked over at Greg and then at Morgan. "What do you mean married?"

Tony sighed. "She's my wife."

"Tony..." Denise said only to be cut off.

"Dee, I know you think I'm a piece of shit because I cheated on Christina or from the way I treated Stevie, but I'm a man now. I've changed. I would never do that to Morgan. I'm in love with her. I've never loved anyone as much as I love her. I've changed, sis. I'm not the same Tony."

"Is this true, Morgan?" Greg asked.

"Yes, we're happy. Aunt Denise, we wanted to tell you, but knew you would be upset," Morgan chimed in, hoping Denise wouldn't go off.

Tony walked up to her. "Dee, I never meant to hurt you. I didn't plan this. It just happened. You out of all people should know love has no boundaries. Look at you and Derrick."

Denise nodded. "Tony, you know Morgan is my niece, but she's like a daughter to me."

"I know. Dee, you don't have to worry. I'm not like that anymore."

"Do you love him?" Denise asked Morgan.

Surprised, she stared at her aunt for a moment before replying, "Yes, Aunt Denise, I love him."

"Then I have nothing more to say. Tee, just remember..."

 276

Tony exhaled. "I know, sis." He reached out to hug her. "Trust me. I'm not going to do anything to hurt her."

Tony reached out and kissed Morgan in front of them.

"So what are you having this time?" Denise snidely asked.

"We're having twins," Morgan replied, beaming.

"Dee, she's good," Tony said, trying to reassure her.

"Oh, I know." Denise winked.

Once Tony and Morgan exited the private area, Denise and Greg looked at each other.

"This shit is crazy for real. You know, I truly believe he loves her," Greg stated.

"Shit, that makes two of us, but that doesn't change the fact that he raped her."

"True! Morgan needs some serious help, Dee. Tony did a number on her."

"Tell me about it. Greg, it took every ounce of me not to stab his ass."

"I know, sis, but he'll get his in due time."

The dinner was wonderful. Tony and Morgan cuddled all night, not leaving each others side. As for Morgan, she fit right in. Since she was smart, she held intelligent conversation.

Morgan was sitting by herself when Denise came over. "Hey, niece, are you having a good time?"

"Yes, but my feet are starting to hurt," she replied, giggling.

"That's pregnancy for ya," Denise teased.

"Thank you, Aunt Denise."

"For what?"

"For not saying anything to Tony, and for accepting him and us. Aunt Denise, I know it's sad the way we started out, but we love each other. He's a great father to my kids, and he loves me very much."

"Morgan..."

"No wait, Aunt Denise. Tony has paid for what he's done to me; he lost his entire family. If I can forgive him, then you can, too."

Denise's eyes started to tear up. Morgan was just like her mother. "You remind me of your mother. She always pointed out the good in a person, even in me. If that's what you want, then I'm fine with it."

"Yes, Auntie, that's what I want."

She embraced her niece. "Then that's what you will have."

Denise was in a daze the whole night. For the first time, she thought about what she had done. Within a couple of months, she killed more than the Son of Sam. Did she make a mistake?

"How are you holding up?" Greg asked.

"It's hard, you know. Morgan wants me to forgive him."

"How do you feel about that?"

Denise looked at him. "Forgiveness is between him and God. I'm just gonna arrange the meeting."

Greg laughed. "Don't worry, Dee. God will forgive him. He will forgive all of us."

Greg was about to say something else, but Tony came over. "Thanks, guys."

"For?" Greg asked, sipping his drink.

"For being there for me. Dee, I know you're not alright with me messing with your niece. But, real talk, sis, that's my heart."

"Tony, you said that already. I get the picture." Denise then leaned closer and stared in his face. "If I find out you hurt her, I promise you that I will cut your fucking heart out, and I mean that from the bottom of mine," she warned.

Tony looked at Denise and then over at Greg. He didn't like the vibes they were giving. Therefore, he smiled, shook their hands, and left.

After the charity event, Morgan and Tony hopped on a plane for a nice family vacation. Instead of going to their private island, Tony rented a two-hundred-foot luxury yacht to cruise Europe. Sunbathing on the deck, Tony and Morgan laid there cuddling.

"Hey ma, what are your thoughts about Denise?'

"What do you mean?"

"You think she was happy with us?"

Morgan sighed. She thought about telling Tony the truth, but didn't want to worry him. "I don't think she was happy, but she'll come around. It's just gonna take some time. Why?"

"I don't know. I was getting a bad feeling from her."

"Oh really? Well, I spoke to her, and she gave us her blessings."

Tony looked at Morgan. "She did?"

"Yep. Don't worry, baby. She'll come around. Like I said, just give her some time. If not, at least it's out in the open. Now we just have to find a way to tell my father."

"What you think he's gonna say?"

"As long as I'm happy, he will give us his blessings."

Tony reached over to hug his wife. "I will make sure you're happy."

*****

For the next two weeks, Morgan shopped and did a lot of sightseeing with the kids. She and Tony had decided to visit her father together, and then it was off to have dinner at her grandparents.

Tony was trembling; it was the first time he'd been inside a prison. Morgan, on the other hand, was fine. When Tony saw Felix come from behind the door, he almost shitted on himself. He hadn't seen him in years, and now he really realized who Morgan's father was.

Damn, Morgan looks just like her father, Tony thought.

Morgan smiled. "Hey, Daddy."

"Hey," Felix said, staring at her.

"Hi, Felix." Tony's voice cracked when he spoke.

"Tony Flowers, I haven't seen you since you were a teenager. How are you?"

Tony smiled. "I'm good."

Felix nodded, then looked at Morgan. "Where are my grandkids?"

"Oh, I didn't bring them this time. I needed to talk to you about something."

"Okay."

"Hmmm," Morgan said, taking a deep breath. "I'm pregnant again."

Felix already figured that, but looked down at Morgan's stomach and then over at Tony.

"Tony's the father. We've been seeing each other for years. I'm married to him."

Felix lowered his head, wondering why Tony wasn't dead. He wanted to break the Plexiglas and choke the shit out of Tony, but he didn't. In fact, he played along with them.

"Tony, I thought you were married to that pop singer."

"Nah, we were never married. Felix," Tony said, taking control of the conversation, "I know Morgan is your princess, and I just wanted you to know that I would never do anything to hurt her. I love her, and with your blessings, I wanna spend the rest of my life with her."

"Don't you think you should've asked first? Isn't that the respectful thing to do?"

"Daddy..." Morgan whined, annoyed.

"I'm just saying, Princess. You don't go and marry someone's daughter and then tell them after the fact. Stunts like that can get people hurt. Am I lying, Tony?"

"No, sir, you're not lying, and I'm sorry for not asking for your blessings beforehand. But, I love this woman. That's all I know."

Pissed, Felix listened while nodding. He glanced at Morgan, who was smiling. "Princess, I don't know what to say."

"Daddy, Tony loves me and the kids."

"I see. Princess, give me and Tony a couple of minutes alone."

Morgan glanced at Tony and then her father. "Okay," she said, excusing herself to the restroom.

"Felix..." Tony said.

"Now you listen to me, you punk son of a bitch. You're lucky this glass is between us, or I would've ripped your fucking heart out. You come up here asking me for my blessings after you married my daughter."

"I know, sir," Tony responded, scared.

"That's my daughter. You understand me? You may have her fooled, but I know better," he said, giving him a Robert Deniro look.

"Felix, it's not like that. I love her! I would never do anything to hurt her or my kids."

"For your sake, I hope not. Tony, just because I'm in here doesn't mean I can't reach you out there. In this case, money can't buy you safety."

Tony nodded. "You have my word."

"And you have mine."

"I hear you."

Morgan returned. "Is everything alright?"

"It's perfect, Princess. Right, Tony?" Felix winked.

"Yes."

*****

Morgan wasn't home a week before going into labor. She and Tony welcomed Justin and Justine Flowers into the world. To make things even better, they had just closed on their mansion in Lake Minnetonka. Morgan really didn't want to move, but Tony was right. Until they found out who was behind all the killings, they couldn't take that chance.

Besides, Morgan didn't like the limelight. Every time she went out with the children, someone was snapping photos of them. It seemed like every other day their photos were in a magazine or posted on a blog site. Some even compared her to Christina. At least they didn't say harsh things about her or the kids. Many of them couldn't believe Tony married someone better than Christina. While Morgan didn't have her money, she sure was better looking. In addition, they loved their kids. People couldn't believe they were Tony's kids.

Although Tony made Morgan travel with security, it didn't stop her for doing normal things with the kids. Today, she and Denise were taking the kids out. Surprisingly, they had gotten closer.

"Hey, niece." Denise smiled.

"Hi, Auntie." Morgan kissed her on the cheek.

Lil' Derrick grabbed his cousins by the hand and took off into the park, making Denise and Morgan laugh.

"Derrick, be careful!" Denise yelled.

"Where's Derrick?" Morgan asked.

"Derrick and I are not together anymore. It didn't work out," Denise lied.

"Awww, I'm sorry to hear that. Where is he now?"

"I don't know. We haven't talked in months. But, how are you doing? How's married life? And the twins?"

"Married life is wonderful, Aunt Denise, and the twins are great!"

"Good! How's Tony treating you?"

"Tony is doing great. Everyone warned him."

"Everyone like who?"

"Oh, we went to see my father."

"You did?"

"Yeah, we had a long talk. My father gave us his blessings."

"That's good."

"Oh, Tony and I are relocating."

"Why? Where?"

"Well, Tony doesn't want anyone to know, but we're moving to Lake Minnetonka. Until he knows who's behind all the killings, we're moving. You heard about his mother and Al, right?"

"What about his father?" Denise asked.

"He passed a few weeks after Tony's mother died. He was real sick."

"Oh! When are y'all moving?"

"We just closed on our house, so in a couple of weeks we are moving. But, don't tell anyone—safety precautions."

Denise smiled, confused. "Safety precautions?"

"Yes, Tony is having this high-tech security company install a system in the new house. We are meeting them in a couple of weeks to see how the system works."

"Oh, okay. Listen, Morgan, in case Tony starts acting up, I wanna know the exact location, the security code, and anything he's installing. I know he said he loves you, but just in case. You hear me?"

Morgan laughed. "I know."

*****

Fall had just started, when Tony and Morgan finally settled into their new mansion. Morgan had to admit, things turned out to be perfect. The kids were healthy, and Tony finally had some peace of mind.

"Hey, are the twins sleeping?" Tony asked.

"Yes. Tell me why we had more kids," Morgan asked with her hand on her hip.

"Because you do it so well," Tony replied, then laughed and kissed her on the lips.

"Yeah, whateva." Morgan pushed his face away.

As Morgan stared out the window watching Lil' Anthony and London in the yard, Tony hugged her from behind. "What's on your mind?" he asked.

"Do you realize how blessed we are? I mean, considering everything we've been through, our family is happy and safe."

"Yes, baby. I thank God for y'all. Don't think I could've made it without you."

Morgan leaned her head back against Tony's chest. "I think moving was the best thing for us. I feel safe."

"Yeah, for the first time, I do, too."

"Babe, do they know who killed your family?"

"Nah, the police still don't have any leads, but you know they don't give a fuck."

"Don't worry. They will catch the people," she said.

"Have I told you how much I love you, Mrs. Flowers?" Tony smiled and kissed her on the back of the neck.

"No, you haven't, Mr. Flowers."

They were about to kiss, when Morgan heard the babies crying. She and Tony giggled.

"Alright, Mommy's coming."

Tony stood there smiling and watching his children play.

"Daddy!" They called for him to join them.

Meanwhile, Morgan was upstairs tending to the babies, when she saw a shadow fly past the room. Thinking it was Tony, she walked over to the doorway.

"Tony," she called out.

Slam!

Morgan opened the door to the other room. "Babe," she called, but there was no one inside. Looking around, she saw the window was open.

That's strange, she thought while closing it.

Chapter Twenty-Four
Tony

Even though Tony missed New York, he couldn't risk his family getting hurt. Within a year, he had lost his entire family and best friends. There was no way he was about to lose his wife and kids. While watching *Law & Order*, Tony thought about the police and their investigations. He couldn't believe the police didn't have any leads. He wondered if they were actually behind it since he knew a lot of them didn't like him. Also, Tony found it very odd that Detective Clyde and Sharon were killed.

Meanwhile, Morris hadn't called him back. Tony had left several messages for him, knowing he had heard the news by now. Tony knew for sure once he spoke to Morris that together, they would find the killers. Another thing that bothered him was he didn't even say goodbye to Greg and Denise. Though they weren't on the best of terms, at the end of the day, it was because of them that he was able to enjoy the fruits of his labor.

However, there was one person he didn't miss, and that was Christina. That bitch had the nerve to sue Tony for her publishing rights. But, it was all good. Even with all the tragedy Tony was going through, he still managed to win. If it wasn't for Morgan convincing him to give Christina the majority of her publishing rights, Tony would not have given her shit. While he didn't give a shit about her marriage to Rashid, Tony felt like he had built her and she played him.

"Daddy," London said, walking into the room.

"Hey ma, what's up?"

"Read to me."

"Now?"

"Yes. It's almost my bedtime."

Tony laughed. Morgan sure did have them trained. Turning off the television, he carried his daughter into the bedroom, where he read to her until they both fell asleep.

The following morning, Tony flew to New York City for a business meeting. Then it was off to Los Angeles where he would receive an award and perform. This time, he left Morgan and the kids at home.

Ahhh, the smell of New York, Tony thought as he jumped into his awaiting car service. On a tight schedule, he headed over to his midtown office. It was amazing what his new team did with it. Everything was state of the art. Smiling as he walked into the conference room, Tony realized he missed this so much. Once everyone was seated, Tony got right down to business, from listening to tracks to signing off on contracts. Since Mookie always wanted to branch out and tap into pop, rock, and jazz, Tony fulfilled his dream.

Next, it was off to meet with his accountants and business manager. He called Greg and Denise a few times, but their phones went straight to voice mail. Hopefully the next time he was in New York, they could all hook up and have dinner for ole times' sake. Sadly, they were the only ones left. Mike was murdered in Chicago. According to the streets, he was coming out of a club with some chick, when a dude walked up on him, shot him in the face, and then walked off. No one had seen anything. That's why Tony knew it had to be either the police or someone they knew.

After Tony met with his business manager and accountants, he hopped on his private jet heading to Los Angeles. Tony phoned Morgan from the plane, making sure everything was alright. She and the kids had just returned from grocery shopping.

Instead of going to his hotel, Tony headed over to the Kodak Theater to do a sound check. It'd been over a year since he had been on stage. Like the late Michael Jackson, writing was the only way Tony knew how to express his pain. After sound check, he headed back to the hotel, checked in with Morgan again, and then got ready for his big night. That night, Tony didn't walk the red carpet. Instead, he went through the back entrance to avoid the reporters.

Tony took to the stage and killed it, dedicating his performance to the people he lost, something like Diddy did for Biggie. He received a standing ovation, and there wasn't a dry eye in the house. Even Christina, who was in attendance, was touched by his performance. Back in his dressing room, Tony received a call from Morgan and the kids who were praising him over the phone. His eyes got watery when Lil' Anthony said, "You're the greatest daddy."

During his acceptance speech, Tony thanked everyone who supported him, acknowledging the people he lost and closing with love for Morgan and the kids. Initially, he was supposed to fly right out, but after that wonderful performance, everyone wanted to meet with him. Against his better judgment, Tony went to Aaron Styles' party. Everyone in the industry was so happy to see him. Although Tony was an asshole when it came to business, tonight, many saw a different side of him.

On his way out, Tony bumped into Rashid. At first, they stared at each other, unsure of what to say especially since everyone was watching. However, Tony put his hand out to shake Rashid's.

"We're good."

Rashid smiled. "Great performance."

Tony winked, smiled, and then headed home.

A couple of days had passed, and people were still talking about Tony's performance, saying, "The king of New York is back." His new manager wanted him to go back on tour while the energy and love was good, but Tony declined. Losing his families made him realize that life is too short. Therefore, he had to cherish the important things, and for him, playing with his kids and helping his wife cook were two of the many things. Like David Chappelle said, "It's the lifestyle that will drive you crazy." Everything was at your disposal, from drugs to women.

Morgan had given up her dreams for Tony, so tonight, he was taking her into town to have a nice romantic dinner. Then they were going to take a nice walk. Since they lived right outside a small town, Tony didn't have to worry about people recognizing them. Everyone kept to themselves.

Dressed down, Tony and Morgan went to Fletcher's Restaurant, which was small and intimate. Over a glass of wine, southern fried chicken, mashed potatoes, and light music playing in the background, they laughed and talked for hours. Just like normal couples do, Tony even pulled his wife up to dance.

Gazing into her eyes, Tony whispered, "I'm finally happy."

"Me, too," she whispered back.

"I love you, Morgan Flowers."

"I love you more, Tony Flowers."

In a love zone, Morgan and Tony strolled hand in hand as they walked to their car.

"Baby, if you ever wanted to go back on tour, it's fine with me. I'll support you in whatever you do."

"I know you will, but I don't wanna do that. It wouldn't be the same without Tia and Mookie. They were with me from the beginning."

"Yeah, but I'm pretty sure they would want you to live your life."

"I'm doing that right now. Morgan, being on stage was great. Sure, I could zone out and do my thing, but what happens when I come off stage? At the end of the day, the problems are still there."

"You're right. Hey, did you have a chance to see my aunt or Greg?"

"No. I left them several messages, but they haven't called me back. They're probably busy. With everything going on, I know they're keeping a low profile."

"A low profile for what?"

Tony paused. Morgan didn't know about her aunt. "Ma, you don't know about Dee?"

"Know what?"

"Your aunt is crazy."

She laughed. "Tell me something I don't know."

"No, ma, before Derrick and the kids, Denise was something else. She was Greg's hit man."

"Who?" Morgan said, raising her eyebrow at Tony.

"Denise. You didn't know she was a hit man? She's the type of chick that when you cross her, she'll wait and get you when you least expect it."

Morgan froze. "Denise kills people?"

"Killing people isn't the word. She puts that work in. A lot of people were scared to death of her while growing up."

She lowered her head. *Oh my God. What if Denise is behind this?* Morgan looked over at Tony. She needed to tell him, but what if she was wrong. She needed a little more evidence before telling him.

Later that evening, Morgan was in the kitchen drinking some water, when she thought about what Tony had said about Denise. *A killer?* On her way up to the bedroom, Morgan heard a noise.

"Cindy," she called out, thinking it was the nanny as she opened the door. However, there wasn't anyone in the room. She glanced around and noticed the candlestick holder on the floor. *It must've fallen,* she thought. She shrugged her shoulders and closed the door back. Then Morgan heard the shower running. She smiled.

"Wait for me," she said while laughing.

As Tony thrust in and out of Morgan, she glanced up and saw Denise standing in the doorway.

"Oh my God!" she screamed. Morgan jumped up in a cold sweat and glanced around the room. *It was just a dream,* she thought, looking over at her naked husband. Morgan went downstairs to get something to drink. Just as she was about to go back upstairs, she heard someone in the next room. So, she went to the door and opened it. This time, she was grabbed from behind by a person who covered her mouth.

"Take your kids and get the fuck outta of here."

Morgan paused. She knew that voice. "Aunt Dee, is that you?"

At first, the gunman didn't say anything, so Morgan repeated, "Aunt Dee?"

The gunman released Morgan and then removed the mask. Just as Morgan thought, it was Denise.

"Get the kids and get out of here."

"Tony was right. How could you?"

"Morgan, take the kids and leave now. This has nothing to do with you."

Crying, Morgan replied, "It is about me. It was you who killed those people. You killed Tony's family."

Frustrated and focused, Denise replied while grinding her teeth, "Morgan, take the kids and get the fuck out of here!"

"I'm not leaving. I'm not going to let you kill my husband."

"Your husband? Morgan, he raped you! How can you call him your husband?"

Shaken and crying, Morgan replied, "Who are you to judge? You're no better than him. It's because of you that he raped me. If you wasn't so busy running after some damn man, you could've stopped him."

Denise lowered her head as Morgan's words penetrated her soul. She was right. If she didn't run out that night, none of this would've happened.

"I know, and I kick myself everyday in the ass because I left you that night. That's why I need to make it right."

"By killing everyone? What does that solve? What's done is done." Wiping snot from her nose and tears from her eyes, Morgan said, "I'm willing to forget everything that happened tonight if you just walk out of here and never come around us again."

"Morgan, I can't."

"Yes, you can, or I'm going to the police. I swear I'll go."

Denise stared at her battered niece and thought about Jasmine. Lowering her gun, Denise grabbed Morgan.

"I'm sorry," she told her, as they both started to cry.

"Me, too. Now please, Aunt Denise, just leave."

Denise stared deeply into her beautiful niece's eyes. "I love you, and I'm sorry for everything," she mumbled, then fired two shots into Morgan.

Morgan gasped, holding her stomach "Oh my God..." She looked up into her aunt's eyes. "I...forgive..." she said before collapsing to the floor.

Greg busted in the door. "What the fuck have you done?"

Kneeling over her, Denise looked up at Greg. "She's gone."

"Morgan!" Tony called.

"Dee, we have to get the hell out of here," Greg said.

In a trance, Denise replied, "I can't leave her."

"Dee, let's get the fuck outta here now," he said, yanking her arm.

"Morgan!" Tony yelled again, going down the stairs.

Denise took one last look at Morgan before sneaking out.

As they went back to their hiding spot, they heard Tony scream at the top of his lungs, "NOOOOO!!!"

*****

The death of Morgan practically killed Tony, who wondered why the killer didn't take his life instead. Overwhelmed with grief, he couldn't make funeral arrangements. The one thing that scared him the most had actually happened. He couldn't even tell their children what happened to their mother. London asked for her mother every day. In addition, it was Tony who had to tell Morgan's family the tragic news. Felix was silent over the phone, while Denise and Morgan's siblings went berserk.

As Tony walked into the church with his children, he prayed it was just a nightmare—that he would wake up with Morgan right by his side. But, that wouldn't be the case. Morgan Flowers was gone. Michael and Monique spoke at the funeral, bringing everyone to tears. Felix was granted approval to attend his daughter's funeral. Dressed in a black suit with shackles around his wrists and ankles, Felix got up and spoke. He broke down so much that his mother had to console him. On his way out, he leaned forward to whisper something in Denise's ear.

Denise, on the other hand, was in a total daze, looking spaced-out. Morgan was her favorite niece. Therefore, Tony knew she was taking it hard. But, it was London who broke everyone's heart when she said, "There goes Mommy" and then ran to the casket begging her to wake up.

After the funeral service, Tony and the kids went to his penthouse where they had been staying since Morgan died. He had just laid the kids down for a nap, when Felix's mother stopped by.

"How are you holding up?" she asked, kissing him on the cheek.

"Mrs. Marciano, I'm doing the best I can for the kids, but it's hard."

"I know, dear. Tony, do the police have any leads?"

"Nothing. I even hired an investigator."

"Well, keep me posted. Listen, I know the twins are yours, but I wanted to see if I can get custody of London and Anthony."

"Custody?"

"Yes."

"Mrs. Marciano, the children are mine. I'm their father," Tony explained.

"Oh, I didn't know. I assumed you were just taking care of them."

"No, they are mine, but thanks for the offer. That really means a lot to me."

The housekeeper informed him that Denise, Greg, and Gabrielle were there to see him.

Mrs. Marciano said hello to them before going to check on her grandchildren.

"Tee, how are you holding up?" Greg asked.

"Not good, man. Dee, I'm sorry."

You will be, she thought, but replied, "She was like a daughter to me. I can't believe she's gone."

Greg looked over at Denise, praying she doesn't lose it. He'd never seen her like this. He had to check on her every day. While

Tony appreciated everyone's support and prayers, he couldn't wait for them to leave.

After their departure, while Tony was sitting in his living room, London and Lil' Anthony came in.

"Daddy," Lil' Anthony softly uttered, holding his sister's hand.

"Yes, big man?" Tony said, picking them both up.

"We want Mommy," he begged.

Tony exhaled as tears rolled down his face. "Me, too...me, too."

"She didn't love us no more?" London asked.

Tony stared into his daughter's face and noticed how much she looked like her mother. "No, Mommy loved us with all of her heart."

Just then, the housekeeper informed Tony that an investigator was there to see him. So, he told the kids to go upstairs, and he would be there shortly to tuck them in. After wiping his face, he told the housekeeper to send them in.

"Mr. Flowers," the investigator said.

"Hi! Did you find out anything?"

"Sorry, I wish I did, but I haven't," he said, signaling Tony to sit down. "Tony, this is personal. Do you have any idea who has the money and power to pull something off like this?"

"A lot of people."

"Well, put together a list and let me investigate the people. Only someone that knows you could've done this."

"Alright, I'll get back to you."

Tony paid Frank and then walked him to the door, thanking him for his services. When he returned to the living room, he poured himself a drink and stared out the window. *There are only a few people I know that could pull this off,* he thought.

After that huge fight with Christina, Tony knew it was only a matter of time before Christina told someone about his tape collection. Therefore, he sent his kids to Italy for a visit and went to his New Jersey mansion to clear his head.

As Tony walked into his mansion, he thought, *Damn, I miss my wife so much.* He was in the family room when he heard someone pull up to the house. *Who the hell could that be? No one knows I'm here, not even my security team.* Tony peeked out the foyer's window. It was Greg. *What the hell is he doing here?*

"What's up, Greg?" Tony said in an apprehensive voice.

"You tell me. You alright?" Greg asked.

"Yeah, I just needed to get away from all the madness. My bad, were we supposed to hook up tonight?" Tony asked, leading him into the family room.

"Nah, I heard what happened with you and Chris?"

"Do you believe that bitch? She's lucky I'm going through something, or else I'd have Denise kill her ass. You know, I think the jealous bitch had something to do with Morgan's death."

Waiting for Greg to respond, Tony noticed he was looking around and not paying attention. "Greg, are you alright?"

"Yeah, Tee. What you say about Chris?"

"She came over to the crib wilding out a couple of days ago. She's upset because I married Morgan. You know she never really got over me," Tony said with a touch of humor.

Greg's silence started to scare Tony.

After a couple seconds went by, Greg replied, "Well, you can't blame her. You had a lot of us fooled."

Something about Greg's behavior worried Tony. He stared into Greg's face. "How did you find out about my fight with Chris? Better yet, what did she tell you?"

Greg angrily stared at Tony. "What you think?"

Tony swallowed hard. "I don't know. You tell me."

"Tony...Tony," Denise said, entering the room with her .357 magnum drawn. "How does it feel?"

Scared, Tony slowly backed up. "It was you?"

Denise smiled. "You never did learn, huh? What did you think was going to happen when I found out? You of all people should know better."

"So you killed your own niece. Why not come after me?!"

"That was the plan, but Morgan loved her family so much that she was willing to die for them. Just like your family and friends, you don't deserve that kind of loyalty."

294

Tony looked over at Greg with an expression that asked, *What the hell is she talking about?*

"Tee, it's time to put the cards on the table."

"What are you talking about?" Tony asked.

"Let's start with you raping my niece, motherfucker. How 'bout that?"

Surprised, Tony held his breath.

"You think I wasn't gonna find out? What doesn't come out in the wash comes out in the rinse. Remember that?"

"Denise..."

"You raped her!" Denise yelled as tears fell down her face. "You raped her for years!"

Tony swallowed hard. "It wasn't..."

"It wasn't what?" Denise asked.

"You think I raped her?" Tony picked up the remote and turned on television. Plastered across the screen were Morgan and Tony having sex. Morgan was begging him to fuck her. "Does that look like rape?"

Greg looked at Denise, who responded, "Of course, she's begging you so you wouldn't hit her. That's why. You think I'm stupid."

Tony looked over at Greg, who was putting on a pair of black gloves. He knew they were going to kill him.

"Greg, come on, man! I didn't rape her!"

"This nigga is still lying," Denise said.

"Tee...it's over," Greg said in a calm tone.

Denise was so angry that she placed her gun on the table. Shooting him would be too easy. She wanted him to feel the pain Morgan endured. "With all the bullshit you pulled, Tee, we still would've been cool, but you fucked up when you went after Morgan. That's when you broke the fucking rules."

"What?" he said, acting clueless.

"Oh, don't play stupid, nigga. We know all about Felicia and Morris being your siblings. Morris spilled his guts, literally."

Tony's eyes widened. "Morris..."

"Look at him, Greg. He's shitting on himself. Yep, Morris. I had to admit y'all motherfuckers were good; almost got away with it. I never would've expected y'all to be siblings." She laughed.

It was time to drop the act. "Yeah, they were my family. You killed our father. Did you think you was gonna get away with that? It was payback."

"Your father, nigga? Fuck your father! Do you know what your father was about? He pimped women and had sex with little girls."

With the remote still in his hand, Tony changed the tape. "It doesn't look like that to me." On the screen was a young Denise having sex with an older guy. "I guess the apple doesn't fall far from the tree."

Tony slowly moved back to the sofa. *Damn, I never installed that high-tech security system.*

"I couldn't fuck her mother, but damn, Morgan...now she was sweet," he said, flicking back to their tape. "Look at the way she rides my dick while it's in her ass. She's a natural." He flicked back to Denise's tape. "I guess she learned from the best."

Steaming inside, Denise chuckled. "It's funny that you say that. Tina told us how you like fucking in the ass." Denise winked.

Tony stared at Greg and then Denise. "Is that why you paid Moe off? Because he sucked your dick years ago?"

"What are you talking about?" Tony asked. "Moe never..."

"Nigga, stop lying! We know about Moe and the dudes that you raped years ago."

Frustrated, Greg blurted out, "You're insulting my intelligence. We know that you knew Perry and Paul killed your cousin. We also know you set up Perry and had Paul killed."

With tears in his eyes, Tony lowered his head, praying for someone to come and help him.

"Fuck Perry and Paul! They killed my cousin at your orders. Marion didn't deserve to die. You guys fired first. What was I supposed to do? As for Paul, ha! That nigga was fucking my girl. All of you knew. Yeah, Tony Flowers—always the butt of jokes. Well, not anymore. So what I killed them niggas. Fuck them. They didn't mean shit to me. Yes, I was the mastermind for setting you up, Denise. I'll take the blame for that. Hell, you killed my father."

"Your father deserved to be put in the ground. Don't worry, Tony. You will be there to join him. I'm gonna watch you take your last breath like I did with him."

"You did that already. When you killed Morgan, you killed me. She was my everything, and you didn't have the right to take her away from me."

"You didn't deserve her!" Denise snapped.

"Greg...Dee, please, man," Tony cried, letting go of his tough act. "Yo, I didn't mean to..."

"You didn't mean to what?" Denise asked, injecting a needle into his neck. "Lights out, nigga," she said busting him in the head with the gun.

Just like she did to Morris, Denise and Greg strapped Tony to his dining room table.

"What's going on?" Tony asked in a daze while face down on the table.

"Killing your ass would be too easy. So, right now, you are about to witness unbearable pain," she told him before shoving a pipe up his ass.

"AHHH!" he screamed.

"Ahhh!" Greg and Denise screamed along with him.

"Ahhh! Greg...Dee please...I'll give you whatever you want," he cried.

"You know what, Tee? Some things just aren't for sale," Greg said, ripping open what was left of his asshole. Blood splattered everywhere.

"Turn this nigga over. I want him to see my face," Denise ordered

"Wait, Dee, give this nigga some medication. We don't want him to die on us yet," Greg said.

Denise shot Tony up with some medication and then turned him over. Tony, who was barely conscious, released a sorrow-filled moan.

"I want you to see everything, so even in hell, you will see my face. In your next lifetime, you will know better than to cross me," she told him, then removed his eyelids.

"No...please," Tony moaned. He tried to fight her, but was unable to move. He felt like a quadriplegic.

Greg left the room only to return with a sledgehammer. "Watch out, Denise." In a rage, Greg smashed each of Tony's legs. He came down with such force that you could hear the sound of the bone crushing and the skin tearing.

All Tony could do was yell in anguish. Although he was paralyzed, he could feel every bit of pain.

"Hold up, Greg. Give me the sledgehammer and hold his head up."

Denise smashed Tony's face in, knocking out his back teeth. "Your ass can't cry with a broken jaw."

Blood was everywhere. The right side of Tony's face was open, exposing his skull. Greg threw acid on his wounds so they would stop bleeding.

"I warned you that if you ever crossed me, I would kill you, motherfucker," Denise said, plunging a knife into him with so much force that she cracked one of his ribs.

Even with a broken jaw, he managed to mutter, "Denise...I'm sorry."

"Nah, you're sorry because you got caught."

"Since you think you're God, Tee, we're gonna treat you like one," Greg said. "Dee, let's get some white sheets, tie this lame up, and let him hang from the top of the balcony.

Denise busted out laughing. "Greg, you're crazy, but I love it. Very biblical."

They dragged Tony's battered, bloody body to the top of the stairs. As they were tying him up, they heard a car pull into the driveway. They looked at each other and smiled.

Perfect, they both thought.

Chapter Twenty-Five
Christina

*D*amn, all the money in the world couldn't save Tony's family. He lost everything from his mother to his wife. I guess what they say is true about God not liking ugly, Christina thought.

Christina smirked. *So Morgan is the one who stole Tony's heart.* She could not believe how stupid she was, thinking that Tony could do something from the heart. Morgan was his type–young and pretty. Christina just always felt Morgan was off limits considering that was the niece of Tony's best friend. This was what Tia was talking about when she said Tony was something else. But, no matter how upset Christina was when she found out about them, she still wished them the best. Actually, she was happy that Tony finally grew up and took care of his responsibilities. She couldn't even imagine what Tony was going through. From the reports she heard, he was devastated and had been placed on suicide watch. Her heart went out to their children. They were so beautiful.

Rashid and Christina were married during a small ceremony outside of Los Angeles with just their parents and close friends in attendance. With everything that was going on, they had to postpone their honeymoon. Christina had just started promoting her album and was working on her next tour. She and Rashid decided after this tour, they were going to start working on having babies. They both had received their degrees, and when she sued Tony for her publishing rights, it was Rashid who encouraged her not to give up. Since Paul, Rashid was the best thing to happen to her.

It was late, and Christina had to be up early in the morning. Therefore, she stayed at her favorite hotel. While preparing for bed, she heard a knock on the door.

"Señora Christina?"

Christina came out of the bedroom. It was Carmen.

"Hi, Carmen. It's kinda late, and I'm tired."

"Please," she said.

"Sure," Christina replied, leading her into the living room. *I hope she doesn't want money or help with a green card.*

Scared that someone was in the room, Carmen searched the area. "Sorry...I don't want anyone to hear."

Bewildered, Christina simply said, "Okay."

Carmen took a deep breath. This had been bothering her for many years. After taking a seat on the sofa, she grabbed Christina's hand.

"I've been worried about you for so many years. Every night I prayed for you, asking God to protect you," Carmen said, tearing up.

Still confused, Christina stayed quiet. She knew Carmen was a spiritual person. Something was weighing on her heart.

"What's wrong?" Christina asked.

Wiping the tears from her eyes, Carmen nodded. "Sí, Señora. The night you got sick, I should've done more. I tried..."

Reflecting back, Christina realized she was referring to the night she lost the baby. "Carmen, there was nothing you could've done."

"Yes, I could've. You don't understand."

"What are you talking about, Carmen? You're scaring me."

"That night..." Carmen said, getting up. "Señor Tony came in early, and you was in the room talking to his friend. I caught him listening to your conversation. When he saw me, he went into his office."

"Tony was there?"

"Yes. He came out and told me not to let anyone know he was in his office."

"So he heard everything," Christina said in disbelief.

"I was putting the linen away when I saw Señor Tony standing in the doorway of the bathroom. It looked like he was pouring something on the floor. So he wouldn't see me, I hid in the closet."

"OMG!" Christina gasped. "You don't think…"

"I was in my bed when I heard you scream. I jumped up and ran to you, but Señor Flowers was standing in the doorway. I asked him if he wanted me to call the ambulance. He turned towards me and said no. Señora Christina, I begged him to please let me call someone. Finally, he nodded okay." Carmen cried in relief. "I'm sorry…"

"Oh God, no!" Christina fell back into the chair. "Tony caused me to lose my baby."

"I wanted to tell you so bad, but I was afraid. That's why I quit," Carmen explained.

Christina started to cry. "I can't believe it! How? Why?"

"He knew about you. I saw him watch it on TV."

"You saw him watch what on TV?" Christina asked, trying to make sense of Carmen's words.

"You and the man that was killed. Señor Tony watched y'all on TV. In his office, he has tapes. He keeps them locked away."

Christina's eyes widened. "Carmen, are you telling me that Tony has tapes of me and Paul?"

"Sí. I saw him and his wife. I'm so sorry. I didn't know what to do."

Christina put up her hand. "Carmen, it's not your fault, okay?"

Overwhelmed with guilt, Carmen nodded. "Only if I…"

"Stop it!" Christina said, embracing Carmen into her arms.

"Señor Christina, you know the man that went missing? I heard Señor Tony telling him he needed to help."

"Help with what?"

"Oh, I don't know, señora."

"Did he say anything?"

"No, but Señor Tony pulled out his cell phone and called someone."

Christina hugged Carmen and thanked her again before heading out.

Son of a bitch! Tony knew about me and Paul all this time. That's why he made that slick comment about me fucking hired help. He's the one who leaked the photos to the media.

It was time to pay Tony a visit and get the truth.

Christina cancelled everything and hopped on the next flight to New York. She arrived at Tony's penthouse apartment, but he wasn't home. Even though she didn't live at the penthouse anymore, she still had access to his place. Once inside, Christina went into Tony's office to search for the tapes. It took some time, but just like Carmen said, Tony had some tapes hidden in his drawer. Sure enough, it was Christina and Paul having sex. Christina almost passed out. She couldn't believe her eyes. "Motherfucker," was all she could say. She popped another one in, and again, it was her and Paul having sex in a hotel. "Son of a bitch," she muttered in anger.

Searching his other drawers, Christina came across some more tapes that were labeled "Me and My Baby". Christina popped one in, and it was Morgan and Tony having sex.

"This sick bastard records people having sex."

He even had one of him and Asia.

"What the fuck are you doing?" Tony yelled.

"You're sick! How could you?"

"How could I what?" he asked.

Christina flung some tapes at him. "This, motherfucker! You taped me!"

Tony glanced at the screen. "You were fucking my man, bitch. That's what you get!"

"You killed Paul, and you caused me to lose my baby."

"Shit happens! You think you was gonna slide off with my man and have his baby? Bitch, I made you. Fuck you and him!"

Christina charged him, trying to slap him, but Tony blocked it and pushed her on the floor.

"I'm going to the police," she cried.

"And tell them what? It's my word against yours. Get the fuck outta my house, you slut. And to think I even cared about you." He twisted his face up. "Yo, get this bitch out of my house. If she comes back, have her ass locked up," he instructed his security team.

"I swear on my life you're gonna pay. I promise you that," Christina cried as they carried her out. "That's why your wife is dead, motherfucker!" she screamed.

"You better watch your mouth, bitch!" Tony laughed.

Distraught and angry, Christina went to her old apartment. On her way there, she called Greg. Right now, he was the only person she felt like talking to.

By the time Greg arrived, Christina was drunk, and judging by the way she looked, she'd been crying.

Awww shit, Greg thought. "Hey," he said, greeting her with a kiss on the cheek and smelling the liquor on her breath.

"Hi! Sorry I look like shit," she said, leading him into the other room.

"Are you alright?"

A puffy eyed Christina, responded, "No. Greg, do you remember Tony's housekeeper Carmen?"

"Yeah. What about her?"

"I ran into her. She works at one of the hotels in LA. She told me that…" Christina paused and started crying. "She told me that Tony caused me to lose my baby."

"Tony?" Greg said, confused. "How?"

Christina took a deep breath. "Remember that night you and I talked? We were in the family room."

"Yeah, you told me about Paul."

"We both thought Tony wasn't there, but he was. He came in and overheard us. Carmen caught him listening to our conversation."

Greg's eyes widened. "So he was there?"

"Yes! He heard everything. He also admitted to killing Paul. How could he do this?" Christina cried.

Greg took a deep breath. "I don't know."

Christina looked at him. His response didn't sound right to her. "You knew?" she asked.

Greg looked away.

"Answer me!" she yelled.

"Yeah, we found out he had something to do with Paul and Perry's deaths."

Christina went to the bar and poured herself another drink. "I thought Paul was your friend. You knew Tony killed him and didn't do anything?" she asked with much pain in her voice.

"There's a time and place for everything," Greg stated, trying not to reveal too much.

"A time and place? Did Paul have that? Did my baby have a time and place?"

Greg lowered his head.

"Paul looked up to you. He wanted to be like you, and this is how you repay him? How much did Tony pay you to sweep this under the rug?" she snidely asked. "I'll pay you double."

"It's not about money."

"It's always about money, Greg. Don't give me that bullshit." She fiercely stared at him.

Greg went up to Christina and took the glass out of her hand. "Come on, stop. You know this is not you," he whispered.

"No. Don't tell me what to do. I'm not your fucking wife," she stated, trying to push him away.

However, Greg overpowered her, taking the glass out of her hand. "Come on, it's time for us to talk."

Once he led Christina over to the sofa, Greg started talking. "Chris, we just found out about what Tony did to Paul, Perry, and Morgan."

"Morgan?" she asked.

Greg sighed. "Tony raped Morgan when she was fourteen. He married her to cover it up."

Christina held her stomach. "Rape? Tony raped Morgan?"

Greg nodded. "Yeah. He also had his brother kill Paul. Part of it was because of you and his cousin. It's because of him that Tia and Mookie were killed."

Getting sick, Christina ran into the bathroom and vomited. While rinsing her mouth and throwing water on her face, she cried.

"Are you alright?" Greg asked, handing her a towel.

"Tony raped Morgan. How could he do that? Does Denise know?"

"Yeah, she knows."

"What is she gonna do about it? I mean, now Morgan is gone. She can't let Tony raise those kids. Greg, we have to do something."

Greg hugged Christina. "Oh, something is going to be done."

"So where is he now?"

"He's staying at his house in Alpine, New Jersey."

"Oh really?"

Greg nodded.

"So you're still friends with him knowing all of this?"

Greg laughed. "Knowing is half the battle."

After Greg left, Christina sat there in disbelief. She played back everything in her mind. How could she be so stupid? She remembered one time giving Tony head and seeing dried blood on his penis. Her entire relationship with Tony was built on a lie. He had played all of them. Like the others, Christina laughed to herself. *Tony is a piece of work.* She glanced at the clock.

"Shit. It's getting late," she mumbled.

Christina searched for her cell phone. She knew Rashid and Joyce would be worried about her, considering how she left. She called both to let them know she was fine. Joyce offered to fly out, but right now, Christina really wanted to be alone.

"Fucking Tony," was all she could say.

She was about to call it a night, when her cell phone rang displaying a private number. Her first intention was to send it to voicemail, but something told her to pick it up.

"Hello," she answered.

"Chris, it's Greg, I was just calling to check on you and make sure your ass doesn't do anything crazy."

Christina sighed. "Oh, it's you. I started not to pick up because I normally don't answer private numbers. But, I'm fine. I still can't believe him, though."

"Yeah, well, check it. We decided to try to convince Tony to turn himself in."

"He'll never do that," she told Greg.

"He will if we all confront him together. I figured if you, Denise, and I confront him, he will have no choice but to turn himself in."

Christina looked at the phone. *Is this the same Greg Brightman people feared?* "I don't know, Greg. Tony is a motherfucker," she explained.

"Exactly, but I doubt he's gonna play with us. If not, we'll go to the police ourselves. Like you said, he can't get away with this."

She nodded. "You're right. Okay, so when are we confronting him?"

"Tonight. He's staying at his mansion in Alpine, New Jersey, right off of the Palisades Parkway."

"Oh, I know where it is. I'll meet you there."

Christina took a shower and got dressed. *Damn, how the hell am I going to get there?* The last thing she needed was the media getting a hold of this. That's when it dawned on her to just drive herself. Funny, she remembered Paul making her purchase a car just in case of an emergency, and this couldn't be a better time to use it.

"Alright, Tony," she grumbled.

*****

Two cars were parked in the driveway when Christina arrived. She shook her head. Tony made sure no one would find out about him and Morgan. The house was practically in the woods.

Christina pulled out her phone to let Greg know she was outside, but he didn't answer. Instead of leaving a message, she headed inside. She was about to knock, but someone opened the door from the inside.

Alert, Christina called out, "Greg!" as she entered.

Emerging from behind the door was Greg, sweaty and bloody as hell. "Chris, what's up?" he said, locking the door behind her.

"Oh my God!" she said in shock. "Are you alright?"

"Yeah."

"Where's Tony?"

Greg looked over and up towards the stairs. "He's good."

Scared and confused, Christina just stared at Greg. "What's going on?" she asked in a terrified voice.

Just then, Denise emerged from one of the rooms. "Chris, I'm so glad you could make it."

Christina looked up at Denise, who was also sweaty and bloody. Then she glanced back at Greg. It was a set up. She tried to run, but Greg grabbed her.

"Where are you going?" he whispered.

"Please, Greg, I promise I won't say anything," she cried.

"Ugh..."

Christina heard the sound of Tony's faint moan. With a full grip around her, Greg forced her to look up in Denise's direction.

"You didn't think we was gonna let him get away with it, did you?" Greg asked.

"I know you guys are upset. So am I. Tony killed the love of my life and my baby, but killing him isn't gonna bring our loved ones back. We can call the police and say someone broke in and tried to kill him. Hell, I'll say it," Christina pleaded.

Sadly, Greg and Denise had no intentions on letting her leave there alive. What Christina didn't understand was that even though she didn't kill Paul, by her messing with him, it indirectly caused his death. Even still, Greg could accept that, but the bitch pretended to love Paul. And what did she do after his death? She married Tony. In Greg's eyes, she was no better than Tony. Let's not forget her slick-ass comments she said to Greg.

"We're not going to do a motherfucking thing."

By then, Denise managed to get Tony's mutilated body over the banister. Since Tony believed he was God, Greg and Denise were going to put him on display the same way.

Christina was so terrified that all she could do was cry. Up until then, she didn't feel sorry for Tony, but seeing him hanging there and barely breathing, she wished she could save him.

"Please call the police. He's gonna die," she begged as tears rolled down her face.

"Police? Is she fucking serious, Greg? This nigga caused so many people pain, and you want us to save him? He killed your man and your baby, and you want to save him? Tony was right when he called you a stupid bitch. No one is calling any police. Let me show you the meaning of 'Hell has no fury like a woman scorned.'"

Denise raised a Chinese sword, and with one swift swing, she took Tony's head clean off. His head hit the wall, while his body jerked for a couple of seconds.

As Christina screamed at the top of her lungs, Greg shoved her away from him and pulled out his gun.

"Greg...please," she cried.

"M.O.B. Money over bitches." Greg then smiled before close casketing her ass.

Two Years Later

What they say must be true: Murder is the case to beat. Even with all those bodies, Denise and Greg managed to make it home scot-free. Since they had no suspects, the police believed Tony was the mastermind behind the murders. However, they never found Morris and Derrick's bodies. Everyone just assumed Derrick ran off with someone.

As for Greg and Gabrielle, they were still going strong. The police believed Britney killed Noel and Robin before committing suicide, but Gabrielle knew better. She was pissed that Greg beat her to the punch.

Morgan's children went to live with Felix. That was the best place for them. She remembered Morgan feeling alone because she didn't resemble anyone on her mother's side. She didn't want Morgan's children to grow up like that. So, it was the least she could do.

On the other hand, Denise got professional help. The death of Morgan and Derrick really sent her over the edge. Many nights, she would wake up in a cold sweat, crying about what she'd done. It was Morris who baffled her, though. All those years she'd been fucking him, she never knew his last name. In fact, Denise never knew anything about Morris, unlike Derrick, the only man she had ever loved and killed. Maybe she was a ruthless killer after all.

Some days, she wished she could turn back the hands of time. The one thing she tried to avoid was the one thing she became: a single parent. Lil' Derrick looked just like his father, and Halle had his personality. Nowadays, Denise lived for her kids, making sure she was the best mommy she could be. Derrick would've wanted that.

Every now and then, she checked on Morgan's kids. It was amazing how much they looked like her. London was the spitting image of Morgan. Denise laughed because Tony always wanted a beautiful family, and Morgan gave him that. Denise would never understand why Morgan wanted to protect her rapist. Yes, he was the father of her children, but look at what he had done to become that. Denise could still hear Morgan telling her how painful it was when they had sex or how he would beat her for breathing. He was the only person she didn't regret killing. If she could do it all over again, she would do it in a heartbeat.

Tonight, Greg and Denise were hanging out for the first time in months. They were meeting at Greg's restaurant. Gabrielle was supposed to join them, but cancelled at the last minute.

Gabrielle was in her office at home, when the doorbell rang. She glanced out of the window and saw a black SUV.

Who the hell is that? She thought.

BAM!

As she looked through the peephole, her brains splattered all over the wall.

Across town, Greg and Denise were laughing their asses off. It felt good to smile again.

"Bro, it's getting late. I have to get up early in the morning. I promised the kids I would take them to the zoo."

"Yeah, I know. I have to get going, too. Boo is probably waiting up for me."

"I need you to take me to my car."

"No problem. Let's go."

As they were chilling at a red light, two black SUVs pulled alongside them. While joking and not paying attention, another car pulled up behind them. The light had just changed and Greg was about to pull off, when another car blocked them.

"What the fuck?!" they yelled.

Greg reached in the glove compartment to get his gun, but it was gone. "Shit!" he yelled, thinking it was the police.

The car door opened, and a man dressed in a black trench coat and with shades on got out. Seconds later, a bunch of men jumped out with machine guns.

"Oh shit! It's a hit! Get down!" Greg said.

Tah, tah, tah, tah, tah!

Smoke came from the car as the bullets penetrated the metal. The guy in the trench coat raised his hand for the men to stop, and then ordered them to pull Denise and Greg out of the car. Greg was hit multiple times in the torso. Surprisingly, Denise had only been hit in the shoulder.

Trying to breathe, Greg lashed out, "What the fuck is going on?"

The gunmen looked over at the man in the trench coat, who nodded. Then they riddled Greg's body with bullets, causing his body to jerk.

"Stop!" Denise yelled at their attackers. "GREG!" she screamed, as she heard him take his last breath while falling to the ground.

Next, they dragged her into the middle of the street. At first, Denise didn't recognize the man's face, but when he got closer, all she could think was *Oh my God!*

"I told you that I was gonna keep my promise."

"Felix!" she cried.

"Because of you my daughter is dead! My princess is gone, and her children will be raised without a mother."

Denise lowered her head. Deep down inside, she knew this day would come. Somehow, she wasn't scared. The world was filled with so many scattered lies, and only the truth could set them free. Filled with conviction, Denise looked up into Felix's eyes and smirked. All of a sudden, it started thundering and crackling. She glanced up at the sky and saw a flash of lightning. It was time. Her day had come. But, like a soldier, Denise didn't shed a tear.

"A deal is a deal. Just take care of my children. Will you do that for me?"

"You have my word."

Denise closed her eyes and prayed, asking God to forgive her for all of her sins.

She laughed. "I guess what they say is right. A bullet always tells the truth. Hell, here I come."

She remembered a verse that Jadakiss said: *And you know they say you deserve it whenever you die with your eyes open.* Only cowards closed their eyes, and Denise wanted to see it coming.

Felix smirked. Denise had more heart than most men. He shot her nine times in the head, causing it to smoke. Denise's body dropped like a leaf.

"Is that bitch dead?" his mother asked after Felix jumped in the car.

"Yes!"

"Good. No one fucks with a Marciano," she stated.

Redemption is the only chance of salvation. Denise and Greg forgot one thing. Even the Devil and Angel of Death had to answer to God.

WWW.COM
SNEAK PEEK

Dressed in black Armani suits and black Prada sneakers, Chance, Justice, Patience, and Seven pulled up in front of World Financial Bank, the largest currency distributor in the world. According to Justice, World Financial held a minimum of five hundred million dollars in their vault.

"Bottoms up," Seven said as she hopped out the SUV, with the other ladies following suit.

Justice flashed her badge to the security guard at the entrance. "Hello, sir. We're with the FBI, and we need to see the bank manager."

"Right this way," the guard replied, then led them to a private area located in the rear of the bank.

Knock! Knock!

"Mr. Jude, the FBI is here?" he announced, entering the office.

Mr. Jude stood up from his desk. "FBI?" he repeated, confused.

"Yes," the guard responded.

"Mr. Jude, I'm Special Agent Kennedy. We're here to inspect the room," Chance lied.

"Are you sure? I thought it was no longer needed. In fact, I'm almost certain," Mr. Jude affirmed.

I

"Actually, Mr. Jude, next week is the last week. We just have to make sure the equipment is up and running so they can stream it back to headquarters," Chance answered, thinking quickly.

"Oh, okay, even though I think this is a bit much. No one is thinking about robbing this bank."

"And why do you say that?" Justice asked.

"Because they would never get past the high-tech security system," he answered confidently.

"Well, you never know. They said September 11th would never happen, but look. One can never be too careful," Patience stated.

"True," he replied before leading them to a secure area.

He turned around to glance at the ladies once more, flashing a fake smile while thinking, *Something looks strange about these women.*

"Here we go, ladies," he said, opening the door.

Since 9/11, banks had installed command centers. Ammunition, SWAT uniforms, and high technology equipment were stored in these rooms that only top government officials knew about. The security system could shut down the entire bank, preventing anything from working, even cell phones.

Only a handful knew that on the first Friday of every month, the government took the system offline for thirty minutes to back it up. This was more than enough time for Seven to hack into the system and change the images.

"Done," Seven announced as she signaled for the ladies to pull out their weapons.

Mr. Jude gasped and damn near shitted on himself, while raising his hands in the air. "What's going on?"

"We're here to make a cash withdrawal," Chance informed him, exercising her sense of humor.

Scared to death, Mr. Jude tried to press the pendant on his jacket, but Justice noticed and swiftly busted him in the head with her gun, knocking him to the floor.

"Next time, mi gonna put a bullet in your fucking head," she warned him in her Bajan accent. "Now take the bumbaclot blazer off."

Chance giggled. "We know about the alarm pendant on the blazer," she said, kicking him in the ribs.

"Please, I have a family!" he cried.

"So, don't do anything stupid, or I promise Mayor Bloomberg will be visiting them this evening," Chance whispered in his ear after snatching him up from the floor.

Seven, who was typing something in on the computer, yelled out, "Guys, we have less than twenty minutes before the system reboots! Let's move it!"

The ladies looked up at the clock and then quickly changed into the Swat uniforms that were hanging on hooks in the room.

Chance ordered Mr. Jude into the private vault. "You know what to do," she told him, pushing her pistol into his back.

Bleeding from his head, Mr. Jude did exactly what he was told. Once inside the vault, the ladies started loading the money into large duffel bags. By now, Seven had joined them and noticed Mr. Jude looking up at the camera.

"You're not gonna get away with this," he lashed out with the little courage he had left in him. "Do you know whose money this is?"

Not amused, Chance replied, "No. Enlighten us."

Mr. Jude laughed. "I'd rather not, but I tell you one thing, you guys will never get away with this. They're gonna kill you and your families," he warned. "They have eyes and ears everywhere. They can see you right now."

Trying to scare them, Mr. Jude looked up at the camera.

The ladies paused for a second and then looked at each other, thinking, *If only Mr. Jude knew.*

Growing annoyed, Patience shouted, "Shut the fuck up," and then grabbed a duffel bag from Seven.

Chance looked down at her watch again. "Alright, Seven, let's go outside. Here, Justice, tie Mr. Jude up," she ordered, handing her some tie wraps.

In a final attempt to scare them, Mr. Jude blurted out, "Trust me, they're gonna hunt you down and kill you."

Patience looked over at Justice, who was now putting stacks of money in the duffel bag after having secured Mr. Jude's hands behind his back. Then Patience reached into her pocket and handed Mr. Jude a piece of gum. At first, he refused, pressing his lips tightly together until she placed her gun to his head.

"Open your mouth," she ordered.

After Mr. Jude slowly opened his mouth, Patience shoved the stick of gum inside and forced him to chew. Suddenly, his windpipe closed up, making it difficult for him to breathe. He dropped to his knees in a coughing fit and then began going into convulsions. Within minutes, Mr. Jude was dead from the gum that had been laced with cyanide.

Seven entered the tellers' area and fired shots in the air, causing pure pandemonium, while Chance forced all the back office employees into the tellers' area.

"Everyone move to the center of the building. If anyone tries something stupid, I will not hesitate to put a bullet in you," Chance announced with her semi-automatic handgun in the air.

Frightened, the people did as they were told. One person, who was clearly confused by it all, blurted out, "Aren't they suppose to be police? Is this some kind of joke?"

Justice ran out from the vault with two heavy duffel bags. "Here," she said, handing them off to Chance before running back inside.

Seven laughed to herself as she noticed the puzzled look on several people's faces when they tried to use their phone but didn't have service. *Stupid motherfuckers. I should kill all of them just for being stupid,* she thought.

Again, Justice came out and handed Seven two more duffel bags.

"Ten minutes!" Chance yelled, looking at the clock.

As Seven turned her back to walk towards Chance, one of the security guards tried to reach for his weapon. Bad move. Chance sprayed his body with bullets, making everyone scream in horror. To avoid any other interruptions, Chance and Seven killed the other two guards.

Justice and Patience joined Chance and Seven.

"We're done!" Chance announced.

Just then, a muffled voice from outside the bank shouted through a megaphone, "This is the police! Come out with your hands up."

With a smirk on their faces, the ladies cocked their semi-automatic handguns.

Seven smiled and said, "Right on time!"

"You have thirty seconds or we're coming in there after you!" the voice yelled.

"What you think, Seven? You think thirty seconds is enough?" Patience smiled.

"Thirty seconds? Shit, I can destroy a country in thirty seconds," Seven joked.

Seven pulled out her BlackBerry and typed in a code. "Alright, ten seconds," she uttered to herself.

Ten seconds later, a barrage of bullets came flying through the window and lasted for what seemed like five minutes. Everyone screamed. The police on the outside ran for cover, some trying to return fire.

"Where the fuck are the bullets coming from? Get down! Everyone get down!" the officers could be heard yelling.

Boom! The SUV the ladies had arrived in exploded.

When it was all over, not a single civilian in the bank had been seriously hurt. They only suffered minor injuries from the shattering glass. However, the police officers weren't so lucky. Ten were seriously hurt from the exploding truck.

Laughing, the ladies escaped to their secret hiding spot to lay low until things calmed down.

"What the fuck happened here?" one of the detectives asked.

"We're still trying to figure it out. According to the people inside the bank, the robbers were women posing as police."

One of the head detective's phone rang, and he immediately answered. Once the caller spoke, the detective instantly recognized the voice.

After excusing himself, he whispered into the phone, "I'm already on it. The entire fucking police force is looking into it."

"There's no way in the world anyone could've pulled this off without the help of the government. I want that person and their family dead five seconds ago," the voice on the other end said.

Click!

The detective sighed. Whoever was behind this had just validated their death certificate. He joined the other law enforcement agents who were inside the vault trying to figure out how in the hell someone had robbed World Financial Bank.

"Whoever did this knew the system would be down for thirty minutes," one agent said.

"How? Only a few people know this," the detective whispered.

Watching from their secret location, the ladies were in tears from laughter as they listened to the scenarios the agents created.

"Let's help them out a bit, Seven," Chance said.

Seven nodded, and then pulled out her laptop. "Technology...isn't it a motherfucker?" she teased, while rapidly typing.

The computer in the vault went black, and then one white letter at a time slowly appeared on the screen welcoming them to WWW.COM.

NOW

AVAILABLE

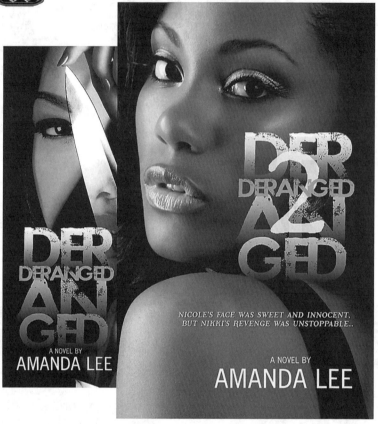

In Deranged, Nikki achieved her goal of capturing Jeremy for Nicole, but fell short as Cowboy spoiled their plans. One year later, Nikki refuses to fail and no longer needs Nicole or her assistance. In Deranged 2, Nicole's face was sweet but Nikki s revenge was unstoppable as she moved heaven & earth to be with her man and live the dream life that they planned together. Once free, AND she sees he's cheating and living their dream life with someone else, Jeremy and his family have nowhere to hide. The question is: Will she finally get what she wants or will she die trying?

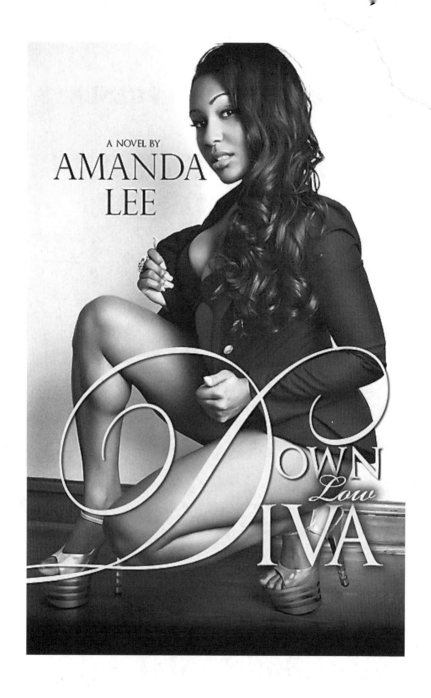

A NOVEL BY
AMANDA LEE

Down Low Diva

Now Available

PUBLICATIONS PRESENTS

DEATH BY THREE

J. MARIE

COMING FALL 2012

CV13
1

GOT BOOKS?

WE DO...

THE CENTRA AT FORESTVILLE
3383 DONNELL DRIVE
FORESTVILLE, MD 20747
301.420.1380

THE MALL AT PRINCE GEORGE'S
3500 EAST-WEST HIGHWAY
HYATTSVILLE, MD 20782
301.853.0010

TLJ BOOKSTORE
WWW.TLJBOOKSTORE.COM
INFO@TLJBOOKSTORE.COM
INFO@THELITERARYJOINT.COM
WWW.TLJESTORE.COM
ORDERS@TLJESTORE.COM